M. Holroyd

Memorials of the Life of George Elwes Corrie, Master of Jesus College, Cambridge,

Rector of Newton in the Isle, Sometime Norrisian Professor in the University of Cambridge

M. Holroyd

Memorials of the Life of George Elwes Corrie, Master of Jesus College, Cambridge,
Rector of Newton in the Isle, Sometime Norrisian Professor in the University of Cambridge

ISBN/EAN: 9783337016128

Printed in Europe, USA, Canada, Australia, Japan

Cover: Foto ©Raphael Reischuk / pixelio.de

More available books at **www.hansebooks.com**

MEMORIALS

GEORGE ELWES CORRIE, D.D.

London: C. J. CLAY AND SONS,
CAMBRIDGE UNIVERSITY PRESS WAREHOUSE,
AVE MARIA LANE.

Cambridge: DEIGHTON, BELL AND CO.
Leipzig: F. A. BROCKHAUS.

MEMORIALS

OF

THE LIFE OF

GEORGE ELWES CORRIE, D.D.

MASTER OF JESUS COLLEGE, CAMBRIDGE;
RECTOR OF NEWTON IN THE ISLE;
SOMETIME NORRISIAN PROFESSOR IN THE UNIVERSITY OF CAMBRIDGE,

DRAWN PRINCIPALLY FROM HIS DIARY AND
CORRESPONDENCE.

EDITED BY

M. HOLROYD.

CAMBRIDGE:
AT THE UNIVERSITY PRESS
1890

Cambridge:

PRINTED BY C. J. CLAY, M.A. AND SONS,
AT THE UNIVERSITY PRESS.

PRINTED BY C. J. CLAY, M.A. AND SONS,
AT THE UNIVERSITY PRESS.

PREFACE.

A HUMAN life is more than a series of events, and the true record of such a life is not a mere narrative of incidents with which its subject has been more or less closely associated. A biography then only deserves the name, when it is the faithful delineation of a character, the portraiture in words of a distinct personality. For such a record the materials must be supplied partly by the utterances, written and spoken, of the individual whose life is described, partly by the observation and reminiscences of others.

The following pages lay no claim to the title of a complete biography. They consist of such memorials as could be obtained from the sources above indicated, and they are presented to the reader without any artificial arrangement, or any attempt to render them attractive by those literary embellishments which make a book more pleasing at the expense of fidelity, and exhibit a skilful picture instead of a truthful portrait.

The work has been undertaken in compliance with a desire expressed by many who knew Dr Corrie in his later years, that the memory of one who had so long occupied an important and influential position in his own University, and had gained the affection and veneration of a large circle both in Cambridge and elsewhere, should not be suffered to pass into oblivion. For the earlier period of a life extended far beyond the common lot, of course no information could be furnished by his contemporaries, whom he survived by many years; and the deficiency has been partially supplied by his own references, made in the course of conversation, to those early times. These were treasured up by friends who enjoyed the privilege of his intimate acquaintance, and they are here reproduced as affording the only, and at the same time a trustworthy, account of days antecedent to the recollection of persons still living.

During the early middle period of his life Dr Corrie was in the habit of writing a Journal, in which he noted not only passing events, but also the impression which they made on his own mind and spirit. The Diary which extends over eight years presents a picture of the man, not only as he appeared to the world—the part which he took in Academic matters, the studies which he pursued, the persons with whom he associated, the work which he performed—but as regards his inner life, its principles, its motives, its aims. They shew not only what he did, but what he was. Few tasks could be more difficult or more delicate, than to decide what should be selected for publication and what suppressed. The accomplishment of such a task may claim a considerate criticism on the part of the reader. An error in judgment may be pardoned, when to err is so easy as to be well-nigh inevitable.

It will be seen from the following Memoirs that during that period of life in which the mental and physical powers are most active, Dr Corrie did not take so *prominent* a part as might have been expected, in public affairs, whether in the University or the Church or in general politics. He was a leader of men, but not in the ordinary acceptation of the phrase. He did not march sword in hand at the head of his troops, but rather directed their operations from a position which commanded the entire field. This was not due to indecision or timidity. It was caused in a great measure no doubt by a consciousness of bodily infirmity (to which frequent reference is made in his Diary); but still more by his habitual suppression of self—the subordination of personal ambition to the promotion of the cause which he had at heart. For mere popularity he cared nothing. He did not believe that truth or right, any more than wisdom, is always in the custody of a numerical majority.

During the concluding period of time included in these Memoirs Dr Corrie, though still more vigorous than many younger than himself, was known as an old man. Men long past middle life so regarded him, and were glad to consult him and to benefit by his extensive knowledge and ripe experience. For the letters which illustrate this period, and more especially for the valuable notices contributed by some of his personal friends, which appear at the end of this volume, the most grateful acknowledgments are tendered, as well as for the assistance readily granted by many other friends, who have thereby in various ways facilitated the execution of the work.

To the Syndics of the University Press, who have generously undertaken the publication of these Memoirs, the author offers her sincere thanks; and in particular to the Chairman, the Reverend Dr Porter, Master of Peterhouse, and to C. J. Clay, Esq., for counsel and help at all times given with considerate kindness, which claims a grateful recognition.

It is not for the writer of a Preface to anticipate the verdict of the reader, either as to the merit of the work itself, or as to the character for the delineation of which such materials as were available have been diligently sought out and put together. But without claiming for the subject of these Memoirs either heroic excellence or immunity from human frailty, it is believed that he merits a place in one of those niches in the Temple of Academic history which were left unfilled by the lamented author of the 'Lives of Twelve Good Men.'

Learned without pedantry, humorous without frivolity, generous without ostentation, dignified without coldness, ever exercising self-discipline without a touch of asceticism—a man of the world—a man of letters,—a man of God—such was George Elwes Corrie. The secret of his influence was the consistency of his life; his consistency was the fruit of his faith in the Christian revelation and the Saviour whom it makes known. His faith, childlike in its simplicity, manly in its intelligence and its strength, was his guide during his long life and his support in the time of failing powers and in the near prospect of death. He was what he professed to be—an English Churchman. In the doctrines of the Reformed Protestant Church of England he found the satisfaction of his faith; in her services to the end of life the fullest expression of his devotion; in her history the credentials at once of her Catholicity and of her Apostolic authority. Loyal in his attachment to her, as the Church of his fathers and the Church of his own long ministry, he loved her as a 'pure and reformed part' of Christ's Holy Catholic Church.

In this hurrying age some may be induced to pause and read the brief memoirs of one of whom it is witnessed[1] that 'he was never in a hurry.' It might seem that his maxim was,

χρονία μὲν τὰ τοῦ Θεοῦ πως ἐς τέλος δ' οὐκ ἀσθενῆ.

It may truly be said of him that during that long life he waited upon God—and he waited to the end. The wine-fats of Cambridge may have many rich vintages in the future, as they have had in the past. But as none can foretell the future, we may be content to adopt the words consecrated by the Lips to which we owe them—'The old is good;' or, shall we retain the loved and familiar version, 'The old is better'?

E. H. P.

---

[1] See p. 345. Appendix I.

CONTENTS.

CHAPTER I.

CHAPTER II.

CHAPTER III.

CHAPTER IV.

CHAPTER V.

CHAPTER VI.

CHAPTER VII.

CHAPTER VIII.

CHAPTER IX.

CHAPTER X.

CHAPTER XI.

CHAPTER XII.

CHAPTER XIII.

CHAPTER XIV.

CHAPTER XV.

CHAPTER I.

IN the rapid succession of passing incidents and circumstances, a life of more than 90 years' duration may be, however comparatively uneventful, not without interest and advantage to the reader, disposed for a while to withdraw from the busy present to follow in these pages the records whether of domestic life, public events, or the personal work and experiences which so long a period obviously comprehends. It is with this conviction, and in accordance with the judgment of many of his most intimate friends, that the memorials of George Elwes Corrie are published.

The family of Corrie was of Scottish origin, and traced their descent from the Macphersons of Clunie, one of whom in troublous times changed his name to Corrie for purposes of concealment. Roger Corrie, born about 1635, was one of the old Covenanters. His grandson John Corrie, who was born in 1722, was present at the battle of Culloden, and was proud of telling his grandchildren of the part he took in the

C.

engagement[1]. His son John married in 1771 Anne, daughter of Mac Nab of Ferlochan, in the parish of Ardchattan, Argyleshire. Their family consisted of four sons and four daughters, the elder of whom were born at Ardchattan, where Mr and Mrs Corrie resided for some years. They subsequently removed, and settled in England, where Mr Corrie took Holy Orders, and was appointed to the curacy of Colsterworth, in the county of Lincoln, which he held for nearly fifty years, being also vicar of Osbournby in the same county, and rector of Morcott in the county of Rutland. In the church of the latter parish he lies buried.

Of the daughters, one only, Mary, survived infancy, and she, joining her brother Daniel in India, was married to John Walter Sherer, of Southampton, Esqre, who became Accountant-General of Bengal. Robert, the eldest son, was a navy-surgeon, and died in the West Indies in 1802.

Daniel, the second son, entered Clare Hall, Cambridge, and took Holy Orders. In 1806 he accepted a chaplaincy of the East India Company. From this time he virtually resided in India, though he twice visited England. His work in India, first as chaplain, then as Archdeacon of Calcutta, and finally as Bishop of Madras, is well known through his memoirs written by his brother, George Corrie. His character is summed up by his brother, who speaks of him as possessing "more than an ordinary share of natural kindness of heart, benevolence of disposition and warmth of affection, so that he could not but be generally beloved." The public testimony to his work is comprehended in the first sentence of his funeral sermon, "All India mourns." He was sixteen years older than his brother George, upon whose early years his character was not without its influence, and his anxiety

---

[1] He fought on the Hanoverian side, and maintained his opinions through life. His grandson would playfully challenge him by alluding to "the Prince." —"Prince!" the old man would answer, " he was no more a Prince than you are!" When speaking of his grandfather, Mr Corrie would add, "We were always on the wrong side in those days."

was manifested in asking from time to time, "How is the boy going on?"

The third son, Henry Corrie, was first educated as a physician, taking his M.D. degree, but he subsequently took Holy Orders and was rector of Blatherwycke in Northamptonshire, and finally of Kettering in the same county. He was a man of considerable power and weight of character, genial in disposition and beloved by all who knew him. The two younger brothers were closely linked, and Kettering was the vacation home of George Corrie during the life of his brother Henry, who died in 1846.

A very old friend of the family, still living, writes of Bishop Corrie and his two younger brothers, "They were a very remarkable trio, and the more so as being brothers, for it is not often that so full a stream runs in one channel."

George John Elwes Corrie, the youngest of the family, the subject of this memoir, was born at Colsterworth, the birthplace of Isaac Newton, on the 28th of April, 1793. His mother died when he was four years old, but her place was supplied to him by his sister Mary, of whose loving care of him in early years he always spoke with the warmest appreciation. The aged and blind grandfather formed at this time one of the family, and the grandsons listened with delight to his stories of bygone battles and adventures. It was the old man's practice daily to retire and repeat to himself chapters of Scripture committed to memory while his sight remained ; and the younger members of the family were often reminded by an old servant that they would never know what they owed to their grandfather's prayers. The paternal grandmother's strongly marked character also was not without its influence, and her oft-repeated saying, "No man ever tried for a gown of gold who did not get a sleeve on't," was not only remembered but diligently acted upon through life, certainly by the youngest of the brothers, and on his part often repeated with zest to those younger friends whom he in after-years delighted to stimulate and encourage.

In the retired parish of Colsterworth, where, as in many country places at that day, the clergyman was not only the spiritual guide of his parishioners but the chief representative of order and obedience to the powers that be, Mr Corrie not unfrequently took the law into his own hands in a manner which would have caused astonishment in modern times. He exercised a firm but benevolent sway among his people, and enjoyed in return their confidence and love. He was a faithful evangelical pastor and preacher, and his church was filled even to crowding with an attentive congregation, a large number of whom were communicants. He numbered among his friends such men as Robinson of Leicester, who with others, was a frequent visitor at his house. He himself conducted the education of his sons; and while teaching them by example as well as by precept, what should be the characteristics of a Christian gentleman, he treated them with such confidence as could not fail to produce in them a corresponding trust and willing obedience.

He was also exceedingly anxious to instil habits of courtesy towards those in a lower rank of life. Walking on one occasion in company with his son they met the chimney-sweeper, who saluted them; observing that his son did not return the recognition, he remarked, "Never let the chimney-sweeper have better manners than yourself."

He would gently moderate his son George's ardour in field sports by saying, "Don't make it your *business;* remember the keeper will always be a better shot than you are."

Mr Corrie's acquiescence in his son's taste for hunting was not very cordial, and the latter would relate how on one occasion, taking a fence into a road, he came close upon his father, who playfully shook his stick at him, the young rider bowing low with uncovered head. On arriving at home he anticipated his father's expression of opinion by saying, "You cannot deny, Sir, that the horse took that fence beautifully!" His early amusements shewed, as they also helped to develope, the steady perseverance in pursuit of any object which was a marked characteristic of his later life. He would spend hours at a rabbit-warren, or in fishing: and the piece of water which was his especial portion still bears the name of Corrie's Pool. As he grew older, he became a good shot, and a keen sportsman, but nothing would induce him to follow game beyond his boundary. Mr Corrie observing to Mr Montague Cholmeley, a neighbour and parishioner, that he trusted his son never exceeded his palings, Mr Cholmeley replied, "If every one was as particular as your son there would be little left for keepers to do." He was greatly attached to horses and dogs, and the exercise of riding, in which he excelled, was continued throughout most of his life.

Illustrative of these rural tastes and of his love of animals the following lines may be admitted:

HUBERT'S FAREWELL TO HIS KENNEL.

Adieu fair abode! my sweet kennel farewell!
I go—but my heart with its throbbings will break;
Change of scene, mortals say, will my sorrow dispel,
But I fear their conjectures will prove a mistake.

O how, when I'm gone can I bear to remember
That out of my kennel I was wont day by day,
To burst forth with rapture, each first of September,
Ere the bright pearly dew had dropped off the spray!

Then hope beamed above me and fluttered on high,
Like a lark when it mounts on the ambient air,
As I tossed up my nose to the grey-mantled sky,
To detect for my master the partridge's lair.

Then to thee I returned when tired with the chase,
Bespattered by mud or drenched by the rain;
And on clean beds of straw often could I retrace
The murd'rous events of the past day again.

In visions I've pointed, oft noting the signs
Which my master is used aye to make with his hand,
In short oft enjoyed all that fancy combines
Out of millions of forms which a dream can command.

But alas! now no more through these fields shall I stray
And hence from my eye falls the tear-drop so big,
And I dread lest, when Hubert is fairly away,
That thou, my dear kennel, wilt harbour a pig!

Then instead of the yellings and growls which abound
In a dwelling apportioned to beautiful dogs,
Thy walls will hereafter be heard to resound
With no noise but the discordant grunting of hogs.

Excuse me, dear kennel, I must sit down and howl
Whilst I think of the changes about to ensue;
That dog must be judged as possessing no soul
Who without great emotion can bid thee adieu.

The keen and active interest he took in these pursuits during his early years laid the foundation of the hardy habits which he retained to old age, and also enabled him to sympathise warmly with the similar tastes of the young men by whom he was surrounded through life.

The important events of the Continental War made a great impression on George Corrie during childhood and early youth, and excited in him an enthusiastic interest in all that concerned the welfare and honour of England[1]. His innate patriotism, thus called out and strengthened by the quickly forming history of the times in which he grew up, was the basis on which rested the political principles of his maturer years.

George Corrie took a warm interest in his father's parishioners, entering into their joys and sorrows, and was long remembered in the parish. An interesting proof of this was given by an old inhabitant of Colsterworth, who, at the age of eighty-four, travelled thence to Newton to be present at the funeral of his former Sunday-school teacher, of whom he afterwards wrote with lively affection, recalling interesting

---

[1] This enthusiasm took the shape natural to his age of forming the village boys into a juvenile regiment, of which he was colonel, and whose object was "to fight the French!"

occurrences connected with the early home life of all the brothers.

Mr Corrie's entrance into the University, of which he was for so many years to be a resident member, took place in October, 1813. He had obtained a Scholarship at Catharine Hall, of which college Dr Proctor was then Master, and Mr Turton, afterwards Bishop of Ely, Tutor. There is necessarily little to relate of his undergraduate life, all his contemporaries of that period having passed away.

His father, knowing his son's great love for horses, and fearing the scenes of temptation into which this taste might lead him, expressed a strong desire that he would not go to Newmarket. This injunction was faithfully respected. Though he was fully aware that his father would never ask him whether his wish had been observed, his loyalty would not permit him to trifle with the confidence thus placed in him.

His impatience of a bad shot surprised him on one occasion into an unexpected position. Coming out of Catharine Hall in cap and gown, he observed a man attempting to shoot rooks in the trees in the front of the college, but in so awkward a fashion that the young undergraduate took the gun from him and at once shot his rook. At this moment the Vice-Chancellor passed by, who turning to him remarked, "Not a very academical pursuit, Sir!"

Mr Corrie kept his college expenses within most moderate limits. His father was so satisfied with the amount of his expenditure that he declined to look at the accounts—a mark of confidence which was most warmly appreciated by his son, and which amply rewarded him for any self-denial he had exercised. He took his degree in Jan. 1817, as 18th Wrangler, on which occasion he was gratified by receiving the following expression of opinion from his old friend and neighbour, Mr Montague Cholmeley, who as his father's intimate friend for many years had had abundant opportunity of observing his character.

From Mr Montague Cholmeley, on Mr Corrie taking his degree :

Sir,

I beg you will accept the enclosed trifle, as a testimony of the high sense I entertain of your truly honourable exertions in the progress of your studies. It is one of the happiest features in the Constitution of this Country, that the best and most esteemed professions are open to every Protestant hero who enters the lists of fame.

For your Father's and Brother's sake, both of whom I esteem with sincere regard, I am glad to hear that you are likely to do honour to your friends, and therefore I am ambitious to be considered one amongst them.

I am, your sincere well-wisher,

MONTAGUE CHOLMELEY.

EASTON, *April* 23, 1817.

Bank of England Note value £10.

The material for a review of the youth and early manhood of George Corrie has necessarily been circumscribed, and what has been related is from his own reminiscences. He always thankfully reverted to the various influences and circumstances which surrounded him at this time, feeling how much under God he owed to them in his subsequent life.

CHAPTER II.

IT had not been Mr Corrie's intention to remain in the University after taking his degree. Mr Turton, however, at once offering him the post of Assistant Tutor, he was led to continue his residence in the College. He was fully alive to the peculiarity of his position, and shewed that he was also qualified to meet it. He called together those who had been his companions, and pointing out to them how difficult it would be for him to exercise any discipline over them, made an appeal to their honour, which met with a cordial and practical response. He would relate how he sat in the gallery of St Mary's as a B.A. Tutor, and that his first appearance on the floor of the Senate House called forth the remark of the Proctor, that " Bachelors of Arts found their place in the gallery ;" to which the young tutor assented, but adding, to the surprise of that officer, " I must first place my men."

Mr Corrie was elected Fellow of his College on May 10th of this same year 1817, and on June 1st was ordained Deacon at Lincoln by Bishop Tomline. His friend Mr Milner, nephew of Dean Milner, was ordained at the same time.

During the examination one of the papers put before them contained a question on the 17th Article. Mr Milner expressed a fear that the bishop might have a prejudice against him on account of his well-known evangelical training, and that his treatment of this question might cause the examiner to reject him. Mr Corrie shrewdly applied his knowledge of the bishop's published opinions on the subject by recommending his friend to begin his answer in the bishop's own words—" This is confessedly one of the most difficult questions in Theology."

Mr Corrie was ordained Priest on Nov. 16th following by Bishop Bathurst at Norwich. His Letters of Orders give these dates. The events of the election to his Fellowship and of his two Ordinations, are marked by himself in a copy of Bogatzky's *Golden Treasury* in the corresponding days. In the first of these entries, by a few words inserted, the commentary is changed into a prayer for salvation and for the satisfying of spiritual hunger and thirst, with a few additional words.

In the second he emphasizes one of the selected texts—" I determined not to know anything among you, save Jesus Christ and Him crucified "—thus shewing his sense of its appropriateness as a guide to one entering on the sacred office, taking for his standard the apostolic principle which he maintained throughout his ministry.

On the third occasion, Nov. 16, the selected text is, " I abhor myself, and repent in dust and ashes." Mr Corrie marks the following words of the Commentary, " 'God be merciful to me a sinner,' is a prayer easy to be said, but hard to be felt. One eye upon the perfection of God's laws, and another upon your own heart, may bring you up to it ;" adding, "A suitable text for the meditation of one who has much cause for self-abhorrence and abasement at the recollection of the cold and often heartless manner in which he returns to God the offering of body, soul and spirit, which are God's by self-dedication."

In 1818 Mr Corrie was elected Dean of his College, an office which he retained until 1849. As time went on it was pleasantly remarked at the annual election of College officers, " We must not interfere with the prerogative of the Dean."

In 1821 Mr Turton resigned the Tutorship, and Dr Proctor appointed Mr Corrie to that important office at a much earlier age than is usual. Mr Corrie in later years speaking of the subject to Dr Proctor remarked, "You made a bold venture, Sir, when you appointed so young a Tutor ;" to which Dr Proctor promptly and kindly replied, "Yes, but you must give me credit for knowing my man." He was naturally well adapted for the work, and from the first found it congenial. But he now threw himself into it with heart and soul, and the combined offices of Tutor and Dean, while enabling him to become intimately acquainted with the character of his men, afforded opportunities of usefulness of which he thankfully availed himself. He could when necessary give an unsparing rebuke, and always took care, as he expressed it, to send away the offender feeling himself to be a culprit not a martyr. He took a lively interest in the tastes and pursuits of his undergraduates, and was consulted by them on all subjects. The choice of a dog was always referred to him, and a stranger might have been somewhat astonished to find the tutor engaged in making a selection from various canine specimens brought by his young friends for his inspection.

The following anecdotes, which have been furnished by one of his old pupils, may serve to illustrate his relations with them.

An incident indicative of Mr Corrie's determination to maintain discipline, irrespective of obsolete rights or privileges, occurs to me. A Yorkshire Scholar, finding a clause in the Statutes which permitted him to continue in College beyond the then usual time at the commencement of the Long Vacation, had failed to apply for his exeat on the appointed day; Mr Corrie sent for him, listened patiently to his statement; but without replying to his arguments, handed him his exeat, and wished him a pleasant Vacation:—the indignant Undergraduate petulantly replied that the treatment was tyrannical and that he should ventilate his wrongs in a letter in the *Record.* Mr Corrie answered "And I will reply in *Punch.*" It is needless to add that neither letter nor reply appeared.

His dislike to smoking was well known: an Undergraduate smelling strongly of the *weed* came into his rooms and was asked to take a seat. "Do you smoke, Sir?" "Yes, both tobacco and cigars."—"And so does my gyp," was the reply.

His extreme unwillingness to take advantage of a youthful indiscretion is shown in the following: A wine party was winding up noisily. He sent the Porter to demand the immediate dispersion of the guests: the demand was not complied with at once; he went himself, but gave some intimation of his approach. Unable to escape, the guests tried to conceal themselves under the table and in the gyp-room, and only the host was fully visible. He requested the host to retire to bed, and said he would not enquire the names of the owners of the " arms and legs " he saw protruding.

A well-known individual long since numbered amongst the dead was reported by the Porter as coming into College at 2 A.M.: and had to appear accordingly—Dr Corrie knew where he had been, and that it was a love of music which had induced him to exceed his time. The excuse given was, that his watch had deceived him: " Take it to the watchmaker, and don't go out of College in the evening till it is thoroughly cleaned and regulated " was his lenient sentence.

But far above and beyond all this there was the everpresent desire to train men not only for active Christian lives on earth, but for the life which is to come, and it was with prayerful consideration that he watched over and guided them as their characters and circumstances required. To these high aims the following extracts bear witness.

From the mother of an undergraduate of St Catharine's College who died.

...Yes, my dear Sir, the good seed you had sown brought forth fruit abundantly, and may the Almighty ever bless your pious labours, as He was pleased to do to the salvation I trust of my son's precious soul.

Mr Hooper remarks on his sermons, &c. :

Mar. 1840.

No one appreciates your sermons as I do. I read none like them, Venn's are the nearest. Did you not at one time read Venn a good deal?

I would give gold to see you for even half-an-hour. I shall never forget while I live all your kindness to me, nor cease I trust to profit by my past intercourse with you.

Mr Baxter writes :

HAWERBY RECTORY, *Mar.* 23, 1869.

My dear Dr Corrie,

...Amid life's ups and downs my College course keeps in my mind as quite an oasis, and as the Scotch say, I *"mind"* the time well when I used to bask in your sunshine, and when a kind word from you spoken *en passant* on the old College staircase acted as a stimulus in my studies. I only wish that I had one like-minded with you near at hand now. I really believe I should be a better man, and more active in my duties.

MOSSLEY VICARAGE, *Mar.* 21, 1883.

Dear Dr Corrie,

I have just received the copy of Dr Turton on the Eucharist which you so kindly sent. Your unfailing kind remembrance of those who when 'in statu pupillari' felt you to be ever their true friend, touches me deeply even now, when old age is fast creeping on. I shall value the book very highly for its own sake but more for yours.

  Believe me, dear Dr Corrie,
    Ever yours sincerely,
      THOS. N. FARTHING.

While indefatigable in the fulfilment of his duty as a tutor, Mr Corrie never lost sight of the importance of a definite course of study, and devoted himself to Theological reading with characteristic thoroughness and perseverance. Always an early riser, he secured time for exercise in company with one of the Fellows before morning chapel. Their goal was usually the second milestone on the Trumpington Road, having reached which they returned in time for College chapel at a quarter past seven. Such was the regularity of their movements that the friend, travelling to London by coach one morning, was accosted by the driver with the remark, " I think, sir, I was rather late yesterday, I met you and Mr Corrie nearer Cambridge than usual."

After the business of the day, followed by the early hall of that period, the long evening at his disposal was as much as possible occupied in reading, which was generally continued to midnight. He was wont to say that his aim had been to fit himself for future work, trusting that for whatever post his College and University friends might at any subsequent time think him qualified, he might not disappoint their expectations.

At this time riding was his chief recreation; in this he was fully in sympathy with his master, Dr Proctor, who was himself an excellent rider, and who, as he became less able to enjoy horse exercise, would frequently offer the use of a horse to Mr Corrie. When thus mounted on one occasion he met Mr Ainslie, the tutor of Pembroke, who noticing the animal he rode, exclaimed, "Does your master keep the tutor in horses?" With his quiet dry humour Mr Corrie replied, " Certainly, does not your master do the same?" and on being assured that such was not the case added, " Then I wonder any gentleman will hold the tuition!"

Mr Corrie not having left any diary earlier than 1836, there is up to that time no record of matters of personal or public interest, nor are there any means of obtaining such notices, all efforts to secure letters of an earlier date having proved fruitless.

The only event in the University of which a note has been made is that of the laying of the first stone of the

New Court of Corpus Christi College, which took place on July 2, 1823, on which occasion Mr Corrie was present.

On Aug. 20, 1823, he was selected to be a Freeman of the borough of Leicester, the qualification being, as stated in the Hall Book of the borough, that he be "a gentleman of sound constitutional principles."

The only relics of his correspondence in the period before us are some letters to one of his nieces, the eldest daughter of his sister, Mrs Sherer, then a child. Two others are also inserted of a little later date written to his youngest nephew, then a boy at school.

With children he was invariably a favourite, winning his way easily to their affection, and the letters following shew his skill in adapting himself to his youthful correspondents.

March 26, 1829.

My dear M. A.

I have long been intending to answer your note, received several months ago, but I have had no leisure for corresponding with young ladies. I now send you a dressing-case, because you being now a Miss advancing in her teens will speedily require such an appendage to your toilette; you will not find any looking-glass in it because I wish the mind to be the only mirror into which you should accustom yourself to look, and because my persuasion is that the more frequently you look into the mind the less necessary will any other looking-glass be considered. Tell Miss Pashy that when she is wise enough to be trusted with a dressing-case, perhaps she will have one, but at present she is to give way to the privileges of your birth-right. She may, however, console herself, by reflecting that as she is the youngest, you will most probably be grey-headed, rheumatic, deaf, lame, blind and toothless before she is. I must conclude by assuring you how much I am

Your very affectionate uncle,

G. CORRIE.

To his niece, Miss Sherer.

Dec. 17, 1829.

My sweet Polly,

I have but a few minutes to say that I send you a book of all knowledge, with the full expectation that you will be an accomplished young lady when I next have the satisfaction of seeing you. The receipt of your welcome note I hereby acknowledge, and assure you that though it is so long since you wrote it, I yet remember its contents, and could answer it without book. In case I have opportunity I shall try to get as far as Devonshire to visit Mr Veale, and, if I can, shall take little Pashy in my way thither or in returning. When I shall leave this I can hardly say. Give my love to your mamma and say that I am right glad to find that I shall have the range of Morcott fields for another year if all be well. As to your uncle Henry I have not heard of him so long that I suppose he has disappeared from the earth, body and soul. With my kindest love to yourself and all, to the end of the chapter imagine me to be

Your dotingly affectionate uncle,

G. CORRIE.

One of the Fellows of this College passes Morcott and will leave this.

To his nephew.

CAMBRIDGE, *Nov.* 24, 1830.

My dear ——

The "diabolical incendiaries" have been playing off their pranks within ten miles of Cambridge, by setting fire to a farm yard. The fire consumed three farm yards and four cottages, doing damages to the amount of £8000 or £10000. When the fire engines arrived from Cambridge the mob rushed upon the men who had charge of the engine and cut the water pipes so that they might render the engine useless. The papers say the people in Norfolk are beginning to break threshing machines. We seem to have arrived at a strange state of affairs.

It is my full intention to leave College at Christmas and bring Mr —— with me, who is amazingly captivated with shooting, tho' I don't think much of his shooting powers, although perhaps it is not quite fair to judge him, he having had so little shooting that he is fain to kill owls, blackbirds, larks, or any other flying animal that may present itself in the absence of partridges. I am quite anxious to see him have a fair chance.

Believe me, yours affectionately,

G. ELWES CORRIE.

CAMBRIDGE, *May* 13, 1835.

Dear ——

I was duly obliged this morning by your agreeable and welcome letter, which I read at least three times over, and as I abominate all approach to the rudeness and incivility of the present House of Commons, I can do no less than sit down and answer your letter by return of post. But how can I express in a manner sufficiently strong the lively satisfaction your letter administered to me, by telling me you are happy! Yet on reflection I thought with myself that the dog ought to be flogged out of his seven senses if he were not happy, because I know that Mr C. feeds his mind, and Mrs C. takes care of his body, and what else can he want? And so you see I reasoned your case out, and my hope is you will make the best use of your time and many advantages, and by this means make all your relatives happy as well as yourself. Indeed I can assure you that lost advantages are acquired miseries: so that every time you are idle or negligent, you may be quite certain that you are purchasing a whole box full of regrets.

To-morrow I hope to see your uncle Daniel and your cousin Anna, who intend passing through Cambridge on their way to Kettering and Leamington.

Did you hear that I had a beautiful hound? On my return to Kettering I had the hound sent to me; but as I did not want it, I sent it back to its sisters, brothers, and friends at the Blatherwycke kennels.

Now, as I have more to do than you have, and have written a somewhat longer letter than you did to me, you must excuse me if I finish by assuring you how much I am

Your loving uncle and godfather,

G. ELWES CORRIE.

CAMBRIDGE, 1836.

Dear ——

It is indeed a *very* "long time since you received my letter," and you had need be very thankful for it. However, on the whole you are not a bad correspondent to write two letters within the twelvemonth, as I conclude that, like myself, you have plenty of work to do, and in that case have not much time for bandying complimentary epistles and vain pleasantries. But why do you not tell me what you are doing? What time you get up? At what time you go to bed? When you play, eat, drink, sleep? I heard of your visit to Kettering, and had a great mind to send for you up here; but then I thought we should only be in each other's way. So our meeting must be deferred till longer days and warmer weather. And you saw young——, did you? Well you saw a picture of what a boy may become who is accustomed to have his own way when a child. I am sure, I hope your good master knocks you down if ever you are so unmindful of your own comfort as to reason when you ought to obey. I heard that the said —— was going to Van Dieman's Land, to be gobbled up by the cannibals of Australasia, but this may be but report. Still the greatest evil that can befall us from God is to have the desires of an evil heart gratified, as indeed God has told us when His Spirit recorded that sentence in the Book of Psalms, "So He gave them up to their own heart's desire." So you are "anticipating a delightful trip into Wales this summer?" Well I hope the weather may be very sun-

shiny for you. If I go anywhere this summer it will be to the
South of Ireland to see how the Paddies are going on.

Now good bye to you, my sweet friend.

From your loving uncle and godfather,

G. ELWES CORRIE.

During the Long Vacation of 1821, Mr Corrie and his
friend and co-tutor, Mr Temple Chevallier, paid their first
visit to the Continent, spending three months abroad. The
journal of this tour as a whole would hardly be attractive
to the reader of these days, but a few extracts are given
shewing the great contrast between the experiences of nearly
seventy years ago and those of the present time, and also
noting the impressions made on the minds of the travellers
by various objects of interest.

*Notes from the Journal of a Tour through France, Switzer-
land, &c. of G. E. Corrie and Temple Chevallier.*

"*June* 25, 1821. We set sail in an English Packet from
Dover, and in about three and a half hours arrived off Calais.
No French boats were in waiting for the passengers, and therefore the Packet was obliged to lay to. After waiting off Calais
for nearly two hours, a French boat rowed alongside of the
Packet. Owing to the roughness of the sea, and to the surf
near the shore, we were more than an hour in reaching the
shore, a distance of not more than two or three miles. We
found the pilots would not venture out to fetch the passengers, and that the sailors who did fetch them were to
be committed to prison for going to sea without a pilot.
We agreed, on seeing the town, that the first appearance of
France was that of desolation. Everything seemed to be
either unfinished or going to ruin. It looked as if the town
had been deserted and had lain desolate for a century or two
and had just begun to be inhabited again.

"*June* 26. We left Calais for Paris in what the French

call a Diligence, but we should call it a stage-waggon. The
horses which drew the vehicle were like half-bred English
cart-horses, very rough in appearance and very tardy in their
movements. The postillion was like the horses, rough, dirty,
and clumsy. To his head was attached an enormous pig-
tail. He wore a pair of large jack-boots made to the best
of my judgment about the Norman Conquest. The Diligence
was drawn by five horses. Three were placed abreast as
leaders, and two as wheelers; on one of the latter rode the
postillion. The traces were made of rope, somewhat like
that we use for harrowing. The tackle very often breaks;
to repair it, the postillion cuts a piece of string off his hat
and a stick off the first tree he comes to, and mends it himself.
In such a manner we travelled towards the capital of France,
changing horses and drivers every 12 or 14 miles. At Cler-
mont we had a good specimen of a French Inn. We passed
through a dirty kitchen to the dining room, in which was
served up a miserably dirty dinner. Everything we saw here
tended to endear England to us. At Chantilly we felt that
all the magnificence of the place had departed. Everything
seemed to indicate that France had never recovered from the
effects of the Revolution ; every chateau we passed merely
advertised us what *had been.* At last we reached Paris. Our
journey hither from Calais, though not more than 185 miles,
had been performed in not less than thirty-eight hours."

Paris was reached on the 28th. Some days were devoted
to it, but the places visited in the French capital are as
familiar to the readers of to-day as London itself.

"In visiting the Pantheon we recalled its history. The
foundations were laid for the purpose of building a church,
but before it was finished the Revolution took place. The
friends of the Revolution were enemies to Christianity and
therefore gave the name of Pantheon to this church. As
they were *liberal* in their principles they intended to have a

Temple for *all the gods*. Thus they were very paradoxical in their practices—one while overturning everything merely because it had been long established, but in their religion turning back to the folly of heathenism, which more than anything else had been established for ages. After however making a trial of heathenism and proclaiming death to be an "eternal sleep," they discovered that the prospect of dying without expectation of a future retribution, was that which caused men to be less fastidious in the commission of crime, and consequently less tolerable as members of society. They emerged therefore one step from heathenism, and declared 'there would be an hereafter.' The name of the Pantheon was then changed to that of 'The Temple of Liberty.' At the restoration of the Bourbons the building was again turned into a church, although it is still better known by the name of the Pantheon.

"In St Stephen's, Paris, the greater number of pictures were representations of miracles which were said to have been performed by St Geneviève: and the guide cordially acknowledged that the propensity of this saint for performing wonderful cures and for assisting people in their difficulties was a profitable thing for those concerned with the Church. At the same time that we cannot but wonder and laugh at the credulity of those who are the dupes of crafty and worldly-minded priests *in the nineteenth century*, one must experience pity for the disciples, and indignation against the teachers of this superstition. No one who has not seen what Popery is in a Catholic country can have any idea of the mummery of it. In this enlightened age, it seems almost incredible that any person would endure the folly of priestcraft so as it must be endured by all who would lay claim to the title of "True Sons of the Church."

"*Sunday, July* 1, was the eighth day after the Fête Dieu, one of the principal festivals of the Church of Rome. We witnessed a grand procession on the occasion which bore more resemblance to a procession in honor of Jupiter, or some other heathen deity, than to the worship of the one only and true God. It was quite horrible to see it. From the procession we went to the Chapel of the British Ambassador. The contrast between the sobriety of the service of the Church of England and the noisy parade of the Church of Rome was highly gratifying, and I was never more pleased or enjoyed a service more in my life.

"*July* 2. We visited the garden of the palace of the Luxembourg, which was laid out very much in the taste of those of the Tuileries. We could not see the Palace; it was occupied by those who were trying the conspirators of Grenoble. I passed by the spot on which the Bastille once stood. I stopped to meditate on all the horrors of the place; but I shuddered not less at the recollection of the monsters by whom the Bastille was destroyed. They professed to liberate the bodies of men from those chains with which they might have been unjustly bound, but they set aside Revelation, and thus brought a thraldom on the souls of men, more bitter than Egyptian bondage. I could not help secretly exclaiming, 'O my soul come not thou into the secret of these men!'"

The diary is resumed on reaching Lyons.

"*July* 9. As I stood on the banks of the Rhone, the appearance of the river suggested many reflexions on the mutability of human affairs, for it seems scarcely anything but a dream to be on the banks of that river on which many of the greatest Roman armies had taken their stand. These had passed away, but not without leaving monuments of their former greatness, which still remain in part, Roman baths and Aqueducts, the Baths in a very perfect state, but the Aqueducts nearly gone to ruin. Sufficient however remains to shew the extent of them. One is surprised in considering the magnitude of the work, both in design and execution. Very beautiful is that short sentence of the Apostle as applicable to man and the works of mankind, 'The world passeth away and the fashion of it, but whoso doeth the will of God abideth for ever.'

Leaving Lyons they entered Savoy at La Tour du Pin. At Les Echelles they heard of the death of Bonaparte: the following Sunday was spent at L'Hôpital.

"*Sunday.*—To us in the midst of a Catholic country this is no day of rest. We felt as if we were in a land in which there was no Sabbath for us. In general the day of God is given to diversion. The village bells were chiming. Many persons were standing at the door of the church waiting for the service to commence, but we knew that the worship in which they were about to join was that in which we dare not participate. Very forcibly was the situation of the Psalmist when he wrote the 63rd Psalm brought to my mind. He was then a fugitive in the wilderness of Judah, and consequently deprived of the service of the Temple. Not dissimilar was our situation, deprived of every opportunity of public worship, and consequently our Sundays seemed to pass away without profit and without comfort. I do consider it to be one of the greatest evils to which a person can be exposed in travelling through foreign lands, that, however desirous he may be, he cannot profitably attend public worship if he be a Protestant.

"At Moutiers our hostess wished to charge us too much for our dinner, and by way of extenuation informed us that meat was *very dear*, being about 4½*d.* a pound."

Passing over the Little St Bernard to La Thuille and Courmayeur, they reached Aosta on July 19.

"Between Moutiers and Bourg we left our carriage and walked, the road being very fine; my companion sketched. I placed myself on an abrupt rock in order to fill my mind with the grandeur of the scene, which was beautiful beyond description. At Bourg we found the most miserable inn in which we had ever taken up our quarters. The approach to our sleeping rooms was over a wooden bridge, below which pigs and cows had their respective sheds ; but we had travelled through France and Savoy and were not unaccustomed to sleep in beds which very few English servants would have cared to have offered to them ! Occasionally in our travels we sat down by the roadside to sketch. This so alarmed some of the country people who could not make out what we were doing, that they enquired of the muleteer whether the *French* were come again.

" An old man informed us that he had lived to see soldiers of all nations in possession of the town. He said all had behaved alike in plundering the inhabitants, but complained of the French because he said *they* came with pretensions of liberty and equality in their mouths, and took the liberty of robbing everybody they met."

From Aosta they crossed the Great St Bernard, encountering a severe storm during the descent, and arriving at Martigny proceeded to Sion.

"We travelled from Martigny to Sion, which is one of the most ancient bishoprics in Switzerland. There is a kind of picture-gallery in a chateau in which the portraits of all the bishops of Sion were to be seen who have possessed the see since A.D. 200 or 300. We paid a visit to a Hermitage and saw one of the hermits. He had been a hermit upwards of forty years ; had never changed his dress. His hands and face seemed as if they had never been washed since he entered the Hermitage. He was altogether a most extraordinary figure. The opinion one forms of a hermit is, that being disgusted with the world, he flies to the desert. The opinion I formed of the man I saw was, that if he had not become disgusted with the world, the world would soon have become disgusted with him. He gave us a sermon on the vanity of the world, and the shortness of life, and concluded by saying that 'he preferred seclusion to the bustle of a city, and that every one ought to live as if each day were to be his last.' I thought on the various methods which men employ to torment themselves, to avoid more completely the torment of the world, and it seemed to be a question of some difficulty to determine, whether idleness and pride, or devotion were the motives which caused a man to turn hermit. The man I saw left an impression on my mind that he did not understand that—

> God alike pervades
> And fills the world of traffic and the shades,
> And may be found amid the busiest scenes,
> Or scorned where business never intervenes.

But this is perhaps judging too severely, and I may be only excusing that mixture with the world, which unmoderated by the Apostolic injunction, 'Use this world as not *abusing* it,' is an enemy to that peace of mind, which they have who whilst they live *in* the world, are not of the world.

"We learnt to-day that very lately the Jesuits in this place went round the town to examine the books which were in it, and that they seized everything which they judged to be heretical or unprofitable. Now it is well known that they would spare no books which would be likely to convey true Christianity to the mind, and I could not help expressing a wish that those of our countrymen who had exerted themselves so strenuously in favour of the entire emancipation of the Roman Catholics in England were under the *surveillance* of the Jesuits for one twelvemonth. I felt confident that a revision of their libraries by these gentlemen of the Church of Rome would do more towards opening their eyes as to the real nature of Popery than all the lectures in the world."

Visiting lakes Maggiore, Lugano and Como, they reached Milan Aug. 3.

"The road which leads to the Simplon commences at Gliss. The new route, which vies with the greatest efforts of man, was made by Bonaparte for the purpose of facilitating the intercourse between France and Italy, and on this road we travelled. On an almost perpendicular mountain which bounds the Saltine on the side opposite the road are several cottages which it seems almost impossible to reach. They give you the idea that the inhabitants of them must have been born there, and that it is probable there they will die, from the mere fact that they cannot get down from the place. In all our travels we have not derived more pleasure from anything than from the road of the Simplon as far as we have traversed it. At Feriolo we saw the people playing at ninepins and other games before the door of the chapel of the convent although it was Sunday. One thing gave us satisfaction, that in the town in which was the convent, there was also a reformed Church, the first we had met with since we left Paris. We saw in a paper yesterday the first intelligence of the Coronation of the King (George IV.). At Milan the conversation at dinner turned on the beauty of the Cathedral. An Irishman in reference to St Carlo remarked that 'he understood there had not been so good a man as St Carlo since the time of our Saviour.' It would have been vain to have disputed the point; no reply was made, all stared as if in doubt what to say. We were obliged again to pass our Sunday without profitable public worship, there being no Protestant service. We heard a very good sermon at the Cathedral from a very venerable old man in the costume of a Doctor in Divinity. He seemed to be a celebrated preacher.

"*Aug.* 25. We left Lucerne, intending to ascend the Righi.

"We took a boat but had not proceeded far when the heavens became black and we began to repent of the step we had taken. Very soon we were obliged to land, the wind blew, and there was every appearance of a storm. We purposed returning to Lucerne, but were persuaded by our guide to go on to the Righi, and about 5 P.M. began to ascend the mountain. Our party consisted of myself and companion, our guide, a man to carry our luggage, and a young woman who was going to a chapel on the top to pay her respects to the Virgin Mary. We presently found we were threatened with a thunderstorm. We walked on as fast as the ascent would permit us. The rain began to fall, we hurried on without any prospect of avoiding it, when on turning round the brow of a hill we saw a house at some distance; we made straight for it, but all in vain; we were quite wet before we reached it. In our speed we had left our company behind, but waited for them, and then proposed to stay at the house, which proved to be an inn, all night. The guide assured us the storm was gone by. The baggage was missing, so the guide went in quest of the carrier. We waited some time, but as neither guide nor man made their appearance we set off by ourselves, fearing we should be benighted. We were joined by the peasantess, who was as much a stranger to the road as we were. When we had gone about 200 yards the storm came on with renewed fury. The lightning was more and more vivid, the thunder seemed to be directly over our heads, and the rain literally poured down. We went on till we arrived at the brow of the mountain, when everything like a road disappeared. Although in much perplexity, we attempted to proceed till we found ourselves completely lost. It was pitch dark, and to advance was to be lost. Our only alternative was to return. By the help of a cross we had noticed, we found the road we had left. Here, our guide came up. He led us on seemingly without knowing the road, over hillocks, and bogs, and stumps of trees, till on a sudden I saw a light at a distance. With more eagerness than good humour, I asked whence the light proceeded. He said, 'From the convent, which is nearly a mile from the inn. I told him to take us there. Turning about, we stumbled down a rock into a bog. At this moment a most tremendous flash of lightning shone upon us so that we could see we were in a perfect wilderness. At the same time we heard the crash of a tree close by which the lightning had struck. Not a little anxious to escape from imminent danger, we hastened on, and in a quarter of an hour reached the convent, and turned into one of the little inns close by. We hastened upstairs, but having no clothes to change we borrowed shirts of the landlord and got into bed. On lying down I found the rain had got through the roof into the bed, and bed, pillows, and covering were all wet, and myself in a violent perspiration from exercise. I had to get up till all was changed, and then returned to rest.

"Our guide called us at 4 o'clock to ascend the Righi. The morning was clear and the prospect beautiful, but after last night's adventures we enjoyed it less than we should have done at any other time. We descended the mountain towards Schwyz. At the foot of it we came to the place in which sometime during 1806 there was a fall of a large mountain, the Rossberg, by which a whole village was buried and 400 souls perished. The appearance of the place is truly desolate. What was formerly a rich valley is now a barren waste. Our guide was very near when the fall happened, and escaped being buried by about an hour. Two persons only out of all the village escaped death,—a young girl, and an infant which was found floating in its cradle on an adjoining lake. The ruins extend over 5 miles, and the road is not less than 200 feet above the level over which it used to pass. The feelings of one's mind are inexpressible, when passing over a spot beneath which so many persons lie buried in one common calamity.

"In the Grisons we had proof of the poverty of the inhabitants. When we enquired for a candle, we had to wait till the landlord *made* one. We asked for tea, and found they had nothing but dried herbs.

"In making our way to Glarus, the guide mistook the road, and we were fain to stop on the road in a village for rest. Our guide said he had found an inn, and we followed him and were shewn into a room where several persons were sitting, among them a remarkably fine old man. Without

any ceremony we ordered some wine, when the old gentleman informed us that we *were not in an Inn.* We began to
apologise and to retire, when he said he should be glad to
give us some refreshment. We thankfully accepted it. We
began to think our host had seen better days. There was a
great propriety and elegance in the manner of the old man
and his wife, and they spoke French with great fluency ; we
made enquiry about a road over the mountain ; the old man
said he would send for a man who would tell us all about it.
Before he came, the old lady proposed we should go upstairs and rest, for which we were grateful, and slept for two
or three hours. In the meantime there was a thunderstorm,
and, the rain continuing, our host desired we should stay the
night. Dinner was provided for us, and the only thing that
made us uneasy was our ignorance as to the real condition
of our host. He told us during dinner that he had been an
officer in the Swiss Guards, who attended the unfortunate
Louis XVIth of France. When the Revolutionary mob made
an attack on the Palace of the Tuileries on the famous 10th of
August, the Swiss Guards were the only soldiers who remained faithful to the king, and were cut to pieces almost to
a man. Our host was one of those who escaped, and fled
to Switzerland. Here he remained till 1801, when the French
Republican army entered the Canton of the Grisons. Another army entered by the valley of the Rhine. Our host
had been made captain, but he and his brave followers could
not withstand *two armies* and were obliged to surrender.
He was taken prisoner and kept as a hostage for two years.
He then returned home. He seemed to gain fresh dignity,
when we told him that the fidelity of the Swiss guards was
admired by every honorable man in England. He observed
that England was a great nation, and had not only resisted
Bonaparte on her own account, but had given liberty to the
world. It would be endless to relate all that passed, but this
is thrown together to record what I considered an adventure.
On taking leave of the old soldier he expressed a wish that

we should visit him again for a longer time, and we quitted a house in which we had received as much kindness and attention as one friend could shew to another. In our journey our guide pointed out gorges and precipices in passing which thousands of Russians perished in their retreat before the French army, 1799.

"At Glarus we passed a Roman Catholic Church (there are both Roman Catholics and Protestants in this canton) in which the congregation were singing vespers. The church was dimly lighted and shewed very palely a row of Saxon arches. I scarcely ever witnessed a more striking scene, and one forgot at the moment that the worship was corrupt. I retired very much impressed by what I had seen and heard, and secretly regretted that the congregation were bowing before the altar of the Virgin Mary, instead of offering up their thanksgivings to Jehovah. In this canton, however, although there are many Roman Catholics, there is much less of the mummery of Popery than in those cantons in which all are Roman Catholics. In some parishes there is both a Protestant and Roman Catholic Church. The intermixture of Catholics with Protestants makes it impossible for the priests to keep their congregations in total ignorance of the Word of God, which is freely circulated among those of the Reformed Church. One thing is very observable, viz. that the *worldly* condition of Protestants is tenfold better than that of Papists. The latter are so impoverished by the expenses of fêtes, and consequently much less industrious in their habits, that you may almost always tell on entering a village the religion of the inhabitants. I consider this circumstance (which must have fallen under the notice of every traveller) as a remarkable illustration of that text, "Godliness is profitable for all things," &c., where by godliness one must understand *true religion* in its full sense. The fact is to be observed in a comparison of *any* country, whether heathen or one in which a corrupt system of divinity is prevalent, with a country in which exists the knowledge of pure and undefiled religion. On this ground, then, I should be an advocate for the universal diffusion of the Word of God, because I believe that in proportion as the light of truth prevails, the moral and worldly condition of mankind is ameliorated. My belief is, I think, founded on observation and experience, which has always a greater weight in biassing my judgment, than subtle reasoning on the propensity of man to pervert Scripture truths, and that therefore an indiscriminate diffusion of Scripture may do harm. The *best gifts* of heaven—nay, the common mercies of life—have been, and will be again, abused, but the Word of God remains yet 'the power of God unto salvation to every one that believeth.'

"At Zurich from a balcony adjoining our rooms we have had a most pleasing prospect of the lake by moonlight. The night quite calm, and an inexpressible softness pervades the surface of the water. The world is hushed in sleep, and the time seems to invite us to meditation. I have some faint idea of the feelings of David when he composed the 8th Psalm ; and truly, in viewing the heavens and considering at the same time that the Almighty's mind is occupied in retaining every star in its proper place, one is led to exclaim, 'Lord, what is man that thou art mindful of *him ?*'"

After leaving Glarus, they spent a few days at Zurich and Schaffhausen, returning to Lucerne.

"At Lucerne we dined with two Frenchmen, whose vivacity was not a little amusing. One of them especially spoke with astonishment of the character of the English. As regards their turbulence on all occasions in which any expression of popular feeling occurs, he observed that the same tumults which, for example, occur on such occasions as an election of a member of Parliament, would be the ruin of any nation but England.

"*Lausanne, Sept.* 16.—This morning we attended service at the English chapel to our no small satisfaction. Since we left Paris in July we have had no opportunity of attending public worship. About 150 English were present. We truly enjoyed the singular beauty and simplicity of our liturgy after having witnessed nothing but the antics of Catholic priests for the last nine or ten Sundays. The prayers were read by a Fellow of Bene't Coll., Cambridge, and the sermon by an old clergyman, I think one of the Irish Deans. In the afternoon we attended the worship of the French Protestants.

"*Sept.* 19.—We visited the Cathedral at Geneva. A secret veneration and awe came over my mind as I stood in the place in which some of the great Reformers had preached. Scenes of persecution came also to my mind when I remembered that I was in the very place where many worthy refugees for religion's sake of my own country had worshipped. I made enquiry at several of the principal booksellers for an edition of the works of Melancthon, but without success. Several of them did not seem to know that such a man had lived."

The last entry in the journal is an account of a conversation with a Genevese fellow-traveller, "who remarked, ' I see you have a Bible among your books; do you believe it?' To this of course we replied, 'Yes.' He then began to produce his Deistical reasons for rejecting a revelation himself, but as they were not new to us we were at no loss to refute them, when he ended by saying, I cannot *understand* the Bible and therefore I don't *believe* it, and I am of opinion that if it should be true, God will not punish any man for rejecting what he cannot understand. We told him that many things were found in it which were difficult, yet not contrary to reason, although above reason. He ceased, and left us astonished at the inconsistency of the man who believes that there is a God, and yet rejects a revelation. Next day he again began to speak of the credibility of the Scriptures. He asked me, 'Do you profit by reading the Bible?' 'I hope so, for I should read no book if it were otherwise;' he rejoined, 'The more I read the Scripture the more my doubts of its truth increase, and I am surprised to hear you say you are benefited by it.' I replied, 'Now you will pardon me if *I* doubt whether you have read it at all.' He acknowledged that he had not read the New Testament."

In 1829, Mr Corrie's father died at the age of 83. On the last day of his life, a Sunday, he had taken part in the morning service, and in the afternoon when walking in the garden was suddenly seized with an attack of angina pectoris. He was with difficulty conveyed into the house, and shortly after expired.

Hitherto Mr Corrie's health had been good, and there had not been the least threatening of coming illness, but in May, 1832, when on a visit to his intimate friend Mr Nevile, rector of Cottesmore, he had a sudden and severe attack of hæmorrhage from the lungs, and for many weeks he lay in considerable danger at Cottesmore Rectory, whence he was removed to Kettering, where his brother Mr Henry Corrie was curate. So critical was his condition, that for six months his medical advisers, fearing a recurrence of the attack, did not allow him to speak, and all communication on his part was by signs or writing only. To his brother's watchful skill and tender nursing he himself mainly attributed, under God's blessing, his ultimate restoration to health. But it was not until after Christmas 1834 that he was able to some extent to resume his duties in College, which had been willingly undertaken during this long and enforced absence by Mr Blakelock, afterwards Archdeacon of Norwich, with the assistance of Mr Philpott, the present Bishop of Worcester, then both Fellows of the College. His own feelings on the subject of sickness and returning health are expressed in the following letter to an old friend.

May 4, 1833.

My dear Chevallier,

Perhaps it may be doubted whether the buoyancy of mind consequent on recovered health is so much to be desired as that subdued and chastened spirit which is inseparable from sickness, especially, if with recovered health we again find our hearts to sympathise with the world, the influence of which is so unpropitious to the growth of an undying life in the soul. Not, indeed, that we ought for a moment to *desire* sickness, when we have the choice also of health, because a merciful God has called us to the practice of no bodily austerities, nor bids us for a moment to delight in that discomfort which renders sickness such a burden to our mortal nature: nor ought we to permit our minds to be so far deluded as to imagine that the animal distaste for the world which affliction superinduces is identical with that purification of spirit, which, as the work of the Holy Ghost, necessarily renders the world insipid to the inner man. Yet still I think it is lawful to cultivate a cherished recollection of any affliction which may have been the means of disengaging the affections from earth; and to regard bodily suffering as a state of blessedness in comparison with any vigour of health which may be combined with a deadness of heart toward God.... Yet if the being called upon to contemplate the dissolution of the bonds of earthly fellowship and love be made instrumental to our regarding the union of our hearts in the fellowship of Jesus Christ as the only true end of our earthly existence and relationship, then may we welcome the very disruption of the heart from the objects of its intensest love, as amongst the choicest and most merciful dispensations by which we can be visited. It is here that the surpassing tenderness of our heavenly Father is especially manifested. He made our spirits, and knows fully the bitterness which those spirits experience when called upon to surrender at His command any object of earthly affection. He beholds every pang we suffer, and imputes no sin to that burst of natural agony with which we resignedly give back to Him, that which from Him was received. He, therefore, lays no affliction upon us merely to outrage our natural feelings, nor commands us to bear His chastisements with stoical indifference: but all His visitations emanate from His Eternal love, which deprives us of nothing which is not to be restored to us in greater beauty and splendour.

Believe me, yours affectionately,
G. E. CORRIE.

That the long period of convalescence had not been without occupation, is manifest from the letters to Mr Temple Chevallier. The proposed Lectures there alluded to were during that time under preparation. The subject of the correspondence with a young friend spoken of in the first of the following letters on the doctrines of the Church of Rome, was one, which, from Mr Corrie's intimate knowledge of Ireland, its priests, and its people, drew out his sympathies in no ordinary degree towards any who embraced such doctrines. He lost no opportunity of so increasing his information on these subjects as to be the more able to refute the specious arguments levelled against Protestantism by the adherents of Popery. The letter dated Oct. 3, 1835, while it contains reference to this controversy, speaks of such a measure of health as, with care, enabled him from this date to continue his work in College, although some time elapsed before he could attempt any clerical duty.

KETTERING, *Nov.* 6, 1834.

My dear Chevallier,

...If God spares me in health, it is my full intention to commence in College during the current year, a course of Lectures on Church History, under the conviction that half the foolery attendant on the religious aberrations of mankind arises from a want of knowledge of what *has been* in the Church of Christ. All the vagaries of the Irvingites about the "flesh of our Lord," and the drivellings of Dissenters about the *purity* of the Church anterior to Constantine, and so forth, can be met only by a fair demonstration of the facts connected with the history of the Early

3—2

Church. From all I have read, I am satisfied that in Church History, as in every other subject, there is "nothing new under the sun," and hence much service might be rendered to sobriety by shewing that the errors and sins of the human mind touching religion are of necessity the same in every age ; subject, of course, to such variety in external appearance as may be superinduced by the local circumstances. In this persuasion I have often thought that the ancient *heretics* were not such monsters as one has been accustomed to regard them, and for truth's sake I should, in reading Eusebius, keep a steady eye on the ancient sayings and doings of reputed heretics with a view to *printing* something more accordant with truth than has yet appeared in the matter of Heresiology. Lardner has written on this subject more moderately than is *wont* by men reputed more orthodox than he, but his leaning is too much to the side of Arianism to admit of his being implicitly relied on. One ought to bear in mind, too, that Eusebius was a patron of the Arian Creed, and that it will be necessary, in consequence, to consider well his narrative so far as it may bear on the parties who may have speculated on the Doctrine of the Trinity. But as it will be as well not to fill my letter with disputations on Church History, I will tell you that, by the mercy of God, I am nearly as well as usual, only heretofore I have been obliged to practise the silence of a Pythagorean. Knowing, I suppose, my exceedingly loquacious habits, the doctors have enjoined upon me to make known my wants and imaginings, either by writing or by signs, and this kind of discipline I have found to be exceedingly serviceable to me. So there is only needed a heart more deeply sensible of the obligations I owe to our heavenly Father, Who always deals out His chastisements more according to His loving kindness than our deserts.

My time of late has been taken up by writing letters of controversy connected with the errors of Popery. A young friend some short time ago embraced the Romish Creed, and in a note I took occasion to point out to him the peril that attached itself to every member of a Church which was so unsound in the great doctrine of Justification as the Church of Rome is; begging him at the same time to examine this subject more closely than I *knew* he could yet have done. There I expected the matter to end, because considering he was the guest of Mr ——, and a French or English Jesuit priest to boot, I took it for granted that they would take pretty good care that he did not slip through their hands. I soon, however, had a long letter in reply stating some of the reasons which had induced my friend to join the "*Catholic*" Church, and attacking the " sandy foundation" of the Church of England, by way of an acknowledgment of my attack on the scheme of Justification cultivated by the Council of Trent. The sentiments expressed in the letter were those commonly to be found in the books of the Roman Catholic champions, such as Berington's *Catholic Faith established by Scripture;* Bossuet's *Exposition of the Catholic Faith*, &c.; Milner's *End of Controversy*, &c., and so far a gratuitous misrepresentation of what the doctrines of Popery really are. My straightforward plan was of course to reject all the *opinions* of these champions as to what Popery *is*, and to turn the attention of my correspondent and his advisers, to the undisguised Canons of the Council of Trent, and the declarations of the Creed of Pope Pius. This, as I expected, most heartily puzzled them, so that, as their champions are wont, my correspondent had in defence of Transubstantiation to betake himself to the "*mysterious*" nature of the miracle performed in the consecration of the Eucharist. I did not answer the " mysterious" argument immediately, and was much surprised by the receipt of rather an earnestly written letter begging that I would continue to write, for that the result of my letters had been to place Popery in a different light to that in which my friend had been led to view it, and stating that, if my arguments continued to convince him of his error, he had resolved to renounce Popery, whatever sacrifice of character &c. might be the consequence. My hopes are that —— (who is far from settled in Popery) may see my letters also. In my last letter I took the bull by the horns by shewing that all the excrescences of Popery were peculiar to it only as being one of many systems of untruth; for that Penance, Fasting, the *opus operatum*, Indulgences, Pilgrimages, &c., &c. necessarily followed from the errors on the subject of Justification. If a man had to increase his Justification by *works*, the institution of penance, &c. as means to that end took place as a matter of course; and I conceived that the discussion of Transubstantiation in the *first instance* was beginning at the wrong end. Albeit I was quite willing in every way to discuss that or any other peculiarity of the Roman Catholics....

Your much attached friend,
G. E. CORRIE.

KETTERING, *Oct.* 3, 1835.

My dear Chevallier,

...This summer has been passed in a state of uninterrupted idleness. I have scarcely opened a book, having in compliance with the wishes of my friends and my own habits, devoted the whole of my vacation to vacuity of mind. Hence I have been found at times walking about in the cool of the evening with four or five dogs at my heels (of various grades from the mastiff to the lapdog), a terror of every unfortunate hare or rabbit that crossed my path—at other times engaged in the construction of a moss house. Thus October has found me laden with the burden of no meditations on the past state of literature, nor of anticipations of its future progress. If God be pleased to continue to me my present good health, I hope to employ my winter in more scholarlike pursuits. And first I hope to bottom the Irish Church question, of which but comparatively little is known. I have got together a good deal, having intended to put all I know in the shape of a Review of Moore's *History of Ireland*, but I hate to be tied to time...I do trust that in God's providence people are becoming more alive to the importance of the Protestant religion. There can be no doubt but that in Ireland a great work is going on in spite of all the resistance and open persecution enacted by the Popish Priesthood. I have two Tracts in hand on Popery for circulation on the —— property in Ireland. You will say I have a good many "irons in the fire," and so in truth I have, but I have been so long laid aside from work that I scarcely know how to find time for picking up my irons. And thus glides away a life which can boast no expectations beyond threescore years and ten !

Ever believe me to be
Your affectionate friend,
G. CORRIE.

In 1835 Archdeacon Corrie visited England that he might receive Consecration to the newly-constituted Bishopric of Madras. At Cambridge he was admitted to his Doctor's degree by Royal Mandate on the 11th of June. His appearance in the Senate-House attracted general attention. Mr Corrie was asked by one present if he knew who was that 'Apostolic looking clergyman.' He was consecrated within a few days, and finally left England on June 19—with a presentiment that it was for the last time. The only remaining reference to this visit is in a letter from Mr Corrie to his young niece, of which some extracts are given.

June 12, 1835.

Your uncle Daniel was admitted to his D.D. degree yesterday amid the admiration of all present. The Professor who presented him made a grand oration to the purport that your Bishop uncle was a wonderfully great man, having translated the Prayer Book into Hindustani and built churches. I have secured a striking portrait of him; he is in his episcopal robes. The whole University ran together as if one of the Apostles or Reformers had risen up. For myself, I have sunk in the estimation of all men, such a slight little man with two such handsome large brothers, yet it was amusing to hear all people addressing my elder brethren as *Mr Daniel* or *Mr Henry*, the distinguished title of Mr Corrie being judged by all as due to myself alone.

CHAPTER III.

FROM 1836 to 1843 Mr Corrie kept a somewhat full diary. Those parts of it which relate to himself reveal him as a constant student of Holy Scripture, and as maintaining a close communion with God and a watchfulness of spirit which bore fruit in the consistency of conduct and example by which he honoured his Divine Master. Of these portions a few extracts may be allowed.

Some passages in the Diary illustrate by contrast with the present, the changes which have been made in University regulations, while in others are found traces of the early stages of some of those greater movements which have since taken place. From youth to old age Mr Corrie was rarely absent from his place in St Mary's, and his journal usually contained some comments on the sermons preached before the University.

1836. *Jan.* 10. I conversed with a friend on the subject of Popery. One is apt to regard the opinions of men polemically. How differently should we feel and speak of opinions if we felt that they were but so many indications of the state of the health of immortal spirits for whom Christ died!

Jan. 17.   In the afternoon I heard —— who was preaching on the Apostolical character of the Church of England.   Two errors he fell into, as I believe.   (1) He said that from some expressions of Irenæus it might be collected that the Creed was repeated in the daily service of the Church during the first two centuries, whereas it was repeated only at the two solemn seasons of Baptism, Easter and Whitsunday, until the year 500.   Then it began to form part of the daily service.   (2) He stated that our Liturgy reached us from the primitive Church through the Roman Missal, an assertion which I believe to be without foundation.   He does not appear to have seen Palmer's *Origines Liturgicæ.*   One thing I have many doubts about the lawfulness of, viz.: reading the newspaper on this day.   The peculiar temptation is that there are just now objects of great national and ecclesiastical importance occurring every day, and as the paper is not my own, I have been tempted to regard the difficulty of obtaining it another day as an excuse for reading it on this.   I fear that in this I do wrong.   I certainly have doubts, and so by God's help will try to rectify this doubtful matter.

Jan. 19.   A long conversation with a German Jew, who seemed surprised at the idea of there being such a thing as the spiritual life of the Lord.   He told me (I suppose by way of compliment) that as the notion was entertained by a person of learning like myself, he supposed there might be something in it: but seemed not to know what to make of me when I replied, that learning was but of little use in matters which must be seen by the light of the Holy Spirit. He was unhappy under the poverty against which he has to struggle, but seemed to derive no comfort from anything that occurred or was said, except from finding that there was somebody who could sympathise with a mind labouring under disappointment.   What a loss he is daily sustaining in his ignorance of the virtue of that atoning blood which cleanses from all sin, and of the consoling power of the sanctifying Spirit! May God lead me to be thankful for even the hope of better things.

Jan. 21. What a scene of distress and turmoil this world is, and how soon will all be forgotten in the calm repose of the grave! Yet it would seem as if the excitement which our affairs occasion us might be to us a presage of their important bearing upon our eternal state; for it is incredible that God should make us capable of being so careful and troubled about many things, were it not that every subject of our anxiety, if viewed, as it ought to be, in the light of eternity, and improved as by God's grace it might, would tend to discipline us for a higher and holier state.

Jan. 24. I have had fears that I am about to have a return of illness (hæmorrhage). Yet I would thank God that I have been able to resign all my life into His hands who will never cast off a sinner looking for salvation only through the redemption which is in Christ Jesus.

Jan. 25. I would hope that in conversations I have had with some of my pupils who are about to leave College, my anxious desires for their best interests may be fulfilled to our mutual happiness.

Jan. 27. I had a call from Bishop Chase of Illinois. The object of his visit to this country is to raise funds for building and endowing a College in Illinois, that new district having, from being almost a desert, become a very populous country. The means for spiritual instruction have not kept pace with the population, so all the "Voluntary Principle" can do is to oblige those who care for men's souls to come to this country in quest of pecuniary support. All accounts agree in representing Episcopacy to be greatly on the increase in America.

Jan. 30. I have had much conversation with —— on many matters connected with the Church and Religion. On the former, respecting the danger arising from sectaries, but he seemed to think much more was to be apprehended from the Clergy called Evangelical. On talking of the methods adopted by some zealous persons for the instruction of the destitute population of the metropolis, it struck me how much is lost by the Church having no expansive power as Popery has. Why else might not some of these wandering spirits, which embrace Irvingism or any other "ism" be licensed by a Bishop, and thus kept in external unity with the Church, having also thus their aberrations controlled?... —— mentioned some striking parallels between Popery and Judaism, a subject worth following out.

Jan. 31. Mr —— preached a masterly sermon at St Mary's. I trust his sermons will be of use by shewing that the Church of Rome, as it now is, holds little in common with the early Christian Church beyond an acknowledgment of the Trinity: but it is to be apprehended that his sermons may by possibility confirm an opinion too common, viz. that we must look to the Church of the early Centuries for doctrine, rather than that we should rely entirely on the Bible as the standard of orthodoxy.

Feb. 1. A friend told me that the followers of Mr Irving are busy in this town, and have many converts. One of these converts told my friend that she "confessed" and did penance, and fasted, thus shewing how fast this sect is verging towards Popery. In London the Deacons and Deaconesses are marrying "by commandment." Strange, strange are the windings of the human heart!

Feb. 2. Mr Challis of Trinity was this day elected into the Plumian Professorship vacated by Prof. Airy having been appointed Astronomer-Royal.

... Have had reason to regret that on an examination of my private accounts I have found too large a sum spent on books. There seems an unwarrantable selfishness in this. I trust God will enable me for the present year to watch myself in these respects, and lead me to feel that it manifests a great defect in my Christian character, not rigidly to aim at self-denial when tempted to spend so much on myself, considering that I thereby prove myself an unworthy and dishonest steward of God's bounty.

Feb. 4.   I had a call from Archdeacon Hodgson (Archdeacon of Stafford).   In the evening he called again and mentioned a plan which himself and others had in view, to buy up the advowsons belonging to Corporations which are to be sold under the provisions of the new Municipal Corporation Act.   The plan alluded to contemplates the vesting of the Patronage in the hands of trustees.   If successfully carried out it may be of immense benefit to the Church.

Feb. 15..   During a walk with a friend the subject of going to parties and amusements was mentioned.   The result of the conversation was a conclusion that very little good is done by religious people at irreligious parties, and much harm often accrues to the Christian's own spirit.   I may remark that I always find it difficult so consistently to associate with my friends as to abstain from some manifestation of levity; yet it seems very much out of character to pass over from conversing on the great things of God to the dealing out of pleasantries.   Of this we may be sure, that if one could but see one's conversation written down, it could not fail to shock the mind to witness eternal verities and foolish observations in such immediate juxtaposition as they often are in actual life.   Yet "are not all these things noted in thy book ?"

It appears from this and other references to the subject that the spiritual destitution of the Metropolis was then engaging attention.

Feb. 18.   Had a long conversation with H. J. R. respecting Church affairs.   The destitute condition of our Metropolis happening to be mentioned, H. J. R. said that a friend of ours had suggested that to the London Incumbents might be assigned a certain number of young men who having taken their degree were intended for the ministry. These might be deputed to read the word of God in stated places among the most destitute portions of the Metropolis, to look after the sick, and do other offices of mercy as lay-helpers. On this being mentioned to the Bishop of London, he said "the best way would be to strike at the root of the evil at once," and that he would undertake to procure the building of fifty churches! It has often occurred to me that as in all crowded places like London there will be a rapidly increasing and fluctuating population, which hardly any regular system can provide for, and as there are always spirits in the Church who though not formed for the regularity of Church Establishment would yet form excellent *irregular* ministers; it would be well always to have a certain number of this class of clergymen licensed as *Street Preachers*. Many sincerely Christian men would thus be kept in the Church who else are formed for scruples or dissent.

Feb. 20. Had a call from the Christian Advocate, who expressed his difficulty in fixing on a subject for the Advocate's Treatise for the current year. I suggested the evidences of our Saviour's Divine Nature from the fact that in His personal actions and ministry were embodied the attributes of Deity as expressed in the Scripture. The Advocate had thought of some Treatise connected with Popery, and I took occasion to say that if he wrote on that subject it would be well to shew that the Defences of Popery put forth by its advocates are not in unison with the standard documents of the Church of Rome.

March 4. Had H. J. R. of St John's with me to carry on the Table we are printing in the *British Magazine* on the state of Church accommodation throughout England. I had a long conversation with Thorp of Trinity (who is examining Chaplain to the Bp of Gloucester) on the subject of examinations for Orders. He complained of the want of efficiency which attaches to the requirements of the bishops that a candidate for Orders should bring a certificate of attendance at the Norrisian Divinity Professor's Lectures. I suggested that if instead of a certificate every bishop had taken the matter into his own hands, and examined in the subjects and books lectured on by the Professor, attendance on those lectures would be a very different affair from what it is now. Men would give attention to what they would hereafter have to be examined in, and not as now, consider the Professor's certificate a mere piece of waste paper earned by a waste of time.

Mar. 9. Had some talk with Lodge of Magdalene on the times, especially about the stir being made at Oxford about Hampden. He agrees with me it ought to have been made earlier, but some allowance must be made for the unwillingness of man to begin opposition, so that discontent which now only begins to break forth *may* have been long entertained. Yet we ought never to compromise truth for the fear of man or love of ease. Lodge also agreed with me in thinking that there is some danger in running from the latitudinarianism of Dissent into the formality of Popery. Of this examples are to be found in some of the opinions advocated in what are called "The Oxford Tracts." How prone is man to extremes.

Mar. 22. I had some profitable conversation with Mr L. of St John's on the importance of bringing poorer persons acquainted with missionary objects and other like subjects, in order to the poor's caring for the souls of others.

Mar. 24. How truly does the Scripture teach "With the heart man believeth unto righteousness," for in the heart the greatest ungodliness may reign whilst externally the life may be moral: but when the heart is right with God, it cannot hold communication with any evil desires without a consciousness of sin, and so separates itself in a degree from a pure and holy God. Gracious Lord, let me never rest satisfied with anything short of that complete sanctification which it is the object of Thy infinite compassion and love to work progressively in all the members of Christ by the holy influences of Thy Eternal Spirit.

April 3.   Easter day.   I was able to assist in administering the Holy Communion in the College Chapel.   I missed one individual usually present.   I have frequently observed the first systems of a young man's decline from strict morality to be absenting himself from the Lord's Table.

April 5.   I desire most humbly to thank God for the restoration of my health, so far that I this day read prayers in Chapel after having been silenced for a long time by illness.

April 12.   An account in to-day's newspaper of the blowing up by gunpowder of King William the 3rd's statue in Dublin.

April 16.   To-day I met a civil engineer at Mr Rose's rooms who is employed in the construction of a Railroad from London northward which is to pass through Barnwell.   He gave it as his opinion that though the railroad might be finished, it would "prove a bubble" as it would never pay.

April 27.   This day the election of a Public Orator took place, which ended in the election of Mr Crick of St John's.

April 28 was Mr Corrie's birthday, on which day he always reviewed the events of the past year with solemn feeling.   This year had been specially marked by his own and his brother Henry's restoration to health, and also by the great pleasure and comfort the whole family had experienced in the visit of their eldest brother to England. These events are noted in the Diary as special subjects for thankfulness.

In addition to the fact that the Romish controversy in the abstract formed a necessary branch of Mr Corrie's *Theological Studies*, he, as already mentioned, possessed special opportunities of observing the effect of the Romish system, both locally and individually, on the people of Ireland.   The result of these observations upon his own mind was to confirm his Protestant principles, while his well-known attention to the subject frequently led others to apply to him for advice or information bearing on it, and from this time the matter is constantly referred to in the Diary.

April 30. I have been told to-day by H. J. R. of St John's that at this present time there are 20 young men educating at the Jesuits' College at Stonyhurst for *Oral Controversialists* on behalf of the Church of Rome. I suppose the Papists find it necessary to counteract the effects of the speeches of Messrs M'Ghee and O'Sullivan.

May 1. I went to St Mary's to hear ——. His sermon undertook to point out the difference between the Protestant and Romanist on the great doctrine of Justification. The preacher was experimentally acquainted with the subject, but the sermon was neither forcible, judicious, nor well informed. It forms an era in University preaching, being the first sermon against Popery by a Select Preacher in an afternoon. Some time ago Mandell of Queens' preached against Romanism in the morning, but his was an able sermon. From this time I doubt not Popery will often be mentioned in the University pulpit. It will be well if preachers read before they write and speak.

May 8. —— preached at St Mary's respecting the "jeopardy" our Church is in from the opposition of Infidels, Papists, and Sectarians. For my own part I take comfort from their opposition, considering it as a certain sign of the true religion of which the Church is the living witness.

June 1. In the morning I attended a meeting of the Committee of Barnwell School, and afterwards called at Trinity Hall and Clare Hall with a view of obtaining subscriptions from the Colleges on behalf of the School.

The following letter was in reply to some questions asked by his friend Mr Chevallier, in whose parish of Esh various difficulties arose from time to time from the existence of a Roman Catholic College in the immediate neighbourhood.

C.   4

CAMBRIDGE, *June* 6, 1836.

...So far as I can accomplish my purposes, I trust to spend from now till August at Kettering in reading for my College Lectures in October, which will comprise two Classical subjects, the Gospel of St Luke, and the collateral reading connected with Jewel's *Apology*. Add to this I have to prepare about four Sermons on the Doctrinal Articles of the Church of England to be preached in the Chapel: for Philpott and I have agreed that it would be desirable to have Sunday instruction for our pupils, in these days of rebuke and blasphemy. We intend to preach sundry courses of Lectures beginning with the Articles of our Church, Philpott taking the Historical and I the Doctrinal Articles. It would therefore be indiscreet to begin my travels until I have made some preparation for the future. I *must* read during the summer, and if I defer reading till October, I should return to College a jaded student, instead of a frisky traveller.... With regard to the Priests' cricket-field, you will have to act with caution. One striking feature of Popery is, its invariable practice to countenance a breach of God's institutions whenever implicit obedience is paid to the institutions of Rome. Public opinion corrects the real tendency of Popery in this respect so far as England is concerned, but in Ireland nothing is so common as to have your feelings shocked by Sunday dances, and games of all kinds. Human nature, in fact, finds but little restraint from Popery in matters moral, though in matters ceremonial the Romanists *appear* to exact much. I say *appear*, because the merit attached to penance, stations, fastings and so forth, renders the self-denial of the body a matter of unspiritual gratification, and not of difficulty. I think I should aim at the correction of Sabbath-breaking by privately exhorting my own people, and by the circulation of Tracts on the duties of the Sabbath among the Romanists. You will have to proceed warily and compassionately. One can never sufficiently bear in mind the great disadvantages the poor labour under in having for a long time before them the example of Sabbath-breaking countenanced if not encouraged by the Priests, and with perhaps no warning from the Protestant Clergyman. It is by raising their notions of their duty to God, that one can most effectually hope to check practices which whilst agreeable to human nature, and receiving apparent palliation from the impossibility of amusements to the poor on other days, are countenanced by professed teachers of religion. What a fearful responsibility must be attached to the teachers of a system, which by encouraging the waste of the Lord's day in godless amusements is instrumental in giving the soul a greater distaste for the enjoyments of heaven. I have always regarded Romanism as in this point of view to be most resisted. Our controversy is not so much about the number of Sacraments, and the hundred and one novelties of Popery, as with the foundation of them all—the Doctrine of *Justification* as expounded by the Council of Trent. To this master-error may be traced every other false doctrine, or corrupt practice of the Church of Rome, and to contend with Romanists about other matters first is to contend in vain. Indeed if a Church cannot teach a man how he may appear just before God, what else can it teach that concerns him one farthing to know? You will see in the *British Magazine* rather a good paper on the Romish question under the head "Church Matters." Look at a saucy letter on Bossuet's Exposition signed C. E. G. I expect to be torn in pieces for it. But of late I have found myself marvellously mixed up with church-steeple men: and yet I believe I am considered a bit of a Roundhead by them.

    Believe me, your attached friend,

        G. E. CORRIE.

According to the intention mentioned above we now find Mr Corrie established at Kettering, and the next few extracts from the Diary are from that place.

June 26. The King's Accession. The Service for the

occasion was read in Church to-day, to the comfort and edification of myself and many others. My brother's text was from Dan. iv. 25; he set forth the Divine Sovereignty in the world, tracing all civil government to God, and pressing upon us the consequent duty of yielding obedience to the constituted authorities of the land, and praying for our Rulers.

June 29. To-day the newspapers report the rejection of the Popish Municipal Corporation Bill intended for Ireland. May a merciful God grant that this may be the first step towards our deliverance from the spirit of Popery.

The following letter refers to Mr Corrie's great desire to visit the Protestant Missions at Achill in order to gain information as to the effect produced by them on the Roman Catholic population in that neighbourhood. The visit was not however at that time accomplished.

KETTERING, *July*, 1836.

My dear Chevallier,

...I have a most itching desire to see the Island of Achill, where the missionaries are in so promising a condition, to the no small consternation of the McHale's Popery. On the other hand some of the peasantry are ready to engage in any enormity dictated by their priests. On —— property there is a school in operation which has been of considerable service in setting at naught priestly authority. The priest has done all he can to put it down, but in vain; and I expect much in due time from this first assault on priestly power. But we who live at a distance from Popery are scarcely sufficiently alive to its unfriendly influence on even the worldly prosperity of our fellow creatures: but that system of iniquity is as truly opposed to the welfare of the body, as to that of the soul. It is my purpose to collect as much information as I can scrape together, and, if I have industry enough, to put what I hear and see on paper. I have shut myself up in this place to read hard, for if it pleases God to continue my present health, it is in contemplation to have sermons in Chapel on Sunday evenings, and my attention has been occupied in preparing materials for my share of the duty. Our purpose is to take the Articles of the Church as our Text Book and prepare a series of Lectures on those Articles which involve Church History and Controversial Theology. P. will begin with the 6th Art. and by way of foundation I purpose to discuss the 9th. But where to begin, how to arrange and compress the matter connected with that important part of our Confession, is not so easy to decide. So far as I have any settled plan at present, I should like to give an historical sketch of the progress of the heretical opinions which from time to time obtained in the Christian Church on the doctrine of Original Sin, in the various *phases* those heresies presented, the sources from whence they sprung, and the danger they involved. Then go to the discussion of the *true* Doctrine, contrasting it and pointing out its importance. This would be preferable to taking the Doctrine first, because people are so much under the influence of what is *last* said, that if the Heretical notions were discussed last, they would be remembered the longest. Perhaps it might be better not to mention explicitly the Heresies at all, but simply point out during the discussion of the *true* Doctrine such features in it as may be inconsistent with such and such notions, not stating whether they were best held or abjured. Alas! Alas! what can mortal man do in threescore years and ten! Still he may be thankful that it is "Eternal life" to know "the only true God and Jesus Christ" whom He hath sent, and that this knowledge is within the reach of every sincere enquirer after divine truth whatever be his age or literary deficiencies.

I abide, your truly attached friend,
G. E. CORRIE.

July 6. To-day the anniversary of the Kettering Bible Society was held. Many factious spirits had decided on objecting to Sir G. Robinson's taking the chair, and upon making a disturbance. I and many of Sir George's friends attended with a view of supporting him, but as he took the Chair at once as President of the Society, there was no opposition. He spoke with Christian dignity and good spirit, so I suppose his adversaries were ashamed.

July 10. I could not help noticing in the account of the Institution of the Lord's Supper as the second lesson (Luke xxii.) was being read, that *Judas* was one of the participants of the Holy Sacrament, and that, therefore, the narrator set aside all the notions of dissenters on close communion. And as if to render that matter less tenable, we find afterwards that all the Apostles were at that time ignorant of the true nature of Christ's kingdom, for they were in such a state as to admit of being strengthened even by Peter; not to mention that we find them (Luke xxiv. 11, 25—27) utterly unacquainted with what the Scriptures taught of the sufferings, and person, and office of Christ. One is tempted to ask, would dissenters have admitted the Apostles to their Communion, whilst they manifested so little knowledge of the Gospel of Christ?

July 11. A day of great heat. I went out and worked in the midst of it with a view of teaching a farmer how to burn clay.

July 19. My object in reading over the Revelation repeatedly is to impress in my mind the sequence of events in that "Book of the Cross" as Bengel beautifully calls it. Time only can develope the real fulfilment of many of the things predicted in that lofty and mysterious record, but the order of events may I think be so far discovered as to lead me reverentially to expect the appearance of each event in its true order of succession.

July 27. I have been occupied with my brother in drawing up an address to the House of Lords to be signed by the members of the Kettering Conservative Association to-morrow.

July 30. Mr McPherson told us that my eldest brother's mission to Tinnevelly, had been under God the means of composing the dissensions which had sprung up in that Infant Church, through the pride of *Caste* and the intemperance of some Lutheran Missionaries, who had without cause withdrawn themselves from the Church Missionary Society. How assiduously does the great enemy of souls labour to mar the work of God! J. B. told me that my little Tract on Endowments had been extensively circulated in Yorkshire, and with good effect. Mr Jones of Creaton thought it worth while last year to translate it into Welsh.

Mr Corrie left Kettering in August to pay various visits to friends in the north. Some extracts from his account of those journeys are given.

Aug. My friends at Sheffield took me over various works, in all of which I was deeply interested, it being my first opportunity of becoming acquainted with the processes of the different manufactures.

Aug. 13. I visited the Parish Church, which is a fine building. In it is a bust in memory of a late Vicar of the Parish; it is the first of Chantrey's works, and is very finely executed. The sculptor was born near Sheffield, and began life as a mill boy in that town.

After spending two days at Leeds with his friend Mr Holroyd, Mr Corrie went on to Durham to visit his friend Mr Chevallier, who was at Flas.

Aug. 21. Went to church at Esh; Chevallier preached. The congregation was of the most rural character and almost filled the small church. The sermon was heard with great attention. As I looked round on the simple, homely, appearance of this little flock, and remembered their want of education as contrasted with the literary attainments and

University Honors of the Preacher, I could have concluded as a worldly calculation that the talents and scholarship of my friend were thrown away, but I felt as a Christian that it is the highest distinction that can fall to the lot of the most accomplished to be made the instrument of leading to salvation the poor of this world.

Aug. 23. We went to Durham to attend afternoon service in the Cathedral, where the Bishop, Dr Maltby, appeared for the first time since his translation. The service was read by the Bishop of Chester. I walked solitarily through the empty aisles of the Cathedral, and conned over the monuments, to see if I could meet with a line which could give me a hope beyond time.

Aug. 24. We went to Castle Eden Dene or Glen. I have seen glens in Ireland, Scotland, and elsewhere, but I consider the Glen of Castle Eden finest of all. We wandered on, and returning up the glen had a fine view of Mr Burden's House which stands boldly on the edge of the scenery. Mr B. was the projector of the iron bridge over the Wear to Sunderland, the first iron bridge that was erected in England.

Aug. 26. Messrs Peile of Trinity, Whiteley of St John's (Sen. Wrangler of his year), Cartwright of Christ's and Wailes of Catharine Hall dined with us to-day, so that with Chevallier and myself we were a completely Cambridge party.

Sept. 2. I walked out in the evening three miles to the extreme point of Chevallier's parish, in order to read and explain a chapter in the Bible to some cottagers detached from the rest of the parish. There were about eight or ten persons. I read Eph. ii. 1—10, and endeavoured as God enabled me to set forth the state of man by Nature and by Grace. It pleased God to give me a ready utterance, and the poor people heard me with patient attention. Several of them evidently understood the power of the Divine Life; and I trust we did not meet in vain. On leaving Flas, I passed through Durham, visiting the Cathedral and the Castle, and then stopping a night at York, passed on to Sheffield, to

Mr Knights, the Vicar of St Paul's, and attended a Meeting
of the Society for Promoting Christianity among the Jews.
Mr Alexander, afterwards Bishop, spoke, and then the Meeting
was addressed by Dr McCaul in a long and interesting speech,
in which he detailed the operations and success of the Society.
The Meeting was in all respects a profitable one.

In October we find Mr Corrie again at Cambridge, hoping
for a continuation of health to enable him to fulfil his various
duties. The Diary continues from 10th October, when he was
sworn into the office of Scrutator with Hodson of Peterhouse.
He was at this time occupied in reading Church History,
with a view to a Lecture on the origin of the 39 Articles.

Oct. 14. I dined with the Vice-Chancellor at 5 o'clock.
At tea I had much conversation with the Master of Jesus
(Dr French) on the Ecclesiastical Commission. He thought
that the Government, if it continue as Radical as now, will
make some excuse for taking the administration of the Church
Revenues into its own hands ; so much of it at least as relates
to Bishops and Chapters. Time will show.

Oct. 22. I went to-day with friends to see the University
Printing Office. We were much gratified with the specimens
of printing showed us, especially by what is called the *English*[1]
Bible. This is the Bible in 4to., in a new and splendid type
with marginal references, in a volume scored off by red ink.
One copy is being printed on vellum specially for the King.
The first sheets of this copy on vellum were struck off at the
Installation last year, by the Chancellor, the Duke of Cumber-
land, Prince George of Cambridge, the Dukes of Wellington,
Northumberland, and other Nobles. It is a splendid specimen
of typography.

Oct. 24. I saw Carus of Trinity to-day, who told me that
Mr Simeon was somewhat better, and hopes were entertained
of his recovery.

[1] So called from the name of the type in which the book was printed.

Oct. 25. I called to-day on the Dean of Peterborough (Dr Turton). He told me that Mr Simeon, though now so ill, expected to be able to preach at St Mary's during the next month, for which he is the Select Preacher, and that if he should not be well enough on the first Sunday in the month, he hoped the University would allow some one to *read his* (Mr Simeon's) sermon at St Mary's, that the course might not be interrupted. What the subject is, he does not tell anybody; and the Dean said it was not known, except that the sermons were intended to bear on Mr Simeon's life and ministry, and not to be printed till after his death. I understood the Dean to say that, in case Mr Simeon could not preach, his sermons were to be put into the Dean's possession as Professor of Divinity; to whom was also to be given permission to show the sermons to any select friend; but the contents of them were not to be given to the world till after the author's decease. In the evening I went over some part of a Catechism for a Sunday School with ——.

Oct. 28. I have been asked to subscribe towards the support of the widow and family of a Mr Mark Robinson, with whom I had a slight acquaintance. He was a man bent on effecting a union between the Wesleyan Methodists of the East Riding of Yorkshire with the Established Church. For years he was employed in collecting subscriptions toward the building of Chapels, to be served by Lay preachers in such places as the Church was deficient in room or labourers. The Chapels to be put under Ecclesiastical control, and in all respects to be made auxiliary to the Church. He was greatly opposed, though a Wesleyan, to the present system of that body, which vests all power in the Preachers; and he used to say that Wesley never intended that his preachers should usurp the Priest's Office and administer Sacraments.

Nov. 2. At a Congregation to-day one Grace was to give a retiring Pension of £200 a year to John Smith, the University Printer, and another to enable the University to purchase some additional ground from Peterhouse for £1000, to admit of Basevi's buildings of the Fitzwilliam Museum being more effectively placed. The latter was opposed, but was carried by a majority of 20 to 5 in the Non-Regent, and of 35 to 2 in the Regent House.

Nov. 7. This evening one of my wards, G. J., arrived; much engaged with him in accounts; we read and prayed together before retiring to rest.

Nov. 14. Mr Simeon died yesterday. He has been a man of God for many years, and now rests from his labours.

Nov. 16. To-day we elected J. W. Parker of London to the office of Printer to the University. I had a long conversation with the Christian Advocate on the subject of Justification, and on the Oxford Tracts.

Nov. 17. The papers of to-day note the death of Charles X. of France. He lived an exile in youth, like our Stuarts, learned no wisdom from adversity, and died therefore like them in exile.

Nov. 18. I had some talk to-day with the Dean of Peterborough on Theological matters. It appears he is now engaged in answering some lectures by Dr Wiseman, which the latter addressed to the students in the English College at Rome.

The only remaining letter written during 1836 which has been preserved was about this date, and is now inserted. After referring to a local matter, on which Mr Chevallier had consulted him, Mr Corrie gives him details of his researches into the earlier formularies of faith of the Church of England to which reference has already been made in the Diary.

To Mr Chevallier.

...The moral of all this is plain; for as you had succeeded in your object to the no small content of all around, and to your own heart as well, there comes a "crook in the lot," a bitter in the sweet; and so we can only thank God that our crosses have a use, and when tempted to drink too deeply at the purest earthly springs, it is well (by even unpalatable sips) to be reminded that "the water of life that proceeds out of the throne of God and of the Lamb" can alone truly satisfy the soul. In your difficulty there is something peculiarly trying, because one cannot doubt but that the Romanists will not be idle in making every use of ——'s discontent: but in these matters we must act for God, and in the spirit of God's Word, and leave results to Him who can "make even the wrath of man to praise Him."...Since my return to College I have been unusually well on the whole, and not idle in the main, for I have been engaged in putting together a short history of the origin and contents of the "Formularies of Faith" which appeared previous to the 39 Articles. I begin with the Articles of 1536 and have to wade through and compare the "*Institution of a Christian Man* (1537), and the *Necessary Doctrine*, &c. (1543)." The "Institution, &c." being of *no authority*, I only use it by way of ascertaining the progress and change of religious opinion from 1536—1543. This reminds me that the preface to *Cranmer's Remains* by Jenkyns shows a good deal of reading, and that the book is in many respects valuable, but *I* have been a little surprised by some of his observations respecting the "Necessary Erudition." If you turn to pp. xxxvii and xxxviii of the preface, you will find J. asserting that "the effect of the words of consecration &c. not indeed amounting to an *explicit assertion of transubstantiation* &c. in the Six Articles &c." Now just compare this sentence with the Six Articles which J. gives, p. xxv, and also with the Doctrine of the Sacrament of the Altar as taught in the "Necessary Erudition," p. 262, of "Formularies of Faith put forth in the reign of Henry VIII.," Oxford 1825, which I presume you possess. It strikes me that J. must have been talking without book. These are the words: "the creatures which be taken to the use thereof, as bread and wine, do not remain still in their own substance, but by the virtue of Christ's word in the consecration be changed and turned to the very substance of the body and blood of our Saviour Jesus

Christ, so that, though there appear the form of bread and wine after the consecration as did before, yet must we, renouncing the persuasion of our senses in this behalf, &c. 'believe' it to be the very precious body, &c." If this is not *explicit* transubstantiation what can be? I do not, also, see my way with Jenkyns either as regards almost all the other assertions he makes with respect to the changes undergone in the Doctrines transmuted from the "Institution" to the "Necessary Erudition." I think, from a somewhat close attention to the wording of the two books, that the "Erudition" contains a great deal more Popery than the "Institution," and if you look at the *notes* appended in the latter to the Exposition of the Creed, as compared with the text, you will I think agree with me that the notes were concocted and added at the suggestion of parties who thought the Exposition of the Creed far too Protestant. Indeed some of the Exposition is quite beautiful for the strain of piety which pervades it; and then come the cold, flat, papistical Notes, lest people should believe and be saved. What Jenkyns could, as a Protestant, mean by the subject of *faith* &c. being handled with "success" (p. xxxviii) I cannot divine. Look at the handling of the subject of "faith," and the only success with which it is crowned seems to me to be the setting up of the distinction between a *true* faith which is meanwhile *dead*, and a true faith which being joined with charity and hope, is alive and justifies. Not to mention that charity and hope are the *necessary* fruit of all true faith, the object of the whole discussion of the Article on Faith is to mystify, as Papists ever do, and love to do, the great doctrine of Justification. Pray look at this if you happen to have the "Formularies of Faith," &c. at hand, and then turn to the Decrees and Canons of the Council of Trent, or to the Rhemist's Annotations on James, chap. II. latter end. Now this must suffice, and be assured how much I abide

Your attached friend,

G. CORRIE.

The Diary next contains notice of the funeral of Mr Simeon —whose death had occurred, as we have seen, on November 14th—and further gives some account of three Memorial Sermons preached on the following Sunday by Professor Scholefield.

Nov. 19. To-day Mr Simeon was buried in the Chapel of King's College. I was unable to attend on account of the wet and cold weather, but I am told there was an immense attendance, the Vice-Chancellor, many Heads of Houses, and numbers of all grades in the University and of the Town. Many went away who could not obtain admittance. Any member of the University was admitted who went in mourning. Thus is buried a true servant of God; one who (like us all) had his failings, but who has been enabled to do more good for the Church of Christ in England than any person now living.

Nov. 20. Professor Scholefield preached this morning from 1 Samuel ii. 30, "Them that honour Me I will honour." It was a Funeral Sermon for Mr Simeon. The discourse was introduced by a few general remarks on (1) what it is to honour God: (2) what the reward of such conduct is. In the first he noticed that God is honoured by zeal in His service; by seeking His glory with a single eye; by a holy life. (2nd) The reward is success to our labour, honour before men, eternal glory in heaven. In each of these particulars the Professor applied the matter to Mr Simeon, dwelling on the zeal which he had manifested during a life of 54 years as a minister of Christ in this Town; by the singleness of purpose which he always showed in matters of religion, and in those on which the interests of religion depended. As an example, he mentioned that Mr S. never gave away his Church patronage to *friends*, but always with a view of obtaining the fittest persons to serve the Church: then, his holy, consistent life was known to all. The result was that he, 2ndly, received the reward of his endeavours to honour God, by having many souls given as the result of his ministrations. He also received honour from men, for from having been greatly persecuted and opposed as a young and middle-aged person, he lived to be so respected that persons of all grades, both in the University and Town, honoured his remains by attending at his funeral; and now he is receiving the highest honour in the enjoyment of God's immediate presence. The obvious conclusion is that (1) we should give God praise for the manifestation of His grace in His deceased servant, (2) and then in God's strength be anxious to follow that eminent servant in the various acts in which he honoured God. The Church was crowded— great numbers were in mourning. The sermon was impressive. In the afternoon the Professor preached at Great St Mary's to a very crowded congregation from 2 Kings ii. 9—12. This was also a funeral sermon for Mr Simeon. He showed how this history received its parallel in the removal and succession of the ministers of Christ. The ministerial office is parallel to that of Elijah, in its being like his, the mainstay of any kingdom or nation, "My father, my father, the chariot of Israel and the horsemen thereof," being a recognition of the idea that the presence of Elijah at that time was the true stay of the kingdom; and that his being thus taken away, was like a removal of all the means on which the moral safety of the country depended. So it is only by a clergy deeply imbued with the prophetic spirit that any country can become truly great; worldly politicians may enter on commercial speculation, &c., and the people all the while be sinking lower and lower in the scale of morality, until God casts off the nation; but the ministers of Christ who are dispersed throughout the country become, by the ordinance of God, the means of "exalting the country by righteousness." He concluded by giving a sketch of Mr Simeon's character, which he did with exquisite taste and warmth of feeling. Among other things he stated that Mr Simeon was a Calvinist in all points but on the article of reprobation; that he was singularly honest in his desire to ascertain the real meaning of a text of Scripture without reference to systems of any kind; and that in an epitaph which he wrote some time ago for himself, he desired it to be engraved on his tomb that the whole subject of his preaching was "Salvation by grace, through a crucified Redeemer;" that he had always desired a calm and peaceful death, rather than what is called a "triumphant" one; that in his devotions he used to observe, "he never communed with God so fully, as when using the Liturgy of the Church of England." Such were some of the particulars stated. The whole congregation was deeply attentive, many strangers attended, and some members of the University not usually present. I observed Archdeacon Hodson, Close of Cheltenham, Low of Colchester, Hensman of Clifton, Dr Dealtry of Clapham. The latter I hear preached Mr Simeon's Funeral Sermon in Trinity Church in the morning, and Archdeacon Hodson was to preach there in the evening. Our Master told me he thought highly of the Professor's sermon at St Mary's, and that it was much admired by Professor Smyth and others. In the evening I went to hear the Professor preach again. He promised in his morning sermon (which had reference exclusively to Mr Simeon's public character) to notice some of the particulars of Mr Simeon's private life. His text was Psal. xxxvii. 37. After pointing out in a lucid and striking manner the meaning of "perfect" and "upright," and how necessarily the end of such a one is "peace," the Professor stated how the text was exemplified in Mr Simeon. He mentioned among other things, that when Mr Simeon was first called to a knowledge of the truth as a very young man, he set himself at once by earnest prayer to seek to know more of God's will; yet for several months his state was that of darkness and perplexity. This state of discomfort reached its very highest during Passion week; and in that season especially Mr Simeon seemed to be without the least peace. On the morning of Easter-day he awoke with this line on his mind, "The Lord is risen indeed, Hallelujah!" and from that day to his death he never doubted his acceptance with God. It was stated also that Mr Simeon did

not derive his comfort in his last illness from the contemplation of any particular promises, but from the consideration of
the whole scheme of redemption in all its fulness as extending
from eternity to eternity. " I adore," he said, "the sovereignty
of God for having chosen me a sinner, irrespective of all merit
in me, and notwithstanding my sin ; I adore the mercy of
God for having redeemed me by His Son ; I adore the
patience of God in so long bearing with my ingratitude ; I
adore the faithfulness of God for having kept me true to the
end." The Professor again mentioned Mr Simeon's wish to
have a peaceful, rather than a triumphant death ; "for," he
said, " I desire to pass out of life as an humble, redeemed
sinner, into the presence of God's holiness." These are some
of the striking particulars mentioned ; and no written account
can convey the exquisitely beautiful manner in which they
were related by the Preacher, who concluded by desiring each
individual to examine whether he were "perfect" and "upright," and so had a well-grounded hope of "peace" at the
last. The Professor mentioned the case of poor C. of this
College as one full of peace, and also that of another person.
He concluded by a powerful address to the congregation, exhorting all to be preparing for the great change of death
which must pass upon all. Many wept, many looked sorrowful, all must have been deeply impressed. Poor Mr Simeon !
he has indeed been this day honoured in the estimation of all:
his soul now rests in peace, and his memory may, in this place
at least, not long survive the present generation, but many,
many, will doubtless rise up in the Last Day and call him
blessed. For myself, I have long desired to honour him as
an eminent servant of God, and have desired to defend him
when I have heard him commented upon by those who understood him not; but as a man, a natural character, I had no
sympathy with him. That, in all probability, was because I
understood him not. Now one sees how little all one's
natural tastes are to be heeded, and how all-important is the
renewal of the heart, and the activity of the life in God's

service. For myself I can truly say, I desire no more from the hands of a gracious God than to die as Mr Simeon has died, "An humble, redeemed sinner."

Nov. 26. Willis brought to my recollection that the first sermon Mr Simeon preached this year was one in which he urged his people very much to seek God to their salvation. At the same time, Mr Simeon stated that he was thus in great earnestness, because he thought he should die before the end of the year. This is remarkable. At the time, I remember both Willis and myself attributed this expression to that kind of feeling with which most people begin a new year who reflect at all. However so it has turned out.

Nov. 27. I preached in Chapel. My object was to give a review of the Articles of Religion set forth in 1536, by way of introduction to a course of Lectures which Philpott and myself are about to give on some of the Articles of 1571. I was somewhat nervous, this being my first attempt to preach since Oct. 1832, when I broke a blood-vessel in preaching. That sermon was preached at Blatherwycke. I was enabled to pray earnestly that this recommencement of preaching might be without bodily detriment to me, and prove the beginning of fresh usefulness in God's service.

I took tea with Mandell, who told me much about Mr Simeon's funeral. He said there was great sorrow when Mr Simeon's body was lowered into the vault, and that one of those who almost wept aloud was one I like much, but one very unlikely, as I thought, to have so much regard for Mr Simeon, or to be so much affected by his death as he appears to have been. But death calls forth many sympathies as we look into the graves of others, and are thus brought to meditate on the time when to "die the death of the righteous" will be our only desire.

Nov. 30. Two Graces came before the Senate to-day; (1) for confirming the Report of the Syndicate which recommends £2500 being spent on building the Public Library. It was non-placeted in the Lower House by only five persons. (2) The grace for granting £300 towards building 50 Churches in and about London was carried in the Lower House, but thrown out in the White Hood House. In the Upper House a grace for giving £50 toward the rebuilding of Great St Andrew's Church was thrown out.

Dec. 7. I saw a letter G. Fisher had received from Sir Fred. Pollock, in which he stated that a dissolution of Parliament was expected in February. The reason given was that the present Ministers at the opening of Parliament will try to pass the resolution expressive of their determination to carry the Appropriation Clause in an Irish Tithe Bill, failing in which (as is expected) they will either dissolve Parliament or tender their resignation of office to the King. I am told that the Conservatives are preparing to bring forward Mr Knight, the Chancery Barrister, and Mr Manners Sutton, as Candidates for the representation of this Town.

Dec. 15. I had a long call from Mr W. about the Election of Members of Parliament for this Town. There seem to be many opinions and many differences, and most probably the Conservative cause will be ruined by factious divisions.

Dec. 16. I had a long visit from a friend, who told me it had just been decided at a meeting of the Conservative Society to bring forward Mr Knight and Mr Manners Sutton as Candidates for the representation of this Town in Parliament whenever there may be a General Election.

Dec. 17. The President of Queens', Dr King, told me that nothing can promise better than the unanimity of the Conservative cause in this town. May it prove so!

Dec. 18. I read prayers in Chapel to-day, a duty I have not undertaken for four or five years. May my increased strength be the forerunner of increasing usefulness and zeal in the service of God.

Dec. 20. I walked an hour with ——. He conversed on the wonderful idea of God in all His infinite goodness, &c. &c. We agreed that it is equally a matter of wonder, how a soul that has once tasted of God's redeeming love and been made acquainted with His redeeming mercy and loving kindness, can ever again have any relish for the sin and unsatisfactoriness of earth! Sad indeed is the deadening effect of sin that can thus admit of insensibility to Him whose love is as boundless as the Eternal perfection of His nature.

Dec. 22. In the evening I drank tea with —— and went over and corrected the MS. of a Catechism for Children.

Dec. 27. Kettering. Snow continues to fall. The mail from London passed at 10 instead of 3 in the morning, drawn by six horses, there being three post-boys, but no coachman on the box. No mail has come from the north for two days, and the mail from London yesterday which arrived here so late did not get further than Rockingham.

Dec. 28. No coaches of any kind have arrived or passed through to-day. The old rector of Kettering, Mr Vevers, who is 82 years of age says there has not been such a snow-storm for 60 years.

Dec. 31. The last day of the year! It is indeed a solemn feeling with which the mind looks back on time to return no more. There is something very overwhelming in the idea that the past is gone for ever except so far as it exists in the increased sanctification of the soul which has taken place as time passes! May I duly consider the end for which time is given, and in each recurring year receive strength from on high to enable me to walk without weariness in the paths of God's holy commandments.

CHAPTER IV.

The Diary for 1837 opens with the following remarks on Heb. xiii. 13—14.

Jan. 1, 1837. Strange that there should be any reproach to be encountered in following Christ. Yet so it is—the divine Saviour was a subject for the reviling and contempt of the Jews and others, to whom His personal Ministry was addressed ; and the doctrine of Christ crucified, as set forth by His Apostles and Messengers, was foolishness and a stumbling-block to those who then heard it, and ever has it been thus. "The reproach of Christ" is not always exactly the same in kind, but in degree it varies little. The human heart is so opposed to the humiliating doctrines of the Gospel, that it is only as we are brought to feel the suitableness of these doctrines to the necessities of our wretchedness and sin, that we cordially embrace the reproach which the Cross brings with it. Then we can indeed enter into the spirit of the holy Apostle when exhorting the Hebrew Christians, "Let us go forth unto Him bearing His reproach." Yes, Thou glorious Saviour, to be Thine in body soul and spirit is the desire of every heart that has but once tasted of Thy love in redeeming it from its once unhappiness. Then can we glory in tribulation for Thy sake. No resting-place is here for him whose affections have by grace ascended to where Christ *dwells*, for there only is his home. To be with Christ in that union of spirit which is the Christian's privilege even on earth, is most sweet and consoling; but his daily desires are after that "City which is to come," where he will see his Saviour face to face, and exchange a transitory reproach for an abiding glory. Oh that with the recurrence of each year I might be found more and more absorbed in the pursuit of that continuing rest which remaineth for the people of God!

Jan. 9. I left Kettering for Blatherwycke. I spent the evening in conversing with Mrs O'Brien on subjects connected with faith and Christian experience.

Feb. 8. Had some talk with the Dean of Peterborough on the Church Commissioners' Report. On my complaining that these Commissioners had recommended changes in Cathedral property which were not warranted by any principle of justice, the Dean observed that the Bishop of Lincoln (one of the Commissioners) had told him that they recommended these changes lest the matter should be taken up by others and worse changes be effected. But the Dean answered, "You have issued your Report, as you drew it up— *under the influence of fear.*" This is the truth. Yet the Dean told me that —— was at the bottom of it all, seconded by the Bishop of London, who seems to be ready to sweep away all Chapters. May God deliver us from the hands of the timid and unfaithful.

Feb. 16. Wrote to H. Rose on the necessity of furnishing our friends in Parliament with all possible information on the subject of Church Rates preparatory to the attack about to be made by the Dissenters.

Feb. 19. Heard —— preach on the Supreme Divinity of our Lord. The sermon was strictly argumentative, and, so far as the quotation of texts went, conclusive. Perhaps, the subject being an admitted truth, the sermon might appear dryer than it was. It is well to feel that admitted truths ought still to possess in one's soul such deep absorbing interest as never to appear dry. The fault is in the hearer.

Mr Corrie's interest in politics, which, it has been seen, was strong even in early youth, had increased with his advancing experience. The references to such topics both in the Diary and in the few letters which follow show distinctly that he never swerved from his Conservative principles, and, although it was not until some years later that he became the recognised leader of the Conservative interest in Cambridge, he was already beginning to take an active part in such matters especially as affected the condition and interests of the University.

CAMBRIDGE, *Feb.* 19, 1837.

My dear Chevallier,

  ...I do pity your go-between state, for though you are a Tory set, yet you really are a part of "the Movement." For myself, nothing but your religion and politics in your body-personal, renders the mention of your name as a body-corporate, tolerable to ears which heard in the report of the appropriation of part of the Cathedral property to your use, the sound of *spoliation.* I suppose it is to set at nought the wisdom of the wise, that God permits good to be done under circumstances so equivocal, for if the Chapter of Durham consented to alienate their revenues for purposes not contemplated (is it so?) by the Donors, and in so doing did right; what is all this din of Deans and Chapters about the sacrilege of meddling with other Cathedral property for the sake of effecting objects equally desirable? However, for the present, I believe there is to be no further progress in Church-robbery to be made, but then there are the Church Rates to be thrown overboard....

Feb. 21. I was told to-day there was to be a great opposition in the Senate-House, to a Grace, the purport of which is to enable the Vice-Chancellor to defend the University privilege of licensing Ale-houses, against the New Corporation Magistrates who have commenced a law-suit against the University on that head.

Feb. 22. There was a great assembly of the Senate to-day, owing to there being three important Graces to be passed; one for effecting a material change in the examination of the Non-reading Questionists to take effect in 1841; one to effect a beneficial change in the regulations with regard to the Previous Examination of the Junior Sophs, the most material of which allows such Junior Sophs as are plucked, or have through sickness &c. been prevented from going into the Examination in the Lent Term, to be examined in the *same* subjects in the October of the same year. The third Grace was to enable the Vice-Chancellor to defend the privileges of the University against the attacks of the Radical Corporation. The first two Graces passed without opposition, though many did not like them in all parts. The third was opposed, but carried by a majority of 37.

Mr Corrie's intercourse with the family of the O'Briens of Blatherwycke Park, Northants, and Cratlow Woods, Co. Clare, resulted in a very close friendship between himself and the eldest son Augustus, who in 1841 was returned to Parliament as member for North Northamptonshire, and in 1847 resumed the family name of Stafford. Although many years his junior, Mr Stafford's qualities of mind and heart were such as greatly to attract Mr Corrie's regard. Mr Stafford on his part highly valued Mr Corrie's friendship, and this mutual esteem led to continued intercourse between them until the lamented early death of Mr Stafford.

CAMBRIDGE, *Feb.* 23, 1837.

My dear Augustus,

      ...As I have often said to you, I desire most unwaveringly to repose in the moral attributes of the Ever-living, who for the wisest and holiest purposes may not put down iniquity and falsehood at the moment, but who ultimately causes the wicked to be taken in his own snare. We are now reaping the fruits of that legislative renunciation of God, virtually made on passing the Roman Catholic Bill of 1829. For ourselves, we have nothing to do but to prepare, as God enables us, for such trials and sufferings as may ere long await us, in the hope, nay lofty confidence, that our country, on returning to God, may have peace at the price of our afflictions. I see but little else before us, for it is evident that if this Municipal Bill for Ireland do not pass, the Whigs will go out. But who can govern the country? If it do pass, it must be at a sacrifice, a cowardly sacrifice, of principle in the House of Lords. For who can suppose that Ireland will not be so thrown into the hands of the Papists, as to secure a permanent majority in the House of Commons efficient only for mischief? However, in these anticipations you must not suppose that I have the least idea of encouraging a spirit of despondency. My aim, as regards myself, is boldly to look at the evil and prepare for the worst, acting most energetically for the right, but prepared for any wrong which an infidel legislation may inflict on me. This, also, I should wish to be your spirit. By God's grace let our fall be that of men who respect themselves, if it is to come, and in the meanwhile let us use every human means for our deliverance which God puts into our hands. I am sure we are too often called to feel how much is lost by wavering or indifference, and so we had need guard against being, by this means, accessory to our miseries. For the rest, there is a God who rules in heaven, and He has so mercifully ordered the soul that happiness should come from *within*. No affliction ought or need to be chosen as a mere matter of self-denial; but trials have their limit, if our heart be right with God. Here let us rest, looking beyond the present to brighter and better worlds. But I have done.

Ever your truly affectionate,

G. E. CORRIE.

Mr Stafford shows his appreciation of another side of Mr Corrie's character when he writes to him to introduce a young friend about to enter the University. "I am going "to tell him you are not a folio bound in vellum, but, con-"sistent with local requirements, somewhat alive to the de-"lights of—rat-catching, moreover that you are my dearest "friend and ready to be a hearty one to him."

Feb. 26. I have been looking into Bellarmine on Baptism with a view of tracing the strong affinity that exists between the Romish doctrine of that Sacrament and Professor Pusey's Tracts.

March 3. Three Graces passed the Senate to-day without opposition ;—

(1) To carry into effect certain modifications of the Plan on which it was purposed to build the Fitzwilliam Museum. Among other things it is to be raised 1 ft. throughout, and $4\frac{1}{2}$ ft. in centre.

(2) To invest £7000 Fitzwilliam money.

(3) To enable the Vice-Chancellor to take the advice of civilians in consequence of a dispute with the Parishioners of St Mary's about the Faculty for the Galleries &c. used by the University.

March 28. I have been occupied with looking out pa-rallel authorities for an Act introduced into the House of Lords, to appoint Commissioners to visit the Universities of Oxford and Cambridge, for the purpose of enquiring into and reporting on the Statutes and administration of the affairs of the different Colleges. This Act is paralleled by the proceedings of the Commonwealth and tyrannical Parlia-ments of those times.

The following undated letter, although obviously written rather earlier, is here inserted in connection with the next extract from the Diary on the same subject.

Extract from a letter to Mr Chevallier.

It seems by the public papers that Lord Radnor intends to bring in a Bill *next* Session to admit Dissenters to Degrees at the Universities, and in consideration of this I have decided on employing my leisure hours in drawing up a short history of the operations of Dissent within the Universities (Cambridge more particularly), from the first stirrings of Puritanism to the Commonwealth. I have got together all that is to be found in Strype's *Annals*, and should be very glad if you would put down anything you may meet with bearing on that subject and period. It will be the fault of the friends of things as they now are, if all the information connected with the subject be not got together by the time the enemies of the Church begin to attack the Universities again. It would be well that all the arguments used in Parliament in favor of the admission of Dissenters should be collected and answered, so that, without referring to the speeches of A, B and C, a pamphlet might be got ready containing an answer to all arguments that have been or may be used. The *Mirror of Parliament* will give the speeches. The arguments of the 60 should be met at the same time without allusion to, or mention of the Petitioners. My feeling is that it is one's *duty* to do this, and for that purpose I shall collect these arguments as I can, in the hope that either yourself or the Master of Jesus will digest them into a readable form, with answers to them. I find Baines, the member for Leeds, talking of the College Fellowships and Scholarships being *Roman Catholic* Foundations, whereas my impression is that the greater number of Fellowships and *all* the Scholarships are Protestant and Episcopalian. The Scholarship Foundations are of most importance, because Baines seems to claim a right for Dissenters to participate in these, though he abjures for the present the notion of intruding Dissenters into Fellowships. Cannot accurate information be obtained on this point?

Ever your sincere friend,
G. E. CORRIE.

April 3. I was occupied all day by a Pamphlet on Lord Radnor's Bill for introducing Dissent into the Universities.

April 8. I called on the Dean of Peterborough, who told me he had just finished his reply to Dr Wiseman's Book on the Eucharist. I went to consult the Dean about a Petition to be sent by the College to Parliament against a Bill brought into the House of Lords to interfere with the Statutes of the Colleges and Halls in Oxford and Cambridge. I had been many hours drawing up the Petition, and the Dean kindly corrected it.

April 9. In the evening the President of Queens' (Dr King) came to my rooms to talk about a Petition to the House of Lords. He deplored that there had been no Petition from the *University*, and said that he feared we were becoming divided among ourselves. May a good Providence watch over our Institutions in these perilous times, and give us unity and firmness in resistance!

April 11. I called on the Master of Trinity this morning about a Memorial to the Church Commissioners on the subject of their sad Report respecting Deans and Chapters.

April 13. I found my pamphlet on my table, "Brief Historical Notice of the Interference of the Crown with the affairs of the English Universities," together with a note from H. Rose.

April 16. I drank tea with Mandell. We talked over the difficulties of the present moral and political affairs of the country, and the serious aspect which Popery is beginning to assume; though we agreed that the nation is become more awake to what Popery is. Mandell told me that the President of Queens' had been present at the late debate in the House of Lords on Lord Radnor's Bill respecting the Universities, and that he (the President) had left the House with the impression that Lord Radnor would never bring his Bill forward again in the form of his last motion.

April 21. The Master of Jesus and Mr Tatham, President of St John's, called on me to say there had been a meeting of the Heads, at which a communication was made from our Chancellor, Marquess Camden, stating that it is the opinion of the friends of the University in high places that the different Colleges would do well to ascertain what authority there had been provided for revising their respective Statutes; and, secondly, whether the different Societies were willing to apply to such competent authority for a modification of such parts of their respective Statutes as required modification? The object of the Master of Jesus and Mr Tatham was to call at each College, in order to ascertain the feeling of the different Societies, with a view to having that feeling communicated at a Meeting of the Heads appointed to take place next Monday. I wrote to the Master on the subject.

April 24. Philpott and myself went into the Treasury to ascertain whether the King as Visitor of this College had ever dispensed with different Statutes. We found several such dispensations. This result the Master submitted to the Vice-Chancellor. I have been all day employed in copying the Statutes given to this College by the Founder. They do not much differ from those now in use.

On April 28 he notes his birthday in the following words :

April 28. ...I am this day 44 years old... May God enable me by His Almighty grace to resolve to live for the future in all watchful holiness of heart as well as of life.

May 1. Battiscombe, a Fellow of King's College, was re-baptized in the Baptist Meeting House in St Andrew's Street; he had previously resigned his Fellowship, and is now gone to preach as the Minister in a Baptist Meeting House at Royston. For some time he was Curate to Professor Farish at St Giles' in this town. There he used to have a service and sermon every morning in the week at *six* throughout the winter. Great numbers of the poor went to hear him, and I believe he was of use to many. But for some time his religious notions have been unsettled; and he has ceased from preaching, attending at the Baptist Chapel before mentioned, until he was rebaptized. He seems to have no objection to the Prayer-book beyond a dislike to be tied down to a Form of Prayer. One may hope he will come to a better mind.

May 3. I called on the Provost of King's, Dr Thackeray, to speak with him about the Royal Commission which is much talked of as likely to be sent to the University. He asked me to give him what information I could about the Law of Visitation, and so I am enquiring into it.

May 8. The Master of Jesus and Mr Tatham called on me on the subject of an expected Royal Commission appointing Visitors to the Universities. It was agreed that it was essentially necessary that preparation should be made by informing ourselves of the law of the case, in order to submitting our case to some eminent lawyer, Chancery-Barrister and Civilian. Sir Wm. Follett, Mr Pemberton, and Dr Adams were mentioned as persons each eminent in his department. It was agreed, also, that the Statutes of different Colleges should be examined in order to ascertain what power existed for modifying such Statutes as required modification. It was suggested that a classification of Colleges should be made. This the Master of Jesus is to do. I agreed to examine the subject of the King's legal power to grant a Commission to Visitors at all.

May 11. The Provost of King's called. He told me that many of the Colleges seemed disposed to set about revising their Statutes, but that he considered himself prevented from stirring in the matter by the tenor of the Provost's Oath. There was a meeting in my rooms of Prof. Scholefield, Messrs Webster of Queens', Carus and Perry of Trinity, Langshaw and Isaacson of St John's, for the purpose of forming a Society, the object of which shall be to assist deserving men of piety and talent in prosecuting their University studies, by giving them pecuniary aid.

May 13. Yesterday a Petition went up from the resident B.A.s and Undergraduates to both Houses of Parliament, expressive of their confidence in, and regard for, all who exercise authority in the University. This is in consequence of some uncalled for and ill-natured observations made against the Tutors, &c., by Lords Radnor and Melbourne, &c., in the late Debates in Parliament.

May 16. A second meeting in my rooms respecting the formation of a Society for assisting deserving young men in the prosecution of their Academical studies, when a Prospectus was agreed upon, and Directors' names selected.

May 24. To-day the Princess Victoria attained the age of 18. There was a Dinner in the Town Hall for the Burgesses, the Mayor in the Chair, and in the evening fireworks were exhibited in King's College grounds.

June 2. Saw a letter written by Lord Radnor in which he states that we of the Universities "are very much deceived, if we suppose the country will be satisfied with the mere alteration of such Statutes as enjoin obsolete customs." So his Lordship has shown the cloven-foot, but I trust he will find himself grievously mistaken if he supposes we shall concede to him any *principle* in our alterations.

June 6. I attended a Committee of the Barnwell Schools. It was mentioned that Providence (Baptist) Chapel in Barnwell was to be sold this evening ; it stands contiguous to the Schools. It was agreed to bid for it not more than £600, the sum to be raised by subscription, and several of us became responsible for the payment of the purchase money if a good title can be made. A saving would thus be effected for the Schools, which must be enlarged ere long.

June 12. I called on the Master of Corpus, Dr Lamb, to ask to be allowed to copy the Commissions issued by Henry 8th and Edward 6th for the Visitation of the University of Cambridge, which are contained in the volumes of the Parker MSS. In the afternoon I had some conversation with the Master of Jesus on ecclesiastical affairs. I promised him some notices of the interference of Royalty with Cathedrals, and have been at work on this all the evening.

The death of Bishop Corrie at Madras from apoplexy was a great shock to his family, especially as the announcement of it in the newspapers preceded the receipt of the letters conveying the sad intelligence. It is thus recorded in the Diary.

June 13. In the papers of this morning, the *Record*, *Standard* and *Globe*, there was the painful announcement of the death of my eldest brother at Madras. The Report I believe to be premature and to have arisen out of the account brought of my sister-in-law's death, particularly as I have a letter from my brother dated Jan. 31. Yet God may have this affliction in store for our family, that by thus gradually narrowing the family circle we may learn to look forward to the undying relationships of a future world !

June 14. This morning brought a letter from my brother-in-law, confirming the report of my eldest brother's death which occurred on Sunday, Feb. 5th, after five days' illness. He retained his consciousness to the last, so far as to express his feelings. It appears that apoplexy was the immediate cause of his death. He had not long returned from his Visitation at Hyderabad and complained of being rather unwell, but not materially so. Yet the doctors say his illness had been coming on some time. Thus has another earthly tie been rent asunder. May my soul learn to follow my sainted brother as he was enabled by grace meekly and devoutly to follow Christ !

June 18. I had a letter containing further particulars of my brother's last illness. I have been looking over a sermon preached by him on the death of Bishop Heber, and have felt very sad and melancholy at times. I have had many kind messages of sympathy and enquiry.

A letter on the same subject from Mr Corrie to his niece is here introduced.

St Catharine's Hall,
July 5, 1837.

My dear Mary Anne,

Many thanks for your last letter, which has afforded me as much satisfaction as the communication of particulars relating to a brother's death-bed can. I have received a letter from one of the Chaplains up the country, but it does not contain any new matter or convey any feeling respecting your Uncle which is not repeated in the Madras Paper, part of which I saw in the *Record.* All accounts, however, agree in representing our loss to have been occasioned by apoplexy, and I wish I could feel that the doctors had adopted that active treatment which one is accustomed to see applied to such diseases in England. This, however, is only one of the flimsy reasons and wishes which cross the mind in its unwillingness to yield up without reluctance one of those many objects of affection which the heart creates for itself; and thus in the bitterness of first grief one is apt to complain of the want of skill of man, instead of submissively giving thanks to God for those troubles with which, for the most merciful purposes, He visits us. The object of all God does is to bring us to that state of heart which is "thankful for all He takes away, and humbled by all He gives." If we are but too apt to seek in other objects that solace in part, which is to be found in God alone, it is but a mark of His unfailing love, if, instead of giving us opportunities for becoming besotted with earthly affections, He removes those to a happier state on which our hearts have been accustomed to be set, that thus we may be at once chastened and liberated, and encouraged to seek for relationships which endure evermore. Or it may be that, by the successive removal of our kindred at short—or rapid intervals, we may be gradually taught what we are slow to learn, viz. that God can supply so fully all the relationships

C.6

of father and sister and brother in this life, that we need not fear to trust for undying happiness in Him alone in the world to come. Still I agree with you, that the possession of such a relation as my now sainted brother, is a talent for which we may be expected hereafter to give an account, and it is therefore not unprofitable for us all carefully to enquire into the good we have received from his holy, peaceful example, or into the responsibility we may have incurred, or shall incur, if his example be lost upon us; only our encouragement may be, on finding how far short we fall of his devoted life, that the same Almighty Grace which strengthened him to serve God with a devoted heart, is available for us if we seek it as he did.

June 20. Intelligence reached us of the death of the King. This melancholy event has occurred at a very critical period of the history of this country, an unsettled government, a democratic spirit abroad. Above all a careless disregard of the progress of Popery, and with it, of tyrannical opinions and practices, as manifested in many of the Bills lately brought into Parliament. Yet is the nation in the hands of God, and we ought to pray earnestly that "the course of this world may be so peaceably ordered that the Church may serve God in all godly quietness."

June 22. The Master of Jesus came to my rooms to look at some papers I had written respecting the Visitation &c. of Cathedrals. He told me the Chapter of Ely had authorised him and the Dean to take Counsel's opinion as to whether or not the members of the different Cathedrals were obliged to attend to any summons of the Committee of the House of Commons, which has lately been appointed to enquire as to the letting of Church property with a view of paying Church Rates out of it. I told the Master I trusted they would resist, for that I believed the existence of Church property to be comprised in the question at issue.

June 23. The Vice-Chancellor called the University

together to-day to proclaim Queen Victoria. We met at
10 o'clock. The Proclamation was first made in the Senate-
House, the Vice-Chancellor sitting in the Chancellor's chair,
then again on the South steps of the Senate-House, then at
the Market Cross, and lastly on Market Hill. There was
much cheering. At 12 o'clock proclamation was made by the
Mayor. He was in an open carriage drawn by four horses,
and had in his train a long cavalcade of horsemen. Among
the horsemen were three or four M.A.s *in their gowns.* Two of
them were Fellows of their Colleges. The reason why these
gentlemen preferred the company of the Mayor, is to be
found in their extreme radical politics. The bells have been
ringing, and there has been much firing of ordnance and
squibs, and one's heart aches as one remembers that the poor
King is lying dead in the midst of all this pomp and
rejoicing. I could not but reflect on the unstable nature
of all earthly regards, and how soon the fickle selfishness
of the heart turns from the dead to the living. As I paced
the College lawn in the evening, I thought that speedily will
come the time when the sound of my footsteps will be
numbered among the things forgotten, and that my place
will soon be supplied by those who will know me only as
my name occurs in the College records, and so I heartily
prayed to God to deal with me here as best seemed to His
blessed Will, and then to receive me to His glory, in antici-
pation of which I should be content to pass into oblivion here
on earth, when, and as soon as, God should see fit to call me.

June 26. The Master of Jesus was with me soon after
nine a.m., bringing with him the Case it is intended to
submit to the Counsel, respecting the power of the House of
Commons to call for, and examine, the members of the
Cathedral at Ely, with a view of ascertaining how they let
their property. This Case consisted of nothing but a synopsis
of a paper I had previously sent to the Master on the subject,
containing references to Acts of Parliament which protect
Cathedrals.

June 27. To-day at Corpus Lodge I copied a Commission given by Cardinal Pole to visit the University.

June 28. I was occupied in copying the Commission given by Queen Elizabeth, to Cecil, Parker and others to visit the University of Cambridge. I copied it from the Parker MS. in Corpus Christi College, through the kind permission of the Master.

July 8. To-day the King was buried, and in consequence the Vice-Chancellor and the University met in the Senate-House at a quarter before eleven. We then proceeded in the order of degree to St Mary's, where a sermon was preached by the Master of Christ's College. The senior Proctor read the Litany; the Anthem was from Ps. xvi., the last four verses.

July 10. This evening Spring Rice came from London to canvass the electors. Notice was given of his expected visit, and a band of music went round Barnwell to collect ragamuffins to meet him at Stone Bridge. A cavalcade was formed of some forty men on horseback and a great many boys. Men were scanty, and the whole a failure.

The Provost of King's called on me this morning to ask me about the nature and authority of College Seals. It has been the custom in King's College for the Provost's Seal only to be affixed to certain documents, such as Petitions, &c., but as the Petition sent from King's College against the Bill lately brought into Parliament by Lord Radnor about the Universities, was signed and sealed only (according to custom) by the Provost, some persons have maliciously given it out that the whole affair was a scheme of the Provost's, and not a Petition from the Society. The Provost very naturally seemed annoyed. He told me also that he could not consent to any alteration in their Statutes consistently with his Oath, and he said that he could not conscientiously administer any Statutes that might be given different from the present ones. I told him that if any new Statutes were forced upon him, I certainly would not resign the Provostship, but leave others to prosecute me and eject me if they chose.

July 14. I joined the Vice-Chancellor and his company at the Thatched House Tavern to carry an address to the Queen. The procession was admitted at St James's Palace, and we were ushered into the Royal presence. The crowd was so great it was impossible to see the Queen, except just the top of her head. I heard her Majesty read her answer. It consisted of expressions of satisfaction at the presentation of the Address, of her confidence that those who ruled in the University would take care to instil sound principles into those entrusted to their charge, of her intention to do all in her power to encourage them, of her wish to see well-considered improvements introduced—of her acceptance of the Bible which the University presented to her, and of her intention to order it to be placed in the Library of Windsor, and to consider it one of the choicest treasures of the place, &c. &c. The presentation then took place, but the crowd was so great and the heat so insupportable, that I was fain to make my way out. The Duchess of Kent stood behind the Queen and a Lady in waiting at her side.

At this date we find Mr Corrie's first acquaintance with the Irvingites. The daughters of the old friend with whom he made his home when in London had joined this sect, and this circumstance led to his being brought into contact with others holding these opinions.

July 14. I dined at Dr R.'s, where I met with sundry Irvingites. The conversation turned on the unity of the Church, and of the position of the Church of England. Many very wild notions were started, very much profound ignorance of the Church's constitution displayed, and many popish sentiments maintained. The impression left on my mind is that the great body of the educated Irvingites will die in the Church of Rome. However, the whole argument was carried on in a calm, peaceful spirit, and I trust some of us may be the better for it.

July 16. I have to-day especially felt how wretched divisions in religious opinions are, since I have not had the satisfaction this day of worshipping in the "unity of the Spirit" with all those dear to me in this house. Whilst I was uniting in the supplications of the Church, others I love were joining in the worship of a congregation which I cannot but regard as in grievous error. My heart felt much as I was called to use in family prayer this evening the petition, "That it may please Thee shortly to accomplish the number of Thine elect and to hasten Thy Kingdom." Yes, O Lord, may Thy Spirit be speedily poured out from on High, that Thy servants "may be one" as Thou art in Thy Triune and adorable God-head!

July 17. Occupied in drawing up a Memoir of my deceased brother for the *British Magazine.* I had also much conversation with Mr —— respecting the Irvingites, who seem from his account to be every day departing further from the truth. Some even go so far as to say that the Christian need not withdraw himself from the society of the world. All kinds of differences of opinion exist among them, and their notions of justification and sanctification, —— told me, are very erroneous.

July 26. The Election for the Town terminated in favor of Messrs. Rice and Pryme. After the Election there was a regular row. For some cause or other the Mayor thought fit to send Maberley of King's to the station-house, and also Earnshaw of St John's, who is acting for the Senior Proctor. This so outraged the populace that they broke the window of the station-house and would have pulled it down had not the Vice-Chancellor interfered on behalf of Earnshaw. The Vice-Chancellor had also to read the Riot Act, for neither Mayor nor Corporation Magistrate dare appear to do it. Afterwards I saw Maberley marched by the police across Parker's Piece to be committed to prison, but the populace ran on before, and formed so dense a mass at the Town Gaol door that the police could not effect an entrance. I could not see whether violence was used, but Maberley was rescued and taken by the mob to the hustings, from whence he harangued them. The crowd afterwards conducted Maberley through the town, but what became of him I do not know. In fact I can make neither head nor tail of the cause of his and the Senior Proctor's apprehension. One sickens at the sight of so much disorder.

The remainder of this summer was spent at Blatherwycke, where Mr Henry Corrie was now rector.

Aug. 22. I made various calls at the cottages to-day; the poor seemed very glad to see me. In the evening I buried two boys who were drowned on Sunday last. There were many people present, and I took the opportunity of addressing them, with the hope that God by His Almighty Spirit would bless the words to the conviction and conversion of some souls present. The people listened with great attention. It was an affecting occasion.

Sept. 4. I have been out all day deer-shooting, but only one deer was killed.

Sept. 6. I have again been occupied in shooting deer. After dinner the squire related all the circumstances of the Limerick county election, with much spirit and feeling, and evident gratification at the high estimation in which Augustus seems to be held by the Limerick gentry.

Sept. 15. Mr O'Brien and I called on Lord Carberry. The conversation turned on the state of Ireland. Lord C. observed with great naiveté, "We must get rid of the Priests!" Would that we could verify his words!

Sept. 16. I went out to try to find a deer which had been wounded by Lord Exeter's keepers, and had been driven into this park. In about two hours I saw one which seemed to go awkwardly. I got into a tree and had the deer driven, but none answered the description, so I lost my shot.

A letter of this date to Mr Chevallier, after giving a

playful account of the outdoor life he was then enjoying, proceeds to a graphic description of the effect of the teaching of Popery on domestic life and on the individual conscience.

BLATHERWYCKE, WANSFORD, *Sept.* 16, 1837.

...Since I have been here I have scarcely opened a book owing to the special love I have for the air of heaven, and the facility with which I can here obtain it. What reading I have had has been in some of the trees of the park, as I have been waiting for deer in my old pursuit of slaying them. Yet you must not imagine that I have returned to my shooting habits, for I have practised self-denial to such a pitch that I have refrained from taking out a certificate for killing hares and partridges. Only the deer shooting is so airy and intellectual that you must excuse me for returning to the practice of it. But then it is not without its *moral* hints, for I find my old limbs less facile at climbing trees, and I am constrained to believe that I am an older chap than I was, and therefore ought to be more sober.

My brother has returned from Ireland, full of the working of Popery in that unhappy country. Nothing can be more fearful than the state of things there. Only imagine your servants some morning informing you that the Priests had forbidden them from coming in to your family worship, or from doing anything for you! Yet this is really the case often in Ireland; and the parties concerned must either submit to the domination of this priestly tyranny or become *absentees.* Immediately on the termination of the county of Limerick election, the housemaid of my friend sent her master word that she could not come in to prayers as usual, for that the priest had forbidden it under the most fearful penalties, had hunted her off her knees, and refused to hear her confession and bade her tell her master so. He had courage to face this trouble, and told his servant she must quit his house instantly, but that he would give her the best of characters. After a sharp struggle, however, the servant set the priest's curses at defiance, and kept her place. During this fight an amusing instance of female casuistry came to light. "Old Peggy," an ancient domestic and veteran confessionist, let out that she had always unburdened her soul to the priest in *Irish*, and then, quoth she, "his reverence passed no remark on my going to your Honor's prayers. I'll engage *he thought* I could not understand a hap'orth of em." Nothing could have provided against the reservation and capaciousness of such consciences as that of old Peggy, but you may understand that a habit of thus cheating "God's representative," as the priest is considered, must lead to the undervaluing of the truth of God Himself. No length of residence among them, and no experience of your kindness, can deliver you from their falsehood and peculation. Surely the great general purposes which God has declared toward the human race, are inconsistent with the long continuance of such a system as Irish Popery! and thus we may expect a not distant termination to a superstition which is at variance with all those great principles which hold society together; only we may perhaps not yet be prepared as a nation to turn to God, with full purpose of heart, and till then we may well be permitted to suffer national detriment.

...On Church matters one may hope that better principles are getting abroad, yet we have a long way to travel before we reach, as a nation, those accurate notions which actuated our forefathers....If I live to return to College, and have time, I intend to send a letter or two to the *British Magazine* on the subject of Dr Lingard's *History of England.* He is a mischievous Papist; his book therefore meets with the patronage and approbation of the human heart. But really one's life is too short to point out a tithe of the falsehood that is daily propounded, and after all few men care to be convinced of the truth. The Psalmist meant a good deal when he wrote, " as soon as they are born they go astray and speak lies."

Sept. 17. I had an interesting conversation with the Squire on the duty of living up to one's convictions.

Sept. 21. I went out early in the morning with the Squire to shoot deer. We remained out till five in the evening, and killed four deer.

Sept. 22. Mr Jackson of Stamford called; he shewed me a ring with a carnelian in it with the head of Julius Cæsar engraved upon it. This ring was formerly the property of Sir Isaac Newton.

Sept. 25. I was out deer-shooting all day. Four deer were killed.

Sept. 27. I walked to Harringworth, and called at the Parsonage, which I found buried in trees which I planted some fifteen or sixteen years ago.

Sept. 29. This morning I rose at half-past five, and proceeded to Uppingham to meet the London coach. We reached London in safety about seven in the evening. We travelled but slowly !

Oct. 20. A meeting in my rooms for the purpose of forming a Society for assisting young men of piety, talent and diligence through their academical course. Several resolutions were agreed to, and the Society was named, " The Cambridge Clerical Education Society[1]."

Nov. 1. At a Congregation to-day a Grace was passed for the purpose of substituting *Declarations* in the place of the *Oaths* hitherto taken by Freshmen at matriculation, and B.A.s ad incipiendum.

The next subject of general interest is the Laying of the Foundation Stone of the Fitzwilliam Museum.

Nov. 2. At twelve I went to the Senate-House to join a procession which started thence to lay the Foundation Stone

---

[1] This Society is still in existence (1890). Since its foundation it has assisted a large number of undergraduates, some of whom have risen to positions of high dignity and great usefulness in the Church.

of the Fitzwilliam Museum. A gallery was erected all round the open space: the whole was completely filled, and the space round where the stone was to be laid was open to the sight of the whole assembly. A copper box was let into the stone below, in which was placed one of each of the coins of the realm and a brass plate with the following inscription :

HAS · ÆDES

RICARDVS · VICECOMES · FITZWILLIAM

ADMIRABILI · MVNIFICENTIA · ET · IN · ALMAM · MATREM · PIETATE

PECVNIIS · TESTAMENTO · LEGATIS

EXTRVI · JVSSIT

IN · QVAS · LIBRI · PICTÆ · TABVLÆ

ALIAQVE · ELEGANTIORVM · ARTIVM · MONVMENTA

IPSIVS · DONA

RECIPERENTVR.

LAPIDEM · AVSPICALEM · STATVIT

GILBERTVS · AINSLIE · S.T.P.

COLLEGII · PEMBROCHIANI · CVSTOS

ACADEMIÆ · ITERVM · PROCANCELLARIVS

QVARTO · NON · NOVEMB · ANNO · DOMINI · MDCCCXXXVII

REGINÆ · VICTORIÆ · I

JOANNE · JEFFREYS · MARCHIONE · CAMDEN · ACADEMIÆ · CANCELLARIO

GEORGIO · BASEVI · ARCHITECTO.

The Vice-Chancellor, Dr Ainslie of Pembroke, then took a silver trowel and proceeded to lay the stone. The multitude then set up nine hearty cheers. The Vice-Chancellor then made a short speech, all being uncovered. The sentiment was good; he spoke of the necessity of aiming at God's honor and glory even in erecting a Museum. Three cheers for the Vice-Chancellor followed. The Public Orator (Mr Crick of St John's) then made a Latin speech, elegant enough, but very long-winded, but it was heard with patience. Another *faint* cheer followed. Then followed cheers for the Queen, the Queen Dowager, the Duke of Wellington, three groans for the Whigs, and three groans for the Proctors, &c. &c., and the meeting dispersed. All the houses were covered with people and the windows also filled with persons; the whole ceremony passed off without a jarring mischance. About seventy persons dined with the Vice-Chancellor in the Hall of Pembroke College.

During this year Dr Hollingworth resigned the Norrisian Professorship of Divinity, and, after much consideration—partly on account of his health, fearing the possible effect of the increased strain on his voice—Mr Corrie, with the concurrent advice of Dr Proctor and other friends, decided on being a candidate for the office. The first entry on the subject in the Diary occurs on

Nov. 13. The Master of Trinity called on me to inform me that I ought to leave a formal notice with him and the other Electors of my intention to be a candidate for the Norrisian Professorship now vacant. I accordingly wrote a notice as desired and am now committed to stand for the Professorship.

Nov. 23. I had a call from an Undergraduate of Corpus, introduced by one of my own pupils, with a view of having some of his scruples respecting the validity of his baptism discussed. He was baptized and bred in the Kirk of Scotland, but, having since he grew up examined the Word of God and come to the conclusion that Episcopacy was the Scriptural Church Polity, he has accordingly conformed to our Church. As yet, however, he feels unconnected with us, having by no public act united himself to our Communion. I told him that, if he could himself be satisfied of the validity of his baptism, the best plan would be for him to ratify his baptismal vows by being confirmed the first opportunity that offered. This plan he was disposed to adopt, and seemed to be a thoughtful, well-informed youth.

Nov. 24. I saw the Master of Trinity to-day. We settled to have a preliminary meeting before long by way of initiating a Society in aid of that for "promoting the employment of Additional Curates." Then we had a long conversation about a Petition from the University against the decision of the Ecclesiastical Commissioners respecting the suppression of the Bishopric of the Isle of Man.

The remainder of the Diary for this year contains nothing of general interest.

CHAPTER V.

THE year 1838 was one of the landmarks in Mr Corrie's University life, for in the spring he was elected Norrisian Professor of Divinity. Though the election was not until May, the subject was necessarily much before him. His own words from his Diary will best tell his feelings at this time. Other subjects of interest are touched on in turn, and some intercourse with a then aged member of Catharine Hall takes us back to the days of Whitfield and Wesley. The first entry is on the renewal of the Church Commission at the commencement of Queen Victoria's reign. The second entry of this year's Diary has reference to his re-editing the works of some old Cambridge Divines for the Syndics of the University Press.

1838. *Jan.* 2. The Master of Trinity told me to-day that the Church Commissioners have resolved to attack the Deans and Chapters. It was thought that, as the Commission expired with the demise of the Crown, and some of the Commissioners were heartily sick of the business, the Commission would not be renewed. It appeared, however, that by some quirk the Commission could be continued; so the Great

Seal has again been appended to it, and the sign manual obtained.

Chevallier arrived from Durham this evening. He had travelled with a man who had been almost everywhere, and among other places in Russia. This man said that very little was known and understood in England about Russia, but that it was a kingdom extending its dominions on all hands as secretly yet as surely as possible.

Jan. 13. Parker, the Printer to the University, called on me about reprinting some of the works of the old Cambridge Divines. I had proposed a reprint of Stillingfleet's works, but the Bishop of London, to whom Parker mentioned my intentions, suggested that, for a trial, a less voluminous writer might as well be taken in hand, and named Mede or Smith. In this I think his Lordship has judged rightly, but not as to the author; so I have fixed on Archbishop Bramhall's works. If the Syndics of the University Press will defray the expense, I hope to have health and strength to fulfil my intentions, for I feel it to be a disgrace to our Body that some of our greatest Cambridge Divines should have their works printed at Oxford. At dinner, Earnshaw, who is one of the examiners, told me that a Queens' man left the Senate-House after having done only two papers, and gave as his reason for doing no more that the questions were *too easy* for him!

Jan. 14. Scholefield mentioned to me to-day that our precious Ministers, in repealing an Act of Parliament connected with the stamps of Almanacs, had got rid of one of the privileges of the University Press, but never apprized us of it till the privilege was taken away *sub silentio.* Alas! alas!

Jan. 15. I have felt some suspicious symptoms of my complaint in the chest, which brought me so low, and threatened my death. May a gracious God in Christ Jesus keep me in readiness for death whenever it may come!

Jan. 31. I went to the Senate-House, where a Grace

was brought forward by Whewell to enable Lord ——
to proceed to the degree of B.A., a nobleman, not having
passed the Previous Examination. The object of the Grace
was to give the noble Lord an opportunity of becoming a
candidate for the Medal, which he could not do if he were
not B.A. Many thought the passing of such a Grace would
not be fair to others who might be candidates for the Medal
if they had not another term to keep, i.e. were not B.A.s.
However it being nobody's special business to 'non placet'
the Grace, it passed both Houses without opposition.

Feb. 1. I had a note from the Master informing me that
Dr Adams of Sidney and myself were the two nominated
candidates for the Norrisian Professorship. Though I was
gratified by the intelligence, I felt a sinking of heart at the
responsibility attached to the idea of being ultimately the
Professor, and so I prayed to God that He would not permit
me to be selected for the office unless it should be for the
promotion of His glory and my own salvation with that
of many souls.

Feb. 2. I called on each Master to leave my card as one
of the nominated candidates for the Norrisian Professorship.

Feb. 16. Langshawe asked me to-day to draw up the
Report of the Auxiliary Church Building Society, to which
I assented.

Feb. 19. An opposition was expected to a Petition from
the University to both Houses of Parliament against an-
nexing the Bishopric of Sodor and Man to that of Carlisle.
The petition however passed without opposition, though
there were many suspicious looking M.A.s there.

Feb. 20. Went to London to see Sir Wm. Beechey about
my eldest brother's portrait. He had made a good figure of
my brother, but the colouring was wrong. There were some
very good pictures of public persons, one of Blücher, one
of Platoff, and one of the Queen Dowager.

[It is difficult in these days of express trains to realize

that a journey from London to Cambridge could occupy nearly seven hours!]

Feb. 23.   I left London at three o'clock, but the roads being bad, I did not reach Cambridge till near ten!

Mar. 14.   In the Senate-House to-day a Grace was brought forward with a view of having Select Preachers at St Mary's in the morning as well as afternoon. It was rejected in the Black Hood House by a majority of sixteen to five.

Mar. 31.   Mr Mortlock of Christ's called on me, and I gave him some queries to submit to lawyers in London, respecting the Visitation of Colleges and the alteration of their Statutes.

April 27.   My mind has been the subject of various emotions to-day.   I thought I cared little whether I obtained the Norrisian Professorship or not, but I find, as the time of election draws near, that I am more anxious about it at times than is consistent with a simple desire to possess nothing but for the glory of God.   May God order everything for my worldly disappointment rather than that I should seek the Professorship for earthly ambition's sake.

As the time of election drew near he was enabled to await the result without undue anxiety.

April 30.   The Master seemed to be in doubt respecting my election to the Norrisian Professorship.   I told him I hoped he would not annoy himself about it, for I was prepared for losing the election.   It has pleased God to keep me in cheerful abiding on His will.   I have been far less disturbed in mind than I could have anticipated, and have felt no anxiety respecting the future lot which a gracious God may in Christ Jesus ordain for me.   I humbly desire strength to honour Him more simply and fully than I have hitherto done.

May 2.   The election to the Norrisian Professorship took place to-day at Magdalen College Lodge.   Dr Adams and I were both summoned into the room where the Heads were assembled, and both read the Oath prescribed by the Founder of the Professorship, and subscribed the same. We then retired. After a short time I was summoned into the room again, when the Vice-Chancellor informed me that I had been elected into the Professorship. I was congratulated by the Heads and subscribed the Vice-Chancellor's book, who fixed to-morrow for administering the Oaths of Supremacy and Allegiance to me. This has been to me a day of excitement and mingled feeling. And now, on my having been elected into an important office, I desire most humbly to be delivered by God's blessed Spirit, and for my Saviour's sake, from pride of station, and to be enabled to seek only God's glory in simplicity of heart and constancy of purpose. Such surplus of income arising from the Professorship as may remain after buying books connected with the Lectures attached to the office, I will endeavour by God's help faithfully to appropriate to religious purposes each year; that my possession of the office may be marked by a more steadfast devotion of my time talent and substance to the Lord Who has redeemed me!

Thus the uncertainty was at an end, and Mr Corrie was in the providence of God placed in that position of usefulness for which his reading during many years had specially prepared him. In connection with this office he not only proved himself a most earnest and diligent student of Theology, but also devoted himself with laborious and patient research to the exposition of the Ecclesiastical History of England and Ireland, in relation both to Romanism and Protestant Nonconformity. From the commencement he issued a Syllabus of his lectures with a view to their greater utility.

A touching letter from his father's friend, Mr Hugh Monckton, addressed to Mr Corrie on his election to the Professorship is inserted here.

My dear George,

I was at Fineshade yesterday, so did not see your letter till this evening, else I would not have missed a post in thanking you for

thinking of me among so many and on such a day.   When you say
you need even my prayers, believe me, dearest George, that I *cannot*,
I may almost say, pray for myself without praying for you, and that
my affection for you and interest in your welfare were conceived too
early in my life ever to cease unless with life itself, nor I trust
altogether even then.   I had called yesterday at Blatherwycke and
seen your letter.   Your brother had read it with a mixture of feelings,
yes, dear George, of strange and almost overwhelming feelings,
thankfulness certainly, but I verily believe more of fear than of joy,
and I hardly now know how to congratulate you on your success.
From all that Henry tells me, my dread is lest you should, in your
present state of health, wear yourself out with over-exertion of body
as well as of mind.   I cannot but hope that some friend on whose
piety and judgment you can rely, may be able to persuade you that,
with a single eye to God's glory, and the *permanency* of any good you
may do in your College, your desire should be not so much to be a
missed man at your death or resignation, but rather to be as little
missed as possible; and that can only be by making others work
with the help of your experience.   To a man who loves his work and
is habituated to it, it must ever be a matter of self-denial, but it
is clearly a *duty* when Providence calls him to it, sometimes to look
on while others labour, when he would rather himself be doing,—but
is it not the best evidence that he can have or give of his real conviction of what he professes to believe, that whoever be the labourer,
the whole efficacy, "the excellency" of the power by which any good
is to be done, is of God, that he himself is nothing and God is all!—
May you my own truly beloved George be blessed with a right perception and knowledge of what things you *ought* to do, and with grace
and power faithfully to fulfil the same, and may the love of God in
Christ Jesus ever be with you.

Remember me always as most affectionately yours,

H. A. MONCKTON.

To Mr Harvey, late Canon of Gloucester, he writes, "In
thanking you for your kind wishes respecting the Professorship, I would at the same time beg you to remember that
I much need your prayers, in order that God may enable me
to discharge the important duties that His providence has
assigned to me, in such a manner as that His name may be
honoured, and the best interests of His Church promoted by
my instrumentality."

May 3.   After seeing the Master of Trinity on the subject, I went to the Vice-Chancellor's and took the Oaths of Allegiance and Supremacy, and Oath of Office, and was admitted by the Vice-Chancellor.   I called on the Master of Corpus to thank him for his vote and to look at some Parker MSS. I then called on the Masters of Clare, Queens' and Christ's, to thank them for their votes, and also on Power of Trinity Hall, who would have voted for me if the Vice-Master had had a vote.   I then went to a meeting of the Society for educating young men at the University, when money was voted to three students, £15 to one and £10 each to the others.   I met Dr Adams, with whom I had a pleasant chat ; he was very cordial.

He submitted his proposed plan of Lectures to Mr Chevallier, who writes :

COLLEGE, DURHAM, *May* 16, 1838.

My dear Corrie,

......The course of Lectures which you have planned seems to me well calculated to find employment for yourself for 50 years' Lectures and to be of use to your hearers.........I do not wonder at your finding a difficulty in introducing an examination.   But I am certain that the lectures, be they as valuable as they may, will be thrown away upon *ordinary men* who are always extraordinarily idle and careless unless their attention is fixed by the necessity of passing an examination.   But the delay of a few terms till you see your way, is far better than precipitation, for a false step is not easily retraced.......

Your sincere friend,
TEMPLE CHEVALLIER.

May 26.   I called on Archdeacon Hollingworth (who is on a visit in Cambridge) to ask him about some practical matters connected with the Norrisian Professorship.   In the course of conversation he told me he had applied to the Trustees of the Professorship to have some alteration as to the reading of Pearson on the Creed.   He had obtained Lord Wodehouse's permission, who is the representative (by his

7—2

wife) of Mr Norris, but the Trustees said the thing could not be done, although there seemed no reason.

Again he writes to Mr Chevallier:

CAMBRIDGE, *May* 31, 1838.

......I am to call on Dr Hollingworth to-day with regard to my public Lectures. It so happens that the founder of the Professorship mentions the subject of Prophecy, as among those he wishes to have touched upon, and therefore, if I am spared, I may not omit to direct the attention of my audience to Prophecy among other things. During the first year I shall be more concerned to provide for the delivery of a sufficient number of profitable Lectures on subjects bearing more directly on the preparation of men for the Christian Ministry. I was not at all surprised by your Papistical opponents in the Church-rate matter. If (as the history of the world shews) they can but get rid of Episcopacy combined with true doctrine, sectarianism in all its forms will speedily disappear in a return of sectaries into the bosom of the "ould" Church. For, as an element of human society, religion must have something like comprehensive polity so long as the visible Church is not identical with a congregation of sincere Christians. Else three-fourths of professing Christians will oftentimes find themselves out of the pale of the Church, what with excommunications, party strifes and so on, unless men take refuge from each other's narrow views, in endless divisions. In other words, since all who seem to be or profess to be Christians are not so, and do not live as Christians, there must be a Church-government calculated for man as he is, and not for man as he is assumed to be. But, for this, republican Church-polity has no provision, since neither in Church nor State is man virtuous enough to admit of the working out of a republican principle. So I have no patience when I hear of the foolery talked, about the perfectibility of human society to be brought about by education and such like schemes. When we look at the present state of the Continent and find those cities which took the lead in the Reformation, now besotted with Popery, and connect the process by which they became so with what we see going on in our own country, I, for one, should not be surprised at the prevalence of Popery in this land, to a far greater extent than one can contemplate with comfort. That system is essentially the religion of human nature, and will, therefore, take root and spread, wherever human nature and favouring circumstances are found. I have done with speculations for this time. I wish you could procure for me a copy of your clerk's verses on ——s death. One feels the value of such memorials. Whatever may be the case with respect to the next world, certainly the works of those who die in the Lord " follow them " in this life, and one seems for the time convinced that it is only our labours of love on behalf of the souls and bodies of our fellow-creatures that are really enduring,—"Charity never fails." Then comes the sorrowful consciousness that we seldom live up to our convictions, and seldomer still embody in our daily practice the prayers we daily utter before the Throne of Grace. So that to the end of time our only refuge from despair is that declaration, "the blood of Jesus Christ His Son cleanseth us from *all* sin." This is, indeed, the glorious *mystery* of redemption, that God can be just and yet the Justifier of every one that believes in Jesus.

Farewell for the present,
Ever your true friend,
G. E. CORRIE.

June 2. I went to the Senate-House to-day, to a Congregation for the purpose of passing a Grace to alter the mode of Examination for Honours. The principal feature in the change is the doing away with the old system of *Classing*.

June 5. I had a long conversation with the Dean of Peterborough, respecting the Ministerial scheme for extracting Church-rates from the Cathedral property. There will be doubtless found among the different Chapters men who would resist the inquisitorial power of the House of Commons, if it were necessary.

June 12. I travelled to London to see Sir W. Beechey's picture of my late brother.

In the midst of his responsible duties he never lost an opportunity of adding to his own store of knowledge. When in London he availed himself of Teachers of various languages, e.g. Danish and Irish, devoting an hour before breakfast to this object. The Irish language was essential to him in his researches into the early history of the Irish Church.

June 14. I had a lesson in Danish from a Baron Von Bülow, a most excellent Prussian nobleman, who lost all his property in the Continental wars of Bonaparte.

June 15. I had another lesson in Danish, and then went to the Adelaide Gallery. There was a Lecture given on making gas for lighting the streets. The Lecturer was an operative, but a man of great intelligence. It was most interesting.

June 19. We formed a party to go to Westminster Abbey to see the preparations for the Coronation. The accommodation is said to be sufficient for 7000 persons. Sydney Smith was there, talking at a great rate. My brother and I went to Sir Francis Chantrey's about a monument to my eldest brother.

June 22. My brother was at a meeting to-day of the S.P.G. in Willis's Rooms, the Archbishop in the chair. The speakers were most decided in their views of the duty of Government to support the Church. An important meeting.

June 23. I intended to return to Cambridge to-day, but owing to the crowd of carriages in the street occasioned by the great number of gentry going to see the Queen's Crown, I was prevented from reaching the coach in time. I went to Millfield ; on our way, the Queen Dowager passed the omnibus in a carriage with four black horses. All the gentlemen in the omnibus took off their hats, which Her Majesty acknowledged by bowing. It is pleasant to see the respect with which all persons treat her.

Mr Corrie spent the next three months at Cambridge in diligent preparation for his public Lectures, which were to be delivered in the ensuing October Term. There are but few notes of this time, not only from his close application to reading, but from the complete loneliness of a Long Vacation residence in Cambridge at that period. He has been often heard to say that no one could *now* realize the quietness, which was so extreme that sometimes he could hardly bear to hear his own footsteps.

The account of the dinner given to the Poor on Parker's Piece, on occasion of the Queen's Coronation, will be read with interest by those who have lately witnessed the similar entertainments in honour of the 50th anniversary of that auspicious event.

June 27. A meeting at the Vice-Chancellor's for choosing the Select Preachers for the ensuing Academical year. The Vice-Chancellor, the Dean of Peterborough (Regius Professor of Divinity), and the Master of Peterhouse were engaged in electing Whewell into the Casuistry Professorship. After this was done, the Vice-Chancellor, the Regius Professor of Divinity, the Senior Proctor and myself proceeded to appoint the Preachers. I hear that Bowstead of Corpus is appointed Bishop of Sodor and Man.

June 28. I went to Parker's Piece to see the dinner given to the Poor of all the Parishes in the Town in honor of the Queen's Coronation to-day. The tables were well arranged, branching in every direction from a kind of Rotunda, on the top of which was a large band of musicians and around which was a railed-in space for such company as chose to pay for tickets. The whole was very orderly. There were foot-races, &c. on Midsummer Green, whence also a balloon ascended. At night there were fireworks.

I found the Dean of Peterborough in Mr Burrell's rooms. We spoke on the want of firmness and principle manifested by Conservatives in Parliament. —— told me that Hook of Leeds had been preaching before the Queen, and had fairly attacked Ministers for their abandonment of the Church to its enemies.

July 19. I sat with Mr Burrell this afternoon : he told me a great deal about Whitfield, whom, as a very little boy, he had once heard preach. He had also heard Wesley preach a Charity Sermon for the Papists who suffered in property by the riots in London which Lord George Gordon headed. Mr Burrell said that Wesley spoke very strongly against their doctrine, and concluded his sermon by saying, " However, they are our brethren notwithstanding their errors, and so I shall have a collection for them directly."

July 20. I sat again to-day with Mr Burrell: he told me a good deal about Mr Romaine, and the scholars who were expelled from Oxford years ago, for holding prayer-meetings in College : one of these students became a celebrated preacher at Whitfield's Chapel in London, and Mr Battis-combe had often heard him preach.

July 21. I have been very busy removing some pictures belonging to the College from a lumber room into the Library.

July 23. Mr S. called on me to-day. He told me that Dr Pusey was formerly a pupil of Dr Maltby's, Bishop of Durham, and entertained the same Theological opinions as his master. Mr Burrell told me that Battiscombe, formerly Fellow of King's and now an anabaptist preacher here, had circulated hand-bills, inviting persons to attend his meeting-house, to hear him preach against Confirmation. One of Professor Scholefield's congregation sent the Professor a hand-bill, and one of the undergraduates of Queens' attended

Battiscombe's synagogue and took notes of the sermon, which were handed over to the Professor, who preached a masterly sermon on the rite of Confirmation to a crowded congregation from the text, "What mean ye by this rite?" He pointedly alluded to B.'s attempt to vilify the rite, and in fact said he was answering the usual dissenting objections. On this B. issued a second hand-bill inviting those who *had* been confirmed to come and hear him preach from the same text, and he has been distributing tracts on the subject. Poor man!

Aug. 11. I had a long conversation with the Master of Pembroke respecting the power of the Crown in College matters. He told me the Statutes of his College were now before the Law Officers of the Crown in order to their modification in some particulars.

Anxious to secure some change before the winter's work began, we find Mr Corrie amongst his friends, and assisting his brother at Kettering.

Sept. 5. Went to London to arrange about sending out my brother's portrait to Calcutta. Called on Mr Pratt and made final arrangements with him. Mr A. called, bringing me a beagle hound.

Sept. 15. At Blatherwycke, I rose early and went into the woods after a deer; Tryon of Bulwick was there with his hounds, but we found nothing. It was truly beautiful and refreshing to sit in the green, lovely wood. I was in the house again by 10 o'clock, and was occupied in writing a sermon for to-morrow. In the afternoon I went to visit sick people, and arranged to administer the Holy Communion to one of them.

Sept. 16. I took the *whole* service in Church this morning, and have much cause for deep thankfulness to God, who has this day given me strength to go through the public services of the Church with comfort.

Oct. 2. —— arrived from Ireland. He told us there had

lately been a meeting of Popish priests in Limerick to decide
on the murder of ——, a gentleman residing in that county,
but that one of the " NAME " gave information to the gentleman in question, and so he passed by another way, and sent
some policemen to the spot where the murder was intended,
and they apprehended three men with blackened faces.

In our walk to-day I called at the Union Workhouse with
a pocket full of spinning-tops and whip-cord, for the amusement of the pauper boys.

The following hearty letter of congratulation and warning
from his attached friend Mr Chevallier may find a fitting
place here.

October 17, 1838.

My dear Corrie,

     I conceive you seated in full-blown professorial dignity not
without some anxiety at the commencement of your important
labours. If it please God to give you health sufficient to encounter
the bodily fatigue necessarily accompanying the addressing a large
audience, and that for so many weeks in succession, I cannot but
feel happy at the prospect of a great amendment in the whole
Divinity course, and thankful that "a great door and effectual" is
open for you precisely in the manner in which your studies and
habits qualify·you to be eminently useful. Would it be improper for
you to engage a friend as curate to do the reading of Pearson, in
your presence of course? I merely mention it, under a fear that the
mere physical exertion of giving utterance to his forcible and clear
but formal language may sometimes be a serious inconvenience to
you......

Ever your sincere friend,
TEMPLE CHEVALLIER.

Oct. 20.   Left Kettering for Cambridge.

Oct. 23.   I had a conversation with Thurtell of Caius
respecting the necessity of instituting an examination for
those who attend the Norrisian Lectures. I wrote to ask the
Dean of Peterborough his opinion.

Oct. 24.   I this day commenced my Lectures as Norrisian
Professor to a room full of auditors, among them Romilly
of Trinity. It pleased God to give me strength to speak

freely, and without much reference to my written paper. May His blessing follow my labours!

Oct. 25. I gave a further portion of my Introductory Lecture, and was enabled to speak with great freedom. The young men heard me with deep attention. May God's Spirit give success to the words uttered in dependence on His aid. Willis told me after that the men took their books (as usual) to the Norrisian Lectures, but did not attempt to read them in consequence of my having expressed myself strongly as to the state of mind in which Ordination ought to be undertaken.

Oct. 27. I had a private Divinity Lecture to-day to the B.A.s of the University and the men of my own College, about 25 in number. I called on the Dean of Peterborough. I told him that the Dissenters in the last *Congregational Magazine* had been nibbling at his book on *The Dissenter and the Universities.* He said "Yes, but I found the Editor had misrepresented me, and so I wrote to the Magazine writer stating that I challenged the writer of the article to bring a single sentence from my book that maintained what he said I did."

Nov. 8. At my public Lecture one of my audience was reading a book of some kind, so I desired him to remain after Lecture, and spoke to him solemnly of the unfaithful state of mind he must be in: telling him also fairly that I would not give him a Certificate. He was a good deal alarmed, and told me he was sorry, and was willing to submit to anything I might enjoin him if I would but overlook his fault. My answer was that as an individual I did not care one straw whether my audience listened or not; but that if any asked me to certify they listened when I *knew* they did not, they asked me to certify a lie, which no man had a right to do. The youth seemed never to have viewed the matter in its proper light, and so, with his assurance of an endeavour to cultivate a better spirit for the future, I let him go. I pray God he may be brought to a right mind.

Nov. 13.   Mr Simpson, a clergyman of Hook Hall, near Goole, called on me about the admission of his son.   He was formerly of this College, and said he was the *only* Freshman in his time.   ———— was the Tutor, but never gave Lectures.

Grave anxiety was felt by many of Mr Corrie's friends lest the exertion attendant on lecturing so frequently and to so many should prove too much for his health. Mr Chevallier thus expresses his thankfulness at the result at the end of the first term of work.

November 20, 1838.

My dear Corrie,

  I have always considered it a matter of great thankfulness that circumstances should have been so ordered as to pave the way for your holding the Norrisian Professorship.   When I look back to the days which are passed, and consider what the degree of usefulness was, which attended those Lectures, albeit given by men of considerable mental thews and sinews, and compare those reminiscences with your description, I feel most grateful for the change, and augur well for the future state of the Church, from so essential a movement in an office of such weight.   I rejoice too that you are able to go through the physical labours of reading Pearson, which must be considerable, seeing that his sentences are constructed on the long-winded principle, although full of pith and moment.   Your plan and arrangement of lectures appear to me to be excellently adapted to your purpose, and calculated to set men reading for themselves, which is the great point........

Ever your sincere friend,

TEMPLE CHEVALLIER.

Nov. 23.   The Provost called to-day to ask me about the Female Refuge lately established, and gave me a subscription for it.   Dr Hubbersty of Queens' was buried to-day in St Botolph's Church.

Dec. 10.   In walking with Willis we passed by Parker's Piece, and there saw some forty gownsmen playing at football. The *novelty* and liveliness of the scene was very amusing.

Dec. 13.   One of my pupils shewed me a letter which stated that the last words of Judge Allan Park, who is just dead, were, " I wish my time were come, but I desire to wait with patience for God's will."   He died in the Lord Jesus.

Dec. 18.   Mr Whytehead of St John's called for his Divinity Lectures' Certificate.   I had some interesting conversation with him, and recommended him strongly to study Anglo-Saxon, with a view of translating some of the Anglo-Saxon Homilies in our Public and other Libraries.

Dec. 22.   I came to Kettering, and in the afternoon walked out for two hours with my hounds.

Dec. 31.   During this year God has given me increased opportunities for usefulness.   May I be also more devoted in serving Him, and in setting forward the salvation of all who come within the region of my influence.

CHAPTER VI.

THERE are but few matters of University interest mentioned in the Diary for 1839. The New Year found Mr Corrie at Leamington with his brother-in-law and sister, Mr and Mrs Sherer, and their family; going thence to Blatherwycke and Kettering, where the Vacation was spent among friends.

On *Jan.* 20 Kettering Church was opened for Evening Service, and lighted with gas for the first time.

Jan. 21. Left Kettering for Cambridge. May I have grace given me to fulfil the duties on which I am about to enter, and be enabled to say with sincerity, " If Thy presence go not with me, carry me not up hence."

Mar. 10. I was engaged with the Master two hours about our College Statutes; then I went to St John's to call on Tatham, about the date of their College Statutes. I had a long talk with him respecting the contemplated changes in Statutes, and urged the necessity of ascertaining with whom the power of sanctioning alterations lies.

April 6. At Kettering to-day Mr G. Bridges called on me, and I had some conversation with him on the importance of petitioning in favour of preserving the Cathedrals.

April 11. The Master called on me this morning and we

had a long conversation respecting the College Statutes, as to the principle on which we ought to proceed in having our Statutes altered if necessary.

April 22. I went to hear Professor Whewell's Inaugural Lecture. There was a large audience. He *read* his Lecture, giving a hasty sketch of the Science of Casuistry before and since the Reformation, and glancing at some of the casuistical writers in England from Perkins to Jeremy Taylor.

April 27. I met the Dean of Peterborough, and had a long conversation with him respecting the attacks now being made on Cathedrals. The Dean said he had called a Chapter of his Church and had expounded to them his views, which were that the Cathedral property was as much that of the Chapters, as the property of noblemen and others was their own. I expressed my astonishment that no Capitular Body had had courage to resist the claim of the House of Commons, to the right of appointing a Committee of that House to inquire into Chapter-property, but the Dean gave me to understand that he was prepared to resist.

April 28. My forty-sixth birthday.... May that portion of life which remains to me be given up entirely to God, and may the Holy Ghost sanctify me daily and make me more fit for God's eternal kingdom.

May 1. The Master of St John's (Dr Wood) was buried this morning. He was a man whose Mathematical writings produced a great change for the better in the studies of this University, and they will live in history when those books now common will have been forgotten.

May 9. I hear that Dr Davys, the Queen's preceptor, is to be the new Bishop of Peterborough, and Professor Peacock of Trinity the Dean of Ely. Blunt of St John's was to-day chosen Lady Margaret Professor of Divinity.

At this time Mr Corrie published his Pamphlet entitled, "Brief Historical Notices of the Interference of the Crown with the Affairs of English Universities," the purport of which is explained in the following extract from the Preface.

"...It seems to the writer, that, in these days, the interference and authority of the Crown, in all matters relating to our Ecclesiastical and Literary Institutions, cannot be too narrowly scrutinised, or too sparingly employed. For we have not now to do with the Sovereign, as possessing an independent legislative existence, as in circumstances to shew a sincere attachment to our Church and Universities, and as powerful to uphold them; but, as the State servant of that Prime Minister who may happen to command a majority in the Commons' House of Parliament; and as being, therefore, oftentimes obliged, however personally unwilling, to exert a hostile influence against every Institution that we have been accustomed to revere. Although, therefore, all who entertain an unfeigned attachment to Monarchy must ever regard the Sovereign personally as an object of loyal and dutiful reverence, it seems to be not the less necessary to be well acquainted with the limits which the Law has assigned to the Royal authority, because a blind acquiescence in the illegal exercise of the Kingly power would only embolden an unscrupulous Minister to use the Prerogatives of the Crown against the Religion and Liberties of his Country."

May 11. The Provost of King's called to thank me for my Pamphlet. He told me a curious incident connected with their College in the reign of William III., to the effect that the Crown tried then to force a Provost on the Fellows by Royal Mandate, but that the Fellows resisted, and sent one of their number to Court, who was rather deaf. They wished to petition Queen Mary who was then regnant (King William being abroad), that the Mandate might be withdrawn. While the deaf Fellow was waiting with others, he was talking over the object of his visit, and as the Queen was passing he was saying aloud, "If the Crown is to force a Provost as formerly, why did they banish King James from the throne?" He did not know the Queen was near, and again repeated the question, "I say, why did they banish King James, if the Crown is to do such acts now?" It is supposed the Queen heard, for the Mandate was never pressed. The Provost also told me a London bookseller had informed him that he had just sent nine copies of Dr Turton's Book on the Eucharist to Rome.

On the subject of the pamphlet he writes to Mr Chevallier:

CAMBRIDGE, May 14, 1839.

My dear Chevallier,

...Events seem to be working toward a crisis of some kind, and the God-denying Act of 1829 may well lead us to fear that for a time at least we shall be left to the tender mercies of a *soidisant Liberal(!!)* Popery. May we be found faithful to that righteous cause with which it has pleased God to unite our destinies. For the rest "the Lord God Omnipotent reigneth," and we know that His Almighty power will be so exerted that the very turbulence of mankind shall only more effectually pave the way for the triumph of the Redeemer's kingdom. If, in the progress of events, therefore, our beloved country is to suffer humiliation and trial, we must aim at foregoing our sorrow for the prostration of our country's prosperity and glory, in that joy which we ought to feel when Christ alone is exalted among the inhabitants of the world at large. But one need not anticipate evil; though one may be prepared to endure it. I have just printed a pamphlet, " Brief historical notices of the Interference of the Crown with the Affairs of the English Universities." It has cost me no end of research, and I had no notion of the labour I had undertaken, though a tenth part of the toil does not appear on the paper. My object has been twofold: to ascertain the history of such changes as have taken place in our Colleges and Universities ; and secondly, to shew *incidentally* how good, sturdy, sound principle has always been quite equal to protecting the right against all the odds of power in the wrong. By the history, I trust, some stop may be put to that sleight-of-hand method of dealing with our Institutions, by which we might find our Colleges changed into

8

C.

Dissenting and Popish Academies: for I believe that what I
bring forward will lead many to understand that, if the great
Institutions of the land are under the protection of the law,
there is something contrary to common sense to suppose that
any interested parties can at any time agree with the Minister
of the Crown to remodel the Wills and Statutes of Founders.
Yet this is the unsophisticated English of all that authority
which people were here led to believe was vested in the
Crown as regarded its power to change or modify Statutes.
I have just touched, also, on the case of Cathedrals among
other Royal Foundations, with the hope of leading the
members of Chapters to examine the preposterous power
now usurped by the House of Commons, when claiming the
right to appoint a Committee to examine into the letting
of Cathedral Property. My very blood boils as I witness
the un-English manner in which the usurpations of that
Assembly are submitted to. The fact you mention respecting
there formerly being a " Durham College" in Oxford—Where
is the story of it to be found? I do not think the Statutes
of Durham Cathedral differ from those of others in reminding
that Chapter of their duty to educate youth, because schools
for that purpose were attached to all Cathedral Churches.
The worst of the case of Durham is, that whilst nobody will
care to look into the history of "Durham College" at Oxford,
all will seize on the fact that the Chapter have agreed to
alienate certain portions of their revenues, and that, without
putting forward much of a principle at the time, beyond that
they could afford to found an University. My belief is that
Sir R. Peel, Stanley and Co., if they had come into power,
would have acted in this manner respecting Church property,
taking Durham for their example. They have no notion
of the ground on which Church property rests, or the uses for
which it was given. Their whole mind is set on the simple
fact that there is a great want of Church Endowments for
the overgrown population of certain districts, and that Parliament will not vote money, or individuals give it, in sufficient

amount. Therefore, Sir R. Peel and the Bishop of London fancy that they can rob the Cathedrals without resistance with the rascally provision of reserving existing life-interests. Oh, if we had but some right-minded men to reject the life-interest bribe with the scorn and detestation it will hereafter be found to deserve! But if we are to be robbed, let the robbery be perpetrated by our enemies, not by our hypo-critical or false-judging friends. The argument used respecting Prebendal Stalls might (as I constantly affirm here) be ad-vantageously applied to the confiscation of every Fellowship in every College, at either and all of the Universities, that is not absolutely required for carrying on the College business. In our own Society three or four Fellows would be amply sufficient, the remaining ten would enrich ten poor Vicars. And why not? Sir R. Peel could not say, on his principle. However I have done. I suppose in 1939 posterity will read this letter (if it survive so long) pretty much as I con over those in our Treasury written in the time of James II. Forebodings that were never realized and evils that were never anticipated. And then may follow the humiliating feeling, " Man disquieteth himself in vain." But, then also may we, by God's mercy in Christ Jesus, be experiencing that uninterrupted tranquillity which none can taste in this world of sin.

Your truly attached friend,
G. E. CORRIE.

May 18. I called on the Vice-Chancellor to suggest to him the propriety of petitioning against the Government Scheme of Education. He asked me to send him the Minutes of the Privy Council on that subject, and he promised to bring the matter forward.

May 20. —— told me he had just come from the Town Hall where a meeting was held to address the Queen, by way of encouraging her to retain her present Ministers, who have obtained the sobriquet of the " Chamber-maid Ministry." In the evening a meeting was called by the Dissenters to vote an address similar to that voted by the Town Council, but no address was voted. A strong body of the Conservative operatives took possession of the Town Hall, and owing to the refusal of the Corporation to admit gownsmen, the latter procured a ladder and tried to get in at a window of the Town Hall, and were met by the Police, and a disturbance ensued. The meeting was dissolved without coming to any decision. The Riot Act had to be read in the Town Hall.

May 22. I had a talk with the Master of Jesus to-day. We agreed to have a meeting on the subject of Education, about the Commencement, and he promised in the meanwhile to promote a Petition from the University. After the Master left me Langshawe brought to me a Mr Page, a clergyman who is commissioned by the Irish Bishops to obtain support for the Church Education Society in Ireland. I told him it would be most important if possible to have that Society united with the English National Society.

May 28. I came to London yesterday, and to-day breakfasted with Augustus O'Brien : Viscount Adare, and Robert Monteith and Locke King were there. We went to a meeting of the "National Society for Educating the Poor." The Archbishop was in the Chair, and most of the Bishops were present. The Resolutions were moved and seconded by the Earl of Chichester, the Bishop of London, Lord Abinger, the Bishop of Salisbury, Dr Hook, Mr Bethell, M.P., Dean Chandler, Lord Sandon, Archdeacon Batten, and Sir Thos. Acland. Thanks were returned by the Earl of Winchilsea and Lord Wriothesley Russell. The Bishop of London's speech was very powerful and eloquent. It was remarkable that when any decided, bold statement was uttered the whole assembly sympathised with it. A Romish Priest tried to address the meeting, but was speedily ejected. The meeting lasted from one o'clock till six o'clock.

July 2. I was occupied all the morning, as yesterday, in collating a MS. of Gildas. I afterwards walked with H.

Goulburn, with whom I had a conversation respecting the Government Scheme of education.

July 6. Mr Gourrier, the minister of the English Episcopal Church in Paris, called to ask for a subscription toward building a new Church. He told me that the well-educated in Paris are ready to embrace Episcopal Protestantism, being convinced of the absurdity of Popery and dissatisfied with Presbyterianism. He also said that Louis Philippe made use of the Popish party only because he could not do without them.

July 8. The Provost of King's called with a MS. book containing narratives connected with the exercise of the Royal power in the University.

July 15. Mr Corrie paid his first visit to Oxford with Mr O'Brien and Mr Augustus O'Brien, on the occasion of the first meeting of the Royal Agricultural Society. He was much impressed with the beauty of the City, greatly admired many of the Colleges, and paid a long visit to the Bodleian Library. He was much interested in the Agricultural Show "which was equal to his expectations." On the 17th the party all dined at the Agricultural dinner in Queen's College Hall, which was very numerously attended.

After dinner Lord Spencer gave the loyal toasts. The Duke of Richmond then gave, "The Chancellor of the University." This was received with great applause. Indeed, as soon as the Duke of Wellington's name was mentioned, the cheering was immense. The health of "the Foreign Ambassadors and Ministers present" being given, the Chevalier Bunsen returned thanks, and was loudly cheered. Many others followed, but I came away.

July 19. They told us at Northampton that the operative shoemakers to the number of two thousand had last night ceased from work, and were parading the streets in a body. We reached Kettering in safety. In the evening there was a meeting of Chartists, to the number of one hundred and fifty.

July 20. I heard to-day that men are drilled in the sword exercise twice a week at a public-house; that at Isham there are as many as fifteen Chartists in that small village, who meet at the public-house twice a week; and that the chairman is constable of the Parish.

The month of August was spent in a visit to Ireland with Mr O'Brien and Mr Augustus O'Brien, where their property claimed their attention.

The statements in the Diary are of great interest, and forcibly demonstrate that the Ireland of 1839 was under the same priestly influence as the Ireland of to-day, with the same results of want and disaffection. Copious extracts are unhesitatingly given, the subject being one which engages especial attention at the present time.

July 29. We left Kettering for Liverpool, stopping at Birmingham, where at night a party of soldiers patrolled the streets with a police officer at their head. Next morning we started for Liverpool, which was reached in $4\frac{1}{2}$ hours. We decided on crossing to Ireland, though the night was stormy. We landed in a rough sea, and at Kingstown found part of the railroad to Dublin had been washed away by last night's gale. Our carriage could not be landed at Kingstown on account of the heavy swell. We therefore had to seek for a car; but here the Irish character presented itself, for after saying we could have any vehicle we wished for, it turned out there was not a wheel carriage on the premises. After however various shufflings and manœuvrings we obtained a covered car and drove to Dublin.

Aug. 1. We left Dublin on our way to Limerick. Our first stage was Black-Church. The inn there is a solitary house, white without, but full of smoke and filth within. We only just peeped into a room, and then got into a carriage. We travelled on to Newbridge. On our way we passed Palmerstown, where the Earl of Mayo has a house. We passed also Jigginstown, the other side of Naas. The squire told us he remembered the heads of some of the rebels of 1798 hanging on the castle at Naas. At Jigginstown are the remains of a house, begun on a large scale by the great and unfortunate Lord Strafford when Lord-Lieutenant of Ireland in Charles I.'s time. At Newbridge we went into the church, which is extremely neat. We were told there were sometimes as many as seventy persons at Church. All the country from Newbridge to Monasterevan is wretched. On approaching the latter place the plantations about the house of the Marquis of Drogheda give a dressed appearance to the country. Monasterevan is rather a better kind of town. The Barrow flows through the place, and was overflowing its banks on both sides the road. Soon after we crossed the Grand Canal. Kildare, through which we had previously passed, seemed a most wretched place. We saw the rock of Dunman at a distance to the left, but the appearance of the country from Emo to Maryborough looked poverty-stricken.

Aug. 2. Leaving Maryborough we passed through Montrath, Campbell Town, Roscrea, Tonnavara to Nenagh; part of the country was wretchedly miserable to look upon, but at Campbell Town, which belongs to the Fitzpatricks, there was an appearance of comfort. At Roscrea I went to look at the remains of the old Cathedral, of a Round Tower, and of the Castle which now forms part of a barrack. The remains of the Cathedral consist of a northern gable, which now forms the gateway to the New Church. After passing Roscrea we came on several gentlemen's houses. Among them that of Lord Bloomfield, who is now absent in consequence of having received several threatening letters. He was greatly improving the country, and of course became obnoxious to those who live by agitation. We walked on towards Tyrone and called at the house of one of the Squire's tenants: he shewed us a small farm which the Squire has in his own hands; the latter had intended it to be a model farm, and was proportionally disappointed to find it managed very little better than the lands of the tenants. We called on another tenant, Ned Welsh, and found him ill in bed from a hurt. He may be considered as a specimen of the larger native farmers, and wretched enough his house was. The first room was that in which all the cooking was done; in this were Ned's wife, daughter, and two or three children. In the second was the sick man, lying on a not uncomfortable bed; but dirty boards formed the floor of the room, so that the dust rose in clouds every foot we stirred. At the foot of the bed stood another for some portion of his household. The walls were adorned with little wretched prints in black frames of the Virgin Mary and other like subjects. We then went on to examine a bog which the Squire had drained last year. We were met by one of the tenants, and with the usual salutation, "You are welcome to Ireland." We looked into the cabin of another tenant, who had eight children eating potatoes. He was a fine young man, and was gratified by a call from his landlord. We turned towards Nenagh, the tenant Burke accompanying us. I entered into conversation with him about the country, by asking him what business there was at the last Assizes. He said, "There was a good deal of business but not much damage done." I asked him what he meant by "not much damage." His answer was, "There were only four convicted, and they were only to be transported." "What for?" "For some murder or attempt to murder." "How many were there tried for murder on the whole?" "Oh, about sixteen or seventeen, but the jury could not agree." I then talked about the Poor Law, and Burke said it was "not liked by the people." On returning to Nenagh, I was looking out of the window and the most wretched objects of poverty were to be seen everywhere. Two or three little urchins, on seeing Augustus and myself, held up their fists in an attitude of saucy defiance at us. Soon after, two drunken miscreants came under the window, and asked for two barrels of ale, taking me for the Squire. Of course I did not seem to hear them, but they talked impertinently and fiercely. Mr Walker, the agent, soon after was looking out, and on

seeing the two men pointed them out to the Squire, as
miscreants who would not hesitate to assassinate any body
for a couple of shillings! On talking to Mr Walker respecting the state of religion, he said he believed both
Popery and Protestantism were at a standstill; that neither
party seemed really to care for religion, and had no ani-
mosity against each other respecting it. He said also, with
reference to the murder of agents, that so far as he could
learn, obnoxious parties were those who took presents as a
reason for granting favourable conditions in taking lands,
a practice which, he was sorry to add, prevailed to a great
extent among agents in this country. He said an offer had
been made to him of a pony for his son, and other considerations, if he would give the party applying the option of some
of the Squire's land about to be vacant. In fact, the whole
system here seems to be one of lying and chicanery. But on
looking at the poverty, wretchedness, and ferocity of the
people, who seem to be without number, one is led to ask
'What remedy is to be applied to all this misery? What is to
be the end of the present state of things?' One thing was
strikingly corroborative of the effect of religious belief on the
worldly affairs of man, viz., that on looking at a field in
beautiful order as compared with one adjoining, I was told
"The tenant is *Protestant.*" That there is no *ignorance*
strictly speaking in Papists that makes them less worldly
wise, may be seen at once by any who will pay the slightest
attention to their ready intelligence. But alas! alas! Popery
seems to be like the blight of heaven resting on this land!

I forgot to note that, on our arrival at Tonnavara,—the
post-boy said in a jocular way to the people that came to see
us refresh the horses, "Are ye the boys that shot Lord
Norbury? What did ye shoot him for?" "No, we did not
shoot him, but at any rate we'd be glad to see the poor
fharmers get their right." The Squire thought the post-boy
asked the question to give us some notion of the ready spirit
with which the people sympathised with the murderers, and

to shew us, that if we were landlords, how many there were who would not mind serving us the same, if it suited their purpose.

Aug. 3. We left Nenagh for Shalee, where there are lead mines. We came to a most miserable cabin, not nearly so good as almost every pig-stye in England, where an old woman and her son lived. After visiting the mines we posted to Limerick ; and then went on to Cratloe, where we arrived in safety.

Aug. 4. The Squire, Augustus and myself set off to Limerick by water to attend Church. The boat was so leaky that we put back again, and it was then too late to go to Church, so we returned to the house, where I read the Morning Service to the few Protestants of which the household is composed. Old Ryant, a Papist, worshipped with us. On walking we met Connor, one of the wood-rangers. He told me that there is now a *Friar* in Cork who cures people of a love for whisky, by means of a charmed medal which is worn about the neck, and is purchased for eightpence. The medals are numbered, and it is calculated that not less than ten thousand have already been sold. The effect of the medal is said to be such that whosoever possesses it is seized with a hatred of whisky, and in fact, would be prevented from the possibility of drinking any more, since if he were to attempt it, the whisky would become maggots. Connor said, that the Friar had shewed one of those who went to him *the whisky actually changed into maggots.* Connor only spoke of what he had heard, yet he firmly believed it. On returning from the wood we met several of the people, who were right glad to see Augustus and the Squire. At prayers in the evening, the whole household attended, Protestants and Roman Catholics alike.

Aug. 5. We left Cratloe for Cappamore and the Limerick estates. We visited some farms, and some mountain land where the Squire had separated off a portion and *limed* it and then planted potatoes. The crop succeeded beyond his expectation. We were accompanied by a crowd of peasant tenantry, and on our return almost all the inhabitants of the place accompanied us either on foot or on horseback. We then went on to Tipperary. After dinner a tar-barrel was lighted in honour of the Squire. Augustus told me that the last time he was in Tipperary was just after he had been a candidate for the county of Limerick, and that the crowd recognized and cheered him. This called forth the attention of the Priests, who dispersed themselves amongst the people, and the result was that by the time Augustus had changed horses, the cheering of the crowd was converted into yells and groans. He accordingly hurried off, but his servant was so enraged at the mob, that he threw a bottle right among them as his master drove off.

Aug. 6. We went to Ballyglass. We were accompanied by Dillon the wood-ranger, and afterwards went to his house and had some refreshment. Part of his house had been newly fitted up, but so truly Irish did the concern seem, that one of the boys had to climb over a high partition wall to open the door of the bedroom. One of the post-boys who drove us, had last year driven Augustus from Tipperary to Michelstown, and on the way had desired a man to get off the carriage, and for his pains was waylaid on his return, beaten and left for dead! In fact the county of Tipperary is full of murder and violence.

Aug. 7. We met Tom Barry. He had been to Cork with his boy to the holy Friar. The boy had a lameness of long standing, and Tom, having heard of the powers of the Friar, took him to be miraculously cured. The Friar, it seems, made the sign of the Cross, uttered some prayer, touched the lame part, and the boy was instantly relieved from pain! This was the story, as told by Tom, and assented to by the boy, though the contrary was manifestly the case. Tom Barry had also joined the Temperance Society. His number was ten thousand one hundred and one, and Father Malone told us that the number was at least twenty-five thousand. Barry said that all who wore the medal immediately conceived a dislike for spirituous liquors, and that an unhappy man who had ventured to drink whisky after possessing himself of a medal had instantly gone raving mad! Father Malone who dined with us, told us that the road between Mallow and Cork was covered with people dead drunk, or nearly so, in consequence of their having drunk very copiously, as a kind of farewell to whisky, previously to their abjuring it at Cork. At first Mr Malone seemed shy and embarrassed, but after some general conversation he became chatty. The holy father was very communicative, and seemed to regard his office as a profession by which he had to live. There was not a particle of apparent religion about him, but on the contrary he seemed to be a mere trading ecclesiastic. He talked a good deal about the people, and seemed to know all their designs. As an example of his merely secular notions I noticed that on the Squire's observing, "Such a one is a remarkably pretty person," Malone answered, "I don't know much about her, for she will be no *profit* to me, since she is not in my parish, and *so* if she were to marry, I should be none the better for it," or words to that effect. In fact Malone came quite up to my notion of a Popish priest.

Aug. 8. At seven this morning we set out by steam-boat to witness a Regatta. One thing struck me among the people to-day, and that was their use of the *English* language in their familiar intercourse with each other. This is very different from the usage of ten years back. I have felt much compassion for the wretched ignorance, profanity, and worldly destitution, which in this country everywhere meets the eye and ear.

Aug. 9. Augustus and I went to Limerick, and called on Archdeacon Maunsell. He told us of a meeting held in the city some time since by the Liberals, for the purpose of establishing a Seminary in which people should be educated without religion. This was the *professed* object of it, but the Archdeacon said he had the best means of knowing that of the principal Professors *three* were to be Papists. This accounted for the ready support which the scheme met with from the Papists. The sound part of the Protestants determined to go to the meeting and out-vote the Liberals and Papists. This they succeeded in doing, so far that the meeting ended in nothing, the Protestant disputants having completely beaten their opponents in numbers as well as argument, although the chairman, Sir Aubrey de Vere, a liberal kind of Protestant, declared that the Papists &c. had the majority. The upshot of the whole business was, that the Protestants were within an ace of being torn to pieces by the mob of Papists, who backed the discomfited Liberalists.

Aug. 11. Attended service at Limerick Cathedral. The service was conducted with great seriousness. The preacher gave a truly scriptural sermon. We stopped to look at Bp. Jebb's monument, which is a full-length figure of the Bishop in sitting attitude.

Aug. 12. We went to Bealcraggy and commenced examining the estate. I stayed behind the rest and talked with one of the people. He told me they were most anxious for a school on the estate, for that the priests did not care to have the people taught to read, though all were longing for instruction. I observed that if a school were established, the priests would not let the children attend. The answer was, "I will engage all the children of Mr O'Brien's tenants will attend school in spite of the priests." He told me also that the children learned as much in a week from the schoolmasters established by such persons as Mr Synge of Corofin, as from a Romish schoolmaster in a month. "But you shot at Mr Synge." "Oh no! there is none more venerated by the people than he." As we left we were loudly cheered. Poor people, my heart was touched as I thought of their bondage and misery!

Aug. 13. We started for Fountain, an estate of the Squire's. The circumstances of this property are peculiarly interesting. The tenant was a kind of gentleman farmer, who spent his money, and became embarrassed in his circumstances. His wife was dead. When he found he could not get on, he went off to Australia, leaving his family of six, all young. The Squire's agent took possession of the estate with the crops on it, and undertook the management of the affairs of the orphans. The eldest son, of nineteen, was made tenant, and his sister, a girl of sixteen, undertook the education of four younger children. In this state we found them this morning, and it was very beautiful to witness the simplicity and youth of the household, whose united ages did not exceed forty-five years. They seem quite unconscious of their deserted situation, and are managing and industrious. We proceeded to visit another estate, but the rain fell so fast we were fain to remain at the house where we had called, which appeared good, but the interior was truly Irish. The furniture old finery, the floors dirty, the windows broken,— everything betokened the most complete slovenliness, and yet the owner (a young man), is worth at least £500 a year in private estate. We proceeded to Ennis.

Aug. 14. Before leaving Ennis, on our return to Cratloe, we visited the House of Industry, which contains four hundred Paupers from different parts of the county Clare. The place was very clean for Ireland, but did not bear comparison with similar institutions in England. It appears that nearly four hundred poor wretches had been discharged from the House this week, owing to a want of sufficient funds for its maintenance. We called at Dromoland on our way home.

Aug. 15. We drove to Dromoland to dine, found a large family party, and spent a pleasant evening amongst old friends.

Aug. 16. We started for Limerick, and then went on to Tralee and Dingle by mail cart. We overtook a peasant and his daughter, who had a horse with panniers, in which they were travelling.

Aug. 17. Mr Gear, the Clergyman of the parish, called on us. We went off for some fishing. On returning we found

Mr Gear, and Mr Moriarty the curate of Ventry. With them we visited the school at Ventry, where forty or fifty children were being instructed in Scriptural truth. They were the offspring of parents who have within three or four years abjured Popery, through the instrumentality of Mr Gear's labours at Dingle in the first instance, and afterwards by means of the ministry of Mr Moriarty, who conducts public Service in Irish, and has established a steady congregation of Protestant converts of about two hundred and fifty. Mr M. gave us a most interesting account of the progress of his ministerial labours, and of the success with which it has pleased God to promote His holy truth among a sequestered and besotted people. Mr M. was asked by Augustus whether he was not afraid of personal injury. He said not, for besides that outward persecution had in a measure subsided, he found the greatest personal safety in the clanship of the country, for he was a native of the country and district. As an instance of the security this afforded, he mentioned the circumstance of a convert from Popery who died a week ago and had wished to be buried in a burial-place named. Accordingly Mr. M. collected two hundred converts from Popery, to follow the deceased to the grave, and he went also. They were much dissuaded from attempting to bury the deceased, because the people of the district in which the burying-place is, had declared their determination that no apostate heretic (as they called the deceased) should be buried there. Undismayed, however, they proceeded, but just as they were entering the ground a woman touched the coffin to obstruct its progress, and a man took off his coat and shewed many other manifest symptoms of resistance and riot. On this Mr Moriarty (who speaks Irish as a native) began to remonstrate with the people; appealed to their feelings and mentioned the deceased's wishes. A crowd collected round him, and he spoke to them so effectually, relating the circumstances of the life and death of the deceased, that the whole of the people turned to join in following the corpse, and said, "He is our brother, and, therefore, if he be gone to hell, we will follow him there." We then went on to Dingle, where we turned into a Popish Chapel. There were a few respectable persons repeating something out of books, which seemed a mere matter of form, for they turned round and looked at us. An old man kneeling before the altar appeared very devout. Mr Moriarty told me, that the first movements toward the abjuration of Popery, were the result of the labours of the "Irish Society." The object of that Society is to employ Readers who shall read the Scriptures to the people in their native language. These Readers had for some time excited a spirit of enquiry among the people, who, as a result, went to Mr Gear for further instruction. There is an advantage in the Readers' system also; viz. that they wander among the people, and are but seldom detected by the priest; the consequence is that their readings have accomplished the desired object before the priests discover the cause. Conversions from Popery have taken place also throughout the three Islands called "The Blasketts." There the priests have fairly been obliged to leave the ground to be possessed by Messrs. Gear and Moriarty. The Scripture Readers employ themselves there, and the gentlemen just named go once a week on a missionary errand to instruct these wild Islanders. Mr Gear stated that he had no doubt but that similar results would follow in almost any part of Ireland, if there were clergymen of a devoted spirit located in the churches, for that people would come to hear. In speaking of causes which contributed to allay the outward persecution which the converts from Popery first experienced, there is to be reckoned the fact that when the priests, by cursing the parties from their altars, so injured them in their profession and good name, the aggrieved persons commenced actions for libel against the priests. By this means the latter are constrained to be cautious. Many other interesting particulars were mentioned, and none more, than that all the congre-

gation at Ventry, even those of the tenderest age, repeat the
Confession and responses of the Church Service.

Aug. 18. We went to the Sunday-School with Mr Gayer,
the curate of this place. We found more than one hundred
children, but the most interesting object was a class of adult
converts from Popery who were reading the Bible in a small
gallery with Captain Forbes, who is settled here. They
displayed an amazing knowledge of the Scriptures for their
circumstances, and striking evidence of the life of God in
their souls. We then went to Church. Mr Gayer preached
a simple and beautiful sermon from Luke xv. 23, 24, with
much sound judgment and Scriptural piety. The people
(about two hundred) were very attentive, not exclusive of the
boys of the Sunday-School, many of whom seemed to listen
intently to the sermon. After the Evening Service, at which
there was another excellent sermon, we drank tea with Mr
Gayer, and found Mr Moriarty there. He told us that no
less than three converts from Popery, and natives of this
town, are clergymen in our Church, there being also two
other natives of the place and converts from Romanism now
candidates for Holy Orders, three out of the five being able
to preach in the Irish language. Our friends interested us
very much with accounts of the natives of the Blasketts.
Three years ago a Scripture Reader was sent to those
Islands, but the natives were so inveterate against him that
they threatened to precipitate him from their cliffs. Now,
however, all are anxious to hear the Gospel of Jesus Christ.
Many were the anecdotes related of those interesting people.
Among others, Mr Gayer mentioned that he met with an
old man about eighty coming down from the mountain with
turf. On questioning him, among other things, "Whether he
believed the priest could forgive his sins?" he answered,
"No, I thought so once, but now I am satisfied he cannot
forgive them; indeed I am so great a sinner that I do not
think I shall obtain forgiveness of my sins at all." He added
"Many years ago I stole twenty sheep, and then twenty more,

and on confessing my theft to the priest, he told me I should be forgiven if I gave him a sheep every Christmas and some fleeces of wool. This I continued to do for some time, but I found it no use, and as I said before, I believe my sins are too great to be forgiven." Mr Gayer related that last week two of the Islanders came to his house, and seemed wild with delight with all they saw, kissed his hands and those of the children, and scarcely knew how to shew their pleasure and gratitude to him. Whilst they were present he had occasion to use a lucifer match, which greatly excited their attention, but nothing was said. On their return to the Island, however, they had some argument with Romanists respecting the power of the priests, when the two Islanders said that it was nothing to that of Mr Gayer, who, in their presence, had actually "brought fire out of a *stick!*" It would be endless to note all that was told us, but it may be noted that the priest's influence is so gone in the Blasketts that he obtained only a small basket of fish and a calf's skin for his dues all last year. Miss Hussey also, the owner of the Island, and a bigoted Papist, almost went frantic on learning the progress made there by the Reformation, and in despair gave over the management of the property to some other Romanists. Indeed the work of God is prospering wonderfully, and it has been a source of the deepest gratification to me to hear of all that has come to my knowledge. May the name of the Lord continue to be magnified!

Aug. 19. We left Dingle for Valentia; on our arrival Augustus and I went to visit a cavern on the other side of the bay. We were rowed across. The moon shone brightly, and we entered the cavern, which appeared the more grand on account of the dusky light. The sea too was all on fire wherever our oars or rudder disturbed the water. Wherever also the wet dripped from the roof, there the phosphoretic appearance followed. The echo was fine, and the dull, distant dashing of the waves within the cavern quite awe-inspiring.

We had a beautiful sail across the bay, and the moonlight literally appeared to sleep on the island and sea, all was so still and beautiful. Seldom have I experienced a day of so much animal and mental enjoyment, and all the party repeatedly expressed the same feeling. May that pleasure which is so freely imparted by God through His works, lead me more earnestly to seek my rest only in that tranquillity and peace which is to be found in God as a reconciled Father in Christ Jesus!

Aug. 20. Augustus and I went to see the cavern again, which was grander than I expected to find it, the excavation being very extensive and lofty. We fired off a pistol, and the echo and turmoil occasioned by the report of the firearms was wonderful. The hoarse dashing of the waves was also striking. After luncheon we set out for the slate quarries. After visiting them we ascended the mountain and had a fine view of the Atlantic and of Valentia. We fell in with an old man who is of the Church of England, who told us there are occasional converts from Popery,—three within the last month. The Knight of Kerry asked us all to dine with him, but this we declined.

Aug. 21. In our walk we went into the Roman Catholic Chapel, which we found wretched in the extreme. There were about forty ragged scholars, some reading, some writing. The schoolmaster appeared an intelligent young man, who talked of going out to Australia. He told us the priest discouraged emigration, and we gathered that he himself had evidently the impression that emigrants was only another name for slaves; of this we tried to disabuse him. In the evening we went on board, and had a short sail before dinner. The porpoises were gambolling about the yacht.

Aug. 22. We sailed from Valentia, but, the weather being unfavourable, we made for Dingle; there we could not obtain a car, so were obliged to stay all night. Next morning at five o'clock we left Dingle by the mail car to Tralee. We then proceeded by mail to Limerick, which we reached about half-past five, and thence drove to Cratloe in a car.

Aug. 24. We crossed the Shannon and then walked about two miles to Vermont, and went on to look at the ruins of " Carrig O Gunnell;" they are extensive, and the situation very fine and striking.

Aug. 25. We went by boat to the Cathedral at Limerick. We heard an excellent sermon by the same clergyman I had heard before. After service we went to look at Bp. Jebb's monument; the sculptor is a Mr Bailey, and it seems well executed.

Aug. 26. We started this morning for Lack. We found the steamer crowded, and we landed at Cahircon and walked to Kildysart, and thence took a car to Lack. Our object was to find the part of the estate where draining had been undertaken by the Squire, which was accomplished at length. We then had a long drive to Kilrush, where we dined and slept.

Aug. 27. We sailed from Kilrush in the yacht, which had been ordered down to meet us there, and after a prosperous voyage reached Cratloe in the afternoon.

Aug. 28. This day Augustus fixed on as the holiday in commemoration of the first residence of the family at Cratloe. There was a great gathering of peasantry, men, women and children. Races and sports occupied the afternoon, and in the evening there was an exhibition of the magic lantern, which afforded infinite amusement. They are indeed a light-hearted, social people, their whole demeanour being marked by the utter absence of all rudeness. One can only marvel at the cruel superstition which habitually converts such beings into relentless savages.

Aug. 29. At half-past six a.m. H. Nevile and I left Cratloe for Limerick. We then took the coach for Dublin, which we reached about ten p.m., and, finding the mail packet left Kingston at half-past eleven, took a car and drove off, but owing to the carelessness of our driver barely reached in time. The night was beautifully fine and the sea tranquil, I therefore remained on deck for some time.

Aug. 30. We left Liverpool at three p.m., for Birmingham, which we did not reach till ten p.m.! The next day we accomplished forty miles to Weedon in an hour and a half.

Sept. 1. How I enjoyed the calmness and rest which a Sunday in England affords, compared with the disquiet of the Lord's day spent in unhappy Ireland!

The Term found Mr Corrie at Cambridge, but there are but few entries of public or University interest of that date.

Cambridge, Nov. 8. I went to Archdeacon Thorp's rooms, to meet a Committee of the Camden Society, the object of which is to promote the study of Ecclesiastical Architecture. To-day I issued the subject for the Norrisian Prize Essay for the ensuing year. "The Holy Scriptures contain sufficiently all Doctrine required of necessity for Eternal Salvation through faith in Jesus Christ."

Dec. 2. Mr Gayer, the curate of Dingle, called. I made his acquaintance in Ireland. We had much interesting conversation on the state of Ireland. In the evening several of my pupils came to my rooms, and Mr Gayer detailed to them a good many interesting particulars respecting his missionary proceedings at Dingle and Ventry.

Dec. 3. In the evening, Professor Scholefield, Carus, Dalton, Willis, and Mandell came to tea. Mr Gayer gave us some particulars of his Mission in Kerry, and we had all much profitable conversation.

Dec. 6. There was a meeting at the Town Hall for Promoting Education among the Poor in the Principles of the Church. The Bishop of Ely[1] was in the Chair.

Dec. 11. Went to the Senate-House, where we had to vote on a Grace for appropriating £500 a year out of the money paid by Members of the University to the Library, to

---

[1] Bishop Allen.

form a Fund for paying the sum now due for building the new Library. It was carried, there being a minority of one.

Dec. 12. H. Goulburn, of Trinity, came in the evening. We had much talk on the subject of National Education.

Dec. 13. I met the Master of Trinity[1], who had been to my rooms to see me on the subject of the National School Society.

Dec. 14. I went to St John's Lodge, to a meeting of the Antiquarian Society. We were occupied with modifying the Rules. The Members present were the Vice-Chancellor[2], Messrs Cookson, Lodge, Smith (of Caius) and Hildyard, Sir Henry Dryden, Bart., Halliwell (secretary), and myself. The final revision of the Rules was left to Lodge, Halliwell, and myself.

The last entry at the close of each year contains the expression of those feelings which with him were not weakened by repetition—his own unworthiness, his gratitude, his renewed self-consecration.

[1] Dr C. Wordsworth.   [2] Dr Tatham.

CHAPTER VII.

NEW YEAR'S DAY, 1840, which was partially spent at Kettering, was begun by an administration of the Holy Communion at 7 a.m., which was largely attended. The next entry is on the day of the introduction of the Penny Postage.

Jan. 10. To-day the New Post-Office Regulations take effect, and letters if prepaid are conveyed throughout the United Kingdom for one penny.

Jan. 23. I went to a meeting of the Board for Promoting the Education of the Poor in the Principles of the Established Church. The Earl of Hardwicke was in the Chair. On bringing up a circular for distribution, I moved that a clause be inserted "with the approbation of the Bishop of the Diocese," in order to recognise more fully our connection with the Church. Objections were made to this, as being unnecessary, and some observed, that the circular was understood to be drawn up on a kind of comprehensive principle. However, Lord Hardwicke said I had better specifically move that the clause be inserted, which I accordingly did. After a short pause (during which Lord Hardwicke said "somebody had better second the proposition, as it involves an important principle"), Frere, the rector of Cottenham, seconded my motion, which was carried without a dissentient voice.

Feb. 1. I have been occupied almost all day in the Library, verifying quotations from the Fathers. Willis is reading Bullinger on the Sacraments with me in an evening.

Feb. 10. This day the Queen was married. I went to the Vice-Chancellor on business, and took the opportunity of obtaining the Vice-Chancellor's *imprimatur* for a reprint of Bullinger's sermons on the Sacraments. I expressed my hope also, that the address of congratulation which the University will present to the Queen on her marriage, may contain some expression of our hope, that her Majesty's aim will be to uphold the Protestant religion. I had some conversation with the Dean of Peterborough[1] respecting the Cathedrals. He told me he was utterly against the concession plans, and that three out of four of his Prebendaries had written to him to say, that they could not, consistently with their oaths, agree to spoliation in any form.

Feb. 14. At the Senate-House, at a Congregation called for voting an address to the Queen on her marriage, the Master of Jesus[2] told me that the Vice-Chancellor[3] did not intend to give any luncheon in London to the Deputation: on which I expressed my satisfaction, for, on the presentation of an Address on the Queen's Accession, I had been disgusted at seeing some of the persons intoxicated in the very Presence Chamber. The Master of Jesus also told me that on that occasion twelve men, professing to be of the University, had gone to the Thatched House Tavern, after the address had been presented, and had ordered a cold dinner in the Vice-Chancellor's name and at the University charge. It has also been decided, that all who go with the Address shall write down their names and colleges on going into the Thatched House.

Feb. 17. At a Congregation at the Senate-House to-day a petition to the Legislature for Church Extension was passed. I had some conversation with the Provost of King's on the subject of an Act of Parliament which is contemplated,

---

[1] Dr Turton.   [2] Dr French.   [3] Dr Tatham.

for giving the Bishop power to alienate tithes from one living to another, or to endow new Churches, when the patronage is in *Colleges.* One of the notable schemes of the day! Why do they not meddle with livings in the patronage of laymen?

The following letter to the late Mr Irvine of Leigh (an old pupil) on the responsibilities of persons of property in spiritual matters has, with another, been kindly supplied by the late Rev. J. Brame, rector of St Peter's, Manchester:

CAMBRIDGE, *Feb.* 21, 1840.

Dear Mr Irvine,

... I am truly glad you have so soon got to work in your parish, and should advise you to ascertain, as soon as may be, what *ought* to be the number of Churches and Clergy for the due supply of the spiritual wants of the place, and then print a statement to put into the hands of men of property, in and about the place, calling on them to fulfil the urgent duty thus devolved upon them, by God's Providence, and the spiritual destitution of their neighbours. The unsettled state of the people will so far work for good, that it will bring to light the awful neglect of those who, having used the labourer for their own profit, have left him to perish in sin, without any adequate effort being made for providing him with religious instruction. We may learn also, how thoroughly impotent for good, education is, without true religion, and how completely futile the "Voluntary System" has proved as a substitute for Establishment.

Yours very truly,
G. E. CORRIE.

Feb. 22. Three young men came to consult me respecting the formation of a Society for encouraging the Study of Ecclesiastical Knowledge, with a view to the defence of the Church of England. I told them to see me again.

Feb. 26. I was told a disorderly crowd went to Buckingham Palace with the Cambridge Address to the Queen; that many could not get into the Palace; that those who did get in made

a disorderly rush and squeeze, so as to break the glass of the
Palace window. This was afterwards confirmed by the Master
of Emmanuel[1]. On mentioning all this to Mr Burrell, he told
me that it was *always* a disgraceful business so far as he had
ever known. That he had gone with three Addresses to
George 3rd, and that then the Universitymen were rude and
ill-behaved in the extreme. I had thought the present ill-
manners was one of the signs of the times.

Mar. 2. I went to the Senate-House to hear the Addresses
to Prince Albert and the Duchess of Kent read. That to
Prince Albert was full of beautiful and touching sentiment.

Mar. 9. I spent some time in our College Library verifying the references to the Fathers as quoted in Bullinger's
Decades; a tiresome business.

Mar. 13. I had an interview with a youth whom I had
desired to call on me to-day, having yesterday observed that
he was reading during my Public Lecture. I spoke very
seriously on the great importance of regarding every preparation for Holy Orders as a sacred duty, and not as a matter of
form. He behaved very well, and I trust some good may
come of our interview, but I refused to admit him to the
Lectures again this Term.

Mar. 18. In the afternoon I went to the Senate-House
to vote on a Grace which was brought forward, to appoint a
Syndicate to consider how far it might be expedient to interfere to regulate the questions set by the Moderators in the
Examination for Honours. It arose out of the many com-
plaints that have been made of the last Examination for
Honours in January, in which the questions were far too hard,
and purposely made so, to disappoint the mere *book-work* men.
The result was that the great body of the men could do little
or nothing. The Grace of to-day was virtually a vote of
censure on the Examiners. It was carried by considerable
majorities in both Houses.

----

[1] Dr Archdall.

The following letter to Mr —— is the first of several to a friend, who constantly referred to him on both personal and parochial matters.

CAMBRIDGE, *April* 1, 1840.

Dear Mr ——

Having finished some portion of my occupation for this Term, I find myself in circumstances to attend to your difficulty respecting oaths. On recurring to your letter it appears to me that much of that may have been occasioned, by your having confounded those Scriptures which forbid profane swearing, with those which relate only to *protestations*, and with others which have reference to oaths, as an appeal to God for confirmation of man's veracity. These severally involve distinct considerations of greater or less importance, and they are not therefore to be confounded as if identical. With respect to profane swearing or taking God's name in vain, I need observe nothing, because you have rightly decided upon the precept, Matt. v. 33. I will therefore put you in mind that for the confirmation of a statement, appeal is not necessarily confined to God, for human testimony may for all the purposes intended by that appeal be sufficient. Hence the Apostle (1 Thess. ii. 5) may as justly say ὑμεῖς μάρτυρες, as θεὸς μάρτυς. But then you would not say that St Paul "*swears*" by these Thessalonians; he appeals to them as having it in their power to confirm that of which God the searcher of hearts was also cognisant. Precisely the same idea is contained in some of those other Scriptures you quote: the objects or persons mentioned, are appealed to (not sworn ˙by), as evidence of assertions made, or of facts to be confirmed. Some of the Scriptures, as Gen. xlii. 15, are in proper sense not oaths but protestations. "By the life of Pharaoh," "as surely as Pharaoh liveth or is alive, so surely," &c. The fact that Pharaoh was alive was unquestionable, and a protestation by that fact, assumed the thing referred to, to be as certain and unquestionable. But when we speak of an *oath*, we usually and exclusively understand, a deliberate calling upon

God to bear witness to the truth of words spoken by us, as when we enter into contracts with our fellow-men :—when, in other words, we make God a party in the transactions of human society.   Are we then at liberty to connect thus the Self-existent with the mortal : the All-holy with the sinful?   My notion is that the lawfulness of taking an oath, is inseparable from the idea of God's providence and government of the world.   If that be true which Jehovah asserts of Himself, "By Me kings reign," &c. (Prov. viii. 15, 16), can there be any acknowledgment of God in the administration of human affairs without, in some manner, directly connecting that administration with Him?   But there is no way of referring the affairs of human society to God more directly than by realising His perfect justice the standard of our Laws; His unsullied holiness, the exemplar of our intercourse with each other : His omnipresence and omniscience, the measure of our candour and sincerity: His unswerving veracity, the prototype of our testimony : His Almighty power, our refuge against injustice and a check upon our perfidiousness.   And so, of all the attributes of the glorious Godhead.   You will observe, therefore, that as these sentiments are inseparable from an Oath, and involved (as men believe) only in an oath, a religious person, in my view, is so far from having scruples about taking an oath, that he holds oaths to be essential to the perfection of human society; that regarding the taking of an oath as a solemn acknowledgment of God's continual regard for, and control of the relations of this life, the Christian by that act engages in an act of devotion.   Therefore it was, that in every engagement and transaction which involved the principles on which the well-being of society rests, holy men of old were wont, by a solemn appeal to God, to make Him a party to what they did and undertook (Gen. xxiv. 3): and what is more, such oaths were recognised (and therefore made lawful) by God, who promised His blessing on the observance of such engagements as were made under the sanction of His great Name.   (Ps. xv. 4: xxiv. 4.)   Nor can this principle be regarded as peculiar to any particular age or dispensation: for in such a command as Deut. vi. 13, if the injunction to fear God, to serve Him and cleave to Him be binding once and for ever, why should "to swear by Him" be (without the slightest hint from the inspired writer) regarded as a ceremonial peculiarity? Hence of the Christian economy also, it was predicted (Isai. lxv. 16) "that he who blesseth Himself in the earth shall bless himself by the God of truth; and he that sweareth in the earth shall swear by the God of truth." And therefore the first Christians did not scruple accordingly to bind themselves by *oath* to the observance of such laws of honesty and morality as are essential to the well-being of Society. And as if to mark the universality of a principle which constitutes God the judge of the world and its transactions, it pleased Him so to affect the natural conscience with reverence for an oath, that people of every nation, religion, or superstition have regarded such a solemn appeal to God, as affording the utmost assurance to human testimony, and the only safeguard against universal distrust (Heb. vi. 16). All, therefore, a Christian has to to do (as I think), is to see that the oath, does not exact of him conditions at variance with the gospel of Christ: *that* being provided against, he may safely confirm his words by an appeal to the Most High, with all reverence and godly devotion.

You will of course receive these observations for what they may be worth, and believe me to be,

Very truly your friend,
G. E. CORRIE.

April 9. I was at a meeting of the Governors of the Boys' School, to decide on agreeing to permit the Board of Education to annex a Training School for Masters to the Boys' School. There was some discussion whether it should be allowed to the Board, to annex their Training School to ours in perpetuity, or only for a limited period on trial; it was decided almost unanimously in favour of perpetuity.

April 20. Thurtell of Caius called on me to say that the

Governors of Addenbrooke's Hospital had agreed to give him £3 towards buying religious books for the patients if I would assist him in selecting them. I told him I would do my best to aid so good an object.

May 8. I had a long walk with the Vice-Chancellor. Amongst other things, he told me that the review of Brougham's Pamphlet in the *Quarterly* some years ago, was usually supposed to have been put together by Canning, although the present Bp. of Gloucester (Monk) had the credit of it at the time.

May 18. Dalton of Queens' called to say a Mr Traill from Ireland wished to be introduced to me, and to state his notion of a restoration of the ten Bishoprics which were suppressed in Ireland by Lord Stanley for the purpose of getting rid of the Church-cess. Soon afterwards Mr Traill came, and I had a long and interesting conversation with him; he gave me his papers and promised to call in the evening. We had much talk about the plan of a restoration of the Irish Bishoprics. Mr Traill said he had held correspondence with several members of the Legislature, but all seemed shy of meddling with the matter. But God's cause can prosper without them.

May 20. I went to the Senate-House expecting there would be some voting on a Grace regarding the re-appointing of a Syndicate to enquire into the mode of examining for Honours. The real object of the Grace, however, was to censure the Examiners of the year. The Grace was thrown out in the Caput by Dr Geldart[1].

May 22. The Election for the Town commenced at eight o'clock, and at the close of the Poll, Sir A. Grant was in a majority of ninety-three. Great struggles were made on both sides; Sir A. Grant made a short pithy speech, and then marched off the ground in a glorious procession. Belancy told me the undergraduates have rendered essential service to the good cause, by their great exertions in watching those

[1] Regius Professor of Laws.

who were all last night prowling about to bribe some twenty voters who are known to be regularly bought; but so narrowly were these gentry watched, that it is believed that with all their cunning they could not succeed in their tricks.

May 23. I went to the hustings to hear the Poll declared. The procession was a grand one. The Mayor declared Sir A. Grant duly elected to serve in Parliament for the Borough of Cambridge. Then Sir Alexander Grant made a most effective speech. When I returned to my rooms I found a note, stating that the Ludlow Election has been gained by a majority of forty-one. We have need to be thankful to a merciful Providence for so disposing the hearts of men.

An elaborate and useful paper on suitable School-books was drawn up, but has been long since superseded.

May 28. I was engaged in an examination of School-books, for the purpose of making out a list for the Diocesan Board of Education in Cambridge. When amongst my own people, there is sometimes a feeling of weariness comes over me with regard to my present occupations, and a desire to have them changed, and to have my natural disposition to fall back upon the quiet affections of my family gratified. But then I feel how deeply all this is connected with a selfishness, little in accordance with that Apostolic resolution, " I am ready to spend and be spent" in God's service. Lord Jesus order my lot in the world as shall best promote Thy Glory!

May 30. Returned to Cambridge and closed my Lectures to-day.

June 3. There was some voting on a Grace to grant £200 to the National School Society. In the Black Hood House the Grace was carried only by a majority of five, and about the same in the Regent House.

June 4. I met the Vice-Chancellor, who told me that just now there is a dispute between the University and Town

Magistrates respecting our privileges. A gownsman was engaged in a fight during the election, and was summoned before the Mayor for an assault. He pleaded his privilege and appealed to the Vice-Chancellor, who accordingly sent notice in the regular way to the Mayor. This notice was however disregarded, and the Magistrates proceeded to convict the gownsman in a penalty of £5. He, of course, refused to plead or acknowledge their jurisdiction. They, however, committed him to the Town Gaol. This being done, the gownsman paid the penalty, and so the matter is to be put to the issue. The Vice-Chancellor told me the conviction was made under some recent Act of Sir Robert Peel's, in which the privileges of the Universities were not reserved.

June 8. A meeting of the Library Syndicate. The first business was to agree to accept a certain number of books which the Rev. Robert James M'Ghee of Harold's Cross, Dublin, offered to present to the Public Library, subject to certain restrictions as to use. One was that the books should only be taken out of the Library by the Vice-Chancellor or Heads of Houses, or to be exhibited before the Houses of Parliament. Another was that the books should be examined in the Library only, in the presence of the Librarian, lest some person should wilfully mutilate them. With the books was sent a handsome mahogany lock-up case, with a brass plate and with inscription, " Documents proving the crimes and cruelty of the Papal Apostasy, presented by Robert M'Ghee." The Vice-Chancellor explained that we had to decide on accepting the proffered books. Then burst forth all kinds of expressions against the idea of collecting books for such a purpose, and a proposition that they should be rejected. It was argued that the books were common and to be met with anywhere, and so it were useless to accept books which might be had for asking for. On this I observed that some of the books could not be had for any price. Among others selected as common was a Macnamara edition of the Bible with annotations. I observed that the very *existence* of the *edition* lying before us had been denied. Then it was proposed we should accept the books, but reject Mr M'Ghee's regulations respecting their use. The object of this was evidently designed to make Mr M'Ghee refuse us the books except with his stipulation. But this idea was negatived. At last it was almost unanimously agreed that the books should be accepted as offered by Mr M'Ghee, provided he agreed that the inscription on the plate of the bookcase he sent were altered to " Books and an historical chart connected with the Church of Rome, presented by &c."

June 9. The Master of Trinity told me there was a serious intention once, on the part of the National School Society in London, to recommend the disuse of the Church Catechism in Schools in the manufacturing districts, where there are many Dissenters. It appears to have been represented to the Society that many Dissenters would, by such a concession, be gained over, but on careful enquiry, there appeared to be nothing but a premeditated scheme on the part of someone or other, to mislead the Bishops and others. Providentially the evidence produced by enquiry, shewed that the Dissenters in the manufacturing districts did not wish for the concession.

June 12. —— called for his Norrisian Certificate. Among other things he told me that one female relative of his wife had already become a Papist, as the result of reading the Oxford Tracts and Dr Pusey's writings, and that the sister of the party in question was wavering in her faith from a like cause. Mr M. told me that when Dr Pusey heard of the lady turning Papist, he asked to have an interview with her (for he was acquainted with her), and went so far as to offer to travel a good distance to see her, but she refused to see him. The newspapers have been full of accounts of the attempt to assassinate the Queen and Prince Albert.

June 14. I took Scholefield's duty at St Michael's. I had the whole Morning Service to perform, and got through it without fatigue, for which I am deeply thankful, as it seems to have pleased God to restore me again to my profession.

June 17. The Dean of Peterborough told me that Gunning, the Esquire Bedell, had been making a violent speech against the Clergy, and charging them with provoking dissatisfaction with the Queen, and that the result was these attempts to murder her Majesty! His own party were disgusted, but Dr Spence of Jesus, who was the only Clergyman present, (the Speech was made in the Town Hall at a meeting called to address the Queen,) got up and required Gunning to name a single Clergyman who had preached disloyally. This, of course, Gunning said he could not do; but said he had been told so.

June 18. Gunning spoke to me to-day about not being able to dine with us on the Ramsden Commemoration. He evidently feels that he is under a cloud for his violent speech against the Clergy. There was a Congregation for the purpose of voting an Address to the Queen. In the evening Carus came in, with Kingdon of Sidney, to ask my advice as to what the Parochial Clergy should do respecting Gunning's Speech. I advised that they extract from the newspaper the offensive passage, state that they deny the truth of everything Gunning there asserts respecting their disloyal preaching, and send their denial to Gunning, signed by *all* the Clergy, requesting that he will take an opportunity of unsaying what they pronounced to be untrue.

June 22. At ten o'clock I left Cambridge, and arrived safely in London about four o'clock, to be ready to accompany the party with the address to the Queen from the University.

June 23. I breakfasted with Augustus O'Brien, and met Blakesley and Colville of Trinity, Milnes, M.P. for Pontefract, Viscount Adare, Locke King, Francis Gurdon and George Bentinck. We had a good deal of talk on Church matters.

June 24. I went to the Thatched House Tavern to meet

the party from Cambridge with the Address to the Queen.
On arriving at the Palace we were ushered into the Presence
Chamber. The attendance at the Address was not incon-
veniently large, but there was no order preserved, so I soon
found myself in the rear, and I saw nothing of the Queen
beyond the top of her head. She read her answer in a firm
voice, and the presentations being but few the ceremony
was soon over, and we backed out of the room. The
Bishops of Durham, Lichfield, Chichester, and Gloucester
were there. At seven I went to dine with the Duke of Northumberland, who, as High Steward of the University, invited
the Vice-Chancellor, and a Cambridge party to dinner. The
party consisted of the Vice-Chancellor, and the Masters of
Clare, Jesus, Downing, and Magdalen, Earls of Bandon and
Brecknock, Lord Powis, Mr Clive, Messrs Jeffery and Cow-
ling of St John's, the two Proctors, and the two Esquire
Bedells, the Registrary, Dr Geldart, and myself. Nothing
could exceed the gentlemanly hospitality of the Duke. The
dinner also was very splendid, as was the dessert. We dined
off gold plate; but yet the whole was in a style of simple
magnificence. There are some beautiful pictures, which the
Duke took much pleasure in shewing. He seems to be a
man of great taste. We came away at eleven o'clock, after
having tea in the Drawing-room, where the Duchess received
us with great cordiality. Some other Ladies were there
whom I did not know; but they seemed to be a part of
Earl Powis's family.

On the occasion of the first visit of the Royal Agricultural
Society to Cambridge Mr Corrie's guests were, Sir Charles
Burrell, Mr O'Brien, Mr Henry Nevile, Mr Augustus O'Brien
and Mr Locke King.

July 15. Myself and party went to the Cattle Show.
The arrangements were admirable, and the collection of
cattle, agricultural implements, &c. on a far larger scale than ·

at Oxford last year. We looked about for three hours. When my party returned, they prepared for the great dinner in a pavilion erected in Downing College, to which I did not go, but entertained a large party in hall. We had a pleasant afternoon, for Mr Westrope, one of our Master's tenants, is a glorious old Tory. The party returned from the dinner about nine o'clock. The speakers most attended to were Sir Robert Peel and the Earl of Hardwicke.

July 16. Colonel Rushbrooke and Sir Charles Burrell joined our breakfast party. Afterwards Augustus and I went to see the sale of oxen and horses on Parker's Piece. After this my friends left Cambridge. I went to see the Horticultural Show in the Pavilion, which was used yesterday for the great dinner. It is a wonderful erection for a temporary building. There was a sermon this morning at St Mary's, by the Master of Downing[1], in aid of Addenbrooke's Hospital.

July 18. I attended a meeting of the Council of the Cambridge Antiquarian Society. It was agreed to print several communications; among others, a Catalogue of the books given to this College by the Founder, with some notes upon the English authors whose works are mentioned in the Catalogue. The Provost of King's[2] called to ask me about the Cambridge Refuge, to the building of which he wishes to subscribe.

At this time Mr Corrie was in correspondence with a member of the Government respecting the proposal for attaching two of the Canonries at Ely to two Professorships in Cambridge; with a perfect knowledge of University affairs, the want of which has so often resulted in crude legislation, Mr Corrie pointed out the flaws in the proposed scheme and offered suggestions which were gratefully accepted. To this subject reference is made in the next two entries.

July 25. I met —— of Corpus, who congratulated me on the probable appending a Prebendal Stall in Ely Cathedral

---

[1] Mr Worsley.   [2] Dr Thackeray.

to my Professorship. I told him I was very sorry to observe the Crown was to have the Patronage of the Stalls, for that my conviction was, that no greater detriment could happen to the University, than the introduction of political interest in the appointment to Professorships. He did not however agree with me.

July 26. I went with Whewell to his rooms to look at a clause in the Ecclesiastical Endowments Bill, which enables the Crown to apply two Prebendal Stalls in Ely Cathedral to the increase of the endowments of any two of the four Professorships of Greek, Hebrew, Casuistry and Norris.

The remainder of the Vacation was spent at Kettering and the neighbourhood, including a visit to Colsterworth.

Aug. 13. Kettering. A meeting was held to-day to form a Protestant Association. There were present Sir George Robinson, Messrs Maunsell, Winslow, Wyman, Roughton, Hogg, Lamb, Barton, and Craig, also Mr Mackworth Dolben, besides Mr Lord, my brother and myself. A provisional Committee and Secretary were appointed, after some discussion as to whether the Bishop of the Diocese should be applied to. Mr Barton, one of the curates, my brother and myself, had a great deal of conversation to-day respecting Sunday-schools; and it was agreed that an attempt should be made to put the Sunday-school in this place on a more efficient footing than heretofore.

Aug. 17. My brother and I went to a meeting here to-day to consider the question of having a railway from London to Manchester by Kettering. It was agreed that a railway would be a benefit to the place, and that all should be done in our power to further the project.

Sept. 8. At Blatherwycke to-day the conversation after dinner was on the Bishops of the Church, and so much disputation was there that my heart ached and I wished myself in my quiet study again. Alas! how very much is the spirit and feeling and gentleness of Christ foreign to the natural heart! So much judging of motives, so much measuring of others by our own standard and not by the law of love and Christian forbearance. O Lord, give me grace not to be weary of the world until I have accomplished whatever Thou hast called me to do for the furthering of the Kingdom of Thy blessed Son! Yet speedily may that Kingdom come.

Sept. 23. I went to Colsterworth to see our old home. I have had many thoughts of sorrow at the remembrance of the past which this visit to the place of my nativity called forth. My mother's grave, my grandfather's and sister's resting-places: the scene of my father's and eldest brother's ministry, the many that were dead with whom I had been acquainted,—the recollection of the many joyous and also of the many unprofitable days I had spent there. All these combined to affect me. O Lord, I know that Thy patience is unwearied in sparing me so long: and by Thy grace I will hope in Thee to the end. Forsake not, then, the work of Thine own hands!

Oct. 6. I went to Kettering to see after my hounds, which I sent off to Mr Isted of Exton, who wished to borrow them.

Oct. 12. A letter from Cambridge informs me that the Marquess Camden, Chancellor of the University, is dead, and that the Duke of Northumberland is a candidate for the office thus become vacant.

Mr Corrie was in the habit of offering special prayer for help on resuming work in Cambridge or entering on any fresh duties. Such is recorded in his Diary on his return to College at this time.

Oct. 17. I had a good deal of conversation with our Master respecting the election of Lord Lyndhurst to the office of High Steward, and he asked me if my name might be used in writing to our M.A.s respecting Lord Lyndhurst's election to the High Stewardship. Robert McGhee of Dublin called to make my acquaintance.

Oct. 23. Stevenson the bookseller called to consult me about printing a fly-leaf of Errata to Bullinger's Sermons on the Sacraments.

Oct. 28. H. Jones of this College and Henry Bailey of St John's called on me to ask what steps I thought ought to be taken to induce the Undergraduates to stand up in St Mary's during the singing, instead of sitting, as they now do. I told them that it would be best to make it known that to sit during the singing was peculiar to Dissenters and Presbyterians, and to use other methods of persuasion among themselves; but by no means to ask for the interference of the public authorities, which they seemed inclined to do.

Nov. 1. Professor Scholefield is the Select Preacher. The object of his sermon was to draw attention to the Oxford Tracts, against which he has undertaken to preach. The sermon was introductory. He gave a brief but comprehensive sketch of the state of the Church of England during the last and present century—and described the Oxford Tracts as breaking in on the unity of the Church. There was a very large congregation.

Nov. 3. I was told to-day that Battiscombe, formerly of King's and now an Anabaptist preacher at Barnwell, is anxious to get back into the Church, but he hesitates about being silent three years.

Nov. 11. At 9 o'clock the polling for the office of High Steward began. At the close of the first day's Poll at 4 o'clock the numbers were—Lord Lyndhurst 420, Lord Lyttelton 292. I understand that when Lord Lyndhurst came into the Senate-House the cheering of Undergraduates was tremendous. They gave three cheers also for our Master. I have had innumerable callers during the day, Allan Young, Augustus O'Brien, and Lord John Fitzroy, Sir Jacob Preston, &c. &c.

Nov. 12. I went to the Senate-House to vote for Lord Lyndhurst. This I did after much hesitation. As I came back from voting the Undergraduates called out, "Three cheers for Professor Corrie," which were given, and then they called for "one cheer more." I felt nervous and unsettled and left directly. I walked with Chevallier to see the new Fitzwilliam Museum, then to the new Church at Barnwell.

Nov. 13. Soon after we had sat down to breakfast in the Combination-room with our visitors, a stranger made his appearance, who said he had been sent to breakfast by a Mr Belaney. He was recognised as the Marquess of Douro. We made him welcome. He had come to vote for Lord Lyndhurst from fifty miles beyond Edinburgh. The mail in which he travelled had been overturned on reaching the Border, and so he was delayed.

Nov. 16. This day is the anniversary of my ordination as Priest. I have been reading over the Ordination Service, and beg of God to forgive the wretched manner in which I have failed to carry out my priestly obligations.

Dec. 3. I had a good deal of talk with Lodge the Librarian to-day, on the subject of the Petition to Parliament in favour of the admission of Dissenters to the University, which was sent from here a few years ago.

Dec. 4. I attended a Congregation at which Addresses to the Queen, to Prince Albert, and the Queen Dowager were voted on occasion of the birth of a Princess.

Dec. 7. Bailey of St John's and another student came to ask me about some "Hints" which they think of putting forth respecting standing up at St Mary's during the singing.

Dec. 11. Willis sent me a letter from an officer of the Fleet before St Jean d'Acre, written on a sheet of paper that contained *an autograph letter in Arabic from Ibrahim Pasha, to the Governor of Acre.* The officer in question found it in Acre, and said in his letter, "This is all the pillage I got." It was a curious thing. The officer stated a fact, viz. that during the blockade of Acre by the English and others, a French steamer was allowed to enter the harbour on the assurance that the object *of the French* was only to bring off any French subjects who might be in the besieged town : it

was however afterwards found that the steamer conveyed
artillerymen, and left them in Acre to fight against the
English. Bailey of St John's called to-day to submit a
proof-sheet of a short tract that is being printed on the subject of standing up at St Mary's Church during the time the
Psalms are sung.

Dec. 12. Butler, one of the B.A. Scholars of Trinity, came
in to have his Translation of Bullinger *de Origine Erroris*
corrected.

CHAPTER VIII.

THERE have been but few letters recoverable of the year 1841, and the Diary does not contain many subjects of University interest; one, however, is important; the first movement taken towards the introduction of more decided Theological study in the University.

Jan. 1. I have to praise God for His great mercy. May the year now beginning be more exclusively devoted to God, in body, soul, and spirit, than former years have been.

Jan. 23. I went to congratulate the Master of Pembroke on having the Senior Wrangler of his College, with other distinguished honours. He told me that Stokes the Senior Wrangler would be elected Fellow of the College to-day.

Feb. 25. I had a talk with Dalton of Queens', on University affairs, more particularly respecting closing the Union Club Reading Room on Sundays.

Feb. 26. I hear the Ministers have had a majority of *five*, on the Bill for altering the registration of voters in Ireland. The Bill makes the Franchise as low as £5.

Mar. 1. I had a discussion with Belaney about a scheme now afloat for uniting five Societies as *Church* Societies to the exclusion of others.

The following letter to Archdeacon Thorp, though of earlier date, relates to the subject of the last entry.

Jan. 25, 1841.

Dear Mr Archdeacon,

As regards the subject of your last note, I am sorry that I cannot assist you at your contemplated Meeting to arrange for establishing "a Committee for receiving and distributing contributions &c. through the five Societies." My notions on that subject are as follows: I do not recognise in the Societies in question any more Church authority than in some others of a kindred nature, which it is purposed to omit in the union you speak of. I should be afraid, therefore, to risk the creating of division among us by any attempt to exalt the five Societies exclusively into Church Societies by our private opinions. So long as the "Five" are left to plead their respective claims to support on their individually distinct and separate grounds, I cannot doubt, but that as a general rule, they will conciliate the good will of most men who are observant of the wants of the world and wish well to our Church. But then I should hesitate before I closed my eyes to the fact that there are other Societies which are equally supported by Churchmen (Dignitaries as well as private men), without offence against any known and recognised Church-law. I should fear that so soon as we should attempt (indirectly though it only might be) to decide by our private opinions what Societies claim to be united as Church Societies and what do not, we should stand in the predicament of having put many of our Bishops and brethren ecclesiastically in the wrong, and so of having made them or ourselves a Sect in the Church. The practical result would no doubt be the injury of the Societies which we designed to serve. Indeed with all my feelings in favour of the "Five Societies," I should yet think it to be my painful duty to separate myself *locally* from them all, if it were my unhappiness to see them placed in a false position, by any unauthoritative union of them. I am sure you will receive this expression of my opinion in the spirit that dictates it; because, though we may happen to differ on the subject to which it refers, I cannot doubt but that we are cordially united in a desire to forward, as far as in us lies, the cause of our common Redeemer, through the instrumentality of our common Mother, the Church of Christ in these Realms.

Believe me to be, dear Mr Archdeacon,

Yours very truly,

G. E. CORRIE.

The Venerable Archdeacon Thorp.

Mar. 2.   I went to a meeting of the Antiquarian Society. Goodwin of Corpus read an interesting paper on the circumstances connected with the consecration of Archbishop Parker.

Mar. 3.   The Master called with a note from Lord Melbourne's Secretary, announcing that the Queen had given £100 to Mrs Holman the mother of my late pupil, as the result of a memorial I transmitted to the Prime Minister on her behalf.   I was asked to-day to become Secretary to the Church Building Society here, which I declined, having no time.

After a notice in the Diary on the subject, a letter follows from Mr Perry, Tutor of Trinity, afterwards first Bishop of Melbourne, enclosing one from the Bishop of London (Blomfield), which opened a subject afterwards frequently referred to in the Diary—the promoting of more direct Theological Study on the part of those intending to take Holy Orders.   It was proposed to appoint a Syndicate to deliberate on the course to be adopted.   The Grace for this purpose was for the time however non-placeted by the Senate.

Mar. 9.   Perry of Trinity called on me to ask about appointing a Syndicate to consider whether it be desirable to institute an examination for Students in Divinity, after they have taken their degree?   He shewed me a letter from the Bishop of London stating an opinion that the University should do something, and saying also that Oxford is already considering the matter. I gave Perry such advice as occurred to me, and helped him to name a Syndicate.

TRINITY COLLEGE, *Mar.* 9, 1841.

My dear Corrie,

I was greatly obliged to you for the statement of your views on Clerical Education, upon which I am very anxious to have some further communication with you. On Sunday I received a note from the Bishop of London, of which I send a copy for your perusal. You will see that he urges very strongly the necessity of "moving forthwith," and I do trust that you will unite with me in endeavouring to obtain a Syndicate for the consideration of the subject. By it all the several matters noticed by you could be discussed; and the appointment of it would shew the friends of the Church that we really desire to adopt a suitable measure so soon as we shall be satisfied upon its details. Shall you be at home any hour this morning that I may call upon you? There is one point, upon which I am disposed to differ from you, viz. the effects of those Diocesan Colleges. Surely they are likely to become, if we do not take care, of considerable importance *for a time*, even if they should *ultimately* dwindle into insignificance. They have been established by *Bishops*, and cordially supported by many excellent and eminent men, who anticipate from them great and highly beneficial consequences. For myself, I fear lest they should be productive eventually of much mischief to the Church; and the only security which I can see against them is the immediate adoption of a system of Theological Instruction in the Universities.

Ever, my dear Professor, yours most truly,
CHARLES PERRY.

LONDON, *Mar.* 6, 1841.

Rev. Sir,

I beg to thank you for having sent me a copy of your letter to the Bishop of Lichfield. I entirely agree with you in your general view of the question of a course of Theological Instruction to be provided by the University, and I would add that no time should be lost, for the work is actually in hand at Oxford, and Cambridge, if it does not move forthwith, will have only the second rate praise of reluctantly copying the example of her Sister University. Why should not those resident members of our University, and no doubt there are many, who think with you, take up the subject at once, conferring of course in the first place with the Regius Professor and the ruling powers?

I remain, Rev. Sir,
Your faithful Servant,
C. J. LONDON.

The Rev. C. Perry.

TRINITY COLLEGE, *Mar.* 12, 1841.

My dear Corrie,

The Vice-Chancellor[1] called me to him in the Senate-House on Wednesday, and expressed himself as by no means unfavourable to the appointment (so I understood him) of a Syndicate, only he wished to turn over the subject a little more carefully in his own mind before any step was taken. Thus I once more cherish the hope of gaining our first object, the full consideration of the whole matter; and my great desire now is, to lay down some distinct and definite plan of Theological Instruction, which we may submit to the Syndicate (when we have one) as the ground-work for their deliberations. Will you turn your attention particularly to this point, and let me know your views upon it?

Ever, my dear Professor,
Yours sincerely,
CHARLES PERRY.

Mar. 10. I went to breakfast with Carus, to meet Mr Tucker, my late brother's examining Chaplain, who produced a letter he had received from a native Hindoo. It was a singular production, exhibiting the intellectuality of the pure Hindoo Theist. Mr Tucker afterwards called on me. We had a long conversation respecting my brother's last illness. He told me that among my brother's papers was found a letter warning him to be on his guard as to the food he ate, for that a Mahometan had resolved to poison him. This was supposed to be a Mahometan who had been brought by my brother's means to a notional acceptance of Christianity, and had expressed a great desire to be ordained by him. As, however, my brother refused this, not being satisfied of the religious state of mind of the party, the man took a mortal hatred to

---

[1] Dr Archdall.

my brother, and most probably (it was thought) had expressed some design of poisoning him.   However nothing more was known beyond the anonymous letter mentioned above.

Mar. 16.   I met a Procession of all the Benefit Societies, with the Earl of Hardwicke, the Vice-Chancellor, and the Mayor, the Freemasons, &c.   They had been to lay the Foundation Stone of the Victoria Asylum.   The whole Procession had been to St Mary's where a Sermon was preached by the Vice-Chancellor.   I hear that the House of Lords has agreed not to oppose the endowment of the popish Monastic Society of St Sulpice at Montreal in Canada.   Thus has Popery got a legal footing in our Kingdom.

The following letter was written at this time to an intimate friend suffering from severe illness.

CAMBRIDGE, *March* 29, 1841.

... I know from experience that it is a solemn thing to be confronted even with the distant prospect of dissolution, because then the memory in busy activity conjures up the ghosts of neglected duties and sins committed.   And, then there is the unsullied holiness of God and the unworthiness of our best estate brought into contrast, until we feel that there is a meaning in that Psalm, "If Thou Lord shouldest be extreme to mark what is done amiss, O Lord, who may abide it."   Yet this, after all, is the exact state into which it is the object of all God's dealings and teachings to bring us, viz. to a sense of our lost condition in ourselves.   And then it is that *Redemption* stands forth in all its glorious suitableness, for we perceive that He, Who, in the first instance, gave His only Son up for us all, will " with Him also freely give *us all things.*"   Wonderful thought!   Why then need we dishonour God's mercy in Christ Jesus, and rob our own souls of the comfort of believing, and living up to, the promise that all things are ours if we be Christ's!?   We go groping about to find some good thing whereon to rest our hope that God will look upon us, and forget that Redemption is for *sinners*, and that in our

best estate we are sinners to be saved by grace alone. This
thought is sufficient to disarm every unbelieving fear, for, as
there is no state of Christian perfection that needs not the
blood of Christ for its further and entire purification; so is
there no depth of sin from which that blood cannot fully
ransom us. If we can but realize this persuasion by the
simplicity of faith, we triumph over those fears of suffering,
or of futurity, which are inseparable from our natural feelings:
because we learn to look more at the redeeming and sanctifying power of the Cross of Christ, than at our own wretchedness.
In all cases this scripture is alone sufficient to work our peace,
viz. " This is a faithful saying, and worthy of all acceptation,
that Christ Jesus came into the world to save sinners."
I would have you constantly repeat this, and then leave God
to dispose of you for time and eternity, for you cannot be
more tenderly dealt with than by a redeeming God.

Ever your truly affectionate,

G. E. CORRIE.

April 1.   I had a long talk with the Master of St John's[1]
on the purport of some regulations respecting the examination for Medical Degrees, which were introduced to the
Senate to-day.   I voted against them on the principle that
it was a bad precedent to bring forward and pass important
regulations when hardly any one was in the University,
almost all having gone down for the Easter Vacation.   The
regulations were however passed.

April 4.   The Provost[2] told me to-day he was sorry to find
that the Vice-Chancellor and others were disposed to go to
the Crown to obtain a modification of the University Statutes.
I told him he might be sure such would be the case, for that
few either knew or cared as to what the authority was, that
could legally be called upon, to sanction the modifications in
question.

April 13.   I lunched to-day at Archdeacon Thorp's to
meet the Bishop of London[3], Dr Christopher Wordsworth, the

---

[1] Dr Tatham.   [2] Dr Thackeray.   [3] Dr Blomfield.

Dean of Bristol[1], &c. On coming away the Bishop of London asked me to walk with him to our College; he was going to call on our Master. He began to converse with me about a projected plan for some Theological examination in the University. He expressed his opinion that the plan ought to be a comprehensive one, and not merely the setting of a few books to be examined in. I told him that any plan would be useless unless the Bishops fixed on some one general system of examination: for as it was, one Bishop examined in one set of books, another in another. He admitted this was a defect, but said that if some efficient plan were adopted for educating theological students in the University, the Bishops would be guided by it in their examination for Orders. He told me the University of Oxford was setting about a plan of Theological Instruction, and that he hoped we should not be behindhand. The Bishop told me he wanted some efficient young men for the new churches now being built in Bethnal Green, and said he should be glad if I could recommend any.

April 14. I called on the Master to return him a Plan for a Theological Examination that has been privately submitted to the Heads of Houses by the Vice-Chancellor. I expressed very strongly my opinion of the futility of the Plan as a *voluntary* thing (as it proposes to be) and its contemptibleness as a system.

April 28. I had a long conversation with the Master of St John's[2] regarding the proposed plan for adding Theological instruction to the present academical studies. He (as most people are) is greatly opposed to it, and spoke very strongly on the subject. I had some talk with —— afterwards on the same subject; he too is opposed to it.

April 29. I went to a meeting of the Clerical Education Society. Phillips of Queens' and I walked together afterwards, and fell in with the Master of St John's who joined us. The conversation was entirely on the proposed Theological

---

[1] Dr Mansell.   [2] Dr Tatham.

examination. The Master of St John's was very strenuous in disapproving of the measure. At dinner the same sentiment prevailed.

April 30. The Provost of King's[1] called; he brought with him a short memoir of Mr Simeon by M. M. Preston of Cheshunt. We had a long conversation about the contemplated changes in the University. He mentioned many things which have passed, to shew that there is a mischievous spirit of meddling among some. He mentioned who were the concoctors of the plan for the Theological examination which has made so much talk. Earnshaw afterwards told me that he and all he had conversed with in the University, were opposed to the Theological speculations of the three Masters. Cookson of Peterhouse came to talk over with me the proposal for Theological examinations.

May 6. I went to the Anniversary Meeting of the Cambridge Antiquarian Society. Sir Henry Dryden read a Paper on a line of encampment which extends from the South Avon to the Avon that runs through Warwickshire. He exhibited numerous drawings. The whole was interesting and well done. I had prepared a Paper on the Studies of the University in ancient times, but Sir H. Dryden's Paper occupied so long a time that I deferred my Paper till an ordinary meeting of the Society. Mr Flack of Icklingham exhibited some curious Roman Remains dug up in that parish.

May 7. The Master of St John's[2] told me that it would be advisable for Colleges who were interested in Tithes to propose a Petition to Parliament against a Bill now before the House of Commons.

May 11. I went to the Anniversary (the 2nd) of the Camden Society. The Report was read. Archdeacon Thorp our President read a beautiful Address, which I proposed should be printed.

May 12. The Provost[3] called to shew me some old

---

[1] Dr Thackeray.   [2] Dr Tatham.   [3] Dr Thackeray.

Divinity books. Speaking of University affairs, he told me
that the spirit of change among several of the Heads is
rather unpromising. He spoke as if some who formerly
were supposed to take a sounder view of things, were now
mixing themselves up with the movement party. He mentioned names, but I do not feel authorised to write more.
I told him that such being the state of things, it became
those Heads who were of sounder views to be the more
constant at the meetings the Vice-Chancellor called. We
went to the Senate-House, there being a Petition to Parliament in favor of Church extension. There was no opposition; but the Provost told me the Dean of Bristol was
opposed to sending any Petition!!! Alas! for our Church.

May 13. The Mayor called on electioneering business,
and also to see if I would patronise the Commencement
Ball! I declined that honour, as the Mayor said he had
anticipated.

May 16. I met with Dr Geldart[1] and we conversed on
the subject of the Theological examinations. He told me
he should be in the Caput in the place of Dr King, who is
ill; but that he should not think of throwing the Grace out
on the 26th, although he should vote against it in the
Senate.

May 17. I went to the Hall of Caius College, to a
meeting of the Society for Promoting Christian Knowledge
formed among the Undergraduates of that College, and I
moved that the Report be adopted.

May 20. I met Arlett of Pembroke, who said the Grace
for instituting a Theological examination which was to have
been brought before the Senate on the 26th, had been withdrawn. I met the Master of Clare[2], who expressed his utter
surprise and sorrow that it had been brought forward at all.
Above all he said that the share the Master of Jesus[3] had
had in the matter was inexplicable. He asked me if I had
ever conversed with the Master about it. I replied in the

---

[1] Regius Professor of Law.   [2] Dr Webb.   [3] Dr French.

negative, and added that I was as much puzzled by the part he had taken as all my neighbours were.

May 22. The Provost called. We had a good deal of conversation respecting a notice of a Grace which came out this morning for the purpose of appointing a Syndicate to consider the question about a Theological examination, and half a dozen other matters of importance. The Syndicate named was, all the Professors of Divinity, the Professor of Moral Philosophy[1], the Moderators of the present and past years, the Examiners for the Classical Tripos and for the Medal. I have not been asked whether or not I would be on the Syndicate, and I told the Provost a liberty had been taken with my name, which I could best rebuke by not having anything to do with the Syndicate if appointed. He thought that I should serve, if for no other purpose, to try and prevent rash changes.

May 24. Hildyard of Christ's called and told me he wished me to make one of a Syndicate, to consider in what manner a Theological Examination may be best established in the University. The Syndicate is to have as many as twenty-one from various Colleges, and to make a Report before the third of Nov. next. A Grace is to be submitted to that effect to the Senate on Wednesday next.

May 26. Philpott came to tell me a Grace proposed by Blakesley of Trinity respecting changes in the Examinations had passed the Caput and was to be voted upon; therefore I went to the Senate-House at two o'clock. The Grace was lost in the Black Hood House, the votes being 45 and 27. I have been distressed by the idle and careless habits of some of my Undergraduate friends. But then if I could be indifferent to their good or evil course, I feel that I should be unfit for my present position. May God give me strength to be faithful, whilst forbearing and gentle! How often too, when my young friends are having a dinner party, do I think of the holy Job who 'offered sacrifice'

---

[1] Dr Whewell.

for his sons in the days of their feasting (Job i. 5). I desire in this respect to be a follower of that Saint of God, whenever my friends and pupils meet together. Be gracious, O Lord, according to Thy mercy in Christ Jesus.

May 28. The Master of St John's[1] has received a letter from the Duke of Northumberland, saying there would be no Installation, for there was every prospect of a General Election, and so all the world would be canvassing at the time the Installation would be held.

May 31. At a meeting of the Library Syndicate it was agreed to accept a present of books from the Rev. Robert M'Ghee of Dublin, connected with the crimes of the Papacy. Some objection had been made to the Inscription on the Book-case, which was now arranged to the satisfaction of Mr M'Ghee, who was introduced to the Syndicate by Lodge the Librarian.

June 6. I preached at St Mary's to-day. My text was 1 Cor. xii. 6. I made use of it only as a motto; my object was to shew the identity of the Old Testament Jehovah with the three Persons and one God of the New. I desire to give God thanks for enabling me to get through the sermon without distress, for I had not preached in St Mary's since my recovery from illness.

June 8. I called on the Dean of Peterborough[2] to request him to name Philpott as a Select Preacher at St Mary's for the ensuing year, in case I should be absent from the University. I told him I would not be on the Syndicate that was projected respecting a Theological examination, for that I was sure the movement men would outvote those who were more sober. He thought the matter would come to nothing.

June 11. On going to the Senate-House I found it was intended to appoint Mr Judkin of Caius one of the Barnaby Lecturers, in order to recover his vote in the Senate. This having in vain been protested against by the Vice-Chancellor[3] and Heads in private, it became necessary to oppose the job

---

[1] Dr Tatham.   [2] Dr Turton.   [3] Dr Graham.

by voting for the other party named, who was Mandell of Queens'. There was some doubt about the eligibility of the latter, and this also was pointed out by the Vice-Chancellor and Heads, but the Junior Proctor persisted in nominating Mandell as well as Judkin, and the Senate chose Mandell.

A letter of some interest follows to Mr Irvine.

CAMBRIDGE, *June* 15, 1841.

My dear Mr Irvine,

...I am much obliged to you for your Sermon and Notices to Parents and Sponsors. By your Sermon I was glad to find that under many discouragements you have also many hopes. I trust the wretched system of falsehood which interested persons have for years practised with regard to the Church, is in some measure wearing away.......Yet God's truth is prevailing, and so we may be content to form the connecting link between the suffering and triumph of Christ's Church, if only we be found faithful at the last. About your Notice to Parents and Sponsors, I suppose you find a difficulty in procuring such Sponsors (parents or others), whom you can approve. It is however of great importance to make an enduring effort to give a far more sacred character to Baptism than our people (under the blight of dissenting influence) are wont to give it. I have often wished our Church had been content to adhere to primitive usage as regards Sponsors, which required the God-fathers and Godmothers to be the parents. However, I suppose the good people of 1603, had some reason for what they did.

I add only that

I am very sincerely yours,

G. E. CORRIE.

June 16. I went to the Senate-House to see the Bishop of Edinburgh (Mr Terrot) admitted to his D.D. degree by Royal Mandate. The Dean of Peterborough made an excellent speech on the occasion. The Orator also read a letter which the Senate sends to Viscount Alford, to thank him for a valuable present of minerals which his Lordship has made to the University. They formerly belonged to Sir Abraham Hume, grandfather of Lord Alford.

The following letters containing remarks on Ordination are addressed to Mr —— about to enter on Holy Orders.

CAMBRIDGE, 17 *June*, 1841.

Dear Mr ——,

It seems to me that you would do well to pause before you decided *against* taking the curacy Mr —— offers you. God seems in His good Providence to have brought a station of usefulness to your door, in which the duty is not beyond your physical strength. So far as it is lawful for one to urge another in matters in which the responsibility is chiefly on your side, I would certainly *urge* you to accept the Curacy. With a perfect knowledge of our utter inability to sustain in our own strength the high office of Ambassadors for Christ, it has yet pleased God to commit the message of reconciliation to sinful, helpless men. It is the glory of God's grace, therefore, that He perfects strength out of the greatest feebleness, and supplies by the indwelling and abundant outshedding of His Blessed Spirit, all that is needed to make men "able ministers of the New Testament." On the other hand, if we wait, before entering on God's work, until we are really worthy of the service, and in all respects in qualification what the high office of the Ministry would seem to demand, we may wait till our dying day. Address yourself to this matter, then, in the spirit of prayer, but with the feeling that you will have some further depths of knowledge to enquire after, from age to age throughout eternity itself. Great and glorious is our privilege when, in simplicity and entire devotion, we give ourselves to God to be by Him enabled to fulfil the duties of an office so intimately connected with His honour.

From my intercourse with you, I may say with much confidence that you will run no risk of presumption in offering yourself for a Bishop's examination.   If the Bishop is satisfied, then you need not fear that you possess less knowledge than is sufficient for the satisfactory discharge of a Deacon's office.   As respects the Oaths, they are such as any man *intending* to do God's work, may take, not only with safety, but with profit to his soul.   For the rest you must cast yourself on God's grace from this moment throughout eternity :—to be in yourself nothing, but in Him all things. Neither would I have you look at Bernard Gilpin or any other holy man as an example.   His desisting from duty was no doubt owing to the malice of the Devil, who, if he could, would suggest scruples from morning to night, if so be that he could thus close the mouth of a Minister of Christ, or deter an otherwise willing heart from undertaking to preach the Gospel.   "We are not ignorant of his devices," said St Paul: and it is part of the duty of us all to see that the devices of Satan do not cheat God out of our services, and therein rob our souls of comfort ;—though all the while we seem to be but scrupulously righteous.   Our Example must be Christ, and that of His favoured followers as they trod in His steps. And when we fall short of our great Exemplar, we may know that the grace of Christ can give life to the deadest heart and triumph to the feeblest or most fearful warrior. Eternity only can fully explain the meaning of the conquests of the Cross, effected, as they seem to be, by such feeble hands as ours :—Yet, we need not doubt, but that Christ's promise is *always* fulfilled when by the exaltation of His Cross in the humblest hands He is pleased "to draw all men unto Him."   Be of good courage, then, for we are "*more* than conquerors through Him who hath loved us."

Believe me to be always,

Very truly your friend,

G. E. CORRIE.

CAMBRIDGE, *Aug.* 6, 1841.

Dear Mr ——,

I do not wonder at your feeling "the pressure greater" as your ordination approaches, for it is under any circumstances a solemnizing consideration that God's minister is one who has taken the vows of God upon him, never to be revoked. Yet it has always seemed to me that if this solemn act of self-devotion is undertaken in the strength of God the Holy Ghost, we have much reason to be thankful that we can so distinctly deliver ourselves from the ordinary frivolities of the world, by virtue of the separation from things inexpedient even, which God's vows imply. We become thus invested with motives to a holier living than we could beforehand be considered as possessing. The more, therefore, we are brought to feel the greatness of the self-devotion that Ordination implies, the more we have cause to thank God for leading us to follow out all that, in this respect, He has been pleased to put into our hearts. Go on then in that strength which can strengthen, strengthen effectually, the feeblest hands, and wait in patience for the light from heaven which will best clear up all your difficulties by enabling you to see the dignity and happiness of being called to be an Ambassador of Christ.

Believe me always,
Very truly your friend,
G. E. CORRIE.

June 27. At Kettering I preached for my brother in the morning. Many years have elapsed since I preached last in this Church, for I have feared to undertake a sermon in so large a Church, lest I should break a blood-vessel. I desire to thank God for this improved state of my health, and to pray that I may labour more abundantly to His honour and glory through Christ Jesus.

July 3. At Cambridge I dined with the Dean of Peterborough[1]. There were present the Bishops Doane and Meade,

---

[1] Dr Turton.

from America, Dr Terrot, Bishop of Edinburgh, Dr Mills, Mr Walpole of Trinity. I was glad to get acquainted with the American Prelates.

July 6. I took the Misses Powys to the Senate-House. There were twenty Doctors created, in all the Faculties together. There was however such a talk in the Senate-House that it was impossible to hear the speeches of the Professors.

To the friend Mr —— about to take orders he thus states his views on the subject of Oaths.

LONDON, Aug. 14, 1841.

Dear Mr ——,

As to the "legality of an oath" I can only refer you to my former letter to you on that subject. To my mind an appeal to God, if lawful ever, can never be so much in place as when a person gives himself up deliberately to *God's* special service. About being "called according to the Church of England," see Ordination Service. You make no such declaration, nor do you subscribe in the 30th Canon to the services for the Martyrdom of King Charles &c.; these four services form no part of the Prayer-book, but are annexed to it, as sanctioned by each individual Sovereign on their accession to the Throne, and die with each Sovereign accordingly. In subscribing to our Liturgy, therefore, we commit ourselves to no more than the approval of those occasional Prayers and Thanksgivings which are issued from time to time on competent authority, and which we are required to use. At the same time, my own belief is that Charles I. was as really a martyr as those of any age who beforehand had suffered for God's truth. He died for the Church of England: and the pains his enemies took to falsify the "Eikon Basilike" shewed how fully they were aware that those private thoughts and devotions of the Monarch were likely to make the epithets "best of men"—"greatest of Kings," not unseemly as applied to Charles I. So again, though the application of Ps. cix. may rather remind "us of our Lord than of an earthly King," we must not forget that they were applied by an earthly King to himself. Nor need we hesitate to give thanks for our deliverance from "arbitrary power" by King William, for whatever may have been *his* real motives, we are concerned only with those he professed to entertain. For my own part, I have seen no valid reason for questioning those motives, although I see many reasons for questioning the honesty of those non-jurors who took much pains to malign him.

One word more and I have done. Be satisfied that the incessant object of Satan is and will be to close your mouth as a preacher of God's truth. Reject scruples, therefore, in such matters as I have referred to, as suggestions of a nature that would retard your usefulness. To a rightly constituted mind and well-informed judgement there is nothing in your case to oppose any serious obstacles to your entering the Church, and to your finding, in the exercise of your ministry, a happiness which cannot be known to a life spent in bondage to scruples, which have in them less of godliness than of a morbid sensibility. "There is light from heaven and that light shall be yours."

Very truly your friend,

G. E. CORRIE.

A long visit was paid to Mrs Gason in London that he might be on the spot to watch the progress of the monument by Wickes to his late brother, which was being executed for the Cathedral Church of Madras.

Aug. 9. I went to see the picture of St Catharine painted by Mrs Criddle for our College Hall. It is a painting of some merit. I afterwards went to see the monument to my late brother, now being executed by a young artist, Henry Wickes, and was much pleased with it.

Aug. 20. Augustus O'Brien and I went to St Paul's to the sermon preached before Convocation by Archdeacon Samuel Wilberforce. Before the Service began we stood in Paternoster Row to see the procession from the Chapter

House (I suppose) to the Church. It consisted of the Judges and Civilians connected with the Ecclesiastical Courts, the Archdeacons and Bishops' Chaplains, the Delegates from the Dioceses, the Bishop of London and the Archbishop. The procession was met at the West door by the Choir and members of the Cathedral. As soon as the Archbishop entered, the organ struck up and continued playing until all were seated. The Bishop of London read the Litany in Latin. A Psalm was afterwards sung. The preacher's text was Ezek. iii. 17, and he took occasion to point out the former as compared with the present state of the Church, and glanced also at her future prospects. The Sermon was in good Latin, and was well delivered.

Mr Corrie visited Mr Rose at Houghton Conquest, with whom he considered an Article on Outlines of Theology for the *Encyclopædia Metropolitana*, which he subsequently contributed.

Aug. 28. I have been here, Houghton Conquest, a few days, and much occupied in discussing with H. Rose a plan for an Article on Theology in the *Encyclopædia Metropolitana.*

The remainder of the Vacation was spent at Kettering among his family, and in constant daily intercourse with many friends in the neighbourhood.

A letter to Mr —— follows, full of sympathy and encouragement on entering on his clerical work.

KETTERING, *Oct.* 13, 1841.

Dear Mr ——,

You may be assured that I sympathise with you in your scruples respecting Subscription and other matters, yet I do not lay much stress upon your difficulties, as the anxiety you have undergone connected with the death of your relative is to me a sufficient reason to account for the *bodily indisposition* out of which, I can have no doubt, much of your mental trial originates. Each has his separate and peculiar cross to bear, and yours no doubt in part consists in bodily ailments re-acting on the mind. I can never, therefore, sufficiently put you on your guard on that point, because your *comfort* is necessarily interfered with more than it need be, if you could not be satisfied (as I am) that much of your late distress is from without—a skilful enemy taking advantage of your sickly body. At the same time it is of importance to know that it is from God alone that all our strength must proceed, whether of the body or of the mind. Let your faith, therefore, be turned continually *out of yourself*. At our best estate, we know nothing and can do nothing, except as we are directed into the path of true life and knowledge by the guidance and teaching of the Spirit of the living God. And our comfort is that this Spirit is the portion of the *weakest* believer in the Lord Jesus ; because, as He received the Spirit without measure, and we are vitally united to Him, it is out of His fulness that we become possessed of that heavenly grace which by nature we cannot have. Then this divine gift is imparted to us not in proportion to the extent of our profession, but to the *sincerity* of *our faith.* If we have faith, therefore, even as but a grain of mustard-seed, we arise and walk, and our sins are forgiven us for His name's sake. Seek daily, therefore, to apprehend more fully the abounding love and mercy of God our Saviour in giving you a sense of your own insufficiency and sin ; and be sure that there is not a single scruple and misgiving that will not yield to the power of redeeming grace sanctifying the soul, until, as you grow in grace, you will gradually become less scrupulous and more conscientious. Regard then your scruples as arising in the first instance, out of bodily indisposition, and as strengthened by a want of a more extended perception of the liberty of the Gospel, which I am certain that, by God's mercy, you will speedily enjoy if you "follow on to know the Lord" as He has been pleased to reveal Himself in Jesus Christ. Do not revert to the *past,* but keep your mind steadily fixed on your ministerial labours, and the privilege of being permitted to invite sinners to believe on the Lord Jesus and be saved, whilst you beg of God to enable you to realise the Scripture, "*We believe* and therefore speak." Satisfy yourself, also, that there need be nothing to cause you any real difficulty in the Book of Common Prayer, which has been subscribed from age to age by men of God "of whom the world was not worthy." Whenever troubled, therefore, say to your spirit, "This is mine infirmity, but I will remember the years of the right hand of the most High," for you, like all other Christians, can be at no loss to remember much of God's mercy to your soul. Do not be too anxious to experience the *comfort* of religion, although you should have to travel onward still further in doubts and darkness. God may very safely be trusted to deal tenderly with us, whether He call us to follow Him in gloom or sunshine. It is, indeed, but seldom that we can be trusted with sensible joy, and that only as it is accompanied with the self-renunciation that becomes sinners redeemed by grace.

Believe me to be,

Very sincerely your friend,

G. E. CORRIE.

Oct. 19. To-day intelligence reached Cambridge that Professor Whewell has been appointed Master of Trinity by the Crown. The Mayor told me that the Conservatives are so strong in the Borough, that he is to be re-elected Mayor for the ensuing year, and that they hope to get in *five* Conservative Aldermen, as well as *ten* Conservative Town-Councillors.

Oct. 20. I went to the Senate-House to vote for a Grace which was to give £100 toward defraying the expenses of building the new bridge by Queens' College ; the Grace was however thrown out. I was told to-day that I had been honourably mentioned in the last *Church of England Quarterly*, in an article on the State of Theological Education in our Universities.

Oct. 25. I attended the Annual Meeting of the Cambridge Refuge to-day and moved one of the Resolutions. Mr Pullen, Fellow of Corpus, called to ask me to undertake collecting in College for the Society for the Propagation of the Gospel, which I undertook.

Nov. 1. We commenced having two dinners in Hall to-day, the number of undergraduates being greater than the Hall will accommodate at once.

Nov. 7. There was notice in the *Standard* to-day that Richard Sibthorpe, of the Isle of Wight, and Fellow of Magdalene College, Oxford, has apostatised to the Church of Rome.

Nov. 8. After the meeting of the Electors for the Crosse Scholarship, the Vice-Chancellor[1] asked the Dean of Peterborough, Professor Blunt, and myself to remain. He wished to ascertain whether or not we would agree to be members of a Syndicate to consider the subject of Examinations in Theology, for a Degree, or after taking a Degree :—taking for our basis the idea that there was to be no curtailing of the Terms now allotted to other studies. I told the Vice-Chancellor that, so far as I was concerned, it would depend on who it was intended should belong to the Syndicate. I should object that any of the parties who had written or taught anything respecting the subject of Theological Examinations should be on the Syndicate. It was suggested that before any steps were taken the Vice-Chancellor should consult with the Heads.

Nov. 9. The picture of St Catharine, painted by Mrs Henry Criddle, arrived to-day. The evening coaches brought the intelligence of the birth of a Prince of Wales.

Nov. 11. The Provost called to tell me he was certain a Syndicate on the subject of Theological Examinations would be appointed without delay, and pressed me to be on it. I told him I could not promise till I knew who would be on it besides, for that I did not like the idea of being out-voted, and then having to attach my name to a report.

[1] Dr Archdall.

Nov. 12. At a meeting of the Press Syndicate we had a long exposition from Mr Parker, the Printer, on the present difficulties of the printing trade, and on the probable necessity the University would be under, of contracting very materially the Press establishment.

Nov. 18. The Vice-Chancellor[1] called to ask me to be on a Syndicate he wished to have appointed to consider whether any or what change could take place in the Examinations of the University so as to secure greater attention to Theology. I told him I had no objection to be on a Syndicate in case the members of it consisted of persons who had not publicly committed themselves to an opinion on the subject. I also said that there ought to be one or two Heads of Houses. He mentioned the Master of Trinity[2], and I advised by all means that he should form one of the Syndicate. The Vice-Chancellor said he should mention it to-morrow at a meeting of Heads.

Dec. 1. At the Senate-House to-day there were Addresses voted to the Queen, Prince Albert, and the Duchess of Kent on the birth of a Prince : and a Grace passed appointing a Syndicate (of which I am one) to consider the subject of Theological Examinations. The Grace passed with but three dissentients.

Dec. 4. I went to a meeting of the Electors of the Crosse Scholarship, when Mr Witt, of King's, was unanimously chosen. Then to a meeting of the Syndicate for considering the subject of Theological Studies in the University. All the Syndicate were present except the Master of Trinity, viz. the Vice-Chancellor, the Masters of Jesus and St John's, the Regius and Margaret Professors of Divinity, the Regius Professors of Greek and of Civil Law and myself. The Vice-Chancellor read a letter he had received from some nameless dignitary of the Church detailing a plan of Theological Study. There were many subjects touched upon. Among others the Dean of Peterborough turned attention to some enquiries he had made of

---

[1] Dr Archdall.   [2] Dr Whewell.

Bishops and Bishops' Chaplains, who seemed to be unanimous in thinking that the great defect in Candidates for Orders was a want of *Classical* not Theological knowledge. There was a long desultory conversation on the subject of a remedy for that defect, on the subject of shortening the number of Terms, &c., &c. I was obliged to leave at half-past twelve for my Lecture, but I understood that some points were fixed on for future consideration.

Dec. 6. I went to a meeting of the Electors to the Crosse Scholarship. It appeared that Mr Witt of King's, whom we had elected, was not a full Bachelor, so we were obliged to declare his election null, and to elect Lovell. I next went to a meeting of the Antiquarian Society, and some interesting communications were made. Sir Thomas Phillips was present.

Dec. 8. At a meeting of the Syndicate connected with adding more Theology to the University Studies, after a great deal of discussion and friendly difference of opinion, it was agreed that we should consider by the time of our next meeting, (1) whether it would be desirable to recommend that all persons before being admitted to their first Degree should be required, in addition to what is now read, to be examined in some portion of the Epistles and Church History? (2) whether Candidates for Honours should be excepted from the additional examination? (3) whether it would be desirable to have an examination *after* the first Degree specially for those who may be Candidates for Orders?

Dec. 10. I went to a meeting of the Committee for superintending the repair of the Round Church. We afterwards had a discussion on the subject of some Papers about to be issued, and I took occasion to express disapprobation of a Paper in the first number of the *Ecclesiologist*, which reflected hardly on the new churches lately built by Perry.

Dec. 16. I had my last public lecture for this Term. I desire to be thankful for the assistance and grace with which God has been pleased to favour me through a laborious Term.

A note to Mr —— on the subject of the Canon regarding Sponsors follows.

CAMBRIDGE, *Dec.* 14, 1841.

Dear Mr ——,

As regards " Baptisms without Godfathers and Godmothers even in the Church," it seems to me to be settled by the circumstances of the case. The Canon that requires that parents should not be permitted to stand as Sponsors, requires also Sponsors to be communicants, but if none but communicants were Sponsors, baptism would have to be discontinued. What seems desirable therefore, is to instruct the people in the requirement of the Church, but to permit parents to be Sponsors when others cannot be had, rather than have children unbaptized. My brother found great difficulty in this matter, but on stating the matter to the late Bishop of Peterborough (Dr Marsh), the Bishop told him, " if he found it impracticable to conform to the Canon, it would be far better to baptize children without Sponsors, than by objecting to leave them unbaptized." And this is the advice I venture to give you.

Very sincerely your friend,

G. E. CORRIE.

A journey from Cambridge to London still occupied some hours, even with the assistance of the railroad.

Dec. 18. I left Cambridge at eight o'clock for London. The coach brought us as far as Spellbrooke, and then was put upon the railroad. We arrived at the George and Blue Boar in London about one o'clock.

CHAPTER IX.

THE opening of the year found Mr Corrie at Kettering, but he shortly returned to Cambridge.

1842. *Jan.* 1. In the morning at seven o'clock we had the Holy Communion administered in the Church to about 60 persons. I assisted the curate in the service, which was calm and refreshing.

Jan. 2. In the morning I preached for my brother, who is still confined to the house. I preached from Isa. xxx. 15, "In quietness and in confidence shall be your strength." I read prayers in the afternoon. I am thankful that by God's grace I have been enabled to minister before Him this day. May the word spoken in His holy name be blessed to the comfort and edification of the heritage of the Lord in this place, for Christ's sake.

Jan. 23. Our chapel was opened to-day, and the gas-lights burned in the evening for the first time.

Jan. 25. Almost every shop in the town was closed, and a holiday kept in honour of the Baptism of the Prince of Wales, which was to take place at Windsor to-day.

Jan. 28. I attended the Syndicate to consider the Theological Studies of the University. A good deal of conversation occurred on the propriety of taking in all the Acts of the Apostles, or only fourteen chapters. Professor Blunt was desirous of having the whole; there was also much discussion whether the word "explain" should follow "translate," but it was decided that "explain" had better be omitted lest we should introduce doctrinal and other questions into the examination. Then the question arose as to whether a suggestion should be made in the Report of the Syndicate touching a provision for the more extended Theological education of men after taking their B.A. degree. This is to come on next time we meet. A very important question also was mooted as to the extending of our regulations to Candidates for Honors, Bachelors of Law, and Bachelors of Medicine. The Dean of Peterborough[1] was commissioned to confer on the subject with the Professors of Law and of Medicine. Afterwards there was a meeting of the Syndics of the Press; one thing proposed was to vote a copy of all books printed at the University Press to the Duke of Wellington, who had asked for them by way of making them an heir-loom.

Feb. 4. I attended a Meeting of the Syndicate for considering the subject of Theological education. The whole Syndicate was present. Dr Turton stated that he had consulted Dr Haviland[2] as to the Students in Medicine being made liable to an examination in Theology previous to a Degree, as well as Students in Arts, but that Dr Haviland utterly refused his consent; the same was the case with the Law Professor[3]. The subject of instituting a voluntary examination in Theology for those who have taken the Degree of B.A. was then discussed. After much amicable discussion it was decided to put the matter to the vote, when there appeared four in favour of an examination and five against it : viz.

---

[1] Dr Turton, Regius Professor of Divinity.
[2] Regius Professor of Physic.   [3] Dr Geldart.

The Vice-Chancellor, Dr Archdall,
Master of Jesus, Dr French,
Dr Turton, Regius Professor of Divinity,
Professor Scholefield, Regius Professor of Greek, } *for.*

The Master of Trinity, Dr Whewell,
The Master of St John's, Dr Tatham,
Dr Geldart, Regius Professor of Law,
Professor Blunt, Lady Margaret Professor of
  Divinity,
Professor Corrie, Norrisian Professor of
  Divinity, } *against.*

It was then proposed that the Master of Trinity and myself should be entrusted with the drawing up of the Report of the Syndicate, which should afterwards be discussed. I wished to decline the labour, but was overruled.

Feb. 14. Mr Guest, Fellow of Caius, called to ask me to join a Philological Society which it is hoped may be established in London, for Oxford and Cambridge men.

I attended a meeting of the Syndicate for considering the Theological instruction requisite for Degrees. The Master of Trinity and myself had drawn up a report in compliance with the direction of the Syndicate, but when we came to discuss it, a question was raised as to the propriety of recommending a plan for voluntary examination, drawn up by the Dean of Peterborough. It had first to be decided whether or not the plan could be proposed in accordance with what had previously been settled. All seemed to agree that we should first have to open again questions that were decided at our last meeting, as the plan to be proposed by the Dean would require the Report just drawn up to be altogether altered. It was agreed to reopen the question. The plan was read, which proposed an Examination, to be conducted by the *three* Divinity Professors in each October Term for B.A.s. On my opinion being asked, I stated that I could not possibly undertake to examine, as I had already more than I could well get through. I said also, that I could not agree to the plan, even if I had time to examine, for that I believed from experience that any voluntary examination would be altogether nugatory; that I considered the matter to be for the decision of the Bishops; that as most men were ready for Orders within half-a-year of their taking their B.A. degree, I did not see what right we had to induce them to remain out of their profession for six months longer than the Church required. At the same time I observed, that I should have waived all these objections, if I had had time to assist in such an Examination as was proposed, on the general principle of doing all I could to try at least to serve the University. The Dean of Peterborough and the Lady Margaret Professor[1] afterwards came to speak to me privately to induce me to alter my opinion; but I told them that the lack of time and strength was a reason I could not change; that the duties of my office in College and of my Professorship were all I could get through, although I was out of bed eighteen hours out of every twenty-four. The Syndicate then separated after it had been referred to the Dean of Peterborough to modify the Report. Before leaving I told the Vice-Chancellor[2] that I thought it would be better for me to stay away from the next meeting as my difficulties only embarrassed the rest of the Syndicate. The Vice-Chancellor however, as well as Dr French, said I had better come, though my own feeling is that I had better not. In the evening a young man of Christ's College came to consult me respecting the case of one who had been baptized by a Presbyterian Minister. The question was, could he *bonâ fide* say he was a member of the Church of England? I told him, as the Ecclesiastical Courts had recently decided that Lay-baptism was valid, no doubt any man who was in the habit of communicating in the Church of England would be regarded as baptized, and so would be regarded as *bonâ fide* a member of the Church of England.

Feb. 19. The Vice-Chancellor called on me to say that

---

[1] Prof. Blunt.   [2] Dr Archdall.

the Theological Syndicate would not meet on Monday, for
that Dr Turton had sent him word that he (Dr T.) was not
ready with the draft of the plan for a Theological Examination which he had been deputed to draw up. I had previously
told the Master of Trinity how matters had ended at the last
meeting of the Syndicate, and of my objections to the proceedings. He said he entirely agreed with me, and in fact
trusted to my being at the last Syndicate after he had been
obliged to leave. I told him, as I had told the Vice-Chancellor previously, that I did not purpose to attend the next
meeting of the Syndicate, as I conceived I should only mar
the proceedings.

Feb. 28.   I attended a meeting of the Theological Syndicate. Dr Turton read a scheme for two Examinations after
the B.A. Degree.   The one was to be in the Greek Testament
and in sundry subjects of Divinity; the other in the Old Testament Scriptures in Hebrew, to be conducted by the Hebrew
Professor.   The Divinity Examination to be conducted by
the Regius and Margaret Professors of Divinity. On hearing
the scheme read, there seemed to be no objection to it in the
main, and so it was agreed to have some copies struck off for
the use of the Syndicate.   The only remark made was by the
Master of Trinity, who said that "he confessed he should
have liked it better if the plan had contemplated all the
three Divinity Professors as Examiners, instead of only the
two already mentioned."   On this I remarked that the omission was entirely by my own desire, as I had objected to
undertake more occupation, having already more than I could
well do.   It was then remarked by several that the plan would
seem to go out as if there were some disagreement among us,
unless I consented to have my name among the rest.   I answered "that every member of the Syndicate had my permission to state the reason why I declined engaging in the plan,
and that I would myself do all I could to free the Syndicate
from the appearance of casting a slight on my Professorship."
However the Syndicate only met to agree to have the plan

printed, and so the conversation ended by our separating.
I afterwards walked with the Master of St John's[1]. The
subject turned on the Theological Syndicate, and I could only
repeat my reasons for declining to be an examiner. He did
not exactly seem to understand that I had no reference to
the *value* of my Professorship, and therefore said the income
might be increased by a small payment made by each party
who asked for a certificate. I told him that so long as I held
the Professorship, I should never think of making money by
it, nor did I think any one who took the Professorship in the
full knowledge of what the income is, should afterwards
complain of its small endowment.

March 4. A pupil brought me the *Norwich Protestant
Herald* to show me a letter that had been quoted in that
paper from the *Tablet*, a Romish paper. It stated that
there was a great sale of Breviaries, Missals, &c. in Cambridge, one reason of which was that the Norrisian Professor
of Divinity recommended all men going into the Church to
provide themselves with a Breviary, &c.! The object of the
letter was to represent me as favouring Puseyism.

The following is to Mr ——, on the subject of the Sacrament of Baptism being administered during Service:

CAMBRIDGE, March 4, 1842.

Dear Mr ——,

.... About "Christening during Service,"
I should not advise you to set about changing customs at
once that have been of long standing. You will, no doubt,
have some right-minded parishioner's child to christen ere
long; and if so I should advise you to put the matter before
him, explain the Church's directions, and point out the good
that might be done by setting an example of conformity.
After one example, you will find but little difficulty, as one
after another will speedily follow. The difficulty of cases of
this nature is not in the reviving of conformity, but in getting

[1] Dr Tatham.

a *Congregation* at large to *take part* in the Holy Office of Baptism. My early experience was always to witness Baptisms during Divine Service, but it may be questioned whether less harm accrues from Baptism after Service, than from the interruption of Divine worship occasioned by the idle, irreverent gazing and indifference with which all not actually engaged in the Baptism *look on.* But little is attained by Public Baptism, if we have not previously instructed our people so to conduct themselves in *heart* and *outward demeanour* as to give a deep meaning to that petition, " Regard, we beseech Thee, the *supplications of thy congregation.*" In aiming at conformity, therefore, let our ministerial diligence be doubled to instil, by God's grace, into the people at large the spirit of the Baptismal Office.

Believe me to be,

Very sincerely your friend,

G. E. CORRIE.

March 6. Dr Sumner, the Bishop of Winchester, preached at St Mary's. His subject was the character of Hezekiah. The sermon was most excellent in all that constitutes plain, hearty, truly religious teaching. Some parts were eloquent —all impressive and well delivered.

March 7. I went to a meeting of the Theological Syndicate. There was a good deal of altering of the wording of the Report on considering the part which implied that an examination for B.A. would not pass unless the other portions passed also. The Vice-Chancellor expressed himself disappointed. He said it appeared to him to be of great consequence that, if all the remaining part of the Report was rejected, that referred to should stand. However, one and all told him that the plan for B.A. had been drawn up expressly as the part only of a general plan, and in itself would be defective. The discussion however was reserved. In the meanwhile we came to No. 4. In that as I did not concur, I said nothing. The Dean of Peterborough expressed his fear that the appending of No. 4 would prevent me from signing the Report. I told him that would depend on what was customary in a Syndicate, for, if it was usual for the minority to sign the decision of the majority without reference to *individual* opinion, I should of course abide by custom. If, on the contrary, my signature was supposed to express my individual opinion, I could not sign the Report.

March 9. I went to a meeting of the Antiquarian Society, and read a short paper on the Philobiblia of Richard de Bury. There were on the table several remains from a Roman Villa lately discovered at Comberton. News reached Cambridge to-day that intelligence had been received from India of the utter destruction of our army at Cabul, consisting of six thousand men.

March 11. A Grace passed the Senate to-day respecting the removal of the Pictures and Books in the Fitzwilliam Museum to the East Room in the Public Library. Professor Scholefield asked me to-day if I should be at the meeting of the Theological Syndicate to-morrow. I told him I should not : he said he wished I would be : but I replied, " I could not sign the Report of the Syndicate if I were there, so that I am better away." He pressed me to go, but I told him I was sorry to be obliged to decline, for my belief was that some portions of the intended Report would do harm, as giving a wrong impression as to what ought to be regarded as Clerical Education.

March 12. I called on the Master to inquire what the custom was in the University as to signing documents in which members of Syndicates did not acquiesce ? He told me that the *dissentient* parties were not expected to sign. He mentioned that he was instrumental in obtaining this liberty for *dissentients* in consequence of having once been called on at a meeting of the Heads to sign a decision to which the Heads had come, but from which he dissented. He was told it had been usual for *all* the Heads to sign every conclusion the majority agreed to. His answer was, " It may be so, but from henceforth my resolution is formed to sign nothing to which on *principle* I object." My object in asking him was that I might be guided in my own action as to signing or not the Report of the Theological Syndicate that is about to be printed. I dined with Carus of Trinity to meet the Bishop of Winchester and his son. The party consisted of the Masters of Corpus and Downing, Professor Challis, Evans, Cooper, and Lord Charles Hervey, of Trinity. I had a good deal of quiet conversation with the Bishop on the state of religious party.

March 13. The Dean of Peterborough asked me what I should do as to signing the Report of the Theological Syndicate. I told him I should do what was usual, although if I could follow my own opinion freely, I should decline signing. He said the custom was for all to sign if the difference of opinion was not material, but if it was, then the parties dissentient did *not* sign. I told him that in that case I should not sign the Report, although I should not feel called upon to give my reasons to persons out of the Syndicate. Professor Blunt and Professor Scholefield expressed their disappointment that I could not sign the Report. The Bishop of Winchester preached. His subject was Hezekiah as exercising the kingly power to the furtherance of religion. In the evening I went to hear the Bishop preach a sermon in aid of the Church Missionary Society. His text was Luke xiv. 23. The discourse was very striking in many parts, and a deep spirit of piety pervaded it throughout.

March 14. At four o'clock I went to dine in the Hall of Trinity to meet the Bishop of Winchester. We broke up at six o'clock to go to Chapel.

March 17. I met Hildyard. He began to talk of the Report of the Theological Syndicate, praising it very much. He observed he was surprised not to find my name to it, and asked if the omission was accidental! I told him it was designed. He observed that the Report seemed to satisfy every one. I answered, I was glad of it, for that the Syndicate had been at great pains.

March 19. I went to a meeting of the Sub-Committee of the Board of Education. The object of our meeting was to agree upon a Classification of School-Books. We agreed to print such portions of the Report on School-Books which Hailstone and myself drew up in the autumn.

March 20. The Master of Jesus told me that the Address to the Queen was carried up by a small assembly, and the ceremony of kissing the Sovereign's hand was dispensed with except as to two members of each University—the Duke of Wellington as Chancellor, and the Vice-Chancellor of Oxford; and the Vice-Chancellor (for our Chancellor could not attend) and the Master of Magdalene, for Cambridge.

April 1. The anniversary of my father's death. May I be living in patient waiting for my latter end!

The following letter is chiefly on the subject of timely preparation of sermons.

CAMBRIDGE, *April* 1, 1842.

Dear Mr ———,

*   *   *   *   *   *

You will find it your comfort and duty, so far to forecast as never to defer preparation for the Sunday. Preparation for the public ministrations is an every-day duty. My advice is always to fix on the subject you intend to preach on *next* Sunday, before you go to bed on *this* Sunday. Then on *Monday morning* do not fail to arrange your plan for a sermon: and so finish it early in every week. On the supposition that you are obliged to be writing late on Saturday night, or between services on Sunday, you will spend your Sunday in hurry and bustle instead of in calm thought and meditation on what you have to say to your people from God. A very little perseverance will, by God's blessing, be sufficient to overcome a habit which, if indulged in, will leave your sermons crude, and expose you to the charge of offering to God of that which cost you nothing. Labour also to impress on your people the importance of that deep spirit of prayer which our Liturgy implies as being inseparable from a spirit that can profit by the preached word. Never flinch from expressing your conviction that no man has a right to preach who is not "sent," whenever occasion serves, but then do not forget, that after all the ministry is a means to an end—the salvation of those who hear. In fact, assert the soundness, in faith and polity, of your own Church, and leave dissentients to find a reason in the sight of God for setting up what is not sound. It is a melancholy truth, but it *is* a truth, that your farmer who threatened to let the chapel to the Independents if the Wesleyans would not go to it, is merely dissent personified. It is division for division's sake.

So far as I have ever understood, sober-minded divines in general look for a national restoration of the Jews to Palestine, as connected with their spiritual conversion. I do not know Hugh White's book on the Second Advent from my own reading, but I used to hear of it as a good book. At the same time I should not recommend a person to read much on that subject except what is in the prophetical parts of the Bible. There is so much danger of theory....I add only the assurance that I am truly glad to hear of your activity in parochial matters. God will abundantly multiply peace upon you as you devote yourself more fully to His service and glory.

Ever your sincere friend,

G. CORRIE.

April 16. Two of my pupils came to me to-day to ask me to patronise the Boat Club. The reason they gave for applying to me was, that as the men generally understood that I disapproved of boating, they declined joining the club, so that a Boat's Crew could not be raised. I told them that though I believed my own pupils were steady, yet so much evil was connected with boat-racing that I could not in kindness to them encourage it. If they boated for recreation and exercise independently of the racing, I told them I would subscribe toward their expenses.

April 22. At a meeting of the Press Syndicate, we agreed to print a Translation of the Theophania of Eusebius, from a Syriac version lately obtained from Egypt by the translator Dr Lee.

April 27. Birch of Gazeley told me there was to be a great prize-fight to-day near Mildenhall if the police did not interfere. I heard that the Proctors and Pro-proctors were by six a.m. at the Toll-bar at the Paper-mills and turned back all gownsmen who were purposing to go in the direction of Newmarket.

April 30. I heard that three men had been rusticated for being present at the prize-fight on Thursday. The Proctors and Pro-proctors went to the fight and detected the culprits there.

May 6. At the meeting of the Press Syndicate to-day, Dr Turton read a letter from Dr Cardwell of Oxford, stating that the editions of the 39 Articles printed at Oxford ever since 1638, had for the most part omitted the word "all" at the close of the 2nd Article[1]. "Actual sins" instead of "all actual sins" correspondent to "pro omnibus actualibus peccatis &c." It was agreed that Dr Turton should write to Dr Cardwell to say that we intended to correct this

---

[1] This omission which first occurred about the date 1629, and had been perpetuated in all copies of the Book of Common Prayer issued by the Cambridge University Press from that time onward, was rectified in 1854. As a member of the Press Syndicate, Dr Corrie with others called attention to the subject, and in subsequent editions of the Prayer Book the word "all" has been restored. The Bishop of Winchester (Dr Harold Browne), who was a member of the Press Syndicate in 1854, writes, ' I remember that Dr Corrie was very anxious that the word "all" should be reinstated in Art. II. in all the Cambridge copies of the Prayer Book, and I entirely agreed with him.'

To Dr Corrie's accurate knowledge and keen power of observation the detection is due of another less important error in the Kalendar of the Book of Common Prayer. In 1604, shortly after the Hampton Court Conference, under the date Sept. 7 the name of ' Eunurchus, Bishop' was introduced. This was a misprint for Evortius (or Evurtius), which has been replaced in all Cambridge Editions, though the imaginary Enurchus (sic) still appears in Oxford Prayer Books and in the Churchman's Almanack (S.P.C.K.) for 1890.

omission and to inquire whether the University of Oxford intended to *cancel* those sheets already in their possession which are printed without the word "all."

There follows another letter to Mr ——— .

CAMBRIDGE, *May* 7, 1842.

Dear Mr ———,

It seems to me always desirable to read the Athanasian Creed on such Sundays as are appointed by the Rubric, when the service of the church is under your own control. In the church of any clergyman for whom you may be taking the duty for the day, I should certainly follow the custom of that church whatever it might be. Nothing is so little to be commended as the taking of a neighbour's duty only to innovate. In your *own* church on the 29th you might be afforded a good opportunity for preaching on the duty of subjects (very little thought of in these days) by using the Services for the Restoration instead of the Services for the day. At the same time there is such a wretched spirit of innovation at work, under pretence of restoring ancient usages, that I should advise you to abide by the custom of the Diocese until you can feel your way better.

Believe me to be,

Very sincerely your friend,

G. CORRIE.

May 11. At a Congregation at the Senate-House two Graces were voted on to-day. The first, to enable the Syndicate of the Fitzwilliam Museum to contract for building a wall between the Museum and Peterhouse Gardens, was rejected. The Grace on Theological Education was carried by a majority of about two to one in the Black Hood, and by fifty-two to nineteen in the White Hood House.

May 12. After the Anniversary Meeting of the Antiquarian Society, the Provost of King's and myself went home with the Master of Clare-Hall to look at an Ancient Catalogue of the Library of that College, temp. Edw. III. It is a curious relic. Among other things the record contained a notice of the election into a Fellowship of Clare-Hall of the martyr, Hugh Latimer.

May 13. At a meeting of the Committee for repairing St Sepulchre's Church, it was agreed that the repairs should be suspended until funds are more liberally provided.

May 14. Professor Blunt expressed to me his great regret that I was not an Examiner with himself and the Regius Professor in the Theological Examination, but I told him I could not examine, both for want of time, and because I should stultify myself by taking part in a system which I could not recommend to the Senate.

May 22. I am told that Dolman, the Romanist bookseller in London, is buying up all the copies he can get of the English Translation of Bertram on the Lord's Supper, and MᶜGhee's "Memorial of a Jesuit for the Conversion of England." It is supposed the Papists are destroying these books.

June 8. I left Cambridge to-day for Kettering.

June 12. Mr Scott, of Hull, arrived from Burton Latimer, to preach a sermon in aid of the Church Missionary Society. There was a very large congregation, and more than £15 collected.

June 13. There was a public meeting to-day in behalf of the Church Missionary Society. Sir George Robinson was in the chair, and there were present on behalf of the Society Mr Scott and Mr Trapp. Also Mr Mackworth Dolben, and Messrs Craig, Hume, Bull, Broughton, Burdett, Bingham and Chas. Nevile. The whole was a meeting of great interest.

June 18. My brother, Chas. Nevile and myself walked out to the Rectory lands on the Harborough Road, to look at a beautiful spring of water which a person named Preston proposes to bring to Kettering so as to supply the whole town. The level of the spring seems to admit of this.

June 19. Mr Bull told us that the effect of the meeting at Clipstone last Thursday for the purpose of establishing a

Church Missionary Association, at which my brother was present, had been good.   Many of the Dissenters who attended said that they had no idea that the Church-parsons could have spoken as they did.

June 20.   Preston came to me about drawing up a letter to circulate among the land-owners and inhabitants of Kettering, to invite them to assist in bringing water from the Warren Hill to the town.

June 23.   I called on Mr Lamb respecting Preston's plan for conveying water from the Warren Hill to the town.   I found him ready to give every assistance; so I took Preston's prospectus to Dash, to be printed.

June 26.   We had a collection in the church to-day, in obedience to the Royal Letter, in aid of the distressed operatives in the manufacturing districts.

June 29.   I returned to Cambridge.   I met the Master of Clare.   We had a long talk on the subject of editing Latimer's Works for the Parker Society.   I told him if I had time it was a subject I should much delight in.

The following entries in the Diary give an account of the installation of the Duke of Northumberland as Chancellor of the University.

July 2.   After breakfast I went to the Town-Hall to meet the Governors of Addenbrooke's Hospital, and then walked in procession with them and the Bishop of Winchester to Great St Mary's, where the Bishop preached a sermon for the charity.   The sermon was very good, and the collection amounted to £123.

July 3.   At nine a.m. Philpott, Hildyard, Sharpe and myself, the only Fellows in residence, went to call, by desire, on the Duke of Cambridge, who is occupying our Master's Lodge. Before calling I saw Philpott, who told me that last evening he was waiting to see the Duke accommodated, and that the Duke kept him talking till one o'clock in the morning.   When we called we found

His Royal Highness going to breakfast, but he desired that we should be introduced; so Philpott announced our names separately, the Duke taking each cordially by the hand. After a short talk we withdrew. A little before ten a.m. I called at the Lodge and conducted the Duke to St Mary's. There we met the Archbishop of Canterbury and Sir Robert Inglis. Some delay occurring in opening the chancel door, the Duke said, "Let us go in at the other," so we entered at the south door. Then I asked him to go on the Throne, but he persisted in going into some seat anywhere, but I expressed to him my fear that he would be sadly inconvenienced. He then consented to go upstairs, but still would go with Mrs Howley, the Archbishop's lady. However he soon found himself in a crowd, and so was fain to go on the Throne, where the Archbishop was sitting. There he made the responses so loud that he was heard above the clerk and whole congregation. Having seen His Royal Highness seated, I went to my rooms and put on my cassock, and then returned to St Mary's and remained throughout the prayers. Whilst prayers were going on there was a regular fight in the gallery set apart for the town or public. This created some interruption, which the police speedily quelled. When prayers were ended, the Duke of Cambridge, the Archbishop, and others, went into the vestry to meet the Chancellor[1]. I then left the Throne in the expectation that it would be so crowded that there would be no possible breathing. As the Chancellor and the grandees came upstairs I spoke to such as I knew, and then placed myself in the doorway of the gallery and there remained throughout the sermon. The Master of Trinity preached an elegant essay from Ps. cxvi. 12. The Church was crammed full, but it seemed like a day of disquiet rather than like Sunday. I did not go in the afternoon to hear the Bishop of London preach, for I had enough of the morning. I understood he preached well, and to, if possible, a still fuller Church.

[1] Duke of Northumberland.

At four o'clock we dined, and at half-past six we all went to St Mary's to hear the Bishop of Winchester. He preached from Isa. v. 4. He applied the expostulation of the text to the members of the Church of England, by reciting the privileges we enjoy in that community, as having (1) Sound Doctrine, (2) a Scriptural Liturgy, (3) a Parochial Ministry. The sermon was highly refined and good, the congregation large.

July 4. I met an officer dressed as an Aide-de-Camp, looking out for the Duke of Cambridge. I therefore conducted him to the Lodge, and found afterwards that it was Sir Wm. Gomm. I dressed and went to the Chancellor's Levée at half-past nine a.m. It was very well conducted ; on my name being announced he observed, " I think I have had the pleasure of being introduced to you before." I replied that I had had the honour of being entertained by His Grace. On my return I went to my niece's lodgings, and soon after the Duke of Wellington passed with a long procession of Yeomanry. His carriage was drawn by the populace. He looked remarkably well. He was hardly expected, owing to an express having arrived during last night to inform the Chancellor that the Queen had been shot at again. Afterwards we went to the Senate-House, and saw the nobility presented for their Degrees. We had an early dinner and then all my younger party went to the concert. At four o'clock in the afternoon the Mayor and Corporation came in procession to our Lodge to present an address to the Duke of Cambridge.

July 5. I went with my niece to the Senate-House Yard and we remained till after the Installation Ode had been performed. My party went to the collation at St John's. At five I went into the Hall and carved for the party. I had a seven o'clock dinner in my rooms. Augustus O'Brien joined the party. About ten we went to see the fireworks at Jesus College.

July 6. I heard from Philpott that the Duke of Cambridge went alone to see the fireworks last night, and was so crushed among the multitude that his star was unfastened and lost. It was brought to him this morning. After breakfast, my party went to the Oratorio at St Mary's. In the afternoon I went with my niece to hear the band of the Coldstream Guards play on Clare Hall Piece. At five I went to dinner in the Hall of Trinity College, where the Duke of Cambridge, the Chancellor, and a large party of nobility and gentry dined.

July 7. I went with my visitors to see the New Fitzwilliam Museum fitted up for the Ball. The Mayor told me that he hoped the Hospital would be a clear gainer to the amount of £500.

July 9. At half-past three I left by the Rocket Coach for London. We got on the railroad at Bishop Stortford, and reached town at eight.

July 11. Made various calls, and then went with Augustus O'Brien to Lord Lonsdale's, where we lunched; after lunch I went in and sat with the old peer, who was very kind.

July 12. A Mr Roepsdorff, a Dane, called on me with a letter of introduction from Henry Goulburn. He wished to consult me as to the course he should pursue regarding the ministry.

There follows a letter to Mr —— on various subjects.

KETTERING, *Sept.* 8, 1842.

Dear Mr ——,

...I often wonder that the *very nature* of dissent does not discourage persons like Mr ——, from "making agreements with dissenters." Dissent from beginning to end is a mere matter of discipline, which, on dissenting principles, is among the *non-essentials* of religion. What chance is there of ever conciliating (by concessions or otherwise) a class of persons who differ from you, on account of something which, in their opinion, is of as little importance to salvation as the cut of your coat?

I would not have you, however, to be troubled respecting dissent, further than to take care that you give no just occasion for its existence. Your school would have been deserted on Sunday just as much, and on the same principle, to see a person *hanged* instead of baptized. It is human nature and you must be prepared for it. That Methodist ministers, also, should be thought "just as much of as ourselves by many", is not surprising, when Lords and Privy Councillors—men of education—see no difference between the Sacrament as administered by a clergyman and by a Methodist preacher. These are matters which require faith and patience, and a long course of teaching, with an example of Christian holiness.

As to the doctrine of Assurance—the life of God in the soul is like every other life, active, and subject to its own laws. Its tendencies being heavenward, we may, nay ought to, insist on seeing all who claim to have obtained forgiveness of their sins to be walking already as citizens of the heavenly Jerusalem. The Methodist view of "Assurance" is often little better than a dangerous dream. You will find much of human feeling in the teaching of that sect. It is always well, therefore, in teaching, to apply promises to *characters*, as the Bible does, leaving individuals to take the comfort or warning according as their characters may be; e.g. "Blessed are they that hunger and thirst after righteousness &c." There can be no mistake to the soul whether it be hungry or not: then there need be no mistake to it as to whether or not it "be filled." Of course a minister's duty is to take care in teaching, not to *invent* symptoms of natural hunger and thirst, or teach those to be *natural* symptoms which are the morbid results of raging fever, and so of the rest.

Believe me to be,
Very sincerely your friend,
G. CORRIE.

Sept. 21. I went by the Master's desire to the Lodge, taking Mr Burrell's will with me. Philpott read it aloud. It provides that the Master and Dr Turton be the executors, and after some few legacies he gives the residue of his property, of every description, to the Master and Fellows of the College in their corporate capacity, for the purpose of augmenting the incomes of the Livings at present belonging to the College, or toward the purchase of other Advowsons, as the Master and Fellows think best. In this he expresses an earnest hope that those Incumbents who may hereafter be benefited by his bequest, "will be tenderly alive to the promoting of the glory of God and the salvation of precious souls." In a small book containing a statement of his property he had written, "If riches increase, set not your heart upon them," and at the end, " Praise the Lord for all His benefits."

I have found the day to be a season of great trial of feeling. I seemed to read my own speedy dissolution in those deaths and changes which have moved me to the seniority of the Fellows. I earnestly pray that God for Christ's sake will give me grace to stand prepared for the coming of the Son of man, and in the meanwhile to be more diligent in doing the Lord's work, and in watching against sin in all its forms; and in living as a stranger and pilgrim upon earth, until my change come.

Sept. 25. The Master asked me if I intended to be a candidate for the Regius Professorship of Divinity which is expected to be vacant on the promotion of Dr Turton to the Deanery of Westminster. I replied that I had not thought of it myself, although a friend had suggested it to me. He seemed to agree that I had better wait to see who and what were the candidates. I told him that I should take no steps in the matter, although, if circumstances called me forward, I should think it my duty to do my best. I desire most heartily to leave everything in God's hands, feeling satisfied that He may be trusted to order my lot for my soul's profit. For the rest, I desire to be willing to serve Him in obscurity or in public office, so that I may but glorify His great and Holy Name in my life and in my death.

Sept. 26. I left Cambridge this morning for Kettering. Just before leaving College, a note from the Master was put

into my hand, containing his nomination of me to be President
of the College in the room of Mr Burrell.

Several letters to Mr ——, on various subjects are inserted.

CAMBRIDGE, *Sept.* 22, 1842.

Dear Mr ——,

        The difficulty you allude to would, with all others,
yield to a true-hearted desire to serve God for His glory and
the salvation of souls.   There is often great advantage too, in
having to walk circumspectly from *external necessity;* for we
lose much of the blessing of religion in our own souls, and of
influence among our people, by that matter-of-course kind
of piety, which is deficient in high and habitual *motives.*
If therefore, by being in a post of difficulty, we are more
frequently driven by a sense of our own insufficiency to
seek aid and direction from the fountain of all grace and
wisdom, we gain infinitely in mental discipline and wholesome
principle.

On the question of final perseverance, you will find the
pros and *cons* temperately stated in a little book lately published by Hatchards.   The author is Stafford Brown.   One
can hardly suppose that anybody *really believes* that a person
who continues in sin, can be the subject of God's grace.   For
my own part I so utterly disbelieve the *existence* of a *real*
atheist or *real* antinomian, that I should not spend five
minutes in argument with one who maintained that "if he
had received God's grace, however he sinned, he was in God's
favour."

Believe me to be,

Ever truly your friend,

G. CORRIE.

CAMBRIDGE, *Sept.* 24, 1842.

Dear Mr ——,

1. The deacon, as you rightly observed, is subordinate
to the two other officers of the ministry, and so is in pos-

session of a subordinate ministerial commission. At the same time, however, it is to be observed generally that the duties of any office will always be prescribed by the terms of the commission entrusted to it. For instance, the Presbyterian argues that Presbyters alone have power to ordain: our answer is, that Presbyters can only have that power which the terms of their ordination confer on them. If I, as a Presbyter, was not *commissioned* at my ordination to *ordain* others, by what right can I give *myself* that commission? And so of all other offices.

2. There is no Scriptural authority, that I am aware of, for supposing πρεσβύτερος to be ἱερεὺς in the *sacrificial* sense which that term implied under the Mosaic law. The only ἱερεὺς under the New Testament is Christ Jesus. The "gifts and sacrifices" offered by ministers under the Gospel are purely eucharistical, and have nothing to do with "absolution." The absolution which a priest has to pronounce is, in the nature of things, declaratory. God has "given power and commandment to His ministers to declare and pronounce to His people, being penitent, &c." Now, as man cannot read the heart, all absolution pronounced by him must be conditional, not absolute. As a matter of fact, "he that confesseth and forsaketh his sins shall find mercy," so that the *truly penitent* are in God's sight forgiven before man's absolution is pronounced. But then as "repentance and remission of sins" through an atonement is the main argument of the Gospel, the declaration of that "remission" is as inseparable from the ministerial office, as is the preaching of "repentance toward God and faith in the Lord Jesus Christ;" and men can enjoy that declaratory "absolution" only through those instruments whom God has appointed to that end. Observe, however, that there is no room for the idea of *priestly mediation* which is now so falsely insisted upon.

3. I believe the "ἐπίσκοπος" of 1 Tim. iii. is to be regarded as synonymous with what we call a "Presbyter."

But then there is no impropriety in using that Scripture in the consecration of *bishops*, for the whole is descriptive of moral qualifications, and not of official power, and is as applicable to bishop as to priest.

4. As to *archbishops*, they are only *primi inter pares:* and though of very early institution, are yet only for the purpose of ecclesiastical order. The Bishop of Calcutta, for instance, is a metropolitan, though not an archbishop, and to him all the bishops of the southern and eastern possessions of our Sovereign swear " canonical obedience."

5. There is a difference of opinion respecting the meaning of "προεστῶτες πρεσβύτεροι διπλῆς τιμῆς," 1 Tim. v. 17, but the most obvious meaning has always seemed to me to be that those presbyters are to be especially honoured who perform the duties of their office in an exemplary manner (Heb. xiii. 7, 8).

6. I do not see what is gained by calling original sin "*our* misfortune and *Adam's fault.*" If we believe that we are "*born* in *sin*," "the wages of sin is death," wherever found, and we know that it is of the very essence of Divine integrity to reward only according to *desert*. Therefore, infants suffer and die as sinners.

7. The idea in the 2nd Article, "Never to be divided," is truly expressed by *inseparabiliter.* As Christ was God and not man from eternity, so to eternity will He remain both God and man. But this does not in the least imply the continuance of the " *Mediatorship* after the day of judgment.' Our notion of mediatorship is contained in the office of the Christ as *Priest;* but as God-man, He is King as well as Priest and Prophet, and so to Him as "the first-begotten from the dead," and as "the Lamb," shall be ascribed "glory and dominion for ever and ever" (Rev. i. 5, 6; v. 13).

Believe me to be,

Very sincerely your friend,

G. CORRIE.

KETTERING, *Sept.* 30, 1842.

Dear Mr ——,

I would have you bear in mind that the doctrine of Predestination, whether treated in the 17th Article or elsewhere, involves the whole question of God's foreknowledge and man's free agency. Many have been the attempts speculatively to reconcile and explain how fixed purposes in the Almighty are consistent with the contingencies which evermore are connected with the free agency of man. As a question of *practical* divinity it has pleased God to render this difficult question less difficult. As a matter of abstract truth it cannot be doubted, but that all things are *determinate* in the sight of Him with Whom all is one eternal present. What our lives are and shall be, is *now* known to God as fully as if our course were run : whilst *conscience* tells us that He has made our responsibility depend on our accepting, or rejecting His offers of mercy. *This* is our business. God's predestination is *secret to us*, and though unalterably true, can never be the rule of our conduct. We know, that whom He chooses are "chosen in Christ," and so we may take the full comfort of our 17th Article if we be conscious that from the heart we have "received the atonement," and feel within us the workings of God's good Spirit inciting us to holiness. Whilst, therefore, we look only to our interest in Christ as the evidence of our individual safety, yet we need not hesitate to affirm that all the ransomed Church of God are saved only as God has "purposed." We err when we look to God's *secret decrees* as our rule of life and the ground of our comfort, instead of to that eternal love in Christ Jesus which set forth a Saviour, ("the Lamb slain from the foundation of the world,") to be unto us, "wisdom and righteousness and sanctification and redemption." The 21st Article is usually considered as referring to Christian Princes. Yet one can hardly conceive any council being called even under heathen kings if the *Law* objected, so

long as we read in the Scriptures, " Let every soul be subject
to the higher powers."

Receive this as a mark of the sincerity with which I desire
to be your friend,   G. CORRIE.

KETTERING, *Oct.* 7, 1842.

Dear Mr ——,

I was glad to find from your letter that you had
surmounted those difficulties respecting which you last wrote
to me. You must not forget that your progress in knowledge,
as in grace, must be onwards: and that conscience in its
highest and best form, will, by God's strength and teaching,
take the place of those scruples which now, so often, disturb
you.

1. As regards the subject of patronage, you were quite
right in maintaining the position you did. The patronage
before the Reformation was to a much greater extent in the
hands of the Bishops and Monastic bodies, than was the case
in earlier times. By degrees, patrons were induced to give
the patronage of their benefices to their diocesans, or to some
favourite monastery. These bodies often made merchandise
of the benefices made over to them, and sold the presentations. You will find information on the origin of benefices in
Stillingfleet, *Unreasonableness of Separation*, Pt. III., about
section 25. By taking any county history, you may see in
the history of any parish who the patrons of livings were from
the early times, and how the patronage changed hands. You
will find, also, Reynolds' (Archdeacon of Lincoln) " Historical
Essay on the Government of the Church of England, &c." and
Twysden's " Vindication of the Church of England," full of
information as to the encroachments of the papacy in secular
matters.

2. The Gedney case is decided by the judges of the *Ecclesiastical* Courts, and not by the Courts of Common Law: so
that we have no pretence as clergy or churchmen to resist
the decision as that of an usurped power. As an individual,

I regard the *Constitution* of that Court to be faulty in some respects, but still it is a *Church* Court. The supremacy of our Sovereign is best learned from the 37th Article. You will find, however, that it is of the very essence of the papacy, for the Church to claim for itself to be above the correction of temporal law. So soon as ever men are brought together in *society*, they become from that moment the subjects of social law; and except as to the administration of the Word and Sacraments and Ordinations, the law of the land will be that under which all corrections must be made. You cannot deal with men as if they were all spirit, and no body: but this is exactly what popery and all other kinds of dissent attempt to do, when they maintain religion to be a thing of which the State cannot be cognisant.

3. As the 17th Article is silent respecting "reprobation," we are certainly not required to maintain anything respecting that matter one way or other. At the same time you will find very few who would assign the perdition of man to God's eternal decree. The fact is, that (as I before observed) this subject involves the whole question of God's decree and man's free agency:—a matter difficult as to speculative dogmas—intelligible to the most unlettered Christian who embraces "the truth in the love of it." He believes *both*, and gives God thanks for *calling* him into this state of salvation, and gives all diligence to make his "calling and election sure." The pastor *preaches* both, without fear of men's cavillings or vain reasonings.

4. I do not in the least regard anything that Burnet writes on the Articles. I scarcely can make up my mind to mention the book, except as one that may be consulted occasionally for information on some point of historical divinity. Bishop Beveridge on the Articles is a better book, and more learned. As respects the 9th Article, I understand "εἰς κατάκριμα," unto *eternal* condemnation, whether reference be had to infants or others. After all the quibbles of Pelagians and other heterodox sects, the whole course of nature teaches that

everything naturally engendered follows the law of its *kind*.
None "can bring a clean thing out of an unclean;" if, therefore,
we come into the world with an *unholy* nature, or a nature not
righteous, we *cannot* be objects of approbation to a *holy* God.
What justice there may be in regarding children as unholy
being the offspring of fallen parents is another question. The
fact of our being born in sin cannot be explained away
without denying the whole analogy of nature, and taking for
granted the whole matter in dispute. For the rest we may
be sure that the "Judge of all the earth" does "right;" and
so far as I have ever read or considered I believe the doctrine
contained in the 9th Article is the only *rational* development
of the theory of man's condition.

5. The question of "holding a living" is one, which must
for the most part be decided according to individual feelings
and circumstances. I should be afraid to say that the
system as a system is to be utterly objected to, for so many
whose judgment I ought to respect do *not* object to it. As
an *individual*, I do not like it, though in the case you mention,
where all parties are religious, I do not see that the Church
of God would be wronged. In some instances "holding a
living" might be of service, as when by the change of incumbents the parish might really be benefited. You would find
the matter of building a Parsonage no light thing, unless a
plan were given you by the patron and parties interested, and
money sufficient were forthcoming to pay all expenses. "But
sufficient for each day is the evil thereof."

Believe me to be,
Very truly your friend,
G. E. CORRIE.

KETTERING, *Oct.* 11, 1842.

Dear Mr ——,

You need not be at all surprised to find variations
in your state of mind and feelings. This life is a struggle from
beginning to end; and our strength, at all times and under all
circumstances, is to regard God in Christ Jesus as the Source

and Giver of all grace and strength. It does not at all follow that, because you bear the office of an elder, you ought, therefore, to expect to find within yourself the knowledge and experience of an aged person. Timothy, though a Bishop, had yet much to learn from St Paul's teaching. So we can only know of "the things of God" as the Spirit gradually informs and sanctifies our souls. We must look rather to the faithful spirit in which we try to fulfil our mission, than to our actual ability to do all that we could wish. In fact "the treasure" of "the unsearchable riches of Christ," is, at best, but in *earthen* vessels, that the praise and glory may be to God's sacred Name, and not to our natural fitness. *Diligence* in the *duties* of our *calling* is what we must always keep in view; for the rest, the more we regard the operations of God's hand stretched out to help us in every time of need, the more joyful and prosperous will our labours be.

Believe me to be,

Very sincerely your friend,

G. CORRIE.

Oct. 15. I returned to Cambridge and have much reason to be thankful for the mercies of the day. The coach was in some danger of being upset, and I asked myself, "Am I prepared for all extremities?" My faith seemed to waver, as if I should not be ready to meet sudden death. I pray that God would give me grace to try to live more habitually with the Last Day in view, and that I may be in no doubt of my latter end.

Oct. 16. I sat for the first time in my seat in Chapel as President, and could not but cast my thoughts back with sorrow at the recollection that I was occupying a place which had been vacated by the death of Mr Burrell; remembering that very soon (at longest) some one else would have to think of my departure. I heartily prayed that God would give me grace to serve my day and generation according to His Will; and that having done His Will, I might in due time receive the promise of eternal life, through Christ my Lord.

CAMBRIDGE, *Oct.* 19, 1842.

Dear Mr ——,

The matter of *holding* a living at all is so much a matter of individual conscience, that you must decide that question for yourself. So far as the individual case presented to you goes, it is of as unobjectionable a kind as can be, inasmuch as the parties who are the Patrons seem to ensure as much certainty as profession of religion can, that your successor will not be unworthy of them. The offer of assistance also toward building a house is liberal, and the requirements (so far as this world goes) are reasonable. If on consulting your relatives and friends you accept the living, let the plan and building be all the act of the Patrons. In fact deliver it over to their steward as you propose, only giving him the half of the expense, as soon as the required sum is raised on the living. Bear in mind, however, that if you agree to hold the living for ten years, you must, as a gentleman and a Christian to whom truth is precious, vacate the living at the end of that term, to whomsoever it may have afterwards to be given. Nothing would be so much to be deprecated as scruples respecting your successor *then*, which have, and ought to have, their *sole validity now*. I am in the midst of preparations for Divinity Lectures, so that I am obliged to be brief, but I think I have noticed the only important matters that bear on your present circumstances.

Believe me to be,

Very sincerely your friend,

G. E. CORRIE.

Oct. 23. One of my Freshmen pupils came to me in great nervous excitement at the feeling of solitariness. I desired him to remain with me till Chapel, and he went away in much better spirits. I was pleased to find him truly religious.

Oct. 25. I called on the Dean of Westminster; he told me that he was the writer of a Review of the Bishop of

Salisbury's (Dr Denison) Letter to his Clergy on 1 John v. 7. The Review is in the xxxvth vol. of the *Quarterly*.

Oct. 28. At a meeting of the Press Syndicate I was asked to undertake the editing of Latimer's works for the Parker Society, and I consented, on the understanding that it was not to come out until 1844.

Nov. 2. I had a good deal of conversation with Parker, the University Printer, respecting a new edition of Bingham's *Origines*.

There was voting to-day at the Senate-House on the Grace for appointing —— an examiner of the Classical Tripos. The opposition was *not* to the individual, but to the system which is becoming common for private tutors to be examiners of their own pupils.

Nov. 4. The Master of Trinity, Dr Whewell, on being elected Vice-Chancellor this morning, had no Latin speech ready, as he said he had no idea a speech was usual! One scarcely can conceive how a person could have lived so long in the University and know so little of its commonest usages.

Nov. 7. I attended a meeting of the Diocesan Board of Education. The business was, to receive the Report of the Secretary respecting the state of Schools for the middle classes in the County. Nothing could be more unsatisfactory. It was agreed to apply to Mr Allen, the Inspector of Schools appointed by the Privy Council, and ask his advice as to what it would be advisable to do to remedy this state of things.

Nov. 12. I have to thank God for a week of support and comfort yielded to me by the mercy and grace of God in Christ Jesus. I find those who attend my public Lectures daily more interested, and I trust God is doing good by my humble instrumentality. To His name be all the glory through Christ our Lord!

Nov. 23. Great news from India and China, the former notifying the taking of Cabool and Ghaznee.

Dec. 1. —— was with me a long time, respecting the

state and prospects of the Conservative Society in this Town. A friend called to ask me to interest myself about a Petition from the University against the contemplated union of the Dioceses of Bangor and St Asaph. I told him a Petition was in contemplation.

Dec. 23. I am feeling very worn out with one thing or another. May God give me grace to finish my life to His honour and glory, and then, long or short, I shall not have lived in vain.

CHAPTER X.

1843. The opening year found him assisting his brother at Kettering; and, as usual, he begins his Diary with a prayer for God's grace and guidance in the coming year; "that I may evermore dwell in Him and He in me, and that this desire may be perfected in a nearer walk with God, so that, if spared, I may find myself nearer Heaven as each year brings me nearer to eternity."

The only letters recoverable for this year are three to Mr ——, of which the first follows.

Kettering, Jan. 9, 1843.

Dear Mr ——,

(1) I do not see what difficulty you need have respecting the rubric after the Baptismal Service, if you be satisfied that the "*general tenour*" of the Scriptures sufficiently warrants the belief that children baptized and dying before the commission of actual sin are saved. You have no express Scripture for admitting women to the Lord's Table, for practising family prayer, and other matters, respecting which the "general tenour" of the Scriptures is so plain, that there can be no *doubt* whatever as to the right belief on such questions. The general promise, "I will be a God to thee and thy seed after

thee," seems to me to *express* enough for warranting us to conclude that the blessings of the Covenant of Grace are extended to all children who have been initiated into that Covenant in the manner which Jehovah may have ordained. It is only a waste of human life (at the risk of running into all kinds of wild theories) to speculate *how* infants dying before committing actual sin can be saved; for after all we shall have to fall back, upon the question, "How can a child eight days old be capable of the seal of a *righteousness* which is by FAITH?" Yet God has so ordered it; and therefore, for all the purposes of Christian belief, we have, in this Sacramental institution of God, a pledge that there are blessings lost by disobedience to God's commands, as there are benefits following the faithful use of appointed means. The only thing to be borne in mind is that the Sacraments of the *Church* of *God* are for the *people of God;* to the unbelieving all things are *unclean.* *Who* the unbelieving are we cannot certainly discern, but we need not hesitate to say that, whoever they may be, to them the Sacraments of God's Church are administered only to their judgment.

(2) It is of the greatest importance that you should get rid of all those notions which would lead you to reason and judge upon individual cases. You have to do with characters as those characters really are in the sight of God, and as the Last Day will reveal them. Yours will therefore have to be throughout, a ministry of *faith*, not of *certainty*, even in the most hopeful cases. Your warrant is God's assurance that His "word shall not return unto Him void." In the faithful teaching of that word, whether by preaching or the administration of the Sacraments, you may always be certain that God's presence goes with you, though on whom His blessing actually lights, and by whom His word and Sacraments are faithfully used, can be known only to the great Searcher of hearts.

(3) Another point you have to aim at is, to live in less dependence on your *feelings.* There is a great deal of human

nature in much that presents itself to you as being the result of religious scruples. There is no remedy for this but a more devoted cultivation of the life of God in the soul. By this means you will find scruples diminish both in number and intensity: for in proportion as your soul is conformed to God in holy devotion, you will the more readily distinguish what is of God, and therefore, what is lawful. I say nothing, therefore, in answer to your difficulties about the "temporalities" attached to a living, because, as to principle, you might just as well have scrupled about a curate's stipend, which you received out of those very temporalities. If you use your income to God's glory, you are entitled to live by the altar as you minister at the altar; if you do not live to God's glory, your lot would be unhappy even though you exercised your ministry without receiving one farthing for your services.

(4) I do not think you need trouble yourself prospectively about "disturbing the rights and privileges of the Bishops," because you will never be called on to interfere one way or other. Of this you may be satisfied, that you will find yourself opposed to all the "disturbances" which may be contemplated by worldly or ecclesiastical politicians. The "god of this world" will never urge his servants to moot such changes as shall render our Church more efficient for good. All dabblings with "the rights and privileges of Bishops" will, therefore, only be either for the depression of the Church, or for more effectually aiding to *secularise* it; so that you will not have five minutes' perplexity about that matter. The only question you or any Christian will have to ask will be, "Who is on the Lord's side? Who?" Our Saviour's rule will at once supply an answer, " By their fruits ye shall know them."

(5) I must refer you to Wheatly's *Illustrations of the Book of Common Prayer* for all the information I could give you respecting the origin and *rationale* of such of the Services as require explanation. For the rest you will have to decide

upon the accordance of the Prayer-Book with God's word; that being done, you can decide for yourself. You will find God's mind in the Prayer-Book the more fully, the more attentively you study it.

Believe me to be,
Very truly your friend,
G. E. CORRIE.

The Diary of 1843 opens with an account of a visit to Northamptonshire to various friends, among whom Dr Corrie specially mentions the families of Mr Mackworth Dolben and Mr Paul of Finedon, Sir George Robinson of Cranford, and Mr Allan Young of Orlingbury; the intercourse with whom is spoken of as a great refreshment after the weariness to which frequent allusions are made in the Diary for the year 1842.

At the beginning of Term he is settled in College, with the prayer that "God's grace may direct and sanctify me continually that I may enter on my occupations with a desire to bring God glory in all I do."

1843. *Jan.* 25. Intelligence reached Cambridge of the death of Dr Le Blanc, the Master of Trinity Hall. He will be much lamented by all who had the pleasure of his acquaintance.

Feb. 1. Dr Ollivant was this day elected into the Regius Professorship of Divinity. The Provost called to tell me the result of the Election. Dr Mill and Dr Wordsworth were the other Candidates.

Feb. 2. Mr Calthrop of Corpus[1] called to ask my advice as to the propriety of admitting a candidate for Orders without a Divinity Certificate. I told him that so far as I was concerned, I was willing the Bishops should do what seemed best in any case; but if he asked my opinion on the general question, I could have no doubt but that a Certificate should be required from all, or from no candidates.

---

[1] Examining Chaplain to Bishop Bowstead.

Feb. 10.   I went to the Senate-House to a Congregation which had been specially called to petition against the union of the Sees of Bangor and St Asaph.   The Mayor[1] called on me to consult me as to a reprint of Bishop Tomline on the Bible, as a likely text-book for the Old Testament.

Feb. 18.   We kept the Master's birthday in the Combination to-day.

Feb. 20.   I wrote to the Dean of Ely[2] as President of the Philosophical Society, stating that as the Reading Room was kept open on Sundays contrary to existing regulations, it was my purpose to bring the matter before the Society for correction.

Feb. 24.   At the Press Syndicate a question was mooted whether or not we should authorise Parker to print the Prayer-Book simply with the Morning and Evening Services and the Lessons?   After some discussion it was carried in the affirmative.   I afterwards called at the Press to see Parker about printing a small Manual containing the Articles, Canons, and such Acts of Parliament as related directly to the Services of the Church.

Mar. 6.   I saw Thurtell of Caius, and settled with him about giving some tracts away at the Hospital.   I have been grieved at hearing that some of the usual Communicants in Chapel who were not there yesterday, were hindered by their Boat-dinner on Saturday.   Alas! alas! may God give me strength to labour more earnestly for their recovery to a better mind.

Mar. 11.   I have suffered much sorrow to-day on account of the deteriorating effect I perceive the Boating system is working on some of my pupils.

Mar. 21.   Woodham of Jesus came to me about his Preface to Tertullian's *Apology,* which he is editing.

April 6.   To-day I finished my course of Public Lectures for this year.   I give God unfeigned thanks for having

---

[1] Mr Stevenson, Bookseller.
[2] Dr Peacock.

strengthened me thus far: and may the Eternal Spirit of truth bless my labours to the glory of God's Sacred Name in the good of many souls!

April 9. To-day the Morning Service at St Mary's began at 10.30 instead of 11, and is to be continued so. The Parishioners expressed a wish to the Vice-Chancellor[1] to have the hour of Morning Service changed, and so he changed it, and very unadvisedly as it seems to me.

April 28. At a Press Syndicate to-day the Master of Jesus and I were appointed a Sub-Syndicate to enquire into the right of the University to a Pew in St Botolph's Church for the occupant of the house in the Pitt Press.

I am this day 50 years old. May God give me grace to consider how soon I must pass out of this world into an eternal state. I am slow to learn that all worth living for, is to know God, as He has revealed Himself in a Saviour, and to be shewing forth His praise in holiness of heart and life. Let me resolve, in God's strength, to be in earnest for the future, and to be aiming more individually at that progressive sanctification which marks a growing meetness for the inheritance of the saints in light.

May 10. I had an interview with the Vice-Chancellor on one of the Clauses in the Bill on Factory Education. The Vice-Chancellor seemed to think it would be difficult to draw up a Petition in which the Senate would agree, and it was settled that each one should write to his Parliamentary friends. I then had some conversation with the Vice-Chancellor on the subject of the Norrisian Prize Essays and the Lectures, and on the possible or desirable modifications of the Foundation. I told him that I would so far meet any wish of the University to render the Foundation more efficient, that I would agree to forego the Professor's stipend until the expenses of obtaining the modifications through the Court of Chancery were paid.

May 11. The anniversary meeting of the Camden Society

---

[1] Dr Whewell.

was held this evening, at which there was a good deal of fun. An amendment was moved to the Report, the effect of which was in fact a censure on the Committee for undignified expressions in the publications of the Society. The adoption of the Report was then moved and seconded. After a good deal of talk and interruption I asked permission to say a few words, to the effect that enough had been proved by the speakers on the amendment, to shew that caution was necessary, and that an opportunity had been given for bringing the objected matters under. discussion. It seemed to me that the end of the mover of the amendment had been accomplished, and I took the liberty of suggesting that leave should be asked to withdraw it. This was readily acceded to and the amendment withdrawn. Thus the dispute was amicably settled.

May 16. The Master of Sidney College (Dr Chafy) died this afternoon.

May 22. Dr Chafy, late Master of Sidney College, was buried to-day. Maddison of this College (as Vicar of All Saints) was asked to read the Service.

May 23. Mr Phelps, the tutor of Sidney, was this morning elected Master of that Society.

May 24. The Anniversary Meeting of the Antiquarian Society was held to-day. Papers were read, by Sir H. Dryden on "a Burial Ground near Marston, St Lawrence, Northamptonshire;" by Professor Willis on "the English Nomenclature of Architecture during the 15th century;" by myself on "the Studies formerly pursued at our Universities;" and by Mr Clark on "some Roman Antiquities found in the parishes of Littlington and Guilden Morden."

May 29. At half-past ten I went to St Mary's. The sermon was preached by Colenso of St John's from Rom. xiii. 1. He asserted the doctrine of passive obedience and passive resistance. The sermon might, for sorrowful complaining of England past, present and to come, have been preached by Jeremiah the Prophet.

June 1.   I was ordained Deacon as on this day 1817.   I desire to be deeply humbled for the many times I have fallen short, both in heart and act, of the obligations laid upon me by the vows of Ordination.

Then follows a letter to Mr —— on Sponsors &c.

CAMBRIDGE, *June* 7, 1843.

Dear Mr ——,

In reply to your letter of the 5th, I would not have you be disturbed by the small number of communicants. The evil effects of the times of the Commonwealth are still most felt in the utter ignorance and disregard or superstition (as the case may be), which the generality of the people of the country display in the matter of both the Sacraments. You must be prepared, therefore, to exercise much patience on this subject.

With respect to your fears about having persons for sponsors whom you could not but object to, I think it might be well for you to let your people know, as a *general principle*, that you should always like to know a day or two beforehand that it was intended to bring their children to Baptism.   You would thus have an opportunity of instructing the parents in the great duties and blessings connected with the faithful use of that Sacrament, and could indirectly learn who the sponsors were intended to be.

My notion is that there is no principle on which you ought to reject the child of *any* person who offers it for Baptism. The obligations of that Sacrament are strictly *personal* so far as good is to result to the baptized.   Although, therefore, all the parties bringing the child may be living in the neglect of their Christian duties, yet the Minister of the parish may always in after-life keep the baptized in mind of the solemn obligations under which he has been laid, and of the rich blessings which have been promised to a faithful fulfilment of those obligations.

As regards the parties who bring a child to baptism, you can, in fact, draw no line except as a question of *degree*. As to *principle* you are obliged in the most favourable cases to take sincerity on trust:—for who are good, and who are bad, you cannot decide in fifty cases out of every hundred, and might be wrong even in the remaining fifty.

Both therefore must "grow together until the harvest," so far as a Minister is concerned, though he may do much toward encouraging favourable appearances and toward checking *direct* profanation of the Sacraments and ordinances of religion. This is, in truth, what the "Plymouth brethren" have to come to, with all their boasted purity. As to their being "sincere and acting up to their profession," which your friend speaks of, did she ever hear or read of sectarians of any kind who did not profess a *greater strictness* than their *neighbours?* We have the highest authority for knowing that "Satan himself" can put on the garb of an "angel of light," and the history of the Church shews that he seldom appears in any other form, whenever he intrudes himself into the courts of the Sanctuary. It is, however, difficult to deal with such persons as your friend. She is evidently on the move, not knowing anything of the Church she is leaving, and as little of the Plymouth Brethren. The evil, in her case, is the absence of a true conversion of heart to God as a matter of importance to her *personally*. Hence the hankering after change, in the hope of making up from others that which must be found within her own soul. Hence the gropings after "doctrines," "tongues," and "revelations:" but which after all, the "Brethren" have not, even supposing 1 Cor. xiv. 26 &c. did relate to the Church as it now is. Then, again, why she should stumble at the pronouncing all persons to be regenerate in baptism, is difficult to conceive, when she will have to do this in every community she belongs to, if baptism be practised. Baptism, when practised, is at least held to be admission into the Church of Christ, but how can a person be admitted into that Church (whatever you call a Church) without pronouncing him to be a Christian indeed—one i.e. "born of water and of the Spirit." What difficulty then is avoided, on this point, by leaving the Church of England?

That "*we* separated from Rome," is not historically true. As to our succession of Bishops, it may be proved beyond doubt. I send a sketch of the pedigree, which you may copy and return to me.

You had better enquire no further into the case of the young person whom you suppose to have misled you in the matter of Confirmation. There is evidently a lie somewhere, but you will not be able to find out more than you have done. I should, therefore, recommend you to be satisfied with saying to the parties that if they have misled you, the sin is theirs. You must also be prepared for the adhesion to you of persons for the hope of gain. Simon Magus's posterity is not extinct. Your failing seems to be in attending to what people think and say on these points. The Scriptures tell us that "as soon as men are born they go astray and speak lies"; this testimony you will find to be so true that you will in time learn to sift every report and information that reaches you. You must learn to hear everything, but to believe nothing until you examine; and never to let people who tell you anything go away with the impression that you believe any ill report of a neighbour.

The time of singing is, according to Rubric, after the third Collect; but by an Act passed in 1 Edward VI. (1548), you are at liberty to sing at any time, so that the Service is neither "let nor omitted" thereby. An express injunction of Queen Elizabeth admits of singing, also, "at the beginning and end of the Common Prayers." In fact, whatever nonsense people may write now-a-days, a clergyman has not only the times, but the matter, of singing legally in his own direction.

This long letter is written after having dispatched the College Examination. I have, I fear, not touched on all the difficulties your letter mentions, but I trust that you will find not much unnoticed.

Believe me to be,
Very truly your friend,
G. E. CORRIE.

June 9. I have been grieved by the intelligence of the death of Henry Goulburn, to whom I was sincerely attached ; and the indisposition of our Master is of so decided a kind that it may soon be the will of God to subject our Society to great changes for good or harm. I have therefore been called to prayer, that amid every change I may be enabled to maintain the holy integrity of a Christian profession. And do Thou most merciful Father, for Thy Son's sake, grant that I may desire no portion but Thyself, and in Thee find my all ! Amen.

The last letter to Mr ——, this year, is on Episcopal Succession and other subjects.

CAMBRIDGE, *June* 12, 1843.

Dear Mr ——,

1. The date of Justus' consecration to Canterbury is 624, not 694. Wina and Devina are two distinct names, as are also Ceadda and Cedd.

2. All that Bede usually says about consecration is "Episcopum ordinavit," or some such phrase : the verb *ordinare* being that used to express his meaning. Indeed *consecrare* is much more proper to the setting apart of a Bishop to be an Archbishop, than to the consecration (as we call it) of a Bishop. For this *ordinare* is almost always used.

3. A *complete* list of Bishops in Britain from the Apostles to Austin does not exist, but it is not pretended that there was any kind of ministry at that time in the Christian Church except Episcopal. In the Churches of Rome, however, and of Gaul, from whence Theodore, Wina, and Wilfrid obtained ordination, and up to whom we can historically trace our descent, complete lists of Bishops exist. But if this were not the case, since, as I observed, an Episcopal ministry was

universal at that time, it would be as reasonable to deny our descent from Adam, because our pedigree is not historically to be made out, as to deny the descent of any line of Bishops from the Apostles.

4. As regards your question about the 'true Church,' the case is this.—Wherever a Society claims to be a Church of Christ, it must correspond to your description of it, viz. "a congregation of *faithful* persons." In this congregation, also, the Word of God must be preached, and the Sacraments administered according to Christ's Institution, and by men lawfully appointed to the ministry (Arts. 19, 23.). A Church must be all this in *profession* and *constitution:* but like individual Christians, the Church, as a Society, may fall short of living up to its profession, and fall into many corrupt practices in its external ministrations. But as you would not say that a professing Christian, unfaithful to his theoretic belief, was an apostate from Christ, so you would not be entitled to say that a Church, orthodox in belief but corrupt in practice, was an apostate Church. To Churches, as to individuals, the door of repentance and reformation is always open, so that we should deal with an erring Church as with an erring individual, by reminding both of their obligation to live up to the truth of the faith which both theoretically professed. So long, therefore, as, in the darkest ages, any Church in *constitution* and in its *written* and *professed creed*, might be Scriptural, there was in that Church a principle of revivescence to the body at large, and the means of salvation to individual believers. And whatever means were sufficient to constitute an individual a true Christian, must always have been sufficient to constitute a society (*i.e.* a congregation of such individuals), holding the same profession, a true Church in theory.

5. The case of the *present* Church of Rome is widely different from the case of that Church anterior to the decisions of the Council of Trent: just as the case of an individual who by a deliberate act has, in mind and profession, adopted into his creed damnable errors, is different from his case as

a *professing* member of an orthodox Church. The Church of England, for instance, during the last century, fell far short as a body, of the truth of doctrine as taught in her Articles; but so long as those Articles professedly embodied our Creed, it was the Church's sorrow and not her fault that her ministrations were opposed to her professions. Yet all along the Gospel was in the desk. But if during that period the Convocation had added to the Articles the Creed of Socinus, or Pius the IV., the *profession* of the Church would have undergone the same fatal change as that of an individual who becomes a voluntary apostate from the faith of Christ. In judging of Churches, therefore, as of individuals, you must regard the scriptural or the unscriptural character of their Creeds and constitutions, and not be misled by those *practical departures* from a *true* profession which mark Church ministrations in any given age.

6. I do not see why you should be at a loss for reasons for Confirmation. Putting aside the antiquity and probable (though not certain) Apostolicity of the practice, it must surely present itself to the mind of all serious Christians, as most desirable that opportunity should be given to the youth of a parish for solemn and personal instruction, and for an open dedication of themselves to God in the spirit of the Baptismal Covenant. On this the lowest, but not the weakest ground, you may press Confirmation as a rite of great importance.

Believe me to be,

Very truly your friend,

G. CORRIE.

June 16. I saw Professor Sedgwick in the Library, who among other things told me that he was anxious to have been admitted to our College, in consequence of his father having been of the Society, but that owing to the disputes in College at that time the Master would not allow any admissions. I could not but be struck with the strange turns which apparently small matters occasion in a man's future life.

June 22. Mr Bingham called on me, having come to

Cambridge with a view to obtain subscribers to a reprint of the *Ecclesiastical Antiquities.* I went with him to the Pitt Press to shew him a new Greek type, which I thought would do for the Notes in his edition of the *Antiquities.*

Mr Corrie was occupied in collecting material and verifying quotations for the edition of Latimer's *Remains* which he edited for the Parker Society.

June 28. I was occupied all the morning in drawing up a List of the MSS. connected with the works of Latimer which I wish to have copied.

June 30. I went to the Hospital, of which I am this week the visitor.

July 1. We had a dinner in Hall for our M.A.s. I desire to be thankful for a day of rest of soul, and I trust of some profit to others, for our conversation in the Combination Room was on matters of seriousness and devotion.

July 8. I was from ten o'clock till three at Emmanuel copying out a letter of Latimer's which is among the MSS. in Emmanuel College Library.

July 10. I left Cambridge for London.

July 11. I went to the office of the Parker Society to see if any provision were made for copying some MSS. connected with Latimer, but they knew nothing. I then went to the British Museum, and ascertained what I wanted.

July 12. I called on the Chancellor of the Exchequer about an order for admission to the State Paper Office, having previously ascertained that no order had been sent to the office. The Chancellor went with me directly to the Home Office and introduced me to the Under-Secretary, who very kindly had the order made out forthwith. I went to the House of Commons to hear the debate on the Irish question.

July 14. I went to the State Paper Office, where I remained till three o'clock. I then called .at Seeley's to enquire about a copy of Foxe's *Remains of Latimer.*

July 15.   I went to Seeley and Burnside in Fleet Street to enquire after as much of the letterpress of Foxe's *Acts and Monuments* as related to Latimer.   They were very civil and said I should have what I wanted.   I left Town for Cambridge.

July 20.   I left Cambridge for Kettering.

July 31.   I have been occupied all the morning in looking out authorities illustrative of the office of Suffragans to Bishops in England.

Mr Corrie spent the autumn at Kettering, taking charge of the parish during his brother's prolonged absence, and preparing Latimer's Sermons and Remains for the press. He was present at the Consecration of the new church at Orlingbury, in which he took great interest, being the residence of his friend Mr Young.

Sept. 28.   My brother, Mr Bingham and myself went to Orlingbury to the Consecration of the new church.   On arriving we found a large concourse of the clergy and gentry of the neighbourhood assembled to meet the Bishop.   A procession was formed from Mr Allan Young's house, headed by the Bishop, the Archdeacon, the Chancellor, and Dean.   There were at least fifty clergy.   On reaching the church-yard we found several hundreds of people collected, and forming a street down which the procession passed.   On entering the church we found it filled from one end to the other, except Chancel and North-Transept, which were reserved for the clergy.   When all were seated, the Bishop[1] attended by the Chancellor and Archdeacon[2], and one or two others, proceeded from the Communion Table to the West end of the church, and on returning to their places repeated the 24th Psalm alternately, the congregation joining in the responses.   The Bishop then from the Communion Table read the Address used at the Consecration of Churches and the first Prayer, after which the regular Morning Service began, the Rector[3]

----

[1] Dr Davys.   [2] Mr Davys.

[3] The present Rev. Sir Geo. Brooke Bridges, Bart.

officiating. The Venite, Te Deum, Jubilate and Gloria Patri were chanted—the singing being led by a seraphine. After the Morning Prayer the 100th Psalm was sung. The Bishop then preached an excellent, plain, scriptural Sermon from Luke viii. 18, "Take heed therefore how ye hear." After the sermon the Dean of Peterborough[1] read the sentences, during which the Archdeacon, Mr Maunsell, M.P. for the County, and Sir George Robinson collected the alms, which amounted to £304. The prayer for the "Church Militant" was then read by the Dean, and, the Bishop having pronounced the Blessing, the congregation separated. The Bishop returned to Allan Young's from the church attended by the churchwarden as far as the gate, and by the clergy to the house. There a plentiful collation had been provided by our excellent host, who also with true English feeling and Christian hospitality had given to every family 2 lbs. per head of beef for each person, man, woman and child (in order that the poor might entertain their friends). We went to church again at a quarter past three o'clock. The Evening Service was read by the Rector. The Dean of Peterborough preached from 1 Cor. xiii., and a better sermon could not have been delivered. There was a vigour, feeling, and eloquence in the good old man (now 74) which rivetted the attention of all. A collection was made throughout the church by Dr Harrington, Head of Brasenose, Oxford, Honourable A. Powys of Titchmarsh, Dr Langley of Olney, and Lord Alwyne Compton. The collection amounted to £104. The Bishop pronounced the Blessing, and the congregation dispersed, the Bishop and Clergy returning to Allan Young's as before. After Service, Newton Young requested me to draw up an account of the re-opening of the church for the *Northampton Herald*, but I recommended him to apply to the Dean of Peterborough, who agreed to undertake it. After this second Service we returned to Kettering. The day has been most gratifying in every way.

Sept. 29. Bingham told me to-day that the collection

---

[1] Dr Butler.

after the 3rd Service at Orlingbury last evening was £20, so that the collection on the whole amounted to £426.

Oct. 2.   I left Kettering for Cambridge.

Oct. 6.   I went early to Emmanuel College, and was engaged most of the day copying MSS. of Bp. Latimer's.

Oct. 16.   Intelligence comes to-day that O'Connell and others have been held to bail by the Irish Government on a charge of sedition.

Oct. 17.   The Vice-Chancellor[1] issued a notice informing the University, that her Majesty the Queen intends to honour us with a visit on the 25th inst.

Oct. 19.   The opening of Great St Andrew's Church in this town took place to-day.

Oct. 23.   Goodwin of Corpus called to know, whether we of this College intended to make any demonstration at the entry of the Queen into the Town.   I proposed that our men should be drawn up in line, and salute Her Majesty as she passed.   Goodwin called again with Pullen the other Tutor, to say they had seen some other Tutors, and there seemed to be a feeling, that an application should be made to the Vice-Chancellor, to call the University together in a body to receive the Queen.   I could not exactly agree to this, but consented to meet some Tutors at Goodwin's rooms to-morrow morning.   There had been an attempt to collect money towards paying for a triumphal arch in the parish of St Andrew's the Great, but only seven and sixpence was collected during the whole day.   There seems to be a feeling that her Majesty might be so pleased with her reception, that she would grant the Gownsmen a *Term*, which would be a great loss to the trade of the Town!!!

Oct. 24.   At a meeting at 9 a.m. in the Combination-room of Corpus it was agreed that Philpott, Pullen and J. J. Smith should wait on the Vice-Chancellor, to see about some relaxation of the order which limited the admission of the University to Trinity to-morrow to one o'clock.   This the

---

[1] Dr Archdall.

Vice-Chancellor readily entered into, so an order was issued accordingly.

Oct. 25. The University was on the *qui vive* betimes. Preparations were made on a large scale in the way of flags, &c. &c. Peterhouse, Corpus, and our College had platforms erected in front of the Colleges, and we had all our men drawn up to welcome our Sovereign. Soon after two the Queen arrived, preceded by a small detachment of Yeomanry and of the Scots Greys. Her Majesty and the Prince were in a plain travelling chariot, followed by two coaches, in which were the lords in waiting and others. The suite did not consist of more than eight persons. Earl de la Warr was the lord, and the Countess of Charlemont the lady, in waiting; the Marquis of Exeter was in attendance on the Prince. Previously to presenting the University addresses, the whole University met in the Great Court of Trinity, marshalled according to their respective Colleges. The Procession began to form at the Chapel-door of the College, and extended backward past the Great Gate, along that side of the Court, and down the opposite side as far as the Queen's Gate. About half-past three the Procession moved into the Hall of Trinity: the Queen and Prince were standing on a raised space, a canopy of crimson being erected in the centre of the wall behind them. The Address to the Queen was read first. The Queen read her answer in a fine clear voice. Then followed the Address to the Prince, and his answer. After that the Heads of Houses, the Caput, the Proctors, the Orator, the Registrary, and the Bedells were presented, and the University withdrew. We then proceeded to the Chapel of King's College. I had a most excellent place in the Choir. During Service Her Majesty and the Prince were seated under a canopy in the centre of the Chapel just before the Communion rails. It was said to be the place and chair occupied by Queen Elizabeth. After Service the Queen returned to Trinity. In the evening notice was sent to us that the Queen would receive Heads of Houses, Doctors, Professors, and M.A. Fellows of Colleges, at half-past nine this evening. I went with our Master and the Provost at the time appointed, in the Provost's carriage. After waiting a short time we were ushered upstairs according to precedence, and severally presented by the Vice-Chancellor. The Queen received us all very graciously. I returned as I went. It was about ten o'clock. Nothing could have passed off more undisturbedly than this day's stirrings. The Town was very generally illuminated. I walked with Jarrett through the Town between eight and nine o'clock. Everyone good-natured and contented.

I give God thanks for His great goodness and mercy to me this day. I desire also to express my content with the lot His good Providence has assigned me, for I see nothing in exalted rank to envy, but much to honour in our Sovereign. I could not but feel that our Queen needed much the prayers and sympathy of her loyal subjects.

Oct. 26. This morning there was a Congregation, at which Prince Albert was created LL.D., and Mr Phelps, the Master of Sidney, was admitted to the degree of D.D. by Royal Mandate. The Queen afterwards visited St John's, King's, the Public Library, and the Schools. From the Library to the gate opposite St Mary's Church where her Majesty got into her carriage, the pathway was damp, but the Undergraduates immediately covered it with their *gowns* for the Queen to walk upon. She afterwards visited the Library at Corpus, and the Round Church. The Queen left Cambridge for Wimpole at five o'clock. Chief Justice Doherty called on our Master, and said that Lord Lyndhurst told him, that the Queen was much delighted with all she had seen.

Nov. 6. I went to the Anniversary Meeting of the Philosophical Society, where I objected to the passing of a resolution to increase the subscription to the Reading Room, because that room was open on Sunday. After some discussion the Society agreed to bring the matter before the Council, and on that understanding I withdrew my motion. I had a majority on my side in the room.

CHAPTER XI.

1844—1849. As previously remarked, the Diary was not continued after 1843. A few extracts from general correspondence may be given before proceeding with the narrative of the following years.

Cambridge, Mar. 4, 1844.

My dear Mr Moore,

......I may mention to you that in the course of time I shall ask you to preach before the University for a month. This, however, may be a year or two hence if God spares us all. In the mean time I should like you to turn your attention to the nature of the Sacraments of the Old Testament Church, and their connection with those of the New. This subject wants discussing in an uncontroversial spirit, for there is a power of *muddiness* prevailing as to the vital connection of the two dispensations.

Believe me to be always,
Very sincerely your friend,
G. E. Corrie.

Cambridge, Nov. 18, 1844.

My dear Mr Moore,

Your acceptable letter reached me in due time, and I feel your debtor, for not having either yet acknowledged the

arrival of it, or sent my cordial wishes for your happiness
in your new estate.   As, however, the relationship into which
you have entered, is of that enduring kind which can be
likened only to the love and union of Christ to His Church,
congratulations can never be too late nor be misplaced, in
the case of those who realize in all its mystery and beauty,
the married life.   With every kind wish therefore for yourself
and wife,

Believe me, your truly attached friend,

G. E. CORRIE.

KETTERING, *Oct.* 14, 1844.

Dear Mr ——,

The only answer that you can give to the question,
"How can I pronounce a blessing over *individuals* who by
their works shew they are not such and such characters?"
is, that you never are called on to bless individuals as individuals, but as professing members of a congregation to
whom you minister, and who are willing to use your ministry
under the express stipulation that all you do is intended to
apply to the true members of Christ's Church.   On the
ground which you take up, it would be impossible for you
to minister to anybody, because you would never know who
is sincere or not.   The "negatively good profession" is quite
as decisive against the probability of judging it to be sincere
as the really bad, unless, like Antinomians, we maintain that
a man may be a child of true godliness without ever exhibiting a single fruit of the Spirit in his life.   The barren
fig-tree is as really profitless, even in the sight of men, as
the thorn and briar, and therefore, as a mere *question of
scruple*, you must give as much offence by blessing the barren
as the injurious, with this difference indeed, that the "negatively" good may be lulled asleep, whilst the other cannot.
The whole matter, therefore, must ever remain a question of
degree and not of *principle*, and so, after you have wearied
yourself with wandering after every scruple that the Tempter
may dignify with that of conscience, or the Dissenter with

the semblance of religion, you will still have to ask yourself, "How could an all-wise and holy God command His priest to bless a congregation (Numb. vi. 24, &c.) without exception, in whose character so much ungodliness was so habitual (Deut. ix. 6—24)? How could the omniscient Saviour give the Sacrament to a devil (John vi. 70, 71)? How could the Apostle bless the Corinthians (1 Cor. xvi. 23, 24), without exception, after having charged them with encouraging such fornication amongst them as was not so much as named among the heathen (1 Cor. v.)? From the beginning to the end of your ministry, therefore, you will oftentimes have to minister in sacred things to those whom you may have cause to regard with the greatest dissatisfaction ; and though it will always be your duty to lose no opportunity of warning them that are unruly, &c., yet you may without scruple leave the responsibility on the soul and conscience of him who, after warning, may seem to you to profane sacred ordinances. The reason for this must always be because the Great Head of the Church has, mercifully to us, retained in His own hands the separation of the good from the bad. In the meantime, the fact that the Holy and Eternal God causes His sun to rise, and His rain to descend, alike on the evil and on the good, on the just and on the unjust, may well lead us to believe, that we are standing on slippery ground, when we are tempted to withhold a blessing from the most unpromising character who does not refuse or despise it.

If all be well, I return to College to-morrow to my usual avocations, and have need of your prayers that I may strive to do all things to His glory, Who has done and is continually doing so much for us.

Believe me to be,

Very truly your friend,

G. E. CORRIE.

During the year 1844, Mr Corrie completed his edition, for the Parker Society, of Latimer's *Sermons*, to which reference is made in his Diary of Oct. 28, 1842. This volume was followed in 1845 by his edition of Latimer's *Remains*. About the time of the publication of the latter, Dr Wordsworth (who had then retired from the Mastership of Trinity) wrote to him on the subject as follows:

BUXTED, *March* 6, 1844.

My dear Professor,

.........I am very glad that you have undertaken the charge of giving us, through the Parker Society, the Remains of so interesting a person as Latimer, and I have no doubt whatever your edition will be a valuable one...... It would always give me great pleasure, if in any way I could be likely to be of service to you, in your present design, or in any other.......

Yours most truly,

C. WORDSWORTH.

BUXTED, UCKFIELD, *Dec.* 3, 1844.

My dear Professor,

I ought to have written to you long ago, to thank you for your very kind and interesting letter, and for the curious documents relating to the "Blood of Hales," and your own valuable historical remarks on other particulars, which accompanied it. There can be no doubt whatever, I think, that your calculations and conclusions on the subject of Latimer's age are true and incontrovertible. I thank you also for pointing out my mistake: the address in the dedication ought to have shewn me that the Duchess was Katharine, &c. I long much for the sight of your entire edition of the good old Father.

I wish greatly you could be tempted to undertake the volume or two of single, separate sermons, which the Parker Society some time ago promised. The publication, chronologically arranged, would make an extremely curious and valuable one. I hope the main matters are going on pretty satisfactorily, in these unquiet times, in our dear Alma Mater.

I am, my dear Sir, with great regard,

Yours very obliged and faithfully,

C. WORDSWORTH.

Rev. Prof. Corrie.

The following letter to his niece is truly characteristic:

CAMBRIDGE, *Dec.* 14, 1844.

My dear Polly,

Having this day finished Lectures for the present Term, I am unwilling to let a day pass over without congratulating myself on your long, and gossiping, and, I may add, very pleasant letter. I only hope you may enjoy my *Billy-doo* as much as I relished yours, and then forsooth your heart will be gladdened, so far as in this life we are permitted to be glad. If also the kind dear Pashy is still amending, then we may give a little shout for still further gladness. The shout must not be particularly loud, for this world is not for more joy than the heart can bear with sobriety. We seem sometimes to forget this as we perceive some of the clouds of life to pass away which have hung over us for a season, and feel the warm sunshine which has been, for a wise purpose, withheld for a time from shining.

But let us turn to the glad visit of our beloved Queen to our northern county. You would, of course, receive the *Illustrated News,* and see the pictures of the triumphal arches. But as I was possessed with the notion that the arches were not such as the picture gave them, I was more intent on reading what the Kettering people did and said, than in looking at the spurious pictures of arches which grew out of the *brain* of the artist. One is disposed to gather comfort from the dismay which seized Mr —— and his Chartists, when the real feeling of people toward the Sovereign was called forth: but still the signs of the times are but discouraging, and, for my part, I do not see how a hubbub will be avoided, unless God, in His gracious providence, interfere to help us. What a thought it is that out of all the confusion around us there are nothing but the elements of that tranquillity which is characteristic of the "Kingdom" which is to come; and that all is but working out the hastening of that Kingdom! We can enter into our divers chambers for a little while "until this tyranny be overpast."

I have nothing to tell you about myself except that I am in good health considering all things, but I trust never to have so much to do another Term; yet we must work while the day lasts. This, the decease of many strongly urges. I subjoin my kindest love to the household, and thereupon abide

Your truly loving Uncle,
G. E. CORRIE.

Here follow some letters in reply to further questions from Mr ——.

CAMBRIDGE, *Dec.* 18, 1844.

Dear Mr ——,

In reply to your questions I must say,

1. That although I abhor the rejection of Episcopacy by the Scotch as much as you can do, yet it is not easy to award to the existing generation their share of that lamentable transaction. It becomes us therefore to judge mercifully, and to deal accordingly with individual cases as they may present themselves to us, and as charity may suggest.

2. As regards the old man of whom you write, I should certainly require a professed willingness to take upon him all the obligations of the Christian Covenant entered into at Baptism, and moreover, an earnest desire to be a partaker of the Lord's Supper. If he had "little anxiety about the matter," it would be far better for you to press on his conscience the vast importance of preparation for eternity in the general sense, than to urge him to partake of a Sacrament which he does not value. It *is* a "sad thing to leave old people to perish without warning them of this duty," but it would be sadder still to leave them under the impression that the reception of the Lord's Supper could profit them, without a living faith in the Redeemer's Sacrifice.

Believe me to be,
Very truly your friend,
G. CORRIE.

CAMBRIDGE, *July* 3, 1845.

Dear Mr ——,

With respect to your peculiar difficulties I think you will find that the Act of William and Mary to which you refer, only goes to exclude our Sovereign from being in her own person a Papist, and so long therefore, as the Sovereign is personally a Protestant, there does not seem any possible infringement of that Act.

2. With regard to the expressed wish that you do not desire "to deprive any of our fellow-citizens of their rightful *privileges of citizens,*" one may really say that the endowing of Maynooth is establishing and recognizing men who are *not fellow*-citizens, who never *can* be fellow-citizens with us, since they yield allegiance to a foreign power, and we by endowing them, really admit that a foreign "power *has* and *ought* to have authority and jurisdiction within this realm." The Papist is a stranger and alien everywhere but in the Papal States, say what they may. All history shews this to be true.

You will, I doubt not, find many of these practical difficulties more easy to deal with as you become better acquainted with the detail of parish affairs. My belief is that we are too sanguine about characters....We are more surprised at outbreakings of evil in characters of whom we hoped well, than we should be, if we studied our own hearts better.

Believe me to be,
Very sincerely your friend,
G. E. CORRIE.

CAMBRIDGE, *July* 5, 1845.

Dear Mr ——,

The subject of Civil Obedience is not an easy one now that the States of this world have become professedly Christian, but it appears to me always that submission to the "powers that be" is the safest course for a Christian. We may of course choose (if choice be at command) between oppression and persecution, but it is not easy to avoid the force of that command, "Dearly beloved, avenge not yourselves." In our country the question is perhaps somewhat different from that contemplated by St Paul. We are living under an *express social compact*, and it may be said that our Sovereign is as much bound by that compact as we are. In that case our duty seems less restricted as to resistance, when that compact is departed from on the part of the Rulers, but the application of force must always be a case of extremity. "*Passive* resistance," if I may be allowed an Irishism, seems more suited to our profession as Christians than rebellion. I agree with you in believing that the present state of apathy to Popery may partly be traced to our not having availed ourselves of the fifth of November to inform our people of what Popery *is*. With regard to —— I should fear you have unduly vexed his conscience; be on your guard in this particular. After all you can do, you will have to receive a man's professions; if therefore you drive him into a corner by too rigid enquiry, you may make him a hypocrite without in the least satisfying yourself.

Believe me to be,
Very truly your friend,
G. CORRIE.

CAMBRIDGE, *July* 15, 1845.

Dear Mr ——,

I perfectly understand your difficulty about a "*credible profession*," but then, as I said, that is resolved into a mere matter of more or less discipline. The Dissenter professes to be strict, and fills his Meeting-House with mere professors, who do not even satisfy each other that they are what they profess to be. By this artifice he may appear to advantage before men, but, in truth, he openly allows persons to call themselves real Christians and he *treats* them as real Christians, whilst all the while he is encouraging the Antinomian principle that a child of God may yet be without the Christian's faith and practice. The Church of England, like Dissenters, receives persons on profession, but having warned

men that her ordinances are only for the godly, leaves the
parties to decide whether they *are* godly or not, as God and
their conscience may decide. If, in spite of this warning, men
come to the Church's ordinances, she must use the language of
the Church of Christ equally to all ; but then no man is *misled*
as to whether or not that language applies to himself in the
sight of God. Further than this you will find you cannot go ;
for, drive people about as you will, in the end you will find
some of whom you have no belief for *good*, but to whom you
have no *practice* to object against. And then you are, *as to
principle*, exactly where you were when you began, except
that you have distracted yourself and irritated your people to
no purpose. I write in haste, but am

Very sincerely your friend,
G. E. CORRIE.

The shadow of a great sorrow fell on Mr Corrie and his
family in August of this year, 1845; their beloved brother,
Henry, being visited with an attack of paralysis. Mr Corrie
was the only member of the family with his brother at the
time of the attack. Writing in deep distress to summon
his sister he adds :

"In the meantime our support and hope must be the
loving-kindness of the Lord in Christ Jesus ! More we cannot
have, and with less I trust none of us could rest satisfied."

There was a partial recovery, but though his life was continued for more than a year, it was a time of great anxiety to
the tenderly attached brother, whose duties constantly called
him from the side of the invalid. The following letter was
written during that time of trial.

CAMBRIDGE, *Nov.* 14, 1845.

Dear Mr ——,

...Since I last wrote I have been in great trouble
in consequence of the alarming illness of my only surviving
brother, who was seized with inflammation of the brain, in
August, which left me little hope of his life. It has however

pleased God to spare him, though he continues very much of an invalid, and is gone to Leamington for the winter.   Thus does God teach us to depend on His love alone for all the real happiness of this mortal life !   I need your prayers that I may have perfect acquiescence in the Divine Will as revealed in Jesus Christ.

Believe me to be,

Very truly your friend,

G. CORRIE.

On Dr Turton's appointment to the See of Ely in 1845 Mr Philpott became his Examining Chaplain.   On the death of Dr Proctor in the same year, Mr Philpott being elected into the Mastership of Catharine Hall, the Bishop of Ely offered the Chaplaincy to Mr Corrie in the following terms :

ELY HOUSE, LONDON,

15 *Nov.*, 1845.

My dear Professor,

......As the new Master (of St Catharine's) cannot well continue to be my examining Chaplain, will you undertake the office?   In the first instance, I thought that you would not (as Professor) think it worth your notice ; but on well considering the matter, I do not see why you should not render me that assistance.

Believe me,

Yours faithfully,

T. ELY.

Rev. Professor Corrie.

Nov. 16, 1845.

My dear Bishop of Ely,

Let me first thank you cordially for the spirit of true friendship manifested in the note which I this morning received.   Let me next assure you that I could never regard your Chaplaincy as an appointment unsuitable to my position in the University.   When in the first instance I requested your permission to decline the appointment, it was in deference to the wishes of our deceased friend and Master, but now I can have no hesitation in cheerfully placing my best services at your command, for as under any circumstances I should feel it an honour to be selected for your Chaplaincy, I regard the office as rendered doubly valuable by the kind manner in which you have been pleased to offer it for my acceptance. In the meantime I shall always be,

My dear Lord,

Your obliged and dutiful, ·

G. E. CORRIE.

The appointment thus accepted was held to the end of Bishop Turton's life, and while adding materially to their friendly intercourse and mutual confidence, it exercised a considerable influence on the Diocese. The office of Domestic Chaplain was added a few months later. The following reflections on the exercise of a lively faith were written about this time.

A Meditation for any day or night:

Mere worldly men live by reason—the Christian lives by faith. Now as "faith is the substance of things hoped for, the evidence of things not seen," it follows that when in our afflictions and distresses we "hope" in God for deliverance, then faith gives substance to that deliverance before it actually arrives. So, also, if we look for those mercies which God has promised, then faith sees those mercies as if actually present because it has sure "evidence" of their real existence. Let us then not be "faithless, but believing" that *all* things are ours, whether life or death, things present or things to come.

G. C.

SUNDAY NIGHT, *Nov.* 30, 1845.

..... On the error of indulging a fallacious generosity, while losing sight of previous responsibilities.

I am well aware that you have had great exertions to make as regards Schools, &c. and have done much, yet I cannot forget that everybody might do as much, if it were, as in your case, at the expense of leaving unpaid legitimate claims upon them. I am quite sure we may get very wrong on these points with regard to the soundness of our religious principles. For it is not for God's honour to be liberal and charitable at our neighbour's expense. I have ventured to write thus plainly (but I trust not with an unfriendly intent) because I think your letter shews you to be under wrong impressions as regards important religious principles, and sure I am that if our principles of action are not based on simple integrity according to God's word, we may preach to others, and yet be ourselves castaways.

Believe me to be, yours truly,

G. CORRIE.

Nov. 1845.

Some further letters to Mr ——, on parochial difficulties and the spirit in which they should be met, occur about this time.

CAMBRIDGE, *Jan.* 6, 1846.

Dear Mr ——,

With respect to your difficulties regarding ——, my advice is that you fill up the papers without hesitation, on the strength that there is nothing required of you which has not been done by many Christian men, well versed in the Scriptures, before you. My experience would go to discourage a fastidious conscience, whilst I would pray evermore for a *tender* one. I think also we may press too far many of the provisions of the Mosaical Dispensation, specially those which relate to men in their civil relationships.

I think your course with regard to —— has been judicious. It is no use driving a man to extremities in the matter of conscience. If he *say* he is "in charity with all men," we can go no further as to principle, and I think that the absence of the farmer from the Lord's Table may be taken as indicative that the grudge-bearing is not on the side of the other. I am truly glad to hear of your improved health, I doubt not that you will find correspondent rest of mind. I have myself still to sorrow under my brother's

continued illness.   But as my sure trust is in a most merciful
God in Christ Jesus, my desire is only to wait God's will in
every afflictive dispensation.   The time is at hand when *all*
will appear plain.   May God give us grace to wait patiently
for the appearing of our Lord Jesus Christ!

Believe me to be,
Your sincere friend,
G. CORRIE.

CAMBRIDGE, *March* 25, 1846.

Dear Mr ——,

I think that becoming sponsor by *proxy*, is a
matter so settled in this country, that it would be difficult
for you to make any objections to it in the case you have in
view.   It is possible that the parties you have to do with
might understand your wishes and attend to them, and if so,
one cannot but prefer that a sponsor should stand in his own
person.   I do not, however, enter into your view of the good
or bad effect as regards the child.   The answers were made
for the child, the faith promised is for the child.   Now no
state of unworthiness (according to the XXVIth Article) can
obstruct the blessing of the Sacrament to the recipient, if that
recipient prove to be himself faithful.   The evil of ungodly
parents and sponsors is much more in their not putting the
child in mind of the "solemn vow, promise and profession made
in *his* name;" and therefore he may grow up in ignorance.

2.   I should not be too strict about the "artificial flowers."
There may be, in my opinion, more pride and hypocrisy
under a close plain bonnet, than under a veil of silk.   It is
desirable to check a love of *finery*, because it may lead to *sin*
when it can be gratified from no other resources.   But all
this must be done by the inculcation of sound religious
principles and godly sobriety, much more than by placing
"flowers artificial" under an interdict.

Believe me to be,
Your sincere friend,
G. CORRIE.

C.16

LEAMINGTON, *April* 3, 1846.

Dear Mr ———,

1.   I think that the lady mentioned need have no difficulty about being sponsor in such a case, if she have in any way means of putting the child in mind of the vow made in its name with which she can be satisfied. If, on the other hand, she feels that she cannot fulfil the duty of a Godmother, according to her own convictions of that duty, she should decline, giving her reasons to the parties. The responsibility of finding less conscientious sponsors must rest with the parents, not on her who declines to stand from true motives. Only it will be important to bear in mind how far the custom of society (in its best estate) admits of Godfathers and Godmothers interfering in the bringing up of their wards.

2.   I think you should put all your people in mind of the importance of having their children baptized. The obligations laid on parties in Baptism rest with the *baptized* and not so much on the parents. All who are brought to Baptism *willingly*, (from whencesoever they come), should not be refused. I cannot think that we ought to make a child's Baptism, conditional and dependent on the good behaviour of the parents. Baptism is a personal thing ; even though those who bring the party to baptism should neglect their own duty, still the Sacrament remains to the faithful recipient himself.

......A Liturgy *implies* a steady growth in the *Divine life,* and without this it must appear formal and wearisome. With a steady *growth of soul* a Liturgy is *always new* though the same, because petitions acquire a fresh meaning day by day, as we daily become more experimentally acquainted with fresh tokens of the Divine Love, and acquire enlarged views of the great truths of eternal life as revealed to the soul by the teaching of God the Holy Ghost.

Your sincere friend,

G. CORRIE.

April 16, 1846.

......Remember to watch over your own temper and feelings. We are too apt to contract a portion of the bitterness of disputes whenever we engage in them. The all-sufficient grace of God in Christ Jesus must be our refuge, and by that we shall triumph.

There follows a letter to one who had applied to him as Chaplain to bring his name before the Bishop for preferment.

CAMBRIDGE, *March* 26, 1846.

Dear Sir,

In consequence of the intimate social relationship in which it has been my happiness, for many years, to stand to the Bishop of Ely, I feel myself precluded from asking him any favors either for myself or others. As regards your claims on the late Bishop, I should fear that it would be very difficult for his successor to recognise them, considering how many deserving clergymen the present Bishop must himself know, not to mention the different judgment which his Lordship might possibly form respecting the claims which his predecessor might have decided to be deserving of his attention.

Believe me to be, dear Sir,
Very faithfully yours,
G. E. CORRIE.

The following is in reply to a query on the position of the Roman Catholic Church in England, which had been conveyed to him through his niece.

CAMBRIDGE, *May* 29, 1846.

My dear Mary Anne,

What has the "Primitive Catholicity of the Church of England" to do with the Church of Rome in this country? If Dr —— wishes to know how little Rome has to do with us, he will find all that would satisfy an enquirer after truth in *Fullwood's* (Dr Francis) "*Roma ruit*, or, The Pillars of

16—2

the Church of Rome broken." But what proof of the utter groundlessness of Rome's claims can be required beside the facts, that *every* Roman Catholic Bishop, Priest and Deacon now existing in England has foreign Orders, and (2) the whole Romish body in England were, without protest or complaint, for eleven years in communion with the present Reformed Church of England. They would have remained so no doubt to the end of their lives, if an old man at Rome had not told them they ought to *leave* their Parish Churches, and murder Queen Elizabeth! What reasons *can* convince men who are ignorant of these facts of English History?

Your loving Uncle,
G. E. CORRIE.

From the time of Mr Henry Corrie's seizure in August, 1845, his condition had continued very precarious. Having been moved to Leamington, where his brother-in-law Mr Sherer and his family resided, he there remained under his sister's care, Mr Sherer himself also being in declining health. The following lines were penned from Cambridge by Mr Corrie to his sister, on the departure at this time of one of her sons to India.

Oct. 15, 1846,

......My spirit is with you daily, and the more so as the time for Jack's departure approaches. *Our God is everywhere*, and distance is only a term which man has invented to distress his body. The spirit is not bound by space, to those whom nature and a redeeming God make one.

The end came more suddenly than was expected. On Nov. 12 Mr Corrie was summoned to Leamington on account of his brother's increased illness, and on arriving found to his great grief that both brothers had on that day been called to their rest, Mr Sherer having passed away only a few hours before Mr Henry Corrie. The solemnity of the twofold bereavement, albeit cheered by the assured hope of a joyful resurrection, was most deeply felt by the last

surviving brother. The double funeral took place at Kettering amidst the deep and sincere grief of the inhabitants
and of many neighbouring friends. To quote from the
Sermon preached the following Sunday in Kettering Church
—speaking of their departed rector, " He had entwined himself about your hearts, and endeared himself to you all, as
none ever did ;" and speaking of his " scarce less beloved"
brother, "With him all was fervent love for God, and fervent
love for man. All *his* luxury was doing good. Much have
I been built up in faith, instructed and comforted by his
ardent piety." Mr Corrie's own feelings are best expressed
in a letter to one of many friends who had written to him,
the only recovered letter of the kind :

CAMBRIDGE, Dec. 2, 1846.

My dear Blakelock,

I feel much your debtor for the kind expression of
sympathy which your letter that reached me to-day contains.
It is but too true that notwithstanding the kindness of the
sincerest friends, each heart is alone really conversant with
the extent of its "*own* bitterness." This is peculiarly the
case with myself. For though none could come into contact
with my late brother Henry without tasting somewhat of
his natural kind-heartedness, yet, I believe, none were ever
in my circumstances, for knowing and experiencing the depth
and extent of his natural brotherly love. His natural sweetness of temper also, rendered his house such a home, as I
never again expect to meet with in this life. Yet I desire to
trace, even in this afflicting Providence, the Fatherly hand
of a redeeming God in Christ Jesus.

As regards my brother Sherer, he too had very much
about him naturally, which rendered him an object of true
affection to us all. In faith, and hope, and Christian love,
his life was an example to us all.

Respecting the dead we have nothing to desire:—we

trust that they are resting eternally in the more immediate presence of God. But the death of the two, in the same house and on the same day, cast an awe over the whole household, which by God's grace I trust may never be forgotten. Mr Sherer had been declining in health for some time, and his probable dissolution was a reason why we should stand prepared for it. My brother Henry had been so much better that we were indulging hopes of his much longer continuance among us. But on the evening of the 11th of Nov. he was seized with some kind of fit, out of which he never recovered, but died on the 12th, about seven hours after Mr Sherer had passed into eternity. An express was, of course, sent over to me, but I reached Leamington only to find my two brothers dead. I desire, as I much need, your prayers, that amid these trials of the affections, I may be kept from every feeling but that of resignation to the declared will of God respecting me. For the rest I may be content to follow the departed as they followed Christ. I add my kindest remembrances, and that I am,

Very truly yours,

G. CORRIE.

The first work Mr Corrie undertook after the death of his brother was the issuing of the Biography of his elder brother, Bishop Corrie. It had been begun by the surviving brothers conjointly, but necessarily laid aside at the time of Mr Henry Corrie's illness. The work now completed was published in 1847.

On the retirement of the Duke of Northumberland from the Chancellorship of the University of Cambridge, in the early part of the year 1847, the important subject of the choice of a successor to the office being under consideration, the idea of an Episcopal Chancellor was suggested by the late Right Hon. A. B. Beresford-Hope, M.P. in a letter to Mr Corrie, which is here given, with Mr Corrie's reply.

1, CONNAUGHT PLACE,
Feb. 13, 1847.

Rev. Sir,

Will you permit one who has never had the honour of an introduction to you to intrude on you on a matter of very pressing moment—the election of our new Chancellor.

Rumours are, you of course know, afloat respecting a Government Commission to enquire into the Universities. Is not our best hope centred on ourselves, our own good deeds? We should clearly and fearlessly exhibit our ecclesiastical character. And might not we elect a Bishop Chancellor as the best proof of this?

Of the Cambridge Episcopate the names of the Bishops of London[1], Lincoln[2], St David's[3] and Lichfield[4] occur to me as very eminent ones. Time is of course very important in such a matter.

Permit me in anxious expectation of your reply to subscribe myself

Your obedient and humble servant,

A. B. B.-HOPE.

Feb. 14, 1847.

Sir,

Before your letter reached me I had engaged, in conjunction with a few other members of the Senate, to further, as much as in us lies, the election of the Lord Powis into our Chancellorship. It appeared to us, that the persevering zeal with which that nobleman has contended for the integrity of our Episcopate, and his well-known attachment to our Institutions, give promise that our Chancellorship could not, in these days, be entrusted to better hands. At the same time, I can enter, as a general principle, into the sentiments expressed in your Letter, respecting the benefit that might accrue to us from having a Bishop for our Chancellor, although, it is a matter of deep regret to me to know, that some of the most threatening innovations on our Ecclesiastical Institutions, have originated with and are patronised by, some of our present Bishops. Under these circumstances, it has seemed to myself and others that our Chancellorship would for the present be safe in the hands of a lay-nobleman such

---

[1] Dr Blomfield.   [2] Dr Kaye.   [3] Dr Thirlwall.   [4] Dr Lonsdale.

as the Lord Powis; and moreover, if all who wish well to our Institutions, unite to further the Election of such a member of our Body, they may save us from the painful duty of having to obviate any wish (of which there are some whispers) to place over us an exalted personage, who has not been educated among us, nor even nurtured in our Church.

I have thus freely communicated with you, to give you the assurance that no apology was necessary on your part for writing to me on this subject. On the contrary, it is a matter of refreshment to my spirit to find that there are any who care for our Universities, and believe that such Institutions have a deeper meaning than Mammon assigns to the mere walls and revenues of our noble Foundations, for so rife have indifferentism and strange principles become among us here, as elsewhere, that I often feel as if I were one of the last remnants of a bygone race.

Believe me, yours faithfully,
G. E. CORRIE.

A. B. Beresford-Hope, Esq.

Mr Corrie's well-known familiarity with the Romish Controversy led to his being frequently consulted by some of those who from any circumstances were called upon to maintain Protestant truth. In the following instance the Rev. J. Brame, late vicar of St Peter's, Manchester, had been the subject of an attack by a Romish priest in his neighbourhood, on account of a Sermon which he had preached and afterwards printed. Contenting himself with a short reply to his opponent, merely verifying the facts and authorities which had been challenged, he sought Mr Corrie's advice thus:

LEIGH, *May* 1, 1847.

My dear Sir,

If you have an hour to spare I should feel really obliged if you would give me your help and advice under the following circumstances. There is a popish priest here who has hitherto been pretty quiet. He has lately, however, been showing symptoms of an intention to attack the Church.....I have neither ability, nor time, nor books, for a controversy, but, as it may turn out that it is necessary for the Church's good that something more be said, I should feel grateful for some hints and references if you can give me them.

......Believe me, my dear Sir,

Yours faithfully and respectfully,

JOHN BRAME.

CAMBRIDGE, *May* 3, 1847.

Dear John,

My first advice to you respecting the Popish Priest, is to decline any further communication with him, now you have referred him to your authorities. If he writes again, simply acknowledge the receipt of his note as a matter of courtesy, and in case he *impugns* your statements in his letter, only say, "that you have no doubt but that he writes according to the best of his knowledge and belief, but that your information is all the other way." The reason for this advice is, that the man is evidently intending to draw you into a controversy ; and in that perhaps you might have nothing to fear if —— were alone concerned, but you would have to contend against all the Jesuitry and subtilty of Stonyhurst, for no doubt the man would be prompted by *all* the sect in your parts. In the meanwhile with respect to the subjects on which you ask for direction :

1. You will do well first to inform yourself respecting the Romish Congregation by reading Berington's History of *The Decline and Fall of the Roman Catholic Church in England,* or *Memoirs of Panzani.* This book is somewhat scarce, but is written by a Romanist, and contains authentic information. Bear in mind that there is not a single Romish Bishop or Priest now in England whose orders are not *foreign.*

2. All the information you can require on the subject of the Versions of the Scripture, you will find in Grier's "Answer to Ward's Errata in the Protestant Bible." No doubt Middlehurst has not a word to say on that subject which he has not got from Ward. As regards the popish tamperings with the

Bible, a flagrant instance is readily found in their Bordeaux Testament. Grier gives some account of this Testament in the Preface to his "Answer to Ward" above mentioned; and you will see some account of it in Cramp's *Text-book of Popery* (a book you should have), but Bishop Kidder wrote *Reflections on the Bordeaux Testament;* which was *reprinted* a few years ago in London. This enters into particulars. Then again you will find no end of errors and mistranslations of Scripture pointed out by Dr James in his *Bellum Papale*, which has lately been reprinted. I am *told* (I do not myself know by examination) that, singularly and curiously enough, the Romish Archbishop Murray, in Dublin, has been gradually though stealthily *approximating* the Douay and Rhemish Translations used by the Papists to our *English* Version. Nothing, however, but a comparison of different editions could shew this.

3. With respect to the alienation of Church Property, you will find no end of instances of *Papal* doings to that effect in Johnston's (Nathaniel) "Assurance of Abbey-lands to the Present Possessors." In England the confiscation (iniquitous in the extreme) of the possessions of the Knights Templars. It should never be forgotten, too, that it was a *Pope* and *Popish Convocation* and a *Popish* Parliament, that confirmed all that the Popish Henry VIII. and *his* Popish Parliaments had done in that line. The *Reformers* earnestly pleaded for the devoting of the revenues of sin, as exhibited in monasteries, to some *sacred* purpose. The story of the Papal confirmation above alluded to, you will find at length in Dodd's *Ecclesiastical History* (popish), edited by Tierney (a Papist), Vol. II. And as late as 1652, Pope Innocent X. suppressed no end of monasteries at a single blow, whilst the monasteries of Venice were suppressed by the recommendation of his successor Alexander VII., for no purpose but to find money to carry on the war against the Turks; you will see the story in Ranke's *History of the Popedom*, Vol. III.

The Popish tract you enclose is exactly such an one as

has been in circulation for years. The only way to answer it would be to take exactly the same line of Dialogue, and as much as possible the same words, only putting the enormities of Popish Priests and the ten thousand monstrosities of Popery instead of the assertions of the Pamphlet itself. If I have time I will do this for you during the summer. To your people your answer to such trash should be, " If Popery and Papist were inserted wherever Protestant or Protestant religion occurs, the Tract would be true." As regards your own reading, you can do nothing effectual for the Church unless you know *all* Church History well, not less than the Reformation Period. You should bear in mind too, that if you enter into controversy with the priest and he *floors* you, the Church you serve will be damaged, for they are sure to put forth your writings as the *best* defence that can be made. This note, brief and hasty as it is, may shew you that on these points alone there is a good deal to be read, even at the very shortest.

Believe me to be,
Very truly your friend,
G. E. CORRIE.

Mr Brame having written a reply, which was drawn out by a further attack on the part of the priest, sent it for Mr Corrie's inspection, who wrote :

HADLEY CHASE, *Aug.* 20, 1847.

My dear John,

Your Appendix will do you no discredit; nor do I think the priest will meddle further with you. Touching Books of Devotion, you will find a thorough exposure of the old English Breviaries in " Reflexions on the Devotions of the Church of Rome," attributed to Patrick. The book is not scarce, judging from the price. One thing bear in mind, that the existence of the " Congregation of the Index," which was established by the Council of Trent, to be a standing Censorship of the Press for the Romish Communion in all future times, makes all books published by private Romanists, *permissu superiorum*, to be of *authority*. This oversight on the part of Rome has not received the attention it deserves. You will, however, see that as no book can be lawfully put forth and read among Romanists, except as allowed by their ecclesiastical superiors, and *that* according to the provisions of the laws of the "Congregation of the Index," therefore all books that *are* allowed are virtually authorized by the *Council of Trent*. You will see the story of the "Congregation of the Index" in such a book as Cramp's *Text-book of Popery*. If you had thought of it you might have added a knock by stating, under the head, "The mutilation of Churches," &c., that such "mutilations" were in their measure and degree done by *Papists*, inasmuch as they urged on and joined the Puritans in the War against the Church of England, just as they now join other Dissenters. There are some curious proofs of this in Ware's *Foxes and Firebrands*.

Yours very truly,
G. E. CORRIE.

In September Mr Brame writes again to Dr Corrie, "I expect the line they will take will be to shew that the Fathers held the Tridentine novelties, and therefore the Church of England always held them. Besides Soames and Jewel, where can I find easily a string of quotations to prove that they did not hold them?"

HADLEY CHASE, *Sept.* 21, 1847.

My dear John,

The readiest collection of quotations from the Fathers *against* Romanism would probably be Faber's *Difficulties of Romanism*, which was written especially to vindicate the Anglican Church. All the quotations which the Stonyhurst people will bring, will no doubt be from Berington and Kirk's "Faith of Catholics proved from Holy Scripture, and the Fathers," &c., and all these are met by Faber in the book above mentioned. As regards the "interpolations, changes &c." in the Rhemish Testament, nobody can have the slightest idea of what is and has been going on, who has not watched the movements of the Papists. I have always felt that the Trent Church is not a part of the Church of Christ, and that all the mawkish tenderness for that Church which the Oxford School has and does exhibit, is treason against the Church of Christ in this land.

Your sincere friend,

G. E. CORRIE.

Though Mr Corrie held strong convictions on the doctrines and system of Romanism, he did not allow those opinions to influence his friendly feelings towards individual members of the Church of Rome, as may be seen from the following letter he received from the Earl of Denbigh, who has courteously allowed its insertion. In giving this permission Lord Denbigh writes, " I shall only be too happy to testify to my respect and affection for my venerable friend Dr Corrie as often as the occasion for doing so offers itself. He showed me the greatest and warmest kindness at the time when I was standing for the University of Cambridge on Protestant principles ...... and I never remember to have received an unfriendly or unkind word from him, however he may have disapproved of my change."

My dear Master of Jesus,

Your kind little note has given me sincere pleasure and makes me regret more than ever that I had not the good fortune to find you at home.

Although I never allow religious differences to alter my feelings to my friends, yet since I became a Catholic I have so often received the cold shoulder from former warm friends that it is a pleasant change to receive so cordial a greeting from one for whom I have always had so sincere and so affectionate a regard.

I hope if you should be passing through London you will give me the pleasure of seeing you, and

Believe me always,

Yours very warmly,

DENBIGH.

For some time Mr Corrie had been occupied in preparing editions of Twysden's *Historical Vindication of the Church of England*, and Burnet's *History of the Reformation*, both of which were published during this year, 1847. The edition of Burnet's *History* was in an abridged form,—the substance of the supplemental volume being incorporated into the Text,—and was prepared for the use of Students at the Universities and Candidates for Holy Orders. Mr Corrie was indebted to his friend the late Archdeacon Hardwick for much valuable help in the preparation of Twysden's *Vindication* for the press.

The remarks in the following letter to his niece, point to some of the subjects which were absorbing public attention at this date.

CAMBRIDGE, *Mar.* 11, 1848.

My dear...

...... My time has been occupied by sending circulars, by way of securing a Petition from the University against the popish proceedings in Parliament. Most of the people here are apathetic or else favourable to Romanism, and the few therefore who retain anything like true opinion are obliged to rouse: the one party and oppose the other. My hope is that the *rows* going on in the world may awaken *some:* mark my words, you will see *Irish Papists* at the head of every un-English row that occurs, whether in London, Manchester, Glasgow or elsewhere. Robert M'Ghee observed to me years ago, that we should never know the extent of *Irish* treason and disaffection until some social row occurred; and then we should see the meaning of having Papists in Glasgow, Manchester, &c.

Your loving Uncle,
G. E. CORRIE.

The following letters are to his previous correspondent Mr —— on various subjects of interest and importance.

CAMBRIDGE, *April* 4, 1849.

Dear Mr ——,

It seems to me that a school without authority, only ministers to the bad passions of fallen nature, and I have therefore no hesitation in saying, that you had better either burn your school-books or enforce them without respect of persons. If I may judge from the experience of many years in this place, an empty school would be a blessing, compared with the evil done by suffering the disobedient to follow the promptings of a disorderly heart. You cannot compel parents to send their children to you, but you may cause them to respect you, by asserting the importance of giving up the Sunday to God.

2. As regards your non-juring difficulties, I think you lose much of this short life in hunting out for scruples. Unless you have reason to know the contrary, you would do well to take for granted that by the permission of Divine Providence (not to say the direct intervention of God) the Revolution of 1688 was for God's glory, and so a subject of thanksgiving in all ages. Else, you ought to deprecate, if not anathematise, the Americans and others. As regards the question of the Revolution itself however, the principles laid down by the English Convocation in the reign of James I. were (in justification of the casting-off of the Spanish yoke by the Netherlands), "If any man affirm that when new forms of government, begun by rebellion, are afterwards thoroughly settled, the authority in them is not of God, he doth greatly err" (Overall's Convocation Book, Lib. I. Can. 23). Do you believe this? Sancroft (Archbp.), though a non-juror, put forth those Canons for the guidance of the Clergy at the Revolution, although, with much inconsistency, he declined to act out his belief. He swallowed the camel, but strained at the gnat.

3. Now, though I have no respect for the actors in the Revolution of 1688, I have as little for James II. The following is the Oath he took at his Coronation.

Archbishop. "Sir, will you grant and keep and by your Oath confirm to the people of England the Laws and Customs to them granted by the Kings of England your Lawful and Religious Predecessors; and namely, the Laws and Customs and Franchises granted to the Clergy by the glorious King St Edward [the Confessor] your Predecessor, according to the Laws of God, the true profession of the Gospel established in this Kingdom, agreeable to the Prerogatives of the Kings thereof, and the Ancient Customs of the Realm?"

King. "I grant and promise to keep them."

Archbp. "Sir, will you keep peace and godly agreement (according to your power) both to God, the holy Church, the Clergy and the People?"

King. "I will keep it."

Archbp. "Sir, will you to your power cause Law, Justice and Discretion in mercy and truth to be executed to your judgement?"

King. "I will."

Archbp. "Sir, will you grant to hold and keep the Laws and rightful Customs which the Commonalty of this your Kingdom have, and will you defend and uphold them to the honour of God, so much as in you lies?"

King. "I grant and promise so to do."

(The Book of Oaths, pp. 260 and 261.)

Now compare this Oath with *any* history of the reign of James II. that may fall in your way; and then read over the service for the 5th of November. It is remarkable enough also, that one of the Laws of "the glorious King St Edward" is "Rex autem qui Vicarius est Summi Regis, ad hoc constitutus est, ut regnum et populum Domini, et super omnia sanctam Ecclesiam regat et defendat ab injuriosis. Quod nisi fecerit (if he *fail* in *that*) nomen regis perdit."

If, therefore, you would only inform yourself, you might form but a poor opinion of the Whigs either at the Revolution or at any other time, yet you would see that the

Bishops and Clergy, by whom the Revolution was really effected, were not such reckless time-servers as *your scruples* take for granted.

4. Let me, in fine, observe, that as I have nothing more to say, *pro* or *con*, touching this said Revolution (of which so much is said and so little understood), you need not be surprised if I hereafter regard your scruples on that point as things of naught ; or rather, unwholesome vapours issuing out of the lack of that vigour of practical godliness which, by growing daily, becomes an answer to all scrupulous objections to the great facts of God's kingdom upon earth.

Thus I abide, very truly your friend,

G. E. CORRIE.

CAMBRIDGE, *May* 3, 1849.

Dear Mr ——,

I forgot to say that Mr Clay's account of the *Prayer-Book*[1] is an excellent synopsis of history : and would be useful to recommend and give away, now the *tercentenary* of the Prayer-Book is at hand.

Your sincere friend,

G. CORRIE.

As will be seen from the following words in reply to a friend who had asked his opinion on points of Sunday-school teaching, he strongly deprecated losing the precious hour of Sunday-school instruction in amusements, although he willingly provided Scripture illustrations for the little ones.

3. Touching pictures, I should much prefer teaching the *Scriptures* themselves, either orally or by book. It is impossible to separate amusement from pictures, and who would think of *amusing* children into the knowledge and practice of the will of God? The idea is that of the *religion of human nature.*

Your sincere friend,

G. E. CORRIE.

---

[1] The Book of Common Prayer Illustrated, by W. K. Clay, B.D. J. W. Parker, 1841.

Dear Mr ———,

It has never appeared to me worth while to puzzle myself with the *probable reasons* for the change of day as regards the Sabbath, because I do not think the 4th Commandment as interpreted by the Lawgiver himself, ever went further than, or stopped short of, the consecrating to God of a *seventh portion of our time*. The wording of the 4th Commandment sanctions this, and the admitted change of the day under the New Testament so interprets the Command. For my own part I have always been satisfied with the reasons given by Bishop Pearson for keeping the Christian Sunday; and as regards the case you mention of herdsmen, &c., it seems to me to be provided for in *spirit* at least by our Lord's observations, Luke xiii. 15. The *necessity* for a master keeping his servants *always* thus occupied, so as to debar them from God's worship, may be a question admitting of doubt, because in one's own case one can readily contrive to give all servants in turn the opportunity for going to Church. Yet I do not see that you could do half so much good by denouncing the masters as Sabbath-breakers, as by instilling into them the great Christian truth that they are responsible for the souls as well as bodies of all whom God's Providence may have committed to their rule.

...If you mean to secure peace and steadiness in duty, you must rise above that carefulness and troubling, which seems to haunt you, because the people of your parish do not at present manifest that fruit of your labours among them, which the natural heart so earnestly covets to witness. It is but seldom that we are permitted to do more than lament our own inefficiency, with the earnest steady aim to give ourselves wholly to the service of God, in proportion to the deadness and carelessness that may prevail around. We may not lose sight too of that awful, but infallible truth, that our own ministry will oftentimes have no other effect than to become "the savour of death unto death." My advice therefore, is not to trouble yourself about reasons for the change of the Sabbath, &c., but to set yourself earnestly to make *every day a sabbath of rest in God* to the people to whom you minister. Your eyes will never see that great object achieved, but no lower object should be your aim, first of all making yourself a pattern to your flock in steadfastness of purpose in duty, in the mortification of all natural tempers and habits which hinder the growth of the soul in holiness and self-devotion.

Your sincere friend,
G. E. CORRIE.

LEAMINGTON, *May* 9, 1850.

Dear Mr ——,

I understand by Rom. xiv. 5, 6, Gal. iv. 10, Col. ii. 16, what the Church of Christ has always understood by those passages, viz. that the Apostle is speaking of the Jewish Festivals generally. This is indeed manifest from Gal. iv. 10 and Col. ii. 16, in the latter passage of which he mentions the "Sabbath," which points to the very question at issue, viz. the observance of the Jewish Sabbath, as distinguished from the Christian Lord's day. Now every tiro in Church History knows that this sabbatizing was amongst the last lingerings of Judaical weaknesses that remained to the Christian Church down to the middle of the second century. When I spoke of the "change of the Sabbath," I alluded to the fact that whilst in the first instance, the setting apart the seventh day was "because God rested from all His works," in the second (Deut. v. 15) it was to commemorate the deliverance out of Egypt, from which day afterwards the seventh day was reckoned. As respects the obligatory nature of the fourth Commandment, I presume that every Christian ought to demand, "Why is the fourth Commandment less binding than the first?" For in strictness the first Commandment might be said to relate to the Jehovah of Israel, and not to the Triune God as revealed to Christians, and on your principle (viz. that of demanding a proof of the obligation of the Sabbath now) can only forbid idolatry indirectly (if at all) under the Christian dispensation. At the time the first Commandment was given, God in Christ was not specifically declared, and so the Jews (on your principle) may charge us as Christians with a breach of the first Commandment, as they do regard us as guilty of a breach of the fourth, since we do not hallow Saturday. On the other hand, the fourth Commandment, inculcating no more than the hallowing of the seventh day, but strictly inculcating a giving up of a seventh portion of our time to God, can never cease to oblige, on whatever day that seventh may fall, any more than the first Commandment can cease to oblige, under whatever Name and attributes the true God may be revealed. And as the exact day from which the seventh day was first reckoned has been once changed, so may it again be changed if God so order, and yet the fourth Commandment be strictly observed in that change. But, putting all these considerations aside, it may be asked, 'By what Scripture is it proved that any of the ten Commandments have been abrogated?' From first to last they are moral and not ceremonial, and therefore if ever true and binding, must be so for *ever:* and it is remarkable enough that the only one of the Commandments which even seemed to have any local and temporary bearing (viz. the fifth) is expressly quoted by St Paul as binding on Christians (Eph. vi. 3), and therefore *a fortiori,* &c.

2.   My space, as the necessity of the case, does not admit of my going over the question of Baptism. If you will but look at the pre-requisites demanded in order to Baptism, then common sense will shew you that all that is said of the effects resulting from Baptism takes for granted that such pre-requisites exist in the party baptized. As however neither yourself nor any other Minister is endued with the discernment of spirits, you must pronounce and speak the same language to *all* the baptized—i.e. the language of charitable construction. Nor need you hesitate so to pronounce and

speak, because the responsibility of its being true or not in individual cases does not rest with you, but with the parties seeking baptism.   You know that all Christ's promises "He will most surely keep and perform," and you in His name therefore, speak without hesitation, leaving others, "for their parts," &c. as the service teaches.   Reduce your service to the *one* sentence, viz. "N. I baptize thee in the Name of the Father," &c., and add neither prayer nor exhortation, still you would have to answer the question, Into what did you baptize N.?   Of course you could only answer, Into the Church of Christ.   Then you would have to answer the second question, "Is the Church a Congregation of unregenerate, unadopted, unsanctified persons: or a Congregation of faithful men?"   Of course you could only answer again, "A Congregation of faithful men."   Then the use of that single sentence, "N. I baptize thee," &c., would be to all intents and purposes as manifest a declaration that the party so baptized was regenerate by God's Holy Spirit, and received for His own child by adoption, "and incorporated into Christ's holy Church," as you could possibly make by the use of many words.   All you have to bear in mind is that these characteristics can belong to none who are not members of Christ's Visible Church; and, as God our Saviour has instituted Baptism as the Sacrament of admission into His Church, it follows that such characteristics are naturally and necessarily connected with Baptism as rightly received.   But then, as you *can* never know who "rightly" receives that Sacrament, you must pronounce on *all alike*, if you baptize at all.

Your sincere friend,

G. CORRIE.

CAMBRIDGE, 30 *Nov.*, 1850.

Dear Mr ——,

... As regards the Queen being the fountain of power, that does not touch the Scotch Bishops, because they do not derive their secular position from a *foreign* Prince, but from their own congregations, just as the Wesleyans do. Those congregations do not do more than place *themselves* under a Bishop, who claims no power to judge by a foreign law, but by rules which the Law of England admits to be inoffensive.

Your sincere friend,

G. E. CORRIE.

CHAPTER XII.

Mr Corrie's long connection with St Catharine's College
was now drawing to a close. His Tutorial life, including the
time during which he was Assistant-Tutor with Dr Turton,
extended over more than thirty-two years.

Dr French, Master of Jesus College, Cambridge, died in
November, 1849. The Mastership was then in the gift of
Dr Turton, as Bishop of Ely, who at once offered it to
Mr Corrie, and on receiving his acceptance of it, wrote,
"Your determination to accept the Mastership has delighted
me beyond expression; you are the very man for the post.
By all means retain your Chaplaincy, I shall be much obliged
to you for so doing."

The Fellows of Jesus College called on Mr Corrie, expressing their satisfaction at his appointment, and assuring
him of a cordial welcome whenever he should be able to
come amongst them.

The Bishop wrote, "It is a great gratification to me to
learn that your appointment to the Mastership is so well
received by the Society over which you will have to preside.
My hope and belief is that it will tend to good in the University, as well as in the College. So may it be!"

Mr Corrie writes to his old friend (the late) Canon Harvey of Gloucester. "It is most pleasant to find my oldest friends among the earliest and most hearty of those who have been kind enough to congratulate me on my appointment. But your friendship will have performed but a small part of its office if you forget to commend me to the protection of our redeeming God, by whose strength alone I can stand upright in that new path which lies before me."

From numerous kind and hearty congratulatory letters which were received by Mr Corrie, a few extracts are given.

QUEENS' LODGE, *Nov. 24th,* 1849,

My dear Master,

It was with infinite pleasure that I read to-day, in the Cambridge paper, your appointment to the Mastership of Jesus College. I most heartily congratulate you on the event, which I am sure will be no less in accordance with the feelings of the Senate than my own, for they, as far as I can learn, in common with myself, concur in thinking that your experience among the Heads of Colleges will be most valuable and important.

Again offering you my warmest congratulations, in which Mrs King desires to join,

I am, my dear Master, yours very faithfully,

JOSHUA KING.

From Dr Wordsworth, then Canon of Westminster, afterwards Bishop of Lincoln.

CLOISTERS, WESTMINSTER, *Nov.* 24, 1849.

My dear Master,

I hope you will kindly allow me to express the great pleasure, with which I have heard of your appointment to the Mastership of Jesus College. Both on public and private grounds, I beg leave to offer my sincere congratulations, and to unite with many in the earnest prayer that you may be long preserved in health and strength to the College, the University, and the Church.

I am, my dear Master, yours very faithfully,

CHR. WORDSWORTH.

From the Rev. C. J. Ellicott, now Bishop of Gloucester and Bristol.

LYNDON, UPPINGHAM, *Nov.* 26.

Dear Professor Corrie,

I trust I am not precipitate in sending you my most hearty and most cordial congratulations on your new appointment. I have not (living here in the wilds) seen it officially announced, but private letters from Cambridge, and an eager desire to be one of the first of your outlying friends to congratulate you, urge me to this early letter.   Many, many years of health and happiness to you, my dear Professor,

And believe me, yours very sincerely,

C. J. ELLICOTT.

KING EDWARD'S SCHOOL, BIRMINGHAM, *Nov.* 20, 1849.

My dear Professor,

The immediate object of my letter is to express the pleasure it has given me to hear that you have accepted the Mastership of Jesus.   I am much pleased to find that it is not on the whole disagreeable to you to migrate, though I can well understand that it is not without much mixed feeling that you leave our venerable Hall.   What a blessing that you can look back with so much comfort to your residence and labours in it.   Yes, my dear friend, though I can well understand that your own feelings will be those of humiliation rather than of exaltation, yet let me, as having been among the first batch of youths that entered under your Tutorship, thank you, for myself, and my compeers, and my successors in that relation, for the example, advice and influence for which we have been indebted to you.   And may God largely bless you in the new post of comparative leisure, but happily still more extended influence, to which He has Himself called you.   I shall hope to hear that the groves and gardens of Jesus are favourable to your health, and may you enjoy many years of happy usefulness.

Believe me, your very sincere friend,

SYDNEY GEDGE.

From the late Rev. T. Crick, formerly Public Orator.

STAPLEHURST, KENT, *Nov.* 26, 1849.

My dear Mr Professor,

I cannot allow the announcement of an event so important to your own happiness, and to the interests of our University, as that which has just caught my eye, to pass without a word of comment or congratulation to yourself and to Alma Mater. Most sincerely do I rejoice in any revolution of fortune's wheel that bears an increase of happiness or of comfort to those whom I respect and esteem. But my joy is greatly increased when such contingent good to my friends is also an accession of strength to our time-honoured Institutions. You will be told by many, but by no one with more sincerity than by me, that I consider our University greatly indebted to any experienced *Palinurus* who will undertake to navigate any of her craft in such a tempestuous sea ......Accept, my dear friend, my sincere wishes that you may be spared many years to adorn by your uprightness, enlighten by your counsel, and restrain by your sobriety, the Institution over which you are called to preside. ......God bless you.

Yours very sincerely,

T. CRICK.

From the late Rev. Henry John Rose.

I rejoice on your appointment on your own account most sincerely as one of your old and warmest friends, but I may truly add that I rejoice even more on account of the advantages which I believe likely to flow from your appointment to the best interests of our University. I believe that you are peculiarly fitted for the station to which it has pleased God in His Providence to call you, and I sincerely pray that He, who has placed you there, may give you health and strength to bring to effect all the good purposes which I fully believe you to have already matured in your own mind. I feel, too, that from your knowledge of the University you are particularly calculated to assist in resisting evil designs, which will not be wanting ere long, against the better portion of our academical institutions. God bless you.

Yours affectionately,

HENRY JOHN ROSE.

The Rev. R. Dixon writes:

THE COLLEGE, ISLE OF MAN, *Dec.* 17, 1849.

My dear Mr Corrie,

......Allow me to congratulate you most sincerely, on your appointment to the Mastership of Jesus College........ I rejoice that, in these days, your influence will be increased ; because I feel persuaded that you will exercise it to promote the cause of Truth, and to uphold the distinctive doctrines of Church of England Protestantism. May God give you an increase of the spirit of power, and of love and of a sound mind, and if it please Him, may you long enjoy this honourable retreat from the cares of Tutorship.

I am, my dear Mr Corrie, most faithfully yours,

R. DIXON.

It was not only with expressions of affectionate congratulations that Mr Corrie's friends at St Catharine's contented themselves; they were anxious that their feelings should take some permanent form. This was made known to him by the Master of St Catharine's in the following letter.

CATHARINE LODGE, *April* 27, 1850.

Dear Master of Jesus,

I have the gratification of announcing to you, in the name of the undermentioned Committee, that a large number of graduates of St Catharine's Hall, who have been your pupils, being desirous of giving expression to their sentiments of respect and affection for you on the occasion of your ceasing to be Tutor of the College, have joined together to provide, and offer to your acceptance, some suitable and permanent memorial of regard.

Contributions for this purpose to the amount of about £160 have been received from 121 persons. The Committee, to whom the determination of the nature of the memorial has been entrusted, are desirous of consulting your wishes on the subject, feeling assured that whatever form of memorial is most acceptable to you will be most desired by the contributors to the fund.

I am, dear Master, yours very truly,

H. PHILPOTT.

Committee :

Master of St Catharine's Hall (Chairman).	Rev. F. Proctor.
	C. W. Goodwin, Esq.
Dr Ranking.	Rev. D. Moore.
Rev. Professor Jarrett.	Rev. C. Hardwick.
R. C. Hildyard, Esq., M.P.	W. Ogle, Esq.
Rev. S. T. Rusby.	Rev. J. S. Purton (Treasurer).
Rev. S. Gedge (Secretary).	J. Milner, Esq.
Rev. R. Blakelock.	

Mr Corrie thus replied.

JESUS COLLEGE, *April* 28, 1850.

Dear Master of St Catharine's,

I cannot but very deeply feel my obligations to the kindness of yourself and my other pupil friends of St Catharine's Hall, for having united as you have done to offer for my acceptance some memorial of respect and affection. I trust that it would be unnecessary for me to assure you and them that in whatever form such an expression of regard might be presented to me, it would be both gratefully accepted and highly valued. As, however, the Committee to whose determination the nature of the Memorial has been entrusted have been kind enough to allow me a voice in their decision, I venture to suggest that the contributions of my friends should be set apart for the purpose of founding a Divinity Prize within the College in which we were educated. By this means my own feelings would be much gratified in that my name would thus be still connected with a Society to which I owe so much, and, what is perhaps of more consequence, the remembrance of our mutual regard would be secure of being kept alive for time to come, and our Old House be permanently benefited.

Believe me yours sincerely,

G. E. CORRIE.

Mr Corrie had been for some time engaged upon an edition of the *Homilies* which was published in this year, in the preparation of which for the University Press he again received valuable assistance from Mr Hardwick; the following letter from whom, while containing reference to the above publication, gives expression to the deep solicitude felt by so many members of the University relative to the approaching Commission.

ST CATHARINE'S HALL, CAMBRIDGE, 3 *May*, 1850.

My dear Master of Jesus,

I enclose a sheet of the *Homilies*, which has been for some time awaiting your return to Cambridge. I thought you would wish me to do so, although the unsatisfactory account of your health has hitherto dissuaded me from troubling you. I am very sorry to find that your Vacation has in the least degree unhinged you, and shall rejoice in concert with a number of others when I see you back among us. The crisis in our University history adds a public to a private reason for the expression of this wish, there being just now a very crying necessity of advocacy like your own. After much hesitation, and not without much misgiving, I have signed the requisition put forth by the Heads of Houses. I saw no alternative, and was unwilling to be confounded with our University Reformers, a few of whom are taking steps to invite an executive commission. I have since been confirmed in the propriety of my signature by the information that your name is among the Heads of Houses who have signified their general assent to the grounds of the Requisition. By the way, may I suggest that a new edition of your pamphlet on the subject of Royal Interference would be very timely? If your engagements should prevent you from superintending the publication, I am entirely at your service.

Believe me, dear Master of Jesus,

Very faithfully yours,

C. HARDWICK.

Mr Corrie was Vice-Chancellor during the academical year 1850—1851. In addition to the usual responsibilities of the office, the grave subjects in connection with the University Commission claimed his anxious attention. He contemplated the impending changes with serious apprehension, opposed as he felt them to be to long-tried principles and to his own experience. On the eve of entering on his duties he wrote thus:

CAMBRIDGE, Nov. 1850.

Dear Mr ——,

I shall much need your prayers, for my year of office is likely to be a year of trial. In the meanwhile, I desire only to be made instrumental for the good of our University, and in that for God's glory.

Your sincere friend,

G. CORRIE.

The following was his reply to the inquiries issued by the Commission:

CAMBRIDGE, Dec. 2, 1850.

My Lord and Gentlemen,

After having ascertained from high legal authority that the University Commission is without the force of Law, and is moreover regarded as unconstitutional, and of a kind that was never issued except in the worst times, I feel obliged by a sense of public duty to decline answering any of the questions which I had the honor to receive from you a short time ago.

I have the honor to be,

Your faithful Servant,

G. E. CORRIE.

It had been Mr Corrie's desire since the death of his brothers that ultimately his widowed sister, her son and daughter, should make their home with him. His own removal to Jesus College enabled him to fulfil this cherished wish, and thus his house became the centre of their family life.

A further enlargement of interest awaited him, and one most congenial to him as a clergyman. The important rectory of Newton in the Isle of Ely became vacant on the death of Mr Whiteford. The Bishop of Ely, as Patron, expressed in the following letter his earnest desire that Mr Corrie should accept the living:

DOVER STREET, 21 Mar. 1851.

My dear Mr Vice-Chancellor,

......I know how disinterested you are in such matters, but I consider that the Mastership of Jesus is not sufficient of itself, and that it becomes me to do something towards maintaining your position there. All preceding Masters, so far as I know, have held preferment of one kind or another; and I do not see why you should not do the same. Moreover, I am an old man; and this may be the only piece of preferment which it may be in my power to offer. I beg therefore that you will consider whether you can induce yourself to take Newton in the Isle. It is the choicest living in my gift; and it ought to be held by a person of some consequence. I will only add—what yet is needless—that your accepting this preferment will very much oblige me.

Yours very faithfully,
T. ELY.

Once more, do not, I most earnestly entreat you, refuse this offer.

This kind offer he declined, fearing that College duties would prevent his doing justice to the parish. This view, however, was overruled by the Bishop, who in another letter urged upon him his reasons for renewing the offer of the living:

ELY HOUSE, LONDON, *Mar.* 22.

My dear Mr Vice-Chancellor,

.........One great object with me is to introduce a higher tone of thinking and feeling on the subject of Clerical Duty, &c., and I verily believe that you will be able to effect that most desirable improvement in a district which at present I never think of without pain. The foregoing considerations have so much weight with me, that I cannot suppose them to be of little consequence in your estimation. After all I have now stated, I trust that you will not hesitate to take the living.   Yours faithfully,

T. ELY.

These reasons prevailed, and the living was accepted. The Bishop thus expressed his satisfaction:

ELY HOUSE, LONDON, 25 *March*, 1851.

My dear Mr Vice-Chancellor,

Your letter is the kind of letter which I expected you would write. It pleases me much, and I am glad you have accepted the living....... Believe me, yours faithfully,

T. ELY.

The following letter is addressed to the Manager of the Great Eastern Railway, in deprecation of railway excursion trains coming into Cambridge on Sundays:

CAMBRIDGE, 1 *May*, 1851.

Sir,

I am sorry to find that the Directors of the Eastern Counties Railway have made arrangements for conveying foreigners and others to Cambridge on *Sundays* at such fares as may be likely to tempt persons who, having no regard for

Sunday themselves, would inflict their presence on this University on that day of rest. I should be obliged therefore, by your making it known to the Directors that such arrangements as those contemplated by them are as distasteful to the authorities of the University, as they must be offensive to Almighty God and to all right-minded Christians.

I have the honor to be Sir,

Your obedient servant,

G. E. CORRIE,

Vice-Chancellor of Cambridge.

In May 1851, the governing body of King's College passed a resolution which gave up the "present practice of claiming for the Undergraduates of the College the degree of B.A. without passing the examinations required by the University[1]." This information was communicated to Dr Corrie as Vice-Chancellor by the Provost of King's, Dr Okes, and the following is Dr Corrie's reply.

JESUS COLLEGE, 1 *May*, 1851.

My dear Provost,

I beg to acknowledge the receipt of the document from your Society, by which you relinquish for yourselves and your successors the ancient and acknowledged privilege in accordance with which the Undergraduate Fellows of King's College have been accustomed to claim and to receive the Degree of Bachelor of Arts, without having undergone the examinations prescribed by the University for the Undergraduates of all other Colleges.

It will be my duty to inform the Senate of this important decision of your Society, and I doubt not but that the University at large will deeply appreciate the public spirit and high principle by which yourself and the Fellows of King's have been actuated. Believe me to be,

My dear Provost, very truly yours,

G. E. CORRIE,

Vice-Chancellor.

---

[1] See *Memoirs* of Henry Bradshaw, page 21.

Mr Corrie was admitted to the degree of D.D. Oct. 25, 1852, by his friend Dr Okes, late Provost of King's College, who succeeded Mr Corrie as Vice-Chancellor. Mr Corrie had proceeded to the degree of B.D. in 1831.

It was in complete sympathy with the spirit in which the Bishop had acted in presenting him to the living, that Mr Corrie undertook the charge of the Fen parish, with which his name was to be for so many years connected. He was happy in the appointment of a former pupil at St Catharine's, the Rev. J. W. Berryman, as his curate. He and Mrs Berryman devoted themselves heartily to the work before them, and during the eight years their valuable services were continued he felt them to be true fellow-workers with himself, in promoting the highest interests of the parish.

The village of Newton, about three miles from Wisbech, was situated in Marshland, westward of the river Nene; the parish extending further into the Fen, and containing at that time two other hamlets besides distant isolated houses, its length being about six miles.

The church, dedicated to St James, is a handsome one of the 13th century, and contains the tombs of many of the Colville family, formerly proprietors of the soil, one of whom, in the reign of Henry IV., founded a Chantry, with the chapel of St Mary-by-the-Sea, for a Warden and Chaplains. This Chantry being particularly excepted in the Act of Dissolution of Edward VI.'s reign, its lands became annexed to the rectory of Newton. The building was situated within the premises of the present rectory house, where remains of figured tiles and bricks still shew the position of a former floor and wall.

In external matters, the deplorable condition of the parish church first claimed Mr Corrie's attention. There being no School building, the vestry was used for both day and Sunday Schools. It was clear, therefore, that the building of a School House was the first thing to be undertaken. This was done at the rector's expense, who, with the exception of a small sum contributed annually by the parish, made himself responsible also for its maintenance.

With the hearty co-operation of the parishioners the restoration of the church was then entered upon.

A sum being borrowed upon the church rates, which was met by a grant of £42 towards the expenses of the church, from the Incorporated Society for Promoting the Enlargement of Churches and Chapels, on condition of a certain number of seats being secured for the poor, the repair of the nave and roof was proceeded with, and the body of the church re-seated, and an organ, the gift of the rector, was provided. The nave of the church, thus sufficiently restored for Divine worship, was re-opened in 1853. The parishioners welcomed the various plans set on foot for the welfare and improvement of their parish, while their rector's sympathy in all their interests won their affection and confidence. Very soon after Mr Corrie became rector of Newton the bishop, on the death of Mr Fardell, appointed him to the Rural Deanery of Wisbech, and he was thus enabled officially as well as personally to promote the bishop's earnest desires for the spiritual advancement of that part of the diocese. The scene of disorder and confusion on the occasion of one of his lordship's first confirmations, when, for instance, oranges were offered for sale at the open door of one of the churches during divine service, had been painfully impressed on the memories of both the bishop and his chaplain, and it was to open the way to a better state of things that their united efforts were now directed.

An early opportunity was taken, in co-operation with others, of re-establishing in Wisbech the Association of the Society for Promoting Christian Knowledge, which, though formerly in operation, had been allowed to languish.

At the same time an effort was made to bring the claims of Foreign Missions before the clergy of the district, and in 1853 a Church Missionary Association was formed for Wisbech and the neighbourhood.

It was about this time that the first break in the lately re-formed family circle occurred.

Miss Sherer's residence with her uncle was but for a short time ; never in strong health, consumption soon brought her life to a close. She died at Jesus College Lodge in the spring of 1853. Her uncle deeply felt the loss of her companionship, and thus refers to it in a note to his friend the late Provost of King's ....."I am desirous you should not hear by common rumour that it has pleased God to take my niece to His mercy in Christ Jesus. She died in great peace this morning, to our great grief, but, we trust, to her great consolation."

During this year Dr Corrie's edition of Nowell's *Catechism* was completed and published. This was the last volume he undertook for the Parker Society.

In 1854, having attained the age of sixty, Dr Corrie, acting in accordance with the existing regulations of the University, resigned the Norrisian Professorship of Divinity, which he had held since 1838. In connection with this office, he had not only proved himself a most earnest and diligent student of Theology, but had also devoted himself, with laborious and patient research, to the exposition of the Ecclesiastical History of England and Ireland in relation both to Romanism and Nonconformity. His Lectures on these subjects were much appreciated on account of the exact and impartial investigation and sound judgment brought to bear on them. In this capacity also opportunity was afforded, far beyond the limits of his own College, for the display of one of the most marked and attractive features of Dr Corrie's character, his sympathy with younger minds, which shewed itself in the readiness and patience with which he always endeavoured to place his own literary acquirements and experience at the service of any, who by his quick penetration he perceived would be likely to profit by them. In these respects, however, it need hardly be said his interest did not cease with his official responsibilities.

Dr Corrie was one of the Founders of the Cambridge Antiquarian Society, and, for some years, its President; and was a frequent contributor to its *Transactions*. He took a considerable interest in Ecclesiastical Architecture, and was invited to become President of the Cambridge Architectural Society. The following is his reply:

JESUS COLLEGE, CAMBRIDGE, Feb. 7, 1854.

Dear Sir,

I have considered the matter which yourself and Mr Woollaston were good enough to submit to me to-day, and I write to say that I shall have much pleasure in accepting the office of President of the Architectural Society, on condition that the Society adhere strictly to the object which its name implies. That object I conceive to be the encouragement of the study and practice, on correct principles, of Architecture; abstaining at the same time from anything and everything like those circumstances and acts, which acquired for the former Cambridge Camden Society the name and attributes of a sectarian association.

Believe me to remain yours truly,

G. E. CORRIE.

To the Secretary of the Cambridge
　　Architectural Society.

In 1856 the first election of members to the newly established Council of the Senate took place. Dr Corrie was one of the first members. The two following anecdotes relative to the matters dealt with by the Council will illustrate Dr Corrie's keen sense of the ridiculous combined with a certain dry humour.

At a Council Meeting a suggestion was made that there ought to be special places at St Mary's Church for the Members of the Council. Dr Corrie suggested, that the Vice-Chancellor occupying a central place, the other Sixteen Heads should sit each on a footstool at the feet of the Members of the Council, who should have chairs on each side of the Vice-Chancellor.

The other instance was when after the Council of the Senate

had resolved on establishing the New degree of Master of Laws (LL.M.) intermediate between those of Bachelor and Doctor, one of the Members proposed to do the like for the Faculty of Medicine by establishing a new degree of Master in Medicine, the abbreviated title (after the example of A.M. and LL.M.) to be M.M. "Yes," remarked Dr Corrie, "that will do—M.M. Memento Mori."

A further instance of his dry humour is shewn in Dr Corrie's criticism of Dr Donaldson's Book of Jasher, "In healthier times he would have been burnt as a heretic;" on this being reported to Dr Donaldson, he added to some pamphlet he was publishing, "It is sad that in these days there are those high in authority in the University ready to re-kindle the fires of Smithfield." Archdeacon Hardwick drew Dr Corrie's attention to this, who was very much amused with it, and begged the Archdeacon to set Dr Donaldson at rest, "as in these economical days he would not be considered worth the faggots!"

The same characteristics appear in the following, which is contributed by a friend :

Sir James Stephen had just published his Essays, in one of which he had said some startling things, especially, if I recollect right, on the eternity of future punishment. Dr Corrie meeting Archdeacon Hardwick, they got into conversation about the book, when Dr Corrie said, "Who would have thought we should have seen a live Gnostic walking about the streets of Cambridge? You know, my friend, in healthier times he would have been burnt."

The following letter on the alienation of College Property to the University concisely represents Dr Corrie's deliberate views on that subject :

JESUS COLLEGE, CAMBRIDGE, 25 *Oct.*, 1858.

Dear Mr ——,

As regards the Public Meeting to-morrow, one of the Resolutions which I have undertaken to move is, "That it is highly objectionable to tax the Colleges for University purposes, as proposed by the University Commissioners." And my reason for undertaking this is that College endowments were given for College purposes, and not for the use of the University as such : and as regards our own College I am required by our *Statutes* to take care that all our revenues are collected and dispensed for the use of the College and of the Fellows of the same. In the confidence that our revenues would always be disposed of according to our Statutes, our different Benefactors left us certain portions of their property, and I do not see how I could consent to the application of their property to University purposes without being guilty of a breach of trust, and of an abandonment of my Statutable duty to our College. I think, too, as a matter quite independent of personal considerations, that to consent to our Colleges being taxed for University purposes, as distinct from the directions of our several Benefactors, would be admitting a principle of more grave importance than at first sight appears. If you consent to tax Colleges for the University, why not for the support of students at the Dissenting and Popish Hostels that are to be set up at the University? Why not for the maintenance of National and Dissenting Schools? We might, in such cases, complain that our revenues were taxed for purposes which our Benefactors never contemplated in their Wills, but the answer would be, "You consented to set aside the directions and expressed purposes of your Benefactors by taxing your Colleges for the University: and by thus emancipating your revenues from the directions of those persons who gave them, you have set the revenues free for any purpose which may be deemed most advantageous for the State."

You must excuse me, therefore, for saying that this is *not* a question which "each individual must determine by the light of his own conscience and judgment," because it must be decided by the matter of fact whether or not our Benefactors contemplated the appropriation of their property to

College or to University purposes. Now as regards our Bene-factors, there is no doubt about the matter, and therefore for us to *consent* to the taxation contemplated by the Commis-sioners (much more if we voted for their scheme) would be to consent to a vote for the misappropriation of our Funds, and would therefore be a violation of our Corporate obliga-tions laid upon us under the sanction of an Oath.

What the Legislature may do hereafter by Act of Parlia-ment, is not for one moment to be regarded. An Act of Parliament might take away your private property and mine, if the rascality of the day demanded it. Consequences of that kind may safely be left to the decision of God's Pro-vidence. Simple, straightforward, present *duty* is all we have to think about.

Yours very truly,

G. E. CORRIE.

It was not long before Dr Corrie was called on to suffer still further bereavement. The society of his much loved nephew Henry Sherer was so congenial to him, and was so adapted to add happiness to his daily life, that it was a cause of great grief to his uncle when his health failed, and it became evident that he could not long be with them. He died in November, 1858. His aged mother did not long survive him; her death took place the following summer. Dr Corrie was thus deprived not only of his widowed sister, but of those whom he had good reason to hope would have cheered his advancing years[1]. Before the close of the same summer he sustained another serious loss in the deeply lamented accidental death of Archdeacon Hardwick in the Pyrenees. From undergraduate days at St Catharine's Col-lege he had looked up to Dr Corrie as his counsellor. Their close association in literary work, to which reference has already been made, strengthened their friendship, the

---

[1] Dr Corrie was not long alone. Miss Holroyd, the daughter of his old College friend came to him, and was joined by her sisters after their father's death, all remaining with Dr Corrie to the end of his life.

last proof of which on Dr Corrie's part was to become purchaser of the spot at Luchon in which the Archdeacon was interred, in order to secure from any disturbance the ground where his beloved friend's remains had been laid to rest.

Dr Corrie this year prepared an edition of Wheatly *On the Book of Common Prayer*, for the University Press. The assistance of the Rev. W. K. Clay, formerly Vicar of Waterbeach, is gratefully acknowledged in the Preface.

The first Church Congress was held at Cambridge in 1861, at which Dr Corrie was present, and read a paper.

The only other Church Congress which he attended was that at Leeds in 1872, he being then on a visit in that neighbourhood.

The following letters during the year 1863 are all that have been preserved of general interest at this time. They are addressed to the late Canon Harvey, of Gloucester, on different subjects. The first of them is written by him as Bishop's Chaplain :

CAMBRIDGE, 14 Feb. 1863.

My dear Harvey,

The Bishop's Secretaries have forwarded your letter to him respecting a letter which has appeared in the *Guardian* Newspaper, and since then in the *Cambridge Chronicle*. It appears to me, however, that the disrespectful and party-coloured tone of the letter in question will do no harm to anybody but the writer himself. For supposing all the circumstances to be as that writer states them, most people will be ready to give a Prelate, like the Bishop of Ely, some credit for wishing for an exchange of preferment on higher motives than a desire to perpetuate " sectarian preaching."

As a matter of fact the Bishop has never been "applied to by the Simeon Trustees" with respect to the exchange of Trinity Church, Cambridge, for Girton, nor has had any conversation with those Trustees. The proposal for an exchange of Benefices came from a private individual, and all negociations for such an exchange have been carried on solely with the law-agent of that individual. Since those negociations have been going on (for the business is now six or eight months old), it has been stated that the individual in question purposes to endow Trinity Church with an income of several hundreds a year, and then to make over the patronage to the Simeon Trustees; but with this the Bishop has had nothing to do one way or other.

The great object the Bishop has had in view has been to benefit the See of Ely in the matter of patronage, of which the Ecclesiastical Commissioners have robbed the Diocese to the extent of thirty-six livings, since the present Bishop came to the See.

That the contemplated exchange of patronage above mentioned would benefit the See in that respect, is evident enough, so far as money value goes, but more so when it is considered that the patronage of Trinity Church is so circumstanced, that the Bishops of Ely have not been and cannot be free agents in the disposal of it. The main part of the income of that church depends upon the same person being Incumbent and also Lecturer, the Lecturer being elected by the Parishioners, and carrying with him the endowment. However important, therefore, Trinity parish may be, as one among fourteen in Cambridge, the Lectureship, in the present state of things, will, as it has done, decide who is to be Incumbent, and what kind of preaching is to be "perpetuated." The transfer of the patronage will make no change in the latter respect, so long as the endowment rests with the Lecturer. On this ground it was that when the Bishop thought proper to mention to me the offer that had been made to his Lordship to exchange preferments, I took the liberty of stating that I thought "the patronage of Trinity Church the least desirable of any at the disposal of the See of Ely."

But I have done, after I have added that,

I am, my dear Harvey,

Very truly yours,

G. E. CORRIE.

29 *Oct.* 1863.

My dear Harvey,

As regards the Act of Uniformity, I think it would be well for you, as a member of any Committee for considering the subject, to master the Act itself. This you would not find it much trouble to do if you have access to the "Book of Common Prayer with Notes" as edited for the "Ecclesiastical History Society," by Archibald John Stephens; for in the first volume of that book he gives a full expository comment on that Act. The Bicentenary people put forth last year a volume of "Documents relating to the settlement of the Church of England by the Act of Uniformity in 1662," which gives their notions of the Act, in a documentary form, and shews in which way scruples lie: and I conclude your Committee will have to deal with scruples. On that point, indeed, it would amply suffice to refer to Dr Cardwell's account of the Savoy Conference in his "History of the Conferences respecting the Revision of the Book of Common Prayer."

When we have to consider the question of Subscription to Articles of Religion, I think you will find all that can reasonably be urged in Bishop Conybeare's "Discourse of Subscription to Articles of Religion," reprinted in Bishop Randolph's *Enchiridion Theologicum.* If we were called upon to read all that has been written on that subject we should have to wade through the controversy occasioned by Archdeacon Blackburn's Confessional, and the Feathers Tavern Tract of 1772. As a question for present consideration it has always appeared to me that the terms of Subscription required by the 36th Canon both to the Book of Common Prayer and the Thirty-nine Articles would answer every purpose and do away with many objections.

Believe me, dear Harvey,

To be very truly yours,

G. E. CORRIE.

CHAPTER XIII.

To return to the parochial matters which always occupied a large share of Dr Corrie's attention, his care was now especially directed to the Chancel of his church, which was in so dilapidated a state that it required to be rebuilt and reseated. This accomplished, some windows were placed in the chancel, in memory of Mrs Sherer, her son and daughter, by the rector, his surviving nephew, and other friends. Dr Corrie added the gift of a tower clock, and subsequently most of the windows in the aisles were restored by himself and a few friends interested in the church.

For the future, with the exception of a few visits in Northamptonshire, Yorkshire, and Scotland, Dr Corrie's time was entirely devoted to his College and his parish. The life at Newton was very congenial to one who so much enjoyed the freedom of the country. The rectory was a picturesque old house, to which he made some additions, without interfering with its unpretending character, which was in complete harmony with his own simple tastes and habits. The old-fashioned garden with its wealth of flowering shrubs and evergreens was a constant interest to him, while the numerous fine old trees surrounding the house and grounds were almost individually known to and nurtured by him.

After the morning passed in his study, much of his time was spent in seeing his parishioners, by whom he was always welcomed. He thus became well acquainted with their characters and wants. He enjoyed the confidence of the leading inhabitants, who felt that they had in him a friend on whom they could rely, and they willingly co-operated with him in his various efforts for the relief of the poor, and the general welfare of the parish. Their support was especially useful in a determined and successful effort made by the rector at a considerable expense to put down an attempt to establish a third public-house in the village.

Always mindful of the interests of the poor, he rebuilt two of the "Town Cottages," and repaired others, that the aged widows might be more comfortably housed than they could otherwise have been.

The efficiency of both Day and Sunday school was a matter of deep interest to him, and the former, receiving a fresh impetus when placed under Government inspection, never failed to secure a satisfactory report. The Sunday school was remarkably well attended by the children, not only of the labourers, but also of the farmers, whose families also cordially took a share in teaching. Great pains were bestowed by the rector in so selecting books for the teachers that each should be provided with a small compendium of Biblical literature suited both for their own personal instruction and intelligent preparation for their classes. At the happy annual School festivities it was his custom himself to present the children's prizes, always using the occasion for speaking a few simple words of counsel and encouragement.

In testimony that the attention thus given to the religious instruction of the children was not in vain, it may be permitted to quote the following from the Rev. F. H. Cox, rector of Elm :

"Dr Corrie will like to know that I have to-day (as one of the Voluntary Assistant Diocesan Inspectors) visited Newton School, and examined the children in their religious knowledge. I do not know when I have seen a more interesting School, or better evidence of thorough and careful teaching.

March 10, 1884."

During the winter months a night school was carried on, where the rector might occasionally be seen, with a group of boys around him, trying to direct their thoughts higher than their accustomed level.

A carefully selected library was also established for the use of the parishioners.

In the Cambridge and Isle of Ely Book-hawking Association Dr Corrie gladly recognized an admirable means of bringing sound literature within the reach of those who were not likely to seek it for themselves, and warmly encouraged its work in his Fen parish. He was a Vice-President of the Association, and also constantly present at its annual meetings, and both as Master of Jesus College and rector of Newton he gave it his cordial and liberal support.

The members of the women's Clothing Club looked forward with pleasure to their anniversary, on which occasion their rector always addressed to them words of pastoral advice, carefully prepared with a view to any parochial circumstances, and delivered with an affectionate solicitude for their improvement in family practical religion, and an intelligent sympathy in the trials of their lives, to which they often afterwards referred with surprise and gratitude.

After a succession of wet harvests, at the time when the agricultural depression was much felt by the farmers, Dr Corrie invited his parishioners to meet in the schoolroom before the commencement of harvest, for prayer, that God would grant His blessing on their coming labours, and vouchsafe a favourable season.

Himself a liberal supporter of the Church Missionary Society, of which, as well as of the Cambridge and Wisbech

Associations, he was a Vice-President, he endeavoured by example and precept to point out to his people the privilege and blessing of sharing in the work of sending the Gospel to the heathen. By the circulation of the publications of the Society, as well as by the Annual Sermons and Meeting, information was supplied regarding the work, with the view of promoting an intelligent and permanent interest in the subject; and an annual sale of work in the rectory garden—the result of parochial working parties—was looked forward to with much interest, and furnished a material part of the annual remittance.

His parochial sermons were always written, though usually amplified in delivery. Plain, and often homely, they always set forth definite Scripture truths in language which could not fail to be understood, but with a methodical arrangement which denoted something of the careful study and attention given to the preparation of his subject. The character of his teaching cannot be better described than by quoting the words of the Master of Corpus Christi College, from the Sermon preached by him in Trinity Church, Cambridge, the Sunday evening after Dr Corrie's death, and which referring as they do to the whole of his ministerial life it may be allowable to make use of. Intimately acquainted as Dr E. H. Perowne had been with Dr Corrie for many years, and closely associated with him in many ways during a part of Dr Corrie's active life, he with an almost filial affection, during the long period of gradual decline, devoted himself to assist and soothe him, and as the end drew near, was constantly at hand to minister to his spiritual and temporal requirements, to Dr Corrie's great comfort. He was thus well-qualified to bear the testimony contained in the following extract:

"When, yet in the full activity of mind and body, he became Incumbent of a country parish, he devoted himself to his duties as a pastor, not merely conscientiously and sedulously, but with the most loving devotion to his charge. It may indeed be said of him, as of good old John Berridge, 'he loved his Master and His work.' Not in the pulpit only, but in the cottage and in the school, he spoke to his people the Word of God. At a time when, owing to advancing years, many men might have sought rest by withdrawing from public ministrations, he persevered in what was the dearest occupation of his life. Unable from failing sight any longer to prepare written sermons—a task to which he always devoted time and labour—for he used to say in reference to this that he would not offer to the Lord that which cost him nothing—he still spent hours in prayer and meditation every week, that he might come forth on the Lord's day in the fulness of ripe experience and vast stores of reading to explain the Scriptures to his flock, and to proclaim the gospel of the grace of God. He was no mere professional clergyman. He preached, because he knew and valued, the truth as it is in Jesus."

From the time Dr Corrie entered on the office of Rural Dean (the Isle of Ely being exempt from Archidiaconal Visitation)—he never failed to act on Bishop Turton's desire that something effectual might be done for that part of the Diocese which his Lordship "never thought of without pain." Every opportunity was taken by Dr Corrie of obtaining information as to the circumstances of each parish, so as to be prepared to bring plans before the Bishop for increasing the parochial provision of the district as occasion offered. The following letter opens the subject with regard to the parish of Elm-cum-Emneth.

Oct. 10, 1857.

My dear Lord,

The Vicarage of Elm-cum-Emneth having become vacant by the death of the Rev. J. J., I think it my duty to call your Lordship's attention to the great importance of taking advantage of recent Acts of the Legislature for the purpose of obtaining for the inhabitants of those united parishes that spiritual superintendence, which in the present state. of things it is physically impossible to secure to them, but which the Parishioners feel that the large Ecclesiastical revenues annually derived from their Parishes, in common justice entitle them to demand.

That your Lordship may be in circumstances to judge of the urgency of the case, I beg leave to state for your information that the Parish of Elm contains by estimation, 11,050 acres, with a population of 1819 according to the last census. Of this population about 600 are located at a kind of hamlet called Friday-bridge, distant nearly two miles from the parish church : besides a considerable population scattered up and down in places varying from three to six miles from the church. But besides the superficial distance of the population from the parish church, the difficulty of obtaining access to the Services of religion is greatly increased by the nature of the country. A glance at the map accompanying this will shew that the parish of Elm, like every other Fen parish, is intersected by a great number of roads or droves (as they are called), on each side of which are wide deep ditches, which serve for the drainage of the parish, so that localities that appear to be immediately contiguous to each other, are in fact completely separated.   Indeed it is not possible for persons not resident in this portion of England to understand how completely ditches, cross-roads over fen-soils, wide artificial cuts or drains, and other like physical obstacles to locomotion interfere with the possibility of attending Divine Services, in the case of those who live at what seems by the map to be at but a moderate distance from the parish church.

The same causes which operate against the practicability of a population attending the Services of religion of course render it impracticable for a clergyman to afford his distant parishioners that regular spiritual and temporal supervision which they require and are entitled to.   As regards Elm there is also a population, at this present time, of from 200 to 300 scattered within a circuit of two miles around a locality known as Pear-tree Hill, which is (so far as the Church is concerned) totally destitute of public means of grace. To supply an effectual remedy to this unsatisfactory state of things, nothing can suffice but the establishment of regular Sunday services in those parts of the parish of Elm which are remote from the church; and happily there need be no difficulty in procuring such services, if but common justice is done to the people, for, out of the present united parishes, four separate Ecclesiastical Districts might and ought to be formed.

1st, *Elm*, to which might be assigned the care of the present population, exclusive of those living at and contiguous to Friday Bridge.

2nd, *Friday Bridge*, to which might be assigned the care of the population living at and contiguous to that locality.

3rd, *Pear-tree Hill*, with the care of all the population contiguous to that locality, and spread over the extreme southern part of the parish. The population is now between 300 and 400, and on the increase, for farm-houses and premises are being built, up and down.

4th *Emneth*, with its population of 1092 souls, spread over 3390 acres.

I ventured to assert above, that to secure effectual spiritual ministrations for this large and spiritually neglected district, need involve no difficulty, since the Tithes belonging to the Vicar of Elm were commuted at £638. 11*s*. 7*d*. per annum; and those of the Vicar of Emneth at £215 per annum, these together amount to £853. 11*s*. 7*d*.; the Rectorial Tithes of Elm were commuted at £1650. 7*s*. 5*d*., and those of Emneth at £545, which together make £2195. 7*s*. 5*d*. All the Rectorial Tithes of both lordships being now payable to the Ecclesiastical Commissioners, it is not easy to see to what purpose so large an income can be more properly applied, than to the effectual removal of that spiritual destitution of which the inhabitants of the united parishes of Elm-cum-Emneth so loudly and justly complain. The facilities for effecting such removal are, also, many.   There is a noble Church at Elm, and also at Emneth.   There is a good Vicarage House at Elm, and the Ecclesiastical Commissioners possess a Rectory House at Emneth, which might be made over to an incumbent.

Towards the erection of a Church at Friday-Bridge, and of another at Pear-tree Hill, I have been told by an influential inhabitant that a considerable sum would be subscribed, "if the Ecclesiastical Commissioners could be induced to supply competent endowments."   But at any rate there would be no difficulty in obtaining the use of buildings already existing, for Divine Service, until proper churches could be erected.   Both the Vicar of Wisbech and the Rector of Tyd St Mary's, have tried the experiment with regard to outlying portions of their respective parishes, and have found the people ready to lend them barns, and to further the efforts of the clergyman in every way.

I will not, in conclusion, apologise to your Lordship for the length of this communication, because I am well aware that the spiritual destitution of this portion of your diocese has long engaged your most anxious thoughts, especially when taken in connection with the abundant Ecclesiastical resources, by means of which that destitution might at once and effectually be relieved.   My hope, however, is that the Ecclesiastical Commissioners may at length be induced to carry out this plan with respect to Elm-cum-Emneth.

Believe me to be,

Your Lordship's faithful Servant,

G. E. CORRIE.

In a letter to Dr Corrie, Dec. 17, 1857, Bishop Turton says, "A strong memorial, respecting Elm and Emneth, has been laid before the Ecclesiastical Commissioners.   It was founded on your letter to me.   I shall doubtless hear something about it."

The plan proposed, so far as the division of the parishes of Elm and Emneth, and the formation of the parishes of

Friday Bridge and Pear-tree Hill (now Coldham), was subsequently effected[1].

The somewhat sudden death of the aged Bishop Turton, in 1864, terminated on earth a friendship which had been interwoven with Dr Corrie's life from his undergraduate days, and which, in the strong mutual respect and affection which characterized it, made their various official connections a source of much pleasure and satisfaction to both.

With the death of the Bishop, Dr Corrie's commission as Rural Dean naturally expired, to be renewed, however, by the desire of his successor, Bishop Harold Browne, who acknowledged in the kindest terms Dr Corrie's expression of willingness to retain the office.

Bishop Harold Browne, now Bishop of Winchester, was no less anxious than Bishop Turton to provide for the spiritual needs of the Isle of Ely; and the following extract from a sermon preached by the Rev. Canon Hopkins, Vicar of Littleport, at the opening of Thorney Toll Mission Church, in the parish of Guyhirne, in the Deanery of Wisbech, gives an account of various improvements carried out for this purpose. It may be noted that no schemes were ever laid before the Bishop by Dr Corrie without previous careful personal inspection of the localities under consideration:

"Looking back to the year 1851, and comparing it with the present year, 1873, I find a very remarkable change. I have had recourse to the most trustworthy documents within reach, and I can confidently say the figures are within the truth. In 1851, there were nine incumbencies in this Deanery, and there are now fifteen. There were seven houses of residence, and there are now thirteen. The total number of resident Clergy at that time ten, is now twenty-two. There are now sixteen Churches where there were then only

---

[1] It was, however, a great disappointment to Dr Corrie that considering the large population of the parish of Emneth such a small and, as he deemed, such an insufficient income was assigned to that parish.

eleven, and there are twenty-one parochial schools in the place of only five. Besides the new Churches, seven old Churches have been thoroughly restored, renewed, and in part rebuilt. Putting these facts in another shape, in order to have before us a uniform standard of comparison, it may be stated that, during these 22 years, the *increase* in the number of resident Clergy is 120 per cent.; of houses is 86 per cent.; of Churches is 45 per cent.; and of Parish Schools is 320 per cent.

"It will scarcely escape the notice of some who are here that the period from which I began to institute a comparison is the date of the appointment of your Rural Dean, the Rev. G. E. Corrie, D.D., Rector of Newton, and Master of Jesus College, Cambridge, to the living which he still holds. It gives me great pleasure to mention this. The argument 'post hoc ergo propter hoc,' is, I admit, not always valid; but I am confident that those who know the district best will agree with me, that there is a relation here like that of cause and effect. Of course, I do not claim that it is entirely so, but it is so in a very great measure. Of this, at least, I am certain, that no one has watched the course of events with a more lively and prayerful interest, and no one has been more anxious to promote the spiritual well-being of this whole district. You will join with me in the wish and prayer that this life may yet be spared many years to witness a further increase in the various means of grace, and more fruit from the diligent use of them."

Dr Corrie having again accepted a commission as Rural Dean under Bishop Woodford, retained the office until 1878, when he felt it his duty to resign it on account of the increasing infirmities of old age. A kind reply from the Bishop follows:

ELY HOUSE, DOVER STREET, *Jan.* 21, 1878.

My dear Dr Corrie,

    I am very much obliged to you for the Report of the deliberations of your Deanery—one of the most able and important which has yet reached me.

I entirely agree with the opinion expressed that with respect to the Churchyards no compromise can be thought of by Churchmen with any regard to their duty of preserving in its integrity the sacred trust which they have received. I think the suggestion of a committee of inquiry very valuable, and shall take opportunities of testing how it commends itself to influential members of the Legislature. And now I approach the subject upon which I am most unwilling to write. I feel that you have a full right to claim to be relieved from the burden of the office of Rural Dean, and yet I shall most deeply regret the disappearance of your name from the list of Rural Deans and the loss of your co-operation in the work of the Diocese. If it *must* be, I can of course only yield to your wish in the matter, but I do so with sincere sorrow and with real gratitude to you for having so long given the weight of your name and character to an office which depends entirely for its influence upon the personal qualifications of those who fill it. Believe me,

With affectionate respect, yours most truly,

J. R. ELY.

The following letter from the late Rev. John Scott, then Vicar of Wisbech, who had succeeded to the Office of Rural Dean, may be added :

THE VICARAGE, WISBECH, *June* 4, 1878.

My dear Sir,

We have had a meeting of the Clergy of the Deanery to-day, and I have great pleasure in communicating to you a resolution which was unanimously and most cordially passed.

"That this meeting desires to express to the late Rural Dean its deep regret at his retirement, and its deep sense of his long services, his invariable courtesy, and his great hospitality during his tenure of office." I can assure you that this was not passed as a *formal* resolution, but that it conveyed the real feeling of us all. Hoping that it may please God to give you much of His Heavenly blessing as you get nearer the time for entering His rest,

I am, my dear Sir, yours very truly,

JOHN SCOTT.

The Rev. Dr Corrie.

The following letter to the Rev. T. P. N. Baxter, in reply to one from Mr Baxter, announcing his having been appointed a Rural Dean by the Bishop of Lincoln, expresses Dr Corrie's own views of the office and its requirements :

THE LODGE, JESUS COLLEGE, CAMBRIDGE,
16 *Nov.*, 1875.

Dear Baxter,

Your letter of the 4th inst. reached me in the middle of preparation for migrating from the country to College, and so, like many other things, has been left unacknowledged longer than would otherwise have been the case.

I was, however, gratified by the intelligence your letter conveyed, for although the office of Rural Dean is one of no great dignity, the conferring of that office may always be regarded as expressive of the good will and confidence of the Bishop, as regards the individual Clergyman. I may mention in connection with the office in question, that an old pupil of mine (now dead), was expressing his opinion to the Dean of his Cathedral (now also dead), who was given to good humour, 'that he (my ancient pupil) thought that as Bishops were designated "*Right* Reverend," Deans "*Very* Reverend," Archdeacons "Venerable," and so forth, it appeared desirable that " Rural Deans" should have some special designation.' The Dean answered, 'Oh yes, what do you think of our Rural Deans being entitled " *Rather* Reverend?"' The point of the joke was that my old pupil, though an excellent person and a Rural Dean, had not a very reverend external. But apart from my story, I may mention that you will find your new office one of good discipline for yourself, since, to be of use to your brethren, you will have to make yourself extensively acquainted with the bearings of those many questions now *stirred*, both as regards doctrine and discipline. I think, also, you would be of more assistance to your Bishop by reporting the result of your Ruridecanal Meetings, *not* in the form "that such a question was agreed to by the Meeting," but that "on such a question, one clerical brother (without mentioning names) observed 'so-and-so,' whilst another remarked 'so-and-so.'" Your Bishop will thus be made acquainted with *individual* opinion instead of combined results. The Report will take a little more trouble; but not much, if you have at the Meeting one of the clergy to take notes for you of what is said on the occasion. I always follow that plan myself (for among other *dignities*, I bear that of "Rural Dean"), and I am *told* that my Reports are looked for.

This long and rambling note will I fear puzzle you, but in any case I wish it to testify that I abide

Your affectionate *old* Tutor,
G. E. CORRIE.

I have added "*old*," for a person in his 83rd year may assume that epithet without a figure of speech.

The restoration of the West end of the Church had not yet been attempted, but was anxiously desired by both Rector and Parishioners. Accordingly, with the assistance of subscriptions from the inhabitants of the parish and other friends, the work was undertaken in the summer of 1877. An unsightly west gallery was removed, the tower thrown open, all the west windows restored, the Font removed to its proper position, the bells repaired and a chiming apparatus placed in the Tower; and the organ put into thorough repair. The space gained by the removal of the gallery was fitted up with seats, a heating apparatus and lights for evening service were provided; these and other repairs and improvements were accomplished at a cost of about £370. At this time Dr Corrie also carried out his desire to place in the Chancel the Lord's Prayer, the Creed and the Commandments, simply designed in stone—in lieu of the existing wooden Tablets—and harmonising with the architecture of the building. It was a great satisfaction to the now aged rector, to compare the present complete and attractive condition of his church, with that which it had presented when he first took charge of the parish, and his long cherished wish was realized, that he might see the church suitably appointed for the Protestant worship of the Church of England.

The following letter written by Dr Corrie in reply to an urgent request (or demand?) for a return on the Tithe Rent-charge, from a farmer who held land under him as Rector of Newton, explains the principle on which, though shewing on all occasions a practical and liberal sympathy with the difficulties arising from the agricultural depression, he always declined to return anything on the Tithe Rent-charge:

JESUS COLLEGE, CAMBRIDGE, *Oct.* 22, 1878.

Dear Mr ——,

I have received your letter of October 20, and am so far glad that you wrote to me on the subject, in that it has given me an opportunity for explaining the reason why I, like other landlords, have for several years made a return of 10 per cent. on the rent of lands, and why I have refused to make any return on the Tithe rent-charge.

First, Because the Tithe rent-charge is a charge made by Law on owners of landed property. I have therefore nothing to do with fixing the amount to be paid each year by different persons, or the time of paying it. All this has been fixed by law, on the average price, not of wheat only, but of several kinds of grain, for a great number of years, and made on such a principle that Tithe rent-charge should rise and fall as the price of grain rises and falls, so that, in the course of years, the Tithe rent-charge should regulate itself year by year, according to the price of grain, without any other interference.

So much for the principle on which the Tithe rent-charge is charged. But the real question at issue is this. Whatever is the amount of Tithe rent-charge, year by year, the owners of property have the whole amount of Tithe rent-charge returned to them, either with what they receive by an increased rent of their land, which they charge their Tenant on account of the land being chargeable with Tithe; or, when as Tenants, they receive the Tithe rent-charge back again from their Landlord. What I have written will be plainer if I take your own case.

1. In the case of Tithe rent-charge paid on land of which you are yourself the owner, you knew beforehand that your property was subject to the payment of the Tithe rent-charge year by year, whatever it might be, and you accepted your property on the principle that that should be paid, because you became possessed of the property by paying so much less for it than you could otherwise have had to pay if the land had been Tithe rent-charge free. Like other landlords, therefore, you cannot say that, as you did not buy the amount of rent-charge, you might do what you liked with it, but that you might honestly pay the amount of Tithe rent payable on your property year by year, as you would any other debt chargeable on your estate.

2. As the occupier of the property of other persons. For example, if I remember rightly, you occupy a farm or part of a farm under ——, some of which is subject to the payment of Tithe rent-charge to the Parish of ——. On paying your rent from year to year to —— you have received back from him all the Tithe rent you have paid for him. When therefore you ask me to make a deduction on the payment due on Tithe rent-charge, you are really asking me to make you a return on money that has been already repaid to you, either by an increased rent of your own property, or, by your landlord .... I hope you will give me credit for having some reason for still declining to make such abatement of Tithe rent-charge as yourself and others have desired me to make. I hope you will forgive me for writing thus plainly, for you will be good enough to bear in mind, that I am writing in my own defence, and not from any wish to prevent you and my other friends of Newton from communicating with me on any matter connected with your own affairs, in which you may think I can do you service. There are other matters

contained in your letter which I will notice without much delay, in order that my people of Newton may be informed of the manner in which the Tithe rent-charge &c. which I receive from the Rectory of Newton is annually spent. In the meantime, as always with kind regards,

Believe me, yours very faithfully,

G. E. CORRIE.

The many friends whom he had the pleasure of welcoming to his country home saw him under a very different aspect from that which his College life presented. The surroundings of rural life possessed great charms for him. None perhaps gave him more pleasure than the cultivation of trees, for which the spacious old Rectory garden and grounds afforded abundant scope; provided with a ladder and saws, he would himself with a practised hand remove dead and unsightly boughs from one and another of his cherished trees. Illustrative of his acknowledged taste for this recreation, a little anecdote may be quoted. The Tutor and the Bursar of Jesus College came to visit him from Cambridge; being seated at table, the former with becoming gravity said he wished to inform the Master, three of the Society being present, that he had been applied to by a policeman, who stated that a boy had been found climbing a tree on Christ's Piece—then under the control of Jesus College—and had inquired how the College would wish him to be dealt with. What was the Master's opinion? After a moment's pause he replied, "I think, considering the Master is sometimes in a tree himself, the boy might be let off." This was the answer expected by the Tutor. It must be remembered that Dr Corrie was above eighty at the time.

He paid great attention to raising trees and shrubs, and thus his nursery supplied him with the means of contributing to many of the new Vicarage gardens around him, in which he always took great interest. One of his last occupations in his garden was to select all the young trees and shrubs, that were available, for planting in the New Court of Jesus College.

An old friend, struck with his remarkable vigour at the age of 84, had spoken of *him* as "an evergreen": and the thought, combined with his known predilection for trees, suggested the following lines:

> We walked among the summer flowers,
> Scarce a leaf stirred;
> We sought the lime-trees' fragrant bowers,
> Where bees were heard.
>
> How tenderly the stock-dove cooing
> Calls to his mate!
> We pause and listen to their wooing
> By the old gate.
>
> Thus day by day we wander here
> Finding new treasures,
> While coppice, field, and flowers afford
> Abundant pleasures.
>
> And one, the loved and honoured one,
> Whose hand has dressed
> And pruned each wayward bough, now sits
> And takes his rest.
>
> *   *   *   *   *   *
>
> The months have passed away
> Anon the robin's lay
> Thrills on the ear;
> While the sun's level ray
> Gilds the now shortened day,—
> Winter is here.
>
> Where are the bright leaves now
> Which lately clothed each bough,
> Dancing in light?
>
> Yet there is beauty here,
> The summer leaves now sere
> Are fallen and lost.
> But fir and laurel stand,
> Shining on either hand,
> Crisp with the frost.

For they are ever-green,
Winter's blast chill and keen,
May not hurt these :
Firmly their roots extend,
Hardly their boughs will bend,
Bright, living trees !

*　　*　　*　　*　　*　　*

And among these the Master walks,
Noting the growth of all,
Marking where, here and there a tree
By woodman's axe should fall.

They say *he* is an evergreen.
Ah ! kindly thought and true ;
For those who wait upon their Lord
He doth with strength renew.

Not brighter gleam in wintry sun
Those leaves so crisp and hoar,
Than shineth now the silvery head
Of fourscore years and four.

Here, through long years, his roots outspread,
The living stream doth nourish,
Until he at his Master's call
In courts above shall flourish.

L. H., *Newton*, Sept. 1877.

CHAPTER XIV.

ALTHOUGH so conversant with the history of the English Reformation, and led by the necessary preparation for his Professorial lectures to a close and careful study of all matters in connection with it, it happened that, from various causes, Dr Corrie had not as yet published any original work on the subject. He had not, however, abandoned his intention of doing so, and in 1874, in the leisure of advanced age, for he was now eighty-one, he brought out a small volume entitled, " A Concise History of the Church and State of England in conflict with the Papacy during the Reign of Henry VIII.," in which, to use his own words in his preface to the book, the object he kept in view was "to confine the attention of the reader, as much as practicable, to the facts of History, without regard to the persons by whose agency the affairs of Church and State in England were at the time carried on," and to point out how these facts issued in what he was wont to define as "a Re-formation, not a new creation," of the Church of England. In the following letters to a friend he refers to the circumstances which in his opinion increased the importance of this object, and then describes the scope of his intended work :

......Of late I have been impressed with the notion that if I do not work at the Reformation (both my own! and that) of the Church of England, it is likely that I shall pass out of the world, before I have accomplished anything in that line. The line taken by Ritualism of late has also given a more definite form to the kind of book that is wanted for the rising generation. On both sides of the question men and writers have been accustomed (not unreasonably) to mix up the facts connected with the Reformation, and the eminent and wicked persons who were instrumental to that great event. I purpose, therefore, to deal with the facts, without more reference to persons than is absolutely necessary for the circumstances of the case, so as to give people an opportunity for learning how absolutely necessary a Reformation was at the time, and how well it was effected considering the difficulties and obstructions to be contended with. Thus I purpose first reciting all the secular papal abuses existing, when Henry VIII. quarrelled with Rome, and how those abuses (all relating to money matters) were done away with by the several Acts of Parliament: then shew the errors in religion, and how they were got rid of. As matters stand, the Ritualists excite a prejudice against the Reformation by harping on the dark portions of Cranmer's and others' characters as if, but for the selfish and godless character of Henry VIII., no Reformation would have occurred; some good therefore would be done if it could be made clear that nothing, humanly speaking, could be worse than the papal influence in England at that time, and that, for merely worldly purposes, that influence could not much longer have been endured. Whether the object I have now in view will be accomplished depends on my continuance in this life, for I am now decidedly at work.......

Nov., 1869.

I have not lost sight of "The Reformation," more especially as I see room for the book I have in view. The point dwelt upon by our Ritualistic brethren now, is to shew that the Reformation was *completed* by the movements of Henry VIII., and that all which followed was to mar the good work Henry VIII. happily completed. As a trick, this theory is not amiss, for it leaves the Church of England in all respects Popish except in the matter of the papal supremacy. I have been reading a little in that direction, and have in hand Seebohm's "Reformers of Oxford," a book which is highly interesting, as displaying the under-current of religious feeling and opinion, which was felt to a great extent by the religious portion of the educated classes, directly anterior to the Reformation. We may also learn a lesson from the book, if we can read our own unthankfulness for the freedom and light in Divine things which our ancestors so greatly longed for in vain, but which we so little improve as to yearn for the bondage of Rome again....

A few letters may be here inserted of various dates, but which could not be introduced sooner without interrupting other subjects. The first—a reply to an enquiry from the Rev. Daniel Moore respecting books in connexion with a subject with which he was then engaged,—may illustrate Dr Corrie's knowledge of Theological Literature :

Jesus College, Cambridge,
June 6, 1864.

My dear Mr Moore,

As regards the subject of your intended course of Lectures have you looked at Bishop Jeremy Taylor's Tract on "The Divine Institution and Necessity of the Office Ministerial &c."? You will find it in the xivth volume of Jeremy Taylor's works edited by Heber. At the time of Collins the Deist (1710) a treatise was published in one

volume as a sort of set-off to *Priest-craft in Perfection*, and
in which it is likely you would find something to your
purpose.   The volume is entitled, "The Sacred Succession of
a Priesthood by a Divine Right," by Wm. Hume.   A volume
also was put forth in 1653 or 4 by the " Provincial Assembly
of London," in which most of the reasons are solidly given
for the necessity of the Ministry by Divine Institution, and
for the perpetual continuance of that Ministry in the Church.
An eccentric but clever volume was put forth some twenty-five
or thirty years ago by a Yorkshire divine named Oxlee
(John), "On the power, origin, and succession of the Christian
Ministry," and from which a good deal of useful information
might be derived.   It is probable that you may light upon
a book not now much known by a Rev. I. Trasques, called,
" The Power of Preaching," in the form of several sermons
on Luke iv. 32.   I should think the British Museum Library
would supply all the more unusual books, but if not, (with the
exception of the last named) I could supply them out of my
Library....

Believe me to be always,
Very truly yours,
G. E. CORRIE.

The following records Dr Corrie's views on the subject of
Evening Communions as given also to the Rev. D. Moore,
who writes :

I have a distinct recollection of a conversation I had with
Dr Corrie on the subject of Evening Communion, in which he
expressed himself as entirely at issue with those by whom the practice
has been so strongly condemned.   Not only did he see no force in
the argument for explaining, or explaining away the obvious fact,
that the evening was the actual time of the original institution of the
Lord's Supper, but in reference to the alleged desecration of the holy
ordinance by allowing the spiritual food to be received soon after
partaking of carnal food ; he added in his own quaint manner
that since a mixture of the two substances in the recipient was
inevitable, he could not see how the desecration in the case of those

whose participation of the sacred elements had been separated by an interval probably of several hours from their ordinary meal, should be greater than in the case of those who, after communicating, partook immediately of their ordinary meal.

The next is to a former pupil who speaks of it as— " illustrative of the very great interest which he took in the well-being of his old pupils, as well as of the tender jealousy he had, lest any should be influenced for evil by what he considered the lax religious principles of the day, which induced him to write a ' word in season ' in favour of orthodoxy."

BARDSEY, WETHERBY, *Sept.* 3, 1867.

Dear Baxter,

Your letter of August 31 reached me this morning, making me very glad by the information that you have at length found, in the course of God's good Providence, a resting-place in the Ministry. Whatever comfort and independence may be connected with the best of Curacies, there is yet also connected with it the sense of being unfixed. My hope is that it may please God to give you success in your ministrations at Hawerby : and keep you steadfast in the true faith of Christ : for in these days of unsettlement, we have need to be on our constant guard against being moved "away from the hope of the Gospel." * * * *

I am staying in Yorkshire for a few days, but purpose D.V. to proceed to " Newton, Wisbech," and remain there until the usual time for returning to College.

Believe me to be always,

Very truly yours,

G. E. CORRIE.

The two following letters are addressed to Mr Bentley, a former pupil at Catharine Hall. The first is in reply to one from Mr Bentley, apologising for having used Dr Corrie's name after a long lapse of years without renewing the request to do so. In forwarding it for publication, Mr Bentley remarks: "I have preserved it, for I think it a perfect model of high, true, Christian courtesy, such as one does not often meet with."

JESUS COLLEGE, CAMBRIDGE,
24 Jan. 1860.

Dear Bentley,

I accept your apology for giving my name as that of your referee, only on condition that you never hesitate to mention me as one of your friends.

It may be (as you are good enough to observe) that you have received acts of kindness from me, but all I may have done toward your comfort in College has been, and is fully repaid by your steady regard and affection.

Your affectionate old Tutor,
G. E. CORRIE.

JESUS COLLEGE, CAMBRIDGE,
20 Nov. 1875.

My dear Bentley,

I have just received your kind token of remembrance, which I shall place by the side of your former Sermons on Prayer. I cannot but feel very strongly your kind expression of regard which your note of to-day contains. You may be assured that among the happiest days of my life were those spent in our old College, as associated with yourself and others, who were under my care: and I am accordingly sometimes tempted to be dissatisfied with that comparative uselessness which is inseparable from old age. In the meantime I have much occasion for daily thanksgiving, that it has pleased God to give me bodily strength and activity, far beyond that assigned to others of less advanced age than myself.

With every reason for being closely attached to the Society to which I now belong, one cannot help remembering and sympathising with one's old *mother*.

Pray accept this short note as an expression of the earnest desire for your welfare in all respects from,

Your sincerely affectionate,
G. E. CORRIE.

The success of the Jesus College Boat in 1875, gave occasion for an expression of the confidence with which the younger members of the College relied on his hearty sympathy with them. Immediately on their return as head of the river, on the last evening of the Boat Races in that year, they repaired to the Lodge, and sent in an urgent request that the Master would come and speak to them. He was at the time entertaining a party of friends at dinner, who fully entering into the interest of the event, accompanied him, to find the undergraduates assembled in the cloisters eagerly awaiting his arrival. The vigorous cheering soon subsided into perfect silence while, beginning with words of hearty congratulation, and commendation of the perseverance which had met with its reward, their aged Master affectionately urged on them the exercise of the same determination in the graver pursuits of life, with the prospect of corresponding success. The scene was one which would not easily be forgotten by those present.

The life of diligent study and active occupation was now giving place to a serene and cheerful old age, which with one exception—that of impaired sight—continued for some years remarkably free from the infirmities generally incident to the ninth decade of a life. He would often say that "he felt much younger than his years," and when his habitually upright carriage gave way a little to the weight of age, he would exclaim, apparently with some surprise, "I am getting into a habit of stooping!" To quote his own words when speaking of some abatement of strength at the age of 77, "I do not look on this fact, except, I trust, with thankfulness to God, for having preserved to me so long the use of my mental and bodily faculties to a degree so much out of the common way. After living threescore years and ten, on what principle *ought* we to desire to prolong life, except more abundantly to glorify God?"

In 1881 his 88th birthday, passed at Newton, was made very bright by the opportunity it gave of personal congratulations from his friends and neighbours in that locality. A deputation of little girls from the School waited on him in the garden and presented him with two framed illuminated texts, appropriate to the occasion, as a birthday offering from all the school children, which he accepted with a few kind words. Touched with their affectionate thoughtfulness, he eagerly proposed that a tea should, if possible, be provided for them on leaving school that afternoon. This was accomplished, and he himself joined the party, much to the children's gratification. The day closed with a congratulatory telegram sent from the Fellows' table in Hall. Amongst the various letters received on the occasion the two following are selected, the first from the Master of Corpus Christi College, and the second from the Rev. H. A. Morgan, now Master of Jesus College :

April 27th, 1881.

My dear Master of Jesus,

I am sure that I may offer you my congratulations on your birthday and say how thankful I am that you are by God's loving mercy so well and vigorous, blessed with health and strength which many younger men might envy. To your own inner circle of friends, and to myself, this is indeed a source of great happiness, and I am sure that many prayers will be offered that He who has carried you through so many years of useful and honoured labour will continue His gracious care to the end—that your path may be ever brightening to the perfect day. And I well know that beyond that smaller circle there are all over England, and beyond our shores, Cambridge men who love and honor your name—many who owe to you not only right principles and sound learning, and wise plans of study, but "themselves also." For all this we shall specially thank God to-morrow......

April 28th, 1881.

My dear Master,

I cannot refrain from the pleasure of congratulating you very heartily on the return of your birthday. I hope you will long be spared to enjoy a happy life, one which is so deeply valued by those who have the pleasure and advantage of possessing your friendship, and which has tended so much to lighten and brighten the lives and duties of those, who have had the privilege of serving under you in the College.

Hoping that you are now quite well, I am, with best regards,

Very sincerely yours,

H. A. MORGAN.

Some old friends who were visiting him at the time thus afterwards expressed their thoughts, on sending him a book:

STUBTON, 24*th May.*

Dear Dr Corrie,

... ..Will you accept it as a little recollection of the happy birthday we spent with you at Newton? It was to us like a page out of some sweet story of olden times, when simple and happy pleasures brought far more contentment than the restless excitement of our own present condition.......

Yours affectionately,

MADALENE NEVILE.

The failure of sight precluded him from reading, and also by degrees rendered writing impossible, but his excellent memory and power of fixed attention enabled him to follow with pleasure and advantage the subjects of the books he selected to be read to him, and to refer, through others, with remarkable readiness, to passages in any books he might wish to consult. The same habit prevailed still later in other matters. In 1882 during the war in Egypt he listened with his usual attention to the newspaper accounts of it, and on questions of geography would make frequent references to Strabo, an author whom he had studied with care many years before. His indomitable perseverance enabled him to continue some useful work. Having been throughout his Mastership Divinity Lecturer in College, he, even as late as 1882 set questions in Divinity and Church History for College examinations with great interest, and with no remission of his accustomed care.

In the same summer, during his residence at Newton, he also continued to preach once every Sunday, sparing no pains in the preparation of his sermons, while the vigour of his delivery often excited the surprise of his hearers.

An instance of his power of memory may be quoted.   On the winding-up of a College Trust, which at that time passed into the hands of the Ecclesiastical Commissioners, he dictated, without hesitation or reference, an account of the Trust from its beginning, with the circumstances connected with it, and the uses which had been made of it; in reply to which communication he received from the Commissioners a letter of thanks for his very clear statement of the subject.

The difficulty of even signing his name had received the kind consideration of the Library Syndicate, which was courteously expressed in the following note from the Vice-Chancellor of the time :

CLARE COLLEGE LODGE, CAMBRIDGE, March 13, 1878.

My dear Master of Jesus,

   I hope you will not think the Library Syndicate very meddlesome or impertinent when you learn that at their meeting to-day, it being understood that you had occasionally a difficulty in writing from dimness of sight, the Syndicate thought that it might save you trouble if your notes of hand for books borrowed from the Library were allowed to be written and signed by some one else, and accordingly came to a resolution that you might take out books by means of a note of hand written and signed by Miss Holroyd.

The Syndicate has, I know, acted from the wish to do what they thought would be gratifying to one whose real services in the University and in the Library are so well remembered.

I remain, my dear Master, yours sincerely,

E. ATKINSON, V. C.

He still took a lively interest in what was passing in the University.   Among other matters, a Grace brought before the Senate to allow the opening of the Botanic Gardens on Sundays roused his strong disapprobation, and he did all in his power to oppose any encroachment upon the long-established quiet observance of the Lord's Day in the University.   A letter written on this occasion by a non-resident friend, which elicited Dr Corrie's opinion on a collateral subject, is, with his reply, inserted :

OSPRINGE VICARAGE, FAVERSHAM, *May* 24, 1881.

My dear Master,

Though I was not in the Senate-House last Thursday, I can assure you that a call bearing your honoured name would never fail to have my most respectful consideration. Though the opening on Sundays of the Botanic Garden be now, I regret to say, a fact accomplished; if it should be followed by an attempt to open the Fitzwilliam Museum also on Sunday, might an opportunity be given to non-residents to sign a protest against it, and that with more hope of influence than by some of us going up to vote against it? For, if a Grace be rejected by means of non-residents coming up, the question is not really put to rest, because the whole body of the Senate cannot express an opinion, but only such non-residents as by nearness or leisure have the power to present themselves. I am afraid that the decision will be unsatisfactory unless it is made either by the residents alone, if it seems to belong to them properly, or by some means of taking the sense of the whole Senate. May I be pardoned for thus putting my thoughts before you?

Believe me to be, dear Master, faithfully yours,

W. N. GRIFFIN.

The Rev. the Master of Jesus College.

JESUS COLLEGE, CAMBRIDGE, *May* 25, 1881.

My dear Mr Griffin,

The objections to the suggestions contained in your letter (for which I am nevertheless much obliged) are threefold, viz.

1. It is quite usual to bring up absent members of the Senate respecting any questions on which there may be a difference of opinion, and the decisions come to by resident and non-resident voters are always taken to represent the judgment of the *Senate*, by both sides.

2. To have any moral question like that to which your letter refers, to be decided by the votes of the resident M.A.s alone, would be to hand over the granting of a Degree to Bradlaugh by vote of the Senate, we having become so radical a majority of residents.

3. The numbers of the whole Senate being 6400, the consequent trouble and expense of circulating the Protest

against any objectionable measure, would be beyond the power of the few earnest men who would have to carry that Protest into effect. Pray excuse this scrawl, which is owing to my defective sight.

Believe me in any case,

Very truly yours,
G. E. CORRIE.

The following is the last letter he wrote to Mr Walpole as member for the University, expressing in part his grave apprehensions as to the results of the impending new legislation for the University of Cambridge, if left unchallenged :

JESUS COLLEGE, *May 1st*, 1882.

My dear Mr Walpole,

I write to ask you whether or not you are in Parliamentary circumstances to suggest or state, as the case may be, any objections to the Statutes which the Cambridge University Commissioners have sent to Parliament as the Statutes by which we are hereafter to be governed? We are so disheartened here by the little interest which those University and Collegiate Statutes have excited in the members of Parliament, both Lords and Commons, that if some help cannot be obtained from individual members of the Houses, it would seem that the many Church of England objections which can legitimately be made to many of the code of Statutes, will be sanctioned for want of challenge. I must trust your long and valued friendship, to express freely any difficulties you may experience in undertaking any interference in this matter, for whatever be your decision it will not affect the sincere regard and affection with which

I am, yours,

G. E. CORRIE.

The cricket-match played between the Australian Eleven and Cambridge University in June 1882, on the first appearance of "the Australians" in England, called forth much enthusiasm, and Dr Corrie, always an admirer of cricket, was tempted, to the surprise and pleasure of many friends, to emerge from his usual retirement to witness the game, which was won by Cambridge; and he entered with keenness and zest into the success of his University.

In the May Term of 1882 he had the exceeding gratification of seeing a member of his own College, Mr Welsh, Senior Wrangler of his year, and heartily welcomed him, and several others of the College who had also taken good places, to his Lodge to receive his congratulations. His presence in the Senate-House to witness Mr Welsh take his degree was most warmly greeted, and his appearance there on that occasion was the last public act of a University career of more than seventy years.

The summer of 1882 was as usual spent at Newton, and though weak action of the heart had for some time obliged him to avoid any over-exertion, it was a real comfort to him to find that with care he was able to continue preaching until he returned to Cambridge. During the October Term he showed symptoms of a return of the disease of the lungs, which, with the exception of a sudden and short attack in 1875, had lain dormant for fifty years. His deafness, which for his age had been comparatively slight, so greatly increased that, coupled with his inability from his defective sight to read, it threatened to cut him off from all intercourse with others, and for a short time all communication was by signs. He bore the privation with great patience, and consoled himself with the Holy Scriptures, with which his memory was stored. The extreme deafness slightly abating, he was able again to avail himself of artificial help. The expression of thankful relief which lighted up his countenance on finding that the flexible tube would to some extent supply his need, was very touching as he at once asked for the Bible, "that I may once more hear God's blessed Word." Before the end of the year he had an alarming attack of difficulty of breathing, which though yielding to remedies left him more or less an invalid. As he drew near the completion of his ninetieth year in the following spring it was for some time doubtful whether he would live to see the approaching birthday; he however rallied in a remarkable manner, and was able to receive the greetings of his friends. Many were the tokens of affection and respect which reached him. Among other beautiful gifts of flowers one must be mentioned,—an exquisite bouquet consisting of ninety rose-buds—the gift of the Fellows of the College. The kindness of the very numerous friends who came to offer their congratulations was warmly appreciated by him, as were also the affectionate letters which he received on the occasion. He himself was anxious to mark the day by a gift to the Fellows. His note accompanying it and their reply are first inserted, followed by extracts from some others received on the day.

JESUS COLLEGE, *April* 28, 1883.

My dear Dr Westmorland,

Will you be good enough to request the Fellows to accept this Flower-stand for the use of their table in Hall, which, on my 90th birthday, I beg them to receive as a small token of that deep sense which I entertain of the uniform kindness both corporate and personal which I have received from you all during the whole period of my long Mastership.

Believe me, with sincere affection and regard,

Yours sincerely,

G. E. CORRIE.

JESUS COLLEGE, *May* 7, 1883.

My dear Master,

I am requested by the Fellows to thank you for the handsome flower-stand which you have presented to us on your 90th birthday, and also for the kind expressions contained in your letter accompanying the gift. I am also requested to say that we are equally sensible of the uniform kindness we have received from you during the long period you have presided over us, and the interest you have always shewn in our welfare. We trust you may long be spared to be among us.

Believe me to be, with kind regards,

Yours most sincerely,

ARTHUR WESTMORLAND.

April 28, 1883.

My dear Master,

On this day you have completed your ninetieth year, and you can, I doubt not, say that goodness and mercy have followed you during all your long life. The common birthday wish is not suitable to a nonagenarian, but what I do most heartily wish is, that the God and Father of our Lord Jesus Christ may—and I confidently trust He will—prolong your life so far as He sees it to be well for yourself, your friends, and for your beloved College, and that, during the time which still remains to you on earth, He will make the light of His countenance to shine upon you more and more brightly, and keep you in perfect peace even to the end.

I remain, my dear Master, your affectionate friend,

CHARLES PERRY, *Bishop.*

DEANERY, PETERBOROUGH, *May* 1, 1883.

My dear Master of Jesus,

......I hope it is not too late for me to offer you my sincere congratulations on having attained the ripe old age of 90. God has been very gracious to you and to your many friends in sparing you. I do not doubt that every added year of your long life has been a life of more blessing both to yourself and to others. His presence and His love have been with you, and I pray they may be with you richly to the end.

With affectionate regards, believe me,

Most sincerely yours,

J. J. STEWART PEROWNE.

From a young farmer who gave valued assistance in parochial work:

NEWTON, *27th April,* 1883.

Rev. and dear Sir,

I feel it my bounden duty, and I can assure you it affords me great pleasure, to offer you our heartfelt congratulations upon your birthday to-morrow. You have been spared to reach an age far beyond our allotted "threescore and ten," and to which age I think none of us ought to reckon upon attaining.

To review a life of ninety years, abounding with blessings, anxieties, pleasures, and trials must be something extraordinary, and how thankful one must be who has been thus sustained by the Great Preserver. Trusting you may be spared once more to visit Newton "if it seemeth Him good."

Believe me, dear Master, yours very sincerely,

JOHN WING.

A friend formerly his Curate at Newton writes :

WESTON RECTORY, BECCLES,
May 1, 1883.

Dear Dr Corrie,

Your 90th birthday did not pass unnoticed by us, and we have been asking for God's blessing on you in this new stage of your far advanced life. How far better it is to turn our desires for those whom we love into direct petition that He, Who knows best, what for us each best is, should grant to you of His best, than merely to indulge in congratulatory expressions. We have therefore the comfort of knowing that we have thus been permitted to unite our prayers with many of your large circle of friends in bringing down fresh spiritual blessings upon your old age. Do not trouble to acknowledge this, but I could not keep silence.

Believe me, yours very sincerely,

J. HERBERT CLOWES.

DOWNHAM, ELY, *April* 28, 1883.

My dear Dr Corrie,

My lilies must breathe out a welcome to this much-remembered day. Till my time on earth ceases, the 28th will never come round without tender thought of you, and of all the privilege I have had in being reckoned (though so unworthy) amongst your friends.

Yours very affectionately,

L. SHARP.

Similar kind expressions were addressed to him the following year.

SWINTON VICARAGE, *Ap.* 26, 1884.

My very dear Master,

I must not allow this evening to pass without sending you a line to assure you of our very best wishes and prayers on your approaching birthday, that it may prove a very happy one and the harbinger of still happier days, during the time you are yet permitted to remain amongst us. Your life is a very precious one to us all, and we are thankful to the Giver of all good in being permitted to unite once more in praise for having spared you to us so long to aid us with your valuable counsel and example. My children feel this as much as my wife and myself, and we beg to offer our united best remembrances and thanks for all your kind affection to me and mine, during so many years of our pilgrimage.

May we at length meet in a better world, where we shall fully learn how the mutual faith and hope and love of each have been instrumental in one another's good, and proved effectual for the perfecting of the body of Christ.

Believe me, my dear Master,

Your truly grateful and affectionate,

JOHN LEVETT.

In the course of Dr Corrie's researches in English Church History he had become greatly interested in the writings of the enthusiast Henry Nicolas, and the sect called "The Family of Love[1];" and he collected, so far as he was able, the books written by or relating to this sect. These publications are mostly translations into English from the Low-Dutch, some are reprints, and some consist of a group of smaller ones, which again were also printed separately, and all are extremely rare. A list of those collected by Dr Corrie was contributed in *Notes and Queries*, 4th series, 1869, by Mr J. H. Hessels, who was searching English libraries for

---

[1] Also called House of Love (or in Latin *Familia* or *Domus Charitatis* or *Amoris*) or simply Familists. They were a section of the Anabaptists, who had at first followed David Joris, but when he dropped the leadership, it was taken up by Henry Nicolas (who generally called himself by his initials, "H. N."), an Anabaptist who had been mixed up with the Münzer insurrection in his native city of Amsterdam, and had fled thence to Emden in the year 1533. He set himself to oppose all existing forms of religion, and to establish an entirely new one; he gave himself to writing of books, which he put in print, the chief being called *The Glass of Righteousness*. Fuller (*Church History*, IX. 3, § 38) says that Nicolas came to England "in the latter end of the reign of Edward VI., and joined himself to the Dutch congregation in London, where he seduced a number of artificers, and silly women, amongst whom two daughters of one Warwick, to whom he dedicated an epistle, were his principal perverts." The Familists maintained that there was no true knowledge of Christ or of the Scriptures out of their community. It is not improbable that, on the accession of Queen Mary, Nicolas left England like most of the foreign Protestants, and settled for some time again at Emden in East Frisia. But after the accession of Queen Elizabeth he appears to have returned to England, and to have been very active in spreading his religious tenets. The year of his death is not known, nor anything about his residence. On 3 October, 1580, a proclamation was issued "against the Sectaries of the Family of Love," and this was followed by a form of abjuration issued by the Privy Council, in which the members of the sect were required to abjure their most conspicuous heresies. King James I. calls them in his Βασιλικὸν δῶρον, "infamem anabaptistarum sectam, quæ familia amoris vocatur." An accusation against a Familist is mentioned as late as 1627. See J. H. Blunt, *Dictionary of Sects*, &c.　　　　　J. H. H.

material for a biographical account of the celebrated mystic, which he, and the late Dr Tiele, Librarian of the Utrecht University, had in preparation; and to whom Dr Corrie temporarily entrusted his treasures for the purpose.

Dr Corrie now became anxious that these books or a part of them should, during his life, find a place in the University Library, and accordingly invited the late Mr Bradshaw, the Librarian, to select from them all that were not already in the Library, with a view to making that collection as nearly complete as possible. The books were arranged with the utmost patience by Mr Bradshaw, who took great interest in the acquisition, though ·the number still fell short, by one only, of the collection in the Lambeth Library. Dr Corrie received through Mr Bradshaw the very cordial thanks of the Library Syndicate for "this precious gift to the Library."

Dr Corrie had also long been anxious to publicly associate his name with that of his beloved and honored brother Daniel, by the establishment of a small Scholarship in "Bishop Corrie's Grammar School" at Madras. He now entered into communication with the Bishop of Madras (Dr Gell), through whose kind assistance the necessary information was obtained; and in 1884 was founded " Dr George Corrie's Scholarship, to be competed for by those native Christians who shall have passed the necessary examinations; the successful candidate to attend the religious instruction in accordance with the principles of the Church of England under Rule I. of the Fundamental Laws." While referring to his interest in the Madras Diocese, mention may be also made of the Chalice and Paten used by the venerable missionary Schwartz, which, after Bishop Corrie's death, were brought to Dr Corrie by the late Archdeacon Harper on his return to England. While in Dr Corrie's possession they were used at the Ordinations held by Bishop Turton in Jesus College Chapel. On the formation of the new See of Travancore and Cochin, Dr Corrie presented the Chalice and Paten to the first Bishop (Dr Speechly) for himself and his successors in the See.

He had been very desirous to return to Newton for the summer, and though a fresh attack of illness caused some delay, it was with deep thankfulness that he found himself, a few weeks later, once more in the spot he loved so well. He was able also to enjoy short drives, and sitting in the garden, and frequently to join in the Sunday Morning Service, but throughout the summer was liable to severe attacks which caused great anxiety. He returned to Cambridge in the late autumn, and, though the symptoms were from time to time greatly relieved by remedies, it became evident that the aged frame was giving way to the advance of disease. The increased deafness brought his powers of listening to ordinary reading within narrow limits, although he still took an interest in it. Age and infirmity did not deprive him of his natural sociability, and he cordially welcomed (as strength allowed) the many kind friends who visited him. As the summer of 1884 advanced it became evident that no move from Cambridge could be attempted, but he derived great pleasure from drives in the neighbourhood, and seeing once more many localities long unvisited by him. From this time the decline was gradual, but his strong constitution sustained him through many remaining months of weakness. That his sympathies with friends were unabated is shewn by the following note to the late Provost of King's (Dr Okes):

Jesus College Lodge,
Dec. 15, 1884.

My dear Provost,

  I beg you will accept my sincere and affectionate desire that it will please God to add, on this anniversary of your birthday, His inward blessing and support, to those many family affections with which He has been pleased to comfort your great age. For the rest, we cannot more effectually shew our regard and love for each other than by our mutual prayers that whenever it may please God to call upon us to give up the remainder of our lives, we may be enabled cheerfully to obey His call. With much affection to yourself, and love to your children,

Believe me yours,
G. E. CORRIE.

In the early spring days of 1885, supplies of snowdrops, for which his rectory garden at Newton was famous, were sent as usual to him at Cambridge. He took great pleasure in sharing them with his friends, and desired that a bunch should be sent, among others, to the Master of St Catharine's (Dr Robinson), whose kind note of thanks is added:

ST CATHARINE'S LODGE, CAMBRIDGE,
Feb. 14, 1885.

My dear Master of Jesus,

I have received your kind present of a beautiful nosegay of the purest snowdrops. I am very much gratified by this kind remembrance from you, which recalls to my mind many past years, since I first came to College as your pupil nearly forty years ago, and received so much kindness from you in those years. I can at this day recall the influence that seemed to come to us from your sermons in the College Chapel; and now you can still shew us the support and consolation which those same truths can give in the decline of life, "The grass withereth and the flower fadeth, but the word of the Lord endureth for ever."

Believe me, my dear Master,
Yours most truly,
C. K. ROBINSON.

The last letter received by him was from his affectionate and valued friend Bishop Perry, on the last birthday, an extract from which is given:

We can scarcely hope that you may linger longer upon earth, and yet notwithstanding the defects of sight and hearing, you are so free from the infirmities of age, and are kept by the grace of God in such perfect peace, that we have no apprehension of the lengthening of your life, if God sees fit to lengthen it, being productive to you of only "labour and sorrow." We have a sure confidence that, while you live, God will make His face to shine upon you, and enable you to shew forth His praise by your quiet rest in Him; and that when

you die, you will fall asleep in Jesus to awake to glory at His coming
into His Kingdom.   We have therefore no anxiety on your account,
but can commit you to the care of your Heavenly Father, in the
assurance that He will glorify Himself in you both in life and death,
and enable you always to rejoice in Him.

During this time his mind was kept in perfect peace ; and
the grace of thankfulness, always conspicuous in his character,
seemed to increase as the end approached.   The reading
and study of Scripture was, as it had ever been, his unfailing source of comfort.   No day passed without some
attempt, more or less successful according to the variations of
deafness, to listen to some part of God's Word.   Sometimes, if
too much exhausted for his usual portion, he would say, " Read
me some of the strong promises."   At other times a few verses
only were asked for, to supply subject for meditation and
prayer.   When deafness precluded any reading, he would
express regret that he could get "no instruction."   The last
weeks of illness being in the Long Vacation, few of his friends
had any further opportunity of seeing him, but he greatly
valued the daily visits of his friends the Master of Corpus
Christi College and the late Dr Swainson, the Master of
Christ's College.   On the 9th of August he received the Holy
Communion for the last time, at the hands of his attached
friend the Master of Corpus Christi College (Dr E. H. Perowne).
The Tutor (Rev. H. A. Morgan), being unexpectedly in the
house, at Dr Corrie's request united with him in the Service,
at the conclusion of which he said to him, " This has been
a great pleasure to me, for we may not receive this Communion together again, until we partake of it in our Father's
Kingdom."   It was then evident to all that the end could not
be far off; a few days later he was no longer able to leave his
room, but lingered on for nearly six weeks in much weakness.
As the end drew near, he was evidently conscious of it, and
his departure was painless and peaceful on the morning of
Sunday, Sept. 20th.   As the members of the "Church militant"
were assembling for worship on earth, his Master called the

faithful soldier and servant to join the "Church triumphant" "through the blood of the Lamb."

The funeral took place on the following Friday. A large congregation was assembled in the beautiful College Chapel where he had loved to worship. The first part of the Service was conducted by the Dean and Tutor, the hymn "Rock of ages" being sung after the opening sentences were read. At the conclusion of the Lesson, according to custom, the body of the late Master was carried round the Courts of the College, followed by the whole congregation; the hymn "A few more years shall roll" was sung as the long procession moved on. On that bright autumn morning, which seemed to symbolise only changing beauty rather than decay, no shadows marred the peaceful serenity of that unconscious last farewell. A great number of the assembled friends accompanied the family party to Newton, and then, amid a large gathering of affectionate and sorrowing parishioners and friends, including many children with their cottage garden wreaths, mingling with the many floral offerings from other friends, he was laid to rest beside the Church where he had loved to stand among his people as an ambassador for Christ. The hymn "There is a fountain filled with blood," so much valued by him, and so ofted quoted by him, was sung at the grave; the second part of the Service was then read by the Master of Corpus Christi College, followed by the hymn "Now the labourer's task is o'er." The dignity of the College Chapel Service, and the simplicity of the quiet village Churchyard, well represented the characteristics of the life which had now closed on earth.

On Sunday, Sept. 27th, Memorial Sermons were preached, at Newton Church in the Morning by the Rev. W. Carpenter, Vicar of Guyhirne; in the Evening at Holy Trinity Church, Cambridge, by the Rev. the Master of Corpus Christi College.

On Sunday, Oct. 18th, the Master of Pembroke College (Dr Searle), as Select Preacher before the University paid a fitting and affectionate tribute to his memory.

The Chapel Services at Jesus College, on Oct. 25, were made commemorative of the death of the late Master, the Rev. H. A. Morgan, the present Master, preaching on the occasion.

Thus, various friends united in bearing public and affectionate testimony, before very different congregations, to the character of him who had now entered on his rest.

The inscriptions on the Memorial Brass Tablet placed by the Society in the Chapel of Jesus College and on the grave in Newton Churchyard will be found at the end of the volume.

CHAPTER XV.

EXTRACTS FROM LETTERS RECEIVED AFTER HIS DEATH. HIS
POWER OF ATTRACTION, INDIVIDUALITY, AND GENERAL CHARAC-
TERISTICS. HIS TENDERNESS; CARE FOR ANIMALS; SYMPATHY
WITH THE YOUNG, THE WEAK AND SUFFERING. HIS LECTURES
AS TUTOR. HIS FIRMNESS OF PRINCIPLE. LITERARY WORK.
HYMNS.

IN the memorials which have been thus laid before the
reader, the narrative of a long life has been simply told with
but little comment. The impression made on the minds of
those who knew and loved him and of those who had
watched his public career may be traced in the many letters
received after his death, a few extracts from which are
selected for insertion.

The Bishop of Gloucester and Bristol (Dr Ellicott) writes:

"My first feeling in reading your note was one of almost rejoicing
that the dear Saint was with the Master he loved and served so well.
What a fragrant memory he has left behind! Always faithful, always
gentle, always on the right and true side, I can never think of him
without love and gratitude, for many a wise counsel he gave me,
many a kindly help in my studies. It is a pleasure, in life's journey, to
have known such a man."

The late Bishop of Durham (Dr Lightfoot) writes:

"His end was indeed a fit termination to so serene and peaceful
a life. My last visit to him is a most bright and pleasant memory,
and will always remain so. His cheerfulness and contentedness were
the most impressive of all sermons."

The late Bishop of Ely (Dr Woodford) writes:

"I was anxious to hear something of the latter days of the late Master of Jesus, for whom I had a deep respect, and of whom I shall always retain very affectionate remembrances. It was a remarkable life, not only in its length of days, but in its strength of principle and consistency throughout."

The Bishop of Winchester (Dr Harold Browne) writes:

"Though dear Dr Corrie had lived so far beyond the common life of man, we all feel that his departure is a great loss.

"I have long had a very affectionate regard for him. His reception of me as his Bishop, when first I became Bishop of Ely, and his constant support of me ever after, will always be gratefully remembered by me, as also his kindness to my son when he was an undergraduate of Jesus College. He does not leave behind him many truer and better men. May we meet him with joy in the presence of his Lord and ours."

The Bishop of Madras (Dr Gell) writes:

"...I hear that the long life of good Dr Corrie has been brought to a close. That he departed in peace, and trust, and in hope of glory through Jesus Christ, was only what all his Christian friends would expect after his long, consistent and active life in our Master's service, and the manifest singleness of his purpose, and purity of his motives in all that he did. One of the brightest incidents in the four months I spent last year in England was my visit to Jesus College Lodge. In referring, as he did, to many subjects, past and present, he seemed chiefly to be full of devout thankfulness to God for having been so good to him, of benevolence towards men, and of hope regarding the cause of religion in England. May Cambridge never want such leaders of thought, earnest, learned, and sound in doctrine as he was."

The Bishop of Rupert's Land (Dr Machray) writes:

"At last it has pleased God to take to himself our dear friend. I held him in the highest regard. Our sympathies in all questions, both religious and political, were very much the same...His high principle and consistent conduct made him deeply respected by all. I am sure that many now advancing in life have the kindest remembrance of him, and mourn his loss."

The Bishop of Rochester (Dr Thorold) writes :

"I have just seen in the paper that the dear Master has gone home. What a change and what a joy! It is like a great tree gone down, leaving a gap that ferns grow upon, but other trees never quite fill up."

Precentor Venables, of Lincoln, writes:

"It is with a very sincere pang that I realize that one who has been so constant a friend to me for more than fifty years has been taken away, and that I shall never enjoy his society here again. As I have often said, I owe a very large debt of gratitude to Dr Corrie, and any success which may have attended me is in a large measure due to the directions so kindly given to my studies in early youth, and to frequent counsels in later days."

The late Master of Christ's (Dr Swainson) writes :

"I cannot come to Cambridge, but I shall go over the service here, and think of the many, or rather of some of the many, many kindnesses I have received from, and the interesting and *telling* conversations I have had with, the dear old Master!"

The Master of Magdalene (Hon. and Rev. Latimer Neville) :

" If of any one the words are true, ' Blessed are the dead that die in the Lord,' they must be true of him."

The Master of St Catharine's (Dr Robinson) writes :

"It was impossible for me to attend the dear Master's funeral to testify my love and affection for him, but I was not the less mindful of the great loss which his College and University and his wide circle of friends have sustained by his death. For him we cannot mourn ; for death has come to him in a good old age, and perhaps none of us can call to mind, a life more honoured than his. More than all this, we know he died in the firm faith of Christ, supported by all the consolations of hope, and love, and trust, which make death a friend and not a foe. Few have had such a powerful influence for good upon the men of his time; and now we have his memory to be our guide, and a life which will never pass out of our recollection."

The Master of Pembroke (Dr Searle) writes :

"His death-bed is a scene to be remembered, and brings before me that of Elisha; nor do I think it will be less profitable, for I shall love to call to mind his look and words, and specially those which he spoke when I saw him last."

Archdeacon Perowne writes :

" We know, thank God! that it is well with him. Such lives as his, live on and are fruitful.   God give us grace to follow them that are such !

"By very many private friends, and Cambridge men, the good Master of Jesus, so staunch, so true, so kind, so gentle, will be very sincerely mourned."

Dr Westcott writes :

"We all felt yesterday how precious a link of Cambridge with the past had been broken. The bright recollection of the 90th birthday, the rose-buds and cheerful smile, come back to me, and indeed every association which I have with the late Master is full of his ready and helpful kindness, from the time when I attended his lectures, till the time when he encouraged me in preparing for my own. I am specially grateful to him, for the clearness with which he told me to remember, that the evils with which we have to contend now, are not really so great as those which he had known in earlier times. No one could speak with weightier authority on such a question."

The Rev. A. Delmé Radcliffe writes :

" The loss to the Church and to Cambridge is indeed a great one. I am so thankful to have had the privilege of just knowing him, and shall not forget his kind fatherly talks to me, taking one right back into bygone days, and indeed I treasure up the remembrance of the beautiful simplicity of his faith, as a real help to one's own spiritual life."

The Rev. T. P. N. Baxter writes :

"One more link of connection with the past is thus removed. I and many other of his pupils will be stirred by the event, for I suppose there are few men who can command the respect and affectionate regard, which he held in the hearts of those who were brought into close connection with him. His memory will be cherished by us with all due reverence, and I trust that his example will be followed by us to our profit. He, though dead, yet speaks to us in many ways. May our dear Friend's firm, steadfast faith and

consistency of life be profitable to us for our help and encouragement, and may we join him and all the Saints, in the presence of that
Saviour Whom he loved and served, and by Whom he has been
welcomed *Home*. The beautiful language he used when giving me
his blessing shewed most plainly and forcibly how firmly fixed his
thoughts were on, ' Him in Whom he believed.'

"'The kind interest he took in me after my Degree and election
to my Fellowship deepened my feeling and regard ; and the recollection I have of him, both at St. Catharine's and at Jesus College,
always causes my feelings of affection to ' well up' within me with
increasing fervour. There were those, no doubt, who thought him
somewhat 'stiff' and 'unapproachable,' but it never was so with myself ; I ever found his kind look and kind word most helpful both in
my devotion to my studies and in my endeavours to live a religious
life. There was no ostentation—no intrusion—no affectation about
him, but that genuine friendliness of look and manner, and that
thoroughly gentlemanlike, and Christian bearing, which attracted me
very strongly, and made it a happy circumstance to me that I had
rooms on his staircase. I have not yet lost, and I never shall lose,
the very feeling towards him which I then experienced and cherished.
I am quite assured that the world would be ever so much better were
there more of his type in it. Let those of us who knew him, do our
best to follow (so far as we may) in his footsteps, and carry out the
principles which he ever inculcated by word and example."

The Rev. W. H. Allen, his last curate, writes :

" To me the loss seems irreparable; whilst I venerated him as the
very ideal of a Christian minister, I loved him as a father. Where-
ever in God's Providence our lot may now be cast, I shall ever look
back upon my long connection with the dear departed one—nearly
nine and a half years—as a time of great privilege. In his parish he
was always so bright and consistent an example."

The late Right Hon. A. J. B. Beresford-Hope, M.P.,
writes :

"I read the sad news of the departure of the venerable and distinguished Master with deep sorrow. Allow me to assure you how,
with all to whom his career is familiar, I mourn for such a loss to
Cambridge, to the Church, and to society.

"It was indeed a privilege to have known and to be able from personal acquaintance to have revered him. May his wise, unflinching

spirit continue to make its influence felt in the University, which can only flourish, as long as it combines reverence for the past, with hope for the future."

Another writes:

"Earth seems poorer, another link is severed, and the vacant place can never be filled, but Heaven is enriched and Jesus the Saviour is made glad. 'He shall see of the travail of His soul, and shall be satisfied.' We can and do thank Him for the long life of honoured service in which the aged saint was permitted to glorify Him. The memory of the just is blessed ; and we pray that Cambridge hearts, may ever seek to follow closely the example of one, whose consistent faithfulness to the Master's precepts will cause his name to be had in everlasting remembrance. We can ill afford to lose *such* witnesses, but we must ask and believe that God will graciously raise up others to fill up the ranks which of late seem so rapidly thinning."

The Rev. R. Appleton, Tutor of Trinity College, speaks of

"The numerous friends who have had reverence and affection for the oldest member of our body, with all his work so long and so unflinchingly achieved.

"I know that fifty years ago he had been more than once apparently upon the brink of the grave. Surely he lived as if the remembrance of this were never absent from his thoughts. May it not have been so ordered by a wise Providence, with a view to the valuable influence which the example of a real Christian gentleman, would exert over both old and young in the peculiar circumstances of University life ?"

The Rev. O. Fisher, late Fellow of Jesus College:

"To have watched him through the last stages of his long life has been a privilege which I hope will not be lost upon me. Such faith as he had, is rare to witness."

Mr Aikin, a senior member of the College:

"When I look back to my long connection with the College, I can recall nothing but words and acts of kindness from the Master; and his removal from the College makes one feel bitterly how truly the old has passed away, and all things are become new."

From an old inhabitant of his father's parish :

"I retain in my memory lessons I received when a Sunday

scholar which the late Dr Corrie taught me, and can repeat them now although seventy years are passed."

Many of the junior members of the College expressed their grateful sense of his "friendliness towards them," "his courtesy and kindness attracting them with an irresistible charm," while they were also "deeply touched by the request from so aged a man that he might be remembered in their prayers." Not a few spoke tenderly of his removal as "the severance of a link with the past," and of their desire to keep before themselves his bright example.

The above remarks would lead the reader to suppose that the subject of them possessed a considerable power of attraction; and this was truly the case throughout his life; and while this quality won for him many friends, it assisted him in commanding the attention and regard even of those who might widely differ from him, never, however, at the expense of his own convictions. He also possessed a strong individuality of character, gained by the acting out of early principles, the firm mental grasp by which he made a subject his own and retained it, and the disposition which led him to carry out to the utmost of his power any pursuit or duty which was placed before him.

His characteristics have been thus fitly described :

"Distinguished as a theologian, indefatigable as a student, able as an administrator, Dr Corrie was in everything and above all a consistent and exemplary Christian Clergyman."

He was indeed a faithful son of the Church of England, strongly imbued with the Scriptural principles embodied in the Book of Common Prayer and other Formularies. Led by the study requisite for his official position to an intimate acquaintance with her history, he seemed often to those to whom he spoke on the subject, to have himself lived through her varied experiences. In his religious opinions he " desired to be represented as of the old Evangelical party as vindicated by Overton in his *True Churchman Described.*" How he valued the public Ordinances of religion, whether in a country parish Church, or in the Chapels of the two Colleges with which he was successively connected, was shewn by his regular attendance at the services.   As blindness increased in his old age, he would, before going into Church or Chapel, have the Psalms for the day read to him, that he might be enabled to take his part in the service.

When at last obliged by increasing weakness reluctantly to desist from attendance, he, after enquiring whether the bell was going, said gently, " Lord, I have loved the habitation of Thy house," and thus took leave of public worship.   He was remarkably alive to a sense of the union of members of Christ through their living Head : and those near him at the time remember the interest he shewed on the occasion of the burial of an infant whom he had never seen, at whose funeral he officiated for a friend ; and the tenderness with which, quoting the words of the Service, he spoke of him as " our brother," remarking on the provision made for every member of the Church, from the cradle to the grave.   He was not wont, however, to rest in ordinances, but to use them as means of grace, and thus when, through his infirmities, he could no longer avail himself of them, he was none the less in communion with his heavenly Father through a crucified and risen Saviour, in whom he placed all his confidence and hope.

Among his own family, as we have seen, he had always a ready welcome.   His niece has still a vivid recollection that " Uncle George was always the one who led in all our pleasures and amusements, and was a prime favourite with us all :" others beyond his own family enjoy the same happy recollections.   The daughters of the late Professor Blunt were from childhood much attached to him, and a letter of grave, quaint humour is given in reply to a request from one of them, who on leaving Cambridge " could not find among her friends any one so likely as Dr Corrie to take care of her favourite hen."

NEWTON, WISBECH, *Sept.* 17, 1855.

My dear Kitty,

I will very gladly take charge of "Speckle." Her age is no objection, as I am old myself. I think if Speckle has shewn herself to be a good hen, as you intimate, she ought to be kept for the rest of her life, for the sake of what she has been. I do not like the idea of casting off old servants. I have a person always on the premises at Jesus College, whose business it is to feed the bantams, whether I am in Cambridge or not, so there is no chance of Speckle being neglected. I hope she may live and enjoy herself a long time yet, and whenever she may die, I will take care, if I am myself alive, that she has a respectable interment, and that you have due notice. You mention that Speckle will follow you about and eat out of your hand ; what think you of my Peacocks, five of which will follow me about and eat out of my hand ? Besides the grown-up Peacocks and Pea-hens I have four Pea-chickens which I am bringing up to be as tame as possible. I fear, however, I shall have to part with some of them, for they eat a great deal of barley every day.

Felix is lying on my door-mat, at this moment, fast asleep. His residence here, where he can run about and do as he pleases, is very much to his satisfaction. His only grievances are, (1) a cat which will lie before the kitchen fire at the time he wishes to be comfortable in the evening : and (2) a large puppy which persists in playing with him, when Felix would rather not have his company. You would be very much surprised to see what a figure Felix sometimes makes of himself by running among the mud on the banks of the river Nene, which runs half-a-mile from my house. But to return to "Speckle." Be so good as to let some trusty person carry her down to my Lodge, and ask for my gardener, and say that he is to take care of her until I return to College. I shall also have occasion to write to the gardener, and will desire him to be careful of Speckle. My sister desires me to add her kindest regards to your Mamma and you two damsels, in which cordially unites

Your sincerely affectionate,

G. CORRIE.

After Dr Corrie's death in 1885, just thirty years after the letter was written to her, the same lady writes :—

"I feel as though nearly the last link with dear old Cambridge was gone : our happy days at Jesus Lodge will for ever stand out brightly and distinctly in my memory, as some of our very happiest. What a wonderful hold he always kept on the affection of all who ever knew him. Certainly to know him was to love him ; and once having known him no one could ever forget him, with his dear, kind, gentle, courteous ways, which come back upon me *now* as distinctly as though I were back in the old days when we used to trot up to Jesus Lodge and have those delightful visits which made all so bright and pleasant to us children. His unfailing kindness and gentleness to my sister and myself can never be forgotten. Our happiest childish memories are associated with him whose memory will ever be very dear to me."

As years advanced, he was very unwilling to be entirely separated from the junior members of his College, and encouraged their visits to the Lodge that he might continue to hold intercourse with them; and it was touching to see how at his great age he could still enter with freshness into the feelings of those whose career was just commencing. And it was not only with the young and joyous that he sympathised, but especially with the weak and suffering. Witness the almost dying words of the Rev. A. W. South, a junior Fellow of the College, whose exemplary course was so soon brought to its earthly close.

" I do not know how to thank you enough for your kind and consoling letter. It is such a comfort to know that you can thus take thought for me, and find time to send these cheering and strengthening words. It increases that feeling which some of us have always had, that Jesus is the most homelike College in the University. I hardly hope to live through the winter, but I feel, as you remind me, that I am in God's hands, and that it is His to take me when He will."

With regard to his general relations with the Society one of its members writes:

"In his later years, I can only describe the feeling on his part as one of parental affection; I was a complete stranger to him when he inducted me into my fellowship, but I well remember his kind and, as I thought, humble words, 'My friend, you will remember from this time that I am your elder *brother*.' His interpretation of the old Latin oath of fidelity to the College was to me, 'You may think there is much in what you have recited which is meaningless and obsolete, but its intention is as plain to-day as in our Founder's time, that, in a society of Christian gentlemen, you shall remember you are a Christian gentleman.' Does not this seem to illustrate the way in which he put life into the dry bones of antiquity? it was the root of his conservatism."

The following remarks give the same writer's impression of some of Dr Corrie's early Lectures, as Tutor, at St Catharine's College:

"I have done something more than glance over the MS. of the late Master's lectures, and they interest me very much. I suppose they were delivered when he was Tutor of St Catharine's, and therefore date back forty or fifty years at least. I had not known before that he ever had been a professed teacher of classics, though many a talk with him brought to light his great and wide knowledge of classics, though he never to me appeared to acknowledge it to himself. The lectures (on two very dissimilar subjects) illustrate his many-sidedness, and, even more, the minute and painstaking care which he bestowed on his books and his pupils. The lectures on Homer appear to be intended for freshmen or passmen, but those on Cicero are of an advanced order. The clear handwriting and expression show that not a line was set down without great consideration of the needs of his pupils, and the difficulty of the subject. The scholarship is of course now-a-days a little old-fashioned, but it is the stuff out of which our scholars of to-day are made, and, I should say, an excellent specimen of its time."

The following extract of a letter from one whose friendship extended over many years will be read with interest:

"Dr Corrie was a true Christian friend, a very *genuine* man in every respect; so kind and benevolent—so sincere—so strict in adherence to principle. I remember an instance of this which amused me at the time. It was soon after I went to Cambridge as an undergraduate, that a cousin of my own—a young lady who had made acquaintance with Dr Duff of Calcutta, and was deeply interested in his educational schemes—endeavoured to enlist all her friends in the work of collecting £1000 for his projected College in Calcutta, by engaging them to ask only one penny from every person they met; and by dint of labour and perseverance she at length accomplished her purpose. I was one of those commissioned to collect. Dr Corrie was at that time Norrisian Professor of Divinity, and was strong on the subject of the Divine right of Episcopacy. On this subject he had lent me some MSS. of his own to read. It did not occur to me that the fact of Dr Duff being a Presbyterian would stand in the way of my obtaining the penny I asked Dr Corrie to give me. His refusal, therefore, excited a laugh which I could not repress, and in which he good-naturedly joined. 'But,' said he, 'there is no use in holding a principle if you do not act upon it.' Though I did not agree with him in the stringency of the principle, I noted this application of it as a wholesome lesson, which I have always remembered, and in these days of so-called liberalism and charity and compromise of principle, it is well to reflect what serious dangers and disasters might be avoided by acting on the maxim, 'Obsta principiis,' and 'He that is faithful in that which is least, is faithful also in much: and he that is unjust in the least, is unjust also in much,' St Luke xvi. 10.

"Dr Corrie had a great deal of dry humour, sometimes even grim in its expression; as when he said on one occasion dryly, respecting Lord John Russell's measures, 'In healthier times Lord John would have paid for it with his head.' The imperturbable quiet of his countenance and voice in giving utterance to such truculent sentiments was irresistibly comic.

"On my last visit to Cambridge I met Dr Corrie. I was at that time suffering from severe ear-ache, and was accordingly wrapped up, when I was thus accosted by the dear old Master, 'My friend! I *used* to think that I was your senior.'

"He wrote to me when in his 90th year, saying, 'It is wonderful, that I am still able to preach in my College Chapel in my turn, and also every Sunday when in residence in my country parish.'

"When I went to Cambridge to take my Master's degree, I remember dining with him, when he gave his opinion respecting the

Tracts for the Times. He seemed to have little respect for the learning or honesty of most of the tractators. He said that the most charitable view was that they had read their authorities by indexes and picked out what suited their purpose without regard to the context."

In addition to the literary work already spoken of, Dr Corrie's great interest in the early history of the Church in Ireland led him to embody the result of his careful study of that subject in a series of "Five Letters," published in the *British Magazine*, Vols. viii. and ix., with the signature C. E. G., being "a Criticism of the 'History of Ireland' by Thomas Moore, Esq.," 90 and 91 of Lardner's *Cabinet Cyclopædia*, 1835, 1840. The criticism is mainly on the Doctrine of the early Irish Church as to Pelagianism.

He has also left an unpublished MS. of a History of the Mission of Augustine to England.

Dr Corrie had at one time in preparation an edition of Dr Pegge's *Life of Grosseteste*. He has left four MS. books, in which a page is assigned to each page of Dr Pegge's edition, with corrections and amplifications of the notes, and other matter. The whole of this material has been placed in the Library of St Catharine's College, with Dr Corrie's copies of Dr Pegge's Lives of Grosseteste and Weseham. Dr Corrie had also at one time proposed to undertake a new edition of the works of Gildas, and had collected a great quantity of illustrative matter both of the History and Epistle of Gildas; and besides the illustrative notes, he had collated some of the text, and had specially noted the quotations of Scripture which Gildas makes, comparing the Latin with the text of the Vulgate, and with the Septuagint, and had copied out all the passages, with the variations of the versions in a separate column. He also began, but did not go on with, a new translation of Gildas. The whole of this material has also been placed in the Library of St Catharine's College.

From time to time Dr Corrie was in the habit of putting

his thoughts into verse in the form of hymns, or meditations,
a few of which may be acceptable to the reader:

> O Jesu Lord, to Thee alone
> Perpetual praise belongs;
> And the bright choirs before Thy throne
> Pour forth their endless songs.
>
> There, glorious, with the Angel host,
> A joyful countless band—
> The happy spirits of the just—
> Around Thee, Saviour, stand.
>
> And, one with them in bonds of love,
> Their joys in part we know;
> ' They sing the Lamb in hymns above
> And we in hymns below.'
>
> Lord Jesu, give us faith to rest
> Upon Thy love and care;
> Until Thou call us with the blest
> Thy perfect joy to share.

A·BIRTHDAY MEDITATION.

> If Thou, Lord Jesu, wilt direct the way
>   O'er which my future life-long journey lies,
> If Thou vouchsafe to be my constant stay
>   Whilst all my wants Thy bounteous love supplies,
> Then, Lord, lead on—my highest joy shall be
> Undoubtingly to trust and follow Thee.
>
> By Thee conducted, I can fearless tread
>   The tangled maze of this world's wilderness;
> For, if by ways I know not sometimes led,
>   I need not doubt Thy love nor trust Thee less;
> Since Thou, O Lord, canst never guide amiss,
> And where Thou art is safety, peace, and bliss.
>
> Increase then, Lord, my confidence in Thee,
>   And sanctify me to be wholly Thine;
> That I may grow in grace increasingly,
>   And never from Thy heavenly paths decline:
> Uphold me, till my pilgrim course be o'er,
> And I, Thy suppliant, saved, to sin no more.

ALONE, BUT NOT ALONE.

Without Thy presence, Lord, to me
  This earth may well a desert seem,
And all its fleeting joys might be
  No better than a feverish dream.

But where Thou art, there all is light,
  All mental clouds are chased away,
The gloom of sorrow's darkest night
  Is changed into a joyful day.

Why should I then, though all alone,
  Feel lonely, if my God be nigh?
To Him my every grief is known,
  He can my every want supply.

Then teach me, by Thy Spirit's power,
  Daily, O Lord, to live above
This earth, and in my loneliest hour
  Implicitly to trust Thy love.

June, 1862.

The long course has now been traced in its various relationships, aims, and accomplished work, passing through
a peaceful and happy old age to the " rest which remaineth
to the people of God."

APPENDIX.

THE following notes dealing with various points in the life and character of Dr Corrie have been contributed by Dr H. A. Morgan, Master of Jesus College, Mr A. Gray, Fellow and Tutor of Jesus College, Prof. G. F. Browne, and an old member of St Catharine's College. Dr Morgan's paper deals mainly with the work of Dr Corrie as Master, while Mr Gray gives a brief account of the position of the Mastership when Dr Corrie was appointed. Prof. Browne's paper is concerned with Dr Corrie's political work, as is Mr Gray's second paper, while in the fifth appendix an old friend of Dr Corrie contributes some interesting reminiscences of his earlier days as Tutor of St Catharine's College.

I.

As I was for many years intimately associated with Dr Corrie while he was Master of Jesus College, I feel that I may offer a few remarks on some characteristic points which rendered him specially well fitted for the duties attached to that position, and enabled him to carry them out in a manner highly conducive to the interests of the College and the welfare of its members.

In the first place I would refer to the unfailing courtesy which he invariably extended to everyone with whom he came in contact, no matter what the individual's position might be. This winning quality, more especially in the cases of members of the College, very frequently developed into a kindly and sympathetic friendship which was always appreciated at the time, and was often, as I well know, recalled in after years with pleasure and gratitude. Wherever it was in his power to help, or to effect some kindness, he was never appealed to in vain.

One phase of this courteous disposition was shewn by his perfect command of temper in his dealings with others. I have known him subjected to irritation which would have severely strained many a man's patience and self-control, yet he remained calm and self-possessed. With him a common method of disarming an opponent was by returning a perfectly placid answer beginning "My friend", but ending with some sharp thrust of witticism which seldom failed to turn the tables against him to whom it was addressed. He would then proceed to moralise upon the point under dispute, illustrating his observations with a dry humour which left his adversary half disposed to repeat the whole story, even though it told against himself, as an instance of the Master's way of dealing with such attacks. Many are the illustrations which might be given of how happily he struck home under such circumstances, and of the manner in which his characteristic humour, always near the surface, though quite unsuspected under his grave demeanour, was ready to flash out whenever a propitious opportunity occurred. A few instances of his quaint sayings I cannot refrain from mentioning.

On one occasion, when in Switzerland, he hired a carriage and agreed to pay 20 francs for the journey he was about to take, the payment to be made to the innkeeper at the end of the stage. The bill was enclosed in an envelope which on his arrival at his destination Dr Corrie presented. The innkeeper, not aware that the Master knew the contents, took it into his office, changed the o into a 6, and returning it to him said, "Sir, the price of the carriage is 26 francs." "Young man," replied the Master, "you must not only be a great knave, but you must be a great fool, for if you had not been a great fool you would have changed that o into a 9 instead of into a 6;" he then paid the crestfallen innkeeper his 20 francs and left him. When he told me this story he added, "and let me tell you the man seemed more annoyed at my denouncing him as a fool than as a knave."

I have mentioned his extreme courtesy, of which the following answer is an example. A person in conversation with him having been guilty of a falsehood, he exclaimed, "If you repeat that statement I shall be under the painful necessity of informing you that you have told an untruth."

It happened that a kind-hearted Home Secretary had been somewhat too lenient in his decisions respecting condemned criminals until public opinion asserted itself strongly in favour of a capital sentence being carried out in a particular case. When Dr Corrie was informed that the culprit in this instance was to suffer the extreme penalty of the law he said, "You see in these days a man must be in the possession of strong Parliamentary influence in order to get hanged."

Again, though I need scarcely mention it, for it was obvious to all with whom he had any communication, he was the true type of a gentleman in every sense of the word. This too was a quality which he fully valued in others; he would say, "If a man's conduct be not governed by Christian principles, his best safeguard is to be found in the possession of gentlemanly feelings." It so chanced that a thoughtless undergraduate, whose love of mischief got the better of his self-control and reverence, employed a few moments in Chapel in pinning the surplice of the student before him to his chair, with results which do not require description. On this being reported to the Master he remarked, "A Christian would call such conduct profane, a gentleman would term it vulgar."

An interview with him was always delightful, not only on account of his genial and sympathetic nature but from his

large store of information and the sage conclusions which his
keen observation and long experience had enabled him to
form on most questions of interest. As chairman of College
meetings, his tact, temper and courtesy, especially when a
difference of opinion existed amongst those present, helped
much to smooth difficulties and to bring discussions to pleasant
and amicable conclusions, and though his powers under our
College Statutes which existed up to 1882 were very great, for
he possessed a *veto* on all questions pertaining to business and
discipline, he almost invariably refrained from thwarting what
he believed to be the wishes of the Society. He strongly held
the opinion that each College officer should be supreme in his
own department. " You must have an executive" he would
say. Thus he rarely interfered in any way with regulations
drawn up by one of them—any step of his in this respect
would amount to no more than a suggestion. On the other
hand the Fellows well knew what his wishes were, and
their friendly feelings towards him were the means of leading them, as far as possible, to act in harmony with his views.

Again, his long and unbroken experience of Cambridge life
and his intimate acquaintance with the history, customs and
traditions of the University, rendered his advice and opinions
on academic questions, even of a perplexing and intricate kind,
of the greatest value. A conversation with him on bygone
times and well-known University characters was always interesting. There were few University men, of the present
century, in any way remarkable, of whom his memory could
not furnish some racy anecdote or characteristic trait. But it
was not only on University topics that his information was
extensive ; his mind had ranged assiduously and for a prolonged period over so many fields of theological, literary and
political interests that it was difficult to touch on any subject
which had not come within the scope of his researches. Many,
I am sure, will be ready to admit that a conversation with
him had left them both wiser and better informed, and let me
add few could hear him descant on religious belief without

becoming conscious of the refreshing and elevating influence of his tone of mind.

He took a keen interest in the progress of the students, and was especially desirous to help, where it was practicable, deserving men when he knew their means were straitened. He thoroughly disliked the present system of awarding scholarships, by open competition, to young men before coming into residence. He said that the result of this must too frequently be that they would be gained by youths who had received the best training, and whose circumstances therefore were not such as to require pecuniary aid. The rich man's son with his superior advantages would carry off endowments intended for those with small means.

With regard to athletics, whilst he fully approved of manly games and was pleased when success attended the College crews or 'elevens', he greatly deprecated such recreations being overdone. He would urge those who were disposed to indulge in them too freely to remember that to excel in these pursuits was not the *business* of their College careers. In matters of discipline he had no patience with luxurious extravagance, especially when a youth's circumstances did not justify it. In such cases he would appeal with striking emphasis to a young man's better feelings by alluding to the privations which his conduct would entail on others who might remain under his father's roof; but whenever reproof was necessary he always recognized the importance of exercising temper and judgement, so that the transgressor might depart feeling himself to be a penitent, not a criminal.

He was ready and anxious to assist those who were engaged in Theological studies, and he would spare no pains in suggesting and directing the line of reading most suitable for them. In the Lent Term of each year he delivered a course of lectures on subjects connected with Holy Orders; he also took part in the College Theological Examinations; the papers he set were remarkably fair, well calculated to bring to the front the most promising men, and also to give painstaking and industrious students, with moderate capacities, opportunities of shewing their acquirements.

His vitality was extraordinary. On the most bitter mornings he was rarely if ever absent from his place in Chapel, though he would sometimes say, with a humorous hit at the medical profession, that for about half-a-century he had been fighting against consumption. When approaching the age of 90, a short time after he had suffered from a rather severe attack of illness, he was out walking on a very treacherous spring day, without a great coat. He was met by one of our leading physicians, who begged him at once to come into his house, which happened to be near, and to remain there until a carriage could be procured to take him home. "My young friend," he gravely remarked, drawing himself up, "had I listened to the advice given me by members of your profession, I should have been dead 50 years ago."

At another time his physician, when treating him for a very severe cold, was astonished one day to find the Master walking in his garden with only very light clothing—although a keen east wind was blowing at the time. On his reproaching him for this, and observing that two other University dignitaries, both much younger than the Master, who were similarly troubled, were carefully nursing themselves, one in his room and the other in his bed, he completely disconcerted his professional adviser by quietly replying, "Yes, my friend, but you must remember that the gentlemen you have named are far advanced in years."

It would be affectation to refrain from all allusion to his undisguised repugnance to Radicals and Ritualists. On this point he was absolutely firm, for he regarded both as enemies of the Church. But here it is only right to say that no man had more completely the courage of his convictions. It never could be said of him, that he was "all things to all men"; he could not tolerate a person who, in his opinion, was what he called a "trimmer."

Though Dr Corrie was always dignified—I do not recollect having ever seen him in a hurry—he was not what is commonly known as a 'don.' Thus he would delight undergraduates by recounting his own experiences, when young, in hunting and shooting. When the Volunteers were first enrolled he greatly surprised some members of that body in College by requesting them to let him examine the rifle selected for their use, and they were both astonished and delighted by the way in which he criticized and handled the weapon. But an undergraduate was made to feel most thoroughly at his ease in the Master's society when the latter was pleasantly chatting to him in his own drawing-room, brightened as it was by those devoted friends whose tender and affectionate care cheered and smoothed the path of his declining years. In recalling these later years which, towards the end, were frequently disturbed by failing health and its accompanying suffering, no record would be complete in which some allusion were not made to the fervour and intensity of his faith, which never wavered and which at times so beautifully afforded him strength and consolation. And to all who surrounded him the resignation which he then displayed and the vividness with which he appeared to realise and look forward to the unseen, with a simple loving trust, conveyed a striking and never to be forgotten lesson.

H. A. M.

II.

A few words are not unfitting in this place with reference to the important office to which Mr Corrie had just been called. The Mastership of Jesus College, probably from the fact that the nomination to it rested with the Bishops of Ely, as *ex officio* visitors of the College, had been rendered illustrious from its tenure in former times by such men as Archbishop Sterne, Bishops Pearson and Beadon, John Duport and others—some distinguished as administrators of the Church, others, as Dr Corrie himself would sometimes recall in conversation, academic Churchmen of the temperate type, which since the Reformation has been the stamp of Cambridge theology. It could scarcely, however, be regarded as a position of emolument. At the time of Mr Corrie's appointment it was barely worth £400 a year, and until the latest years of his life its value very rarely exceeded £550. It had therefore, in the case of Mr Corrie's immediate predecessors, been invariably associated with Church preferment of one kind or another, an arrangement which, if not actually provided for in the College Statutes, was at least facilitated by the conditions of residence required by them, which in the case of the Master were of a much less stringent character than in that of the Fellows. Of the license thus permitted him Mr Corrie was the last man to avail himself when his absence would have interfered with the supervision of College affairs. The Mastership of a College, in all cases a position of responsibility, was in his instance one of active labour, and one which required and received his unremitting attention. With the Mastership was statutably associated the post of Bursar, into the duties of which he threw himself with characteristic energy[1]. He devoted much labour to the investigation of the history of the College foundation, its estates and their administration, and the knowledge so acquired he practically employed on more than one occasion to the advantage of the Society. Besides the essential duties of his office he took an active part in the educational work of the College, both as an Examiner, and (after his resignation of the Norrisian Professorship) as a Lecturer, the latter function being one not often (at least at the time when he undertook it) associated with the dignity of a College Mastership. 'Read with the object of qualifying yourself for *any* office which you may be called to by your College or the University', was the advice which the Master often impressed on the junior members of the Society; and it must be allowed that

---

[1] The stipend then attached to the office was £30, out of which travelling and other expenses had to be paid.

this object of *practical utility* was never absent from his design in his own multifarious paths of industry.

A. G.

III.

MY personal acquaintance with Dr Corrie commenced when he was already a man of advanced age. I first met him, on anything like intimate terms, in 1867, at the house of an attached friend of his in Scotland, Lord Rollo. From that time onwards I had many happy opportunities of learning his views on political matters, whether of University or of Imperial interest, and on the conduct and policy of that party in the State and in the University to which he belonged. The tradition which I had received as an undergraduate when I entered at Catharine Hall in 1852 was that when Dr Corrie was Tutor the dinner in Hall and the Services in Chapel had to be duplicated each day in order to find room for the large number of undergraduates. And the traditional explanation was, that in times then already far past, of great and sudden changes of opinion in religious and ecclesiastical affairs, he had stood so firm, that parents who desired to shield their sons from incitement towards novel views entered them in crowds under Dr Corrie as Tutor.

With this tradition in my mind, when it was suggested last year that I might write a few words on the political attitude and influence of one whom I had come to regard, as soon as I knew him well, with very warm feelings of respect and affection, I proposed that Canon Hopkins of Littleport, who was Tutor of Catharine when I entered and went out of residence about 1855, should be asked to write some notes on the subject from his earlier point of view. The following extracts from his reply will be read with interest. They confirm the basis of our undergraduate tradition to an extent somewhat unusual with such traditions, and they render unnecessary some remarks which I should otherwise myself have made.

"Dr Corrie's influence politically in the University was very considerable. He was always consulted and looked up to by the leaders of the Conservative party. His support was of very great value; his opposition was almost fatal to the success of a candidate for the representation of the University in Parliament. This preponderating power was due to Professor Corrie's widely extended connexion with the Clergy. They had all passed through his lecture rooms and almost all looked up to him with confidence and respect: often with affection. His opinions were firmly held and emphatically expressed. He was so consistent and so unchanging, that all Conservatives felt quite sure of him. When he had spoken, a very large section of the Electors at once made up their minds and followed him with the utmost confidence. His influence on the politics of the Town was a reflex of his commanding influence in the University contests. As far as I know he never attempted to exert direct influence upon the vote of a College Tradesman. But it was well known where his sympathies went. He was trusted and consulted by the Conservative leaders, and was hated (politically) and feared by the Liberals.

"So far as my knowledge extends, Dr Corrie did not exercise any direct influence upon the religious life and spiritual work in the Town. His help was given to every good object and movement, but he took no direct active part. He was a warm supporter of the 'Old Schools,' as being an important religious agency. He was ready to take the chair when requested to do so at benevolent, educational and Missionary Meetings. Beyond this he did not go."

The impressions which I received from several political conversations with Dr Corrie, who was good enough to speak to me without reserve, were of a somewhat blended character. He dated from times when the management of political affairs was very different from anything I had myself seen, though I had heard a good deal of those times, as a boy, from relatives who had played an active part in them. I think that Dr Corrie was inclined to regret some changes which I regarded as improvements. He certainly felt, for instance, that the possession or control of considerable property in land and houses carried with it the responsibility of securing, as far as might be, that the electoral vote of the property was cast

in favour of whatever might tend towards his two great
objects, the maintenance of Religion by means of the Established Church, and the maintenance of the Throne in unim-
paired dignity.   And he held that a man who was not sound
on both of these fundamental principles was not altogether to
be trusted in other respects.   I could never be quite sure that
he really did feel this.   Even when he sighed for the wholesome times of burning, I used to think that he had a half
comical half kindly feeling how much it would be to the
advantage and profit of those whom he regarded as suitable
for the operation, that they should be burned.   I quite believe,
by the way, that had things so turned, he would himself have
submitted to that discipline, with perfect simplicity, as a
natural part of his duty.   It was not without a very deep
knowledge of Dr Corrie's character that one of the Bishops
wrote to him in 1851, under circumstances which the date will
suggest, —" I hope and believe, old friend, that you would
rather go with me to the fires of Smithfield—if they were to
be once more lighted—than see me yield to the Whitehall
gang of extortioners."

The point that impressed me most in the course of conversations with him on political matters was this, that he
could scarcely bring himself to enter upon a question of
" policy," that is, whether it would be " politic " to take such
and such a course.   He had singularly simple and clear principles, and the only course he could understand was, to carry
them out.   Indeed I believe that the fundamental simplicity
of the mainsprings of his actions not unfrequently gave to
those who did not agree with him the sense that he was acting
with subtlety, that he had hidden motives.   I used to think
sometimes that his only subtlety in these respects consisted in
his leaving opponents to make their mistakes unimpeded, and
to find them out for themselves by the natural consequences.
His advice to those with whom he agreed was,—" Stick to
your principles and do what you honestly can to make them
prevail : they are sound, and they will prevail."   This being

so, it will be understood that at the time to which my personal knowledge is confined, his influence was felt rather than seen. I do not think he had at that time any desire to take a share however prominent or however slight in the detailed work of party politics, though he was always ready to give sage and pithy counsel to those who asked his opinion. As to the town, so far as I can learn from friends in the town who more nearly approached his own age, he never had taken any very overt part in town affairs, had seldom intervened directly. His political friends in the town knew what his objects were; and he knew that they knew, and relied upon their doing what they could to secure them. They were sure of hearty and encouraging approval if they succeeded, and they were safe from all approach to repining and censure if they failed. It was this that made it a personal pleasure to work for him.

Dr Corrie's very interesting publication called *Brief Historical Notices of the Interference of the Crown with the Affairs of the English Universities* (Cambridge, 1839; 106 pages 8vo.), has been referred to in the text of the present volume. The following letter to the Duke of Cleveland, Chairman of the Universities Commission of 1871, will shew how he dealt with the subject in the concrete.

JESUS COLLEGE, CAMBRIDGE,
11 *March*, 1872.

My Lord Duke,

I have the honour to acknowledge the receipt from your Grace of certain papers of enquiry issued by the Universities Commissioners, with a request that I would use "all necessary despatch in procuring answers." To that request it will be my duty to attend as time may be afforded me apart from my official and other duties. In the meanwhile I trust your Grace will forgive me the expression of my fear lest the Commission under which your Grace and others have consented to act should be found an inconvenient

precedent for the Majesty of the People when, a few years
hence, they come to issue their Commission of Enquiry
into the Properties and Incomes of the Nobility and Gentry
of England.

I have the honour to be, with great respect,

Your Grace's most humble servant,

G. E. CORRIE.

When the Cambridge University Commissioners, appointed by the Act of 1877, sent to the Heads of Colleges
and others a paper of questions asking their opinion as to
the chief wants of the University and the manner in which
they could best be met, Dr Corrie commenced his reply as
follows :—

"In the first place I trust the Commissioners will excuse
me for stating it to be my opinion that the present chief
want of the University is exemption from the disturbing
power of Royal or Parliamentary Commissions."

I well remember the unmixed delight with which the
Chairman of the Commission, Chief Justice Sir Alexander
Cockburn, received this sally when I read it to him. "Tell
him," he said, "from me privately, how much I enjoyed it."
It will surprise some of my readers to hear that Dr Corrie's
paper proceeded to recognise that there were from time to
time serious wants, that such wants had been supplied by
individual liberality, "but it may, perhaps, be doubted
whether important objects of this kind should be altogether
dependent on private liberality." His suggestion was, that
when an exigency arose a direct contribution should be
drawn from the Colleges, the rate to be determined by the
body of the Heads of Colleges. The contribution, he added,
should be levied on the gross revenues of the Colleges, as
any other plan "would involve disputes founded on vulgar
inquisitiveness."

In conclusion, I may say that Dr Corrie's never faltering
example of complete and lucid uprightness is a possession

for ever to the younger men whom he admitted to his confidence. If they instinctively take a gentler view than he professed of those who differ from them on fundamental points of what are called politics, and cultivate rather than avoid those friendly relations with political opponents which deprive the necessary business of politics of much of its reproach, it is with the conviction that had he belonged to their generation, the affectionate kindliness of his disposition, the exquisite courtesy of his nature, and the keenness of his sight for moral worth, would have made him their leader in these more modern ways.

G. F. B.

IV.

As the subject of University Commissions was one on which Dr Corrie always adopted a strong and uncompromising line, it may be well to state his views concerning them, especially as the changes introduced by two successive Commissions during his tenure of the Mastership have so far obliterated the outlines of the constitution of the University and Colleges (as existing prior to 1850), as to make it somewhat difficult to comprehend the attitude of the large number of residents in the University who entertained a legitimate objection both to the constitution of the Commission of that year, and to the changes which it proposed to introduce in the statutes of Queen Elizabeth, by which the University and Colleges were governed at that date. As early as 1839 Dr (then Mr) Corrie had published to the world the materials on which he based his own judgment in this matter in his pamphlet entitled, *Brief Historical Notices of the Interference of the Crown in the Affairs of the English Universities.* The pamphlet (which in spite of its title is something more than 'brief') points out the essential change of circumstances attending the authority of the Crown in matters relating to the Church and Universities. 'We have not now to do with the Sovereign, as possessing an independent legislative existence, as in circumstances to show a sincere attachment to our Church and Universities, and as powerful to uphold them ; but as the state servant of that Prime Minister who may happen to command a majority in the Commons' House of Parliament.' While asserting his unfeigned attachment to the Monarchy and the Sovereign personally, the author proves by an elaborate chain of historical evidence that at no time did the right of the Crown to visit and regulate even the Royal foundations in the English Universities receive a legal recognition. Beyond this purely historical objection to the interference of the Crown, Dr Corrie was strongly convinced that such changes as lapse of time had rendered necessary might be most effectively brought about and afford best hope of a permanent settlement by a reformation working from within the University, and in accordance with the existing statutes, which, as Master of a College, he had bound himself by oath to maintain. As Dr Corrie had foreseen, the work of the Commission of 1856 was of a merely provisional character, and was only the prelude to the more sweeping changes introduced by the Parliamentary Commission of 1877. To the inquisitorial investigations of the latter Dr Corrie's objections were again indomitably aroused ; though when changes had been actually effected by it, he submitted to the law of which he disapproved.

A. G.

V.

It is now forty-three years since I last saw Professor Corrie, and so my recollections of him must, in a great measure, be but dim and clouded. Not so, however, my remembrance of his unfailing kindness to me, during the four

years or so that I was privileged to have such intercourse
with him as naturally arises between an undergraduate and
his College Tutor; for to more than this I can lay no claim
whatever.

It was in the October Term of 1842, when I first went up
to Catharine Hall, as the dear old College was then called,
that I first saw the Professor, a thin spare man, a little under
the middle height, with hair even then white, for he was far
from being an old man, although, in my boyish fancy, I
thought him so. He was not the Tutor whose lectures we
freshmen then attended, so I saw but little of him for the
first year of my residence. What intercourse, however, I had
with him was such as to impress me from the first with that
sense of his fatherly kindness which remained ever with me
—deepening and gaining strength, as I saw and heard more
of him. He had, I think, the character of being cold and
stiff and dictatorial, among many of us; but he was never so
with me; and whenever he had occasion to utter words of
warning or of reproof, they were always so given, that I felt
they were fatherly ones, and knew that I deserved them.
His words of encouragement were few, but weighty; and he
never failed to give them when opportunity arose.

I think that he rarely lectured in College; one course
only—it was on the First Epistle to the Thessalonians—do I
remember: but his public lectures, as Norrisian Professor of
Divinity, had to be attended by all who purposed hereafter
taking Holy Orders. During the Easter vacation of 1845, he
kindly gave me private lectures, twice a week, on Herodotus
—the book we had to take in for the College Examination;
and I have a distinct recollection of feeling and recognising at
the time how sensible and scholarly they were.

His dislike to smoking was well known, and many were
the stories of his scolding (if I may use the word) some of
the men for their indulgence in this habit. I smoked, and he
knew it; but somehow he only rebuked me once; and it was
on this wise. I had had occasion to go to his rooms one

morning to get his signature to some paper or other. It was after a breakfast party; and as many of us had been smoking, my clothes must have been redolent of tobacco. When I entered his room, he received me with his usual kindness: he wrote his name, and giving unmistakeable signs of his objection to the smoking, handed me my paper, "There," he said, "take your certificate: good morning." It was a reproof I never forgot, and I took good care not to go into his presence again with the objectionable taint hanging about me. After my undergraduate days I went up to Catharine Hall again for a week, in order to pass what was then known as the Voluntary Theological Examination. Professor Corrie kindly gave me rooms under his own and opening upon his staircase. When I called to bid him good-bye, among other kindly words he said, "I find that you smoke yet: well,—it is not a clerical accomplishment, and besides, you are killing yourself." This was forty-three years ago : and I am thankful to be able to say that though I am still a smoker, I have no reason to think that the habit has marred my usefulness as a clergyman, and better health it is impossible for any one of sixty-six years to have had.

It was, I believe, his custom to invite those men who were on the point of leaving College, after taking their degree, to his rooms after 'Hall' to take wine with him. At any rate he kindly did so to the men of my year. We feared it would be a rather stiff and stately affair; but he soon set us at our ease, and astonished us by his kindly and genial talk, and by the interest which, without a trace of patronage, he seemed to take in our future prospects. He fairly won all our hearts by giving us an amusing account of a pack of beagles which, I think, he once kept, certainly with which he used to hunt,—in Northamptonshire,—describing their good and bad points, and shewing us when a puppy should be kept and when drowned.

I much regret that I cannot remember more of the dear kindly man, but I have written only what I know of my own knowledge and recollection. The apocryphal stories I quite ignore and reject.

I may add that his portrait, a print from the painting by Sandys, now hangs on the walls of my parsonage,—an excellent likeness, bringing him very vividly before me whenever I look at it.

Inscription on Memorial Brass in Jesus College Chapel
in South Transept, Eastern Wall:

IN · PIAM · MEMORIAM

VIRI · DOCTI · GRAVIS · RELIGIOSI

GEORGI · ELWES · CORRIE · S.T.P.

QVI · VOTIS · STVDIIS · MORIBVS · CHRISTO · DEVOTISSIMVS

IN · LAVDEM · DEI · NEC · SINE · LAVDE · HOMINVM

HVIC · COLLEGIO · DIV · PRAEFVIT

TABELLAM · HANC · PONENDAM · CVRAVERVNT

MAGISTER · SOCIIQVE

QVALIS · FVERIT · BENE · MEMORES

———————

NATVS · A · D · IV · KAL · MAII · MDCCXCIII

MORTALITATEM · EXPLEVIT · A · D · XII · KAL · OCT · MDCCCLXXXV

ESTE · ERGO · IMITATORES · CHRISTI

Inscription on the Grave at Newton in the Isle:

IN AFFECTIONATE REMEMBRANCE

OF

GEORGE ELWES CORRIE, D.D.

SOMETIME NORRISIAN PROFESSOR OF DIVINITY

IN THE UNIVERSITY OF CAMBRIDGE,

MASTER OF JESUS COLLEGE,

AND

FOR 34 YEARS

THE RESPECTED AND BELOVED RECTOR

OF THIS PARISH,

WHO DIED SEP. 20, 1885.

AGED 92.

With long life will I satisfy him and shew him my salvation.

INDEX.

CAMBRIDGE : PRINTED BY C. J. CLAY, M.A. & SONS, AT THE UNIVERSITY PRESS.

PUBLICATIONS OF

THE CAMBRIDGE UNIVERSITY PRESS.

Dedicated, by special permission, to Her Majesty the Queen.

THE LIFE AND LETTERS OF THE REVEREND
ADAM SEDGWICK, LL.D., F.R.S., Fellow of Trinity College, Cambridge, and Woodwardian Professor of Geology from 1818 to 1873. By JOHN WILLIS CLARK, M.A., F.S.A., formerly Fellow of Trinity College, and THOMAS McKENNY HUGHES, M.A., Woodwardian Professor of Geology. 2 vols. Demy 8vo. [*Nearly ready.*

THE ARCHITECTURAL HISTORY OF THE UNI-
VERSITY OF CAMBRIDGE AND OF THE COLLEGES OF CAMBRIDGE AND ETON, by the late ROBERT WILLIS, M.A., F.R.S., Jacksonian Professor in the University of Cambridge. Edited with large Additions and brought up to the present time by JOHN WILLIS CLARK, M.A. Four Vols. Super Royal 8vo. £6. 6s.

Also a limited Edition of the same, consisting of 120 numbered Copies only, large paper Quarto; the woodcuts and steel engravings mounted on India paper; price Twenty-five Guineas **net** each set.

"The book consists of three handsome volumes of letterpress, admirably printed on good paper, with wide margins and rough edges, together with a thin volume of plans. The letterpress is well illustrated with reproductions of old prints by Loggan and others, with new views by Mr J. O'Connor, and with measured drawings and details made expressly for this work."—*Times*.

"A work of the very highest merit, at once remarkable for its minute accuracy and its width of scope."—*Academy*.

"To say of it that it is quite the most sumptuous work that has ever proceeded from the Cambridge Press, is to say little. It is hardly too much to say that it is one of the most important contributions to the social and intellectual history of England which has ever been made by a Cambridge man."—*Nineteenth Century*.

THE COLLECTED PAPERS OF HENRY BRADSHAW,
including his Memoranda and Communications read before the Cambridge Antiquarian Society. *With thirteen facsimiles.* Edited by F. J. H. JENKINSON, M.A., Fellow of Trinity College and University Librarian. Demy 8vo. 16s.

"Edited with scrupulous care and fidelity, by Bradshaw's personal friend, Mr F. J. H. Jenkinson, who, besides more obvious work, has bestowed great care on the preparation of the facsimiles, which represent the blurred and half-effaced lines of some of the original documents with admirable closeness.......No one who has to deal with the bibliographical side of literature, and who has regard to the processes by which advances in knowledge are made, can afford to dispense with the *Collected Papers*."—*Saturday Review*.

"Whatever he wrote was marked by thoroughness and accuracy no less than by the real interest and importance of the subject-matter to the history of literature, and the Syndics of the University Press have done credit to themselves and their University by the publication of the present volume."—*Spectator*.

"Under the title of '*Collected Papers of Henry Bradshaw*' the Cambridge Press has issued a volume of the late University librarian. Nearly all of these are on bibliography or allied subjects, and certainly deserved reprinting in their present accessible form, illustrated as they are by excellent plates, reproducing MS. &c."—*St James' Gazette*.

London: C. J. CLAY AND SONS,
CAMBRIDGE UNIVERSITY PRESS WAREHOUSE,
AVE MARIA LANE.

www.ingramcontent.com/pod-product-compliance
Lightning Source LLC
Chambersburg PA
CBHW032016120726
47902CB00013B/979